Ambition

The Chaplain's Legacy Book 6

Mary Kingswood

Sutors Publishing

Published by Sutors Publishing

ISBN: 978-1-912167-61-6 (paperback)

V1

Cover design by: Shayne Rutherford of Darkmoon Graphics

Author's note:

this book is written using historic British terminology, so *saloon* instead of *salon*, *chaperon* instead of *chaperone* and so on. I follow Jane Austen's example and refer to a group of sisters as the Miss Wintertons.

About this book

One man with a secret. A family torn apart by the consequences.

Olivia, the youngest daughter of the Earl of Rennington, has had a difficult year. Denied her first season in town by the illness of her grandmother, there was worse to come — her uncle, the chaplain, was brutally murdered. The discovery that he was not even an ordained clergyman means that her parents' marriage is void, and she and all her siblings are illegitimate. But Olivia has a plan — she intends to outdo her older sister Izzy and marry a duke, and she knows just the man. She's been following his exploits for years. All she has to do is to meet him...

Robert Osborn was once passionately in love with Izzy but when she chose another man, he lapsed gratefully back into his unfettered life as a man of leisure. But when he unexpectedly becomes the Earl of Kiltarlity, he is weighed down with obligations and responsibilities — where is the fun in that? He is astonished to meet Olivia — the very image of her older sister, and what is more, she has no trouble advising him on his new duties. But is his growing admiration simply because she reminds him of Izzy? And can he deter her from her ambition to be a duchess?

Captain Michael Edgerton has been doggedly pursuing the chaplain's murderer for months. Now, with more violence complicating the situation, he has one last throw of the dice to unravel the identity and motive of the killer.

This is a complete story with a happy ever after, but best read after the previous books in the series. A traditional Regency romance, drawing room rather than bedroom. Book 6 of a 6 book series.

About the series*:*

Book 0: The Chaplain: a man adrift, dreaming of a home *(a novella, free to mailing list subscribers).*

Book 1: Disinheritance: a man freed, looking for a new purpose in life

Book 2: Determination: a man pursued, forced to outwit his adversary

Book 3: Anger: a woman alone, trying to choose a different path in life

Book 4: Secrecy: a woman neglected, scheming to secure her own happiness

Book 5: Loyalty: a man of dreams, torn between the past and the future

Book 6: Ambition: a woman thwarted, unswervingly set on making a brilliant debut in society

Want to be the first to hear about new releases? Sign up for my mailing list at https://marykingswood.co.uk.

Contents

Principal Characters	1
1: A Newspaper Report	4
2: Visits	15
3: A Family Dinner	27
4: Harraby Hall	40
5: The Charming Earl	53
6: A Grand Ball	66
7: The Cheese Store	77
8: Briar House	89
9: The Meet	100
10: Lady Euphemia	111
11: Captain Edgerton Has A Theory	125
12: Suitors And Brothers	137

13: A Visit To Grayling Hall 149
14: The Secret Room 164
15: Searching 176
16: Hot Milk At Bedtime 188
17: Reputations 200
18: A Journey North 212
19: Strathinver 224
20: Fishing 236
21: Quarrel And Reconciliation 248
22: Lochmaben Castle 259
23: Of Love And Happiness 273
24: A Kiss 284
25: A Murder Is Planned 296
26: The Captain Understands 309
27: An Ending 319
28: Afterwards 330
Epilogue 341
Thanks for reading! 356
About the author 358
Acknowledgements 359
Sneak preview: Book 1 of Black Sheep: The Duke's Architect 360

Principal Characters

A partial list; for the full list, see my website at https://marykingswood.co.uk under Extras.

The Atherton family of Corland Castle, North Riding of Yorkshire:

Charles, 11th Earl of Rennington (55)

Caroline, Countess of Rennington (50)

Their children:

Walter, the former Viscount Birtwell (29), now married to Miss Winnie Strong

Mr Eustace Atherton (27), living on his own estate nearby, Welwood-on-the-Hill

Josie (Josephine), Lady Woodridge (26), married to Viscount Woodridge; they have two sons

Izzy (Isabel), Lady Farramont (24); married to Ian, Viscount Farramont (35); they have two daughters

Mr Kent Atherton (22), now betrothed to Miss Katherine Parish

Lady Olivia Atherton (18)

The earl's blind sister: Lady Alice Nicholson (48)

Her husband, the earl's chaplain: Mr Arthur Nicholson (55) (deceased)

Their daughter, Miss Tess (Teresa) Nicholson (20), now married to Lord Tarvin

The George Atherton family of Westwick Heights, North Riding of Yorkshire:

The earl's younger brother: Mr George Atherton (50)

Mrs Atherton (Jane, 45)

Their children:

Mr Bertram Atherton (25), now betrothed to Miss Beatrice Franklyn

Mr Lucas Atherton (23)

Miss Julia Atherton (20)

Miss Emily Atherton (18)

Miss Penelope Atherton (16)

Master Philip Atherton (6)

The Franklyn Family of Highwood Place, North Riding of Yorkshire:

Mr Charles Franklyn (46)

Lady Esther Franklyn (33), daughter of the Duke of Camberley

His daughter from his first marriage:

Miss Beatrice Franklyn (21), now betrothed to Mr Bertram Atherton

Their children:

Master Henry Franklyn (7)

Master Charles Franklyn (3)

The Murder Investigators:

Captain Michael Edgerton (37), formerly of the East India Company Army

Mrs Edgerton (Luce, née Willerton-Forbes, 30)

Mr Pettigrew Willerton-Forbes (38), a lawyer

Mr James Neate, a lawyer masquerading as a footman

Mr Alexander Grant Saxby (Sandy, 25), now known as Mr Alexander

Miss Peach, a former governess (deceased)

1: A Newspaper Report

CORLAND CASTLE, NORTH RIDING: SEPTEMBER

Miss Olivia Atherton sat at the elegant escritoire in her bedroom and read the newspaper report avidly. It was the fourth time she had read it, and she still enjoyed the same little thrill as the first time, as if her very blood were fizzing with excitement. Every such report was glorious, of course, but this one was unusually long and detailed.

'An event of the greatest interest to students of the Latin language recently took place in the magnificent medieval setting of Landerby Manor in the county of Lincolnshire.'

Then a great deal about the house and its owners, the Duke and Duchess of Wedhampton, which was of little interest to Olivia. She jumped ahead to the important part.

'Among the many distinguished guests, most notable of them was the Most Honourable the Marquess of Embleton, heir to His Grace the Duke

of Bridgeworth. Lord Embleton graciously attended the entire event, and delighted all present by his contribution to the scholarly recitals, being a number of poems in classical Latin form, written by his lordship's own hand and agreed by all to be of the highest calibre, and comparable to the works of the great poets of the Roman era themselves. Lord Embleton being too modest to read his own works to the assembled company, this pleasant task was undertaken by Mr Bertram Atherton, nephew to the Right Honourable the Earl of Rennington. Mr Atherton performed this office with the greatest eloquence, ensuring that the true beauty of the verses could be fully appreciated by the rapt audience.'

Too modest! He suffered from a stammer, that much she knew, so naturally public recitals would be a great trial to him. Well done, Cousin Bertram, for stepping forward to help his friend. Then there was a great deal more about the other guests and the Latin readings, which she cared nothing about. There was a brief mention of the Franklyns, and Lady Esther's father, the Duke of Camberley was mentioned. How the newspapers loved the nobility! But how frustrating that Bea Franklyn should be there and actually meeting all these illustrious people, when it was Olivia who had studied them obsessively for so many years and knew all about them. And especially one of them in particular.

He had another mention later, for the gentlemen had held a fencing contest one day, which Mr Franklyn, astonishingly, had won, but the marquess had done almost as well.

'The match between Lord Embleton and Lord Grayling was of especial note for the skill exhibited by both gentlemen, Lord Embleton's performance being much admired for his graceful movements and Lord Grayling's for his strength and determination. The match was long and evenly-balanced, but in the end Lord Grayling prevailed.'

Lord Grayling! That a mere baron should defeat a marquess and future duke was not how the world should be run, according to Olivia. She liked the orderly nature of the nobility — the King and the Royal Family at the top, then the dukes, the marquesses, the earls, the viscounts and finally, the barons. Within each rank, they were given precedence according to the date the title was created. It was tidy, with everyone knowing his place in the world.

So it seemed wrong for a baron to be placed above a marquess, even briefly, and that a mere gentleman like Mr Franklyn should defeat all the assembled nobles seemed unconscionable. Not that she had anything against Mr Franklyn, who was perfectly amiable, and allowed Lady Esther to hold the most magnificent entertainments at Highwood Place. Besides, he had not himself defeated her marquess, so she could not object to him on that score.

Not that Lord Embleton *was* her marquess, or ever likely to be, for she had never met him. It was nothing but a game, although an amusing one. Ever since she was thirteen and her older sister Izzy had come back from her first London season glowing with success, with a viscount on her arm and eleven other offers to boast about, Olivia had wondered how she might outdo her. She could not aspire to twelve offers, for she was a mere candle flame to Izzy's shining sun, but perhaps she could manage one. However, it would have to be the best. A duke — nothing would do for her but a duke, and so she had assiduously studied the peerage to make her selection.

It was a depressing business. Twenty-seven dukes, that was all there were in the entire kingdom, and who wanted to live in Scotland or Ireland? A warmer, flatter southern county would be ideal, and preferably close to London. That narrowed her options, and a distressing number of those remaining were either married already or too old or too young. Gradually, she had come to realise that there was just one man who encompassed all her requirements. The Marquess of Embleton. Ralph, for that was his Christian name, was heir to a dukedom in Buckinghamshire, of suitable age and unmarried.

She had begun to watch for the reports of his activities in the newspapers, carefully cutting out each one, the important points to be transcribed into a book she kept for the purpose. For three years now she had tracked every ball he attended, every country house where he was a guest, every shooting party in which he participated, every horse race he watched. Three years, ever since she was fifteen, and he was now thirty and still unmarried. If she had gone up to town for her first season last spring, she would have met him there, and perhaps could have dazzled him with her knowledge of race horses, and the Latin verses she had memorised.

But Grandmama had been so very ill that the season had been postponed and thus Olivia had not met the man who, in her dreams, was to make her a duchess. Nor was it ever likely to happen, not now, not when everything in her life had gone so horribly wrong. Six months ago, she could have gone up to town as the Lady Olivia Atherton, legitimate daughter of an earl, and a catch worthy even of a future duke.

But in June their chaplain, and her uncle by marriage, had been murdered, which was dreadful enough, but the worst part was that he had never been ordained as a clergyman, and therefore her parents' marriage, at which he had officiated, was not legal. Her mother was no longer the Countess of Rennington, her eldest brother was no longer Viscount Birtwell and heir to the earldom, and all six of the earl's children were rendered illegitimate.

Now she was merely Miss Olivia Atherton, still an earl's daughter, still with the same dowry, but cast out of all good society, for surely no one would want to know her. It was depressing, but despite her reduced prospects, she still kept up her careful watch on Lord Embleton. Some girls practised on the instrument or painted in watercolours, but Olivia's favourite pastime was following the marquess's career.

A knock on the door heralded the maid. "Beg pardon, milady, but Lady Alice says to tell you there's a caller."

Company! Olivia jumped up excitedly. As usual, she forbore to remind the maid that she was no longer Lady Olivia. The servants all kept to the same form of address and although it was incorrect, it soothed her a little to still be *'milady'*.

"Who is it, Patsy?"

"Lady Esther, milady."

Now that was interesting. Olivia had not seen her since her return from Landerby Manor, so she could ask about that and perhaps have the felicity of hearing mention of Lord Embleton. *Ralph.*

"Tell Aunt Alice that I shall be down very soon."

A quick look in the mirror reassured her that there was nothing amiss with her appearance, but since it was Lady Esther, the daughter of a duke, she added a necklace to her attire — the amber cross was an elegant combination of demure piety and wealth.

Olivia skipped down the stairs, past Eustace's ridiculous display of armoury on the half-landing, flanked by the Chinese urns, which she rather liked, and into the great hall, the upper walls lined with a vast array of weapons. Corland Castle was not an ancient building, the scene of many battles, but the earl liked to pretend it was.

Her slippers making no sound on the tiled floor, she moved down the great hall into the passage beside the stairs and thence to the drawing room. She arrived just behind another group of callers.

"Lady Strong, Miss Strong, Miss Lily Strong, my lady," intoned Simpson. Then, seeing Olivia coming up behind them, he added, "The Lady Olivia, my lady."

At Corland, even the family had to be announced, so that Aunt Alice, who had been blind since a childhood illness, might know precisely who was in the room. Her own daughter, Olivia's cousin, Tess Nicholson, was inclined to creep into a room unnoticed and take her mother by surprise when she spoke, but Olivia was not so ill-mannered.

Crossing the room quickly, she gave Aunt Alice a hasty kiss, then moved aside for the Strongs to make their greetings. Lady Esther, who had been sitting beside Aunt Alice, now rose and moved across to the earl, who was looking a little bemused.

"Ah, Olivia!" he called out. "Come and sit beside your papa, and tell me all that you have been doing."

She was happy to comply. Poor Papa! He looked so lost these days, for Mama had gone away now that she was not his wife any more, telling him to marry someone younger who would be able to give him legitimate sons. He was dutifully searching for a new wife, but he missed Mama dreadfully. Olivia would not have minded running away, too, but how could she leave poor Papa without anyone to see to his comfort? Her brothers were useless and her older sisters were married. As for Aunt Alice, she was so sunk in grief for her murdered husband that she barely knew what day it was, and had only emerged from seclusion now that a man had confessed to killing poor Uncle Arthur.

So Olivia sat on one side of the earl, and Lady Esther the other, although it was mostly Olivia who kept the conversation going, for Lady Esther seemed sunk in gloom.

Olivia could not wait to get to the important point, however, so as soon as the earl was drawn away to talk to the Strongs, she said, "How did you enjoy your stay at Landerby Manor, Lady Esther?"

"It was very pleasant. The Duke and Duchess of Wedhampton were most gracious. I felt quite at home there."

"And Mr Franklyn was a great success in the fencing tournament, I understand."

Lady Esther made a little moue of distaste. "Well… he enjoys the sport. For myself, I find it deeply unpleasant to watch men fighting, but it is more respectable than some hobbies, so I make no objection."

"And how did Miss Franklyn enjoy her stay? I am sure she was a great success amongst the gentlemen."

Olivia had heard certain rumours about Miss Franklyn's enjoyment, for Bea was not noted for shyness or even for good manners, if truth were told, but she expected a bland response from Lady Franklyn. After all, although she was not Bea's mother, as her stepmother she had always put a good face on Bea's little transgressions.

Much to Olivia's surprise, Lady Esther's face hardened. "Oh, do not talk to me of Beatrice! I can barely speak her name. I intended to bring her with me today, and we set out just as planned, but then Mr Bertram Atherton came galloping after us, jumping hedges and I know not what to catch up with us, and behaving in the most appalling fashion to me."

"Cousin Bertram?" Olivia said, astonished. "Jumping hedges? He never jumps!"

"Well, he did today, forcing the carriage to stop. Then he shouted at me, positively shouted, in the most uncouth fashion, dragged Beatrice out forcibly, and now he has ridden off with her. Such intemperance!"

"Bertram?" Olivia said again, trying to reconcile this passionate young man with her studious, bespectacled cousin, who never lifted his head from his ancient books and was unfailingly polite to everyone. The same Bertram who had sworn never to marry Bea Franklyn and had now apparently ridden off with her.

"You might well look astonished, Miss Atherton," Lady Esther said.

Oh. How lowering. She was *Miss Atherton* to her ladyship, of course. A duke's daughter would never get that wrong, or be kind enough to forget that she was no longer Lady Olivia.

"You will be even more astonished to hear that Beatrice turned down the possibility to be a duchess in order to ally herself with a man who might, or more likely might not, be an earl one day."

"Turn down a duke? Ohhh..." Olivia breathed. "I should never do that. I should *love* to marry a duke. I want to be a duchess above all things."

Lady Esther's face softened and she turned fully to face Olivia. "A worthy ambition indeed. Every woman should aim as high as she can when looking for a husband. Beatrice's offer was not from a duke, but from the heir to a dukedom, which to my mind is even better. So many of the unmarried dukes are in their dotage."

"The Duke of Argyll is only thirty-nine."

"A Scottish peerage!" she said with a grimace. "Inveraray Castle is so far to the north, and think of the weather!"

"Oh, I know. I thought Buckinghamshire would be better situated for weather, and nearer to town, as well."

"Buckinghamshire? Then... you have a particular duke in mind? The Buckingham line is extinct, so you refer, I collect, to the Duke of Bridgeworth, or his heir, the Marquess of Embleton."

"The Marquess. He is thirty years of age and single."

"I was not aware that you were acquainted with Lord Embleton."

Olivia should, perhaps, have been more discreet in her disclosures, for not everyone would approve of her ambition, but Lady Esther was one person who surely would. "I have never met him, but I should very much like to. What is he like?"

"Not a distinguished man in appearance. Rather the opposite, but gentlemanly in his manner and style of dress. Very quiet."

"He stammers."

"Ah. You know about that."

"Izzy told me. I also know that he is a keen sportsman, he fences, rides to hounds, shoots, and keeps race horses."

"You are very well informed."

"I keep all the newspaper cuttings that mention him. I have been following him for several years now."

Lady Esther smiled. This was such a rare event that Olivia barely recognised her. She looked almost approachable. "Ah, if only you were *my* daughter! But I suppose with your mother away and your aunt confined to the castle by her unfortunate condition, there would be no objection if I were to... take you under my wing, so to speak. After all, Beatrice seems to have settled her own future, so now I am at a loose end. Should you like that? I believe I can help you achieve your ambition, Miss Atherton."

"Even though I am not legitimate?"

"You are still the daughter of an earl with a respectable dowry, no doubt, and Olivia — may I call you by your name? — Olivia, you are as pretty as paint, you know. You have all your sister Isabel's beauty and lively spirit, without her wayward turns, and you have a much, much better figure."

"I am very fond of cake," Olivia murmured, lowering her eyes.

Lady Esther laughed, an event so rare that Olivia wondered momentarily if she were about to have an apoplexy. But no, it was merely laughter. Leaning forward a little, she whispered into Olivia's ear, "Gentlemen are attracted to a lady who is fond of cake." Then, in a more normal voice, she went on, "Of course, it would not do to become positively fat, but you are very far from that state. Yes, you have a much better figure. There is a drawing on the wall over there that I should like to examine more closely, if you will be so good as to accompany me."

Surprised but willing, Olivia crossed the room in Lady Esther's wake.

"There! Now we cannot be overheard," she murmured, her voice so low that Olivia had to strain to hear it. "I shall tell you something in the strictest confidence, Olivia. The ducal heir that Beatrice turned down was none other than Lord Embleton."

"Then it is no use!" Olivia cried, before remembering to whisper. "If he is in love with Bea, he will not so much as look at me."

"No, it is very much to the point, for a man who is already thinking of matrimony is ripe to fall into willing hands. He is not so very much in love with Beatrice, I fancy, but he believed her to be in love with him, that was what drove him to offer for her, and I know precisely what gave him the idea — she kissed him."

"Oh! How very—"

"Forward of her? Yes, but that is Beatrice for you, and even though it was inadvertent in this case, it did the trick for it brought him straight to the point. So that is what you must do, when you meet him."

"But how am I ever to meet him?" Olivia said in crushed tones. "He is about to begin his autumn round of visits to relations for the sporting season, and I am confined to the castle."

Lady Esther smiled again. "Then we shall just have to bring him here, shall we not? I happen to know that he is staying with his sister, Lady Harraby, at Harraby Hall, which is three miles this side of Thirsk. If I pen a brief note, just to express my regret that matters with Beatrice did not work out as we had hoped, I could perhaps mention that Lord Rennington is in low spirits just now after his recent difficulties and would undoubtedly be cheered by a visit from a fellow peer... that should do the trick."

"But if he calls to see Papa, he will spend half an hour in Papa's study and then go away again."

"Now, now, where is your ingenuity? Naturally you will ensure that your butler apprises you of such a distinguished visitor, and you can find an excuse to join them. Then you invite him to dinner. He will be too polite to refuse."

"He could come to our big party on Friday."

Lady Esther winced. "With the entire neighbourhood ogling him? And Beatrice will be there, who has just refused to marry him. No, a quiet family dinner, that is what is needed so you have his full attention, and you will have an entire evening to get to know him."

"And to kiss him?" Olivia said doubtfully.

"If the opportunity should arise," Lady Esther said firmly. "A kiss is so definitive, is it not? A man cannot mistake one's intent if one kisses him. It is better if the will to kiss should come from him, but one cannot wait for a man to realise what is needed or one might never get a husband. A lady must go out and seize her destiny in her own hands, Olivia, and I shall help you to do precisely that."

Seize her destiny! How glorious that sounded! And perhaps, with Lady Esther's guidance, Olivia would one day be a duchess.

2: Visits

Robert Osborn, Earl of Kiltarlity, threw down his pen in disgust. How was a man ever to make sense of these endless columns of numbers? And even if such a feat were possible, how could one then decide between the competing claims of his stewards? Three stewards maintained all his estates and holdings, one for the vast Strathinver estate here in Scotland, one for the smaller estates scattered like windblown seeds over the entire Kingdom and the third for the mines, quarries and investments. All of them claimed to have urgent matters requiring decisions, all of them clamoured for his attention, all of them made his head ache. How could he possibly decide?

Just at that moment, the hammering started up again. He groaned. Arms resting on the desk, he laid his head on them and wished… what did he wish? That this burden had never fallen onto his shoulders, primarily. With three older brothers, he had thought himself safe. He could live out his life in careless freedom, flitting from one amusing gathering to another like a bee in search of nectar, with nothing more to trouble him than whether to wear the blue waistcoat or the gold, or if he should attempt a more complicated knot in his neckcloth. But there was nothing amusing about being an earl.

"The mail has arrived, my lord."

Robert groaned again, and raised his head. The hammering was so loud he had not heard the butler enter the room. "Another mountain of bills, I suppose, Winthrop."

"I am sure there will be more pleasant missives, too, my lord. There is a letter from Mrs Haggerty. That should make you smile."

"Ah, yes. Great-aunt Jessica always cheers me up. Anything else?"

"One from Lord Harraby, my lord."

"Harraby! I have not heard from him in an age, not since—" Not since the last of his brothers had died and left him as the sole heir. Not since his world had collapsed into a nightmare of responsibility.

Rifling through the mound of letters, he found the one bearing Harraby's neat franking signature, and tore it open.

'The Right Honourable the Earl of Kiltarlity, Strathinver Castle, near Dumfries, Scotland. Kiltarlity, or Osborn as I still call you in my head, Greetings, my old friend! I trust you are in good health and spirits there in your Scottish fastness, and not receiving as much rain as we are. If we are not careful, the North Riding will be entirely washed away. Jane is very well, but unfortunately is confined to barracks until this baby makes an appearance, so we cannot remove to balmier climes, or seek out congenial company. Necessarily, therefore, the congenial company must come to us. Can you tear yourself away from your duties to come and liven us up for a spell? Your sisters and mother would be company for Jane, and you would be company for me. I have Embleton here at present, and although he is an excellent fellow, he is no conversationalist. He is finally emerging from his misanthropic seclusion,

however. At the advanced age of thirty, he has discovered that there are female personages in the world, and actually offered for one! Can you believe it? We could not, I assure you. Jane did not say a word for fully ten minutes when he told us, so that the servants all panicked and assumed she was having an apoplexy. And as if that were not astonishing enough, the girl turned him down! Can you imagine? Embleton is bemused rather than anything else, but you can see why lively company is required just now, and naturally you came to mind. Do come and cheer us up. If the rain ever stops, I can promise you some good shooting. I remain your very good friend, Harraby.'

Robert jumped up and sped down the corridor to the blue drawing room, where the ladies sat. His mother, still in unrelieved black, was holding forth about something or other, while his sisters were involved in trimming a bonnet. The hammering was louder here, for the builders were working in the very next room.

"How can you hear yourselves think with that racket going on?" Robert said.

"We cannot, of course," Lizzie said sharply. "At least the repairs are underway at last."

"Yes, we shall be much more comfortable once Strathinver is restored to its former glory," Lady Kiltarlity said.

"True, Mother, but we are exceedingly *un*comfortable while the restoration is being undertaken," he snapped. "How would you all like to pay a visit to Harraby?"

"I like Lady Harraby," Lucy said. "How is she?"

"I assume she is well, but she cannot leave Harraby until after her confinement, so Harraby invites us there to provide some company for her."

His mother grunted. "Kiltarlity, I am in no mood for amusement just now, with your father barely cold in his grave."

"Then you may stay here, if you please, Mother. Lady Harraby is chaperon enough for Lizzie and Lucy. Aunt Tina would come and bear you company, I am sure."

"No doubt she would! She is always ready for a free meal, that one."

"She has a very modest jointure," Robert said, making a mental note to check his aunt's annuity and see if it might be increased.

"Then her husband should have made better provision for her," Lady Kiltarlity snapped. "Or else she should have made better provision for herself by marrying more sensibly. But no, if you imagine you three can go jauntering off to enjoy yourselves and leave me here alone to manage everything, you may think again. A change of scene might do me a little good, for heaven alone knows, nothing else is working. My very bones ache, and that foolish apothecary does nothing but give me another tonic. A tonic! Nothing but flavoured water, if you ask me. A bottle of brandy a day would do me more good. So let us go to Harraby and see if that helps. I might be able to offer some useful advice to Lady Harraby. Her first, is it?"

"Second."

"Hmpf. Nevertheless, she does not know everything. I brought seven children into the world who all survived to adulthood, and if four of them have now left the mortal realm, the blame for that cannot be set at *my* door."

She glared at Robert, as if it was his fault that his three brothers had chosen to join the army and had fallen in their country's service, or that his eldest sister had died in childbirth. His sister… well, he could hardly be blamed for that, yet oddly, he somehow felt guilty about his brothers.

At least he would now have a brief reprieve from this dreadful weight on his shoulders.

"I shall write to Harraby at once," he said. "Can we be on the road tomorrow, do you think?"

***

Olivia was exultant — she would be a duchess! At least, she now had a plan and a supporter and a real prospect of meeting her chosen future duke, and if she could not charm him to the altar, it would not be for want of trying.

When all the morning callers had left, she escorted Lady Alice to the gallery, where she liked to sit sometimes.

Seeing the books under her aunt's arm, she said, "Shall I read to you, aunt?"

"No, for Mr Alfred Strong has promised to call and continue the book we were reading yesterday."

"Then I shall go and see Grandmama."

"She is not having a good day, so you might find her asleep."

"That does not matter. I can still talk to her while she sleeps."

Aunt Alice sighed. "You are a good girl, Olivia. I wish Tess were half so reliable as you, but she has a wilful streak in her that there is no eradicating."

Olivia made no comment on that. She had been close to her cousin Tess for many years, and they still shared a bedroom at the castle, but ever since her father had died, Tess had been tearing about the countryside doing who knew what. If she were honest, Olivia rather admired the way Tess always did precisely what she wanted, but they no longer shared confidences as they once had.

"We are not close," Aunt Alice went on. "A daughter should be close to her mother, should she not? I know you miss your mother dreadfully, but I do not think Tess misses me at all when she is away."

Olivia did miss her mother, but she would miss her father more. Her mother was a constant stream of criticisms, whereas her father only saw the best in her and made her feel as if she were someone special and not merely the baby of the family. Worse than that, she was a pale imitation of her older sister. Izzy was the great beauty of the family, the sparkling diamond at any gathering, who sang like an angel, danced divinely, and collected male admirers around her like moths drawn helplessly to her flame.

And Olivia was like Izzy in every way, but less, somehow. Less beautiful, less lively, less witty, less musical, less admired by gentlemen. It was very lowering. And even when Izzy screamed and shouted and broke things, she was still adored and forgiven. Olivia never screamed and shouted. When she became upset, which admittedly was almost as often as Izzy, she wept and then everyone was cross with her. *'Oh, do stop crying, Olivia!'* her mother would say. *'Crying is such a waste of time.'*

Olivia sat with her aunt for a little while, letting her grumble about Tess, but when Mr Strong appeared, she left them and went to see her grandmother. She was old enough to remember the Dowager Countess of Rennington striding about the village in an ancient hat and a startlingly old-fashioned greatcoat, more masculine in style than anything else. She had lived at Langley Villa, a neat little house in the village, but within half a mile of Corland Castle, so she had dined there more often than not. In winter, she had come to the schoolroom to read to her grandchildren, or test them on history or geography. In summer, she had swept them all into her carriage and driven out into the country to look for beetles or wade in the becks. But three years ago she had had what was described as *'a funny turn'*, and since then she had lived in one of the round tower rooms which graced all four corners of Corland Castle, declining peacefully towards death.

Today she was asleep, as she so often was, a nurse sitting at her bedside with her knitting and her faithful maid, almost as old as her mistress, struggling shortsightedly with a piece of mending.

"Ah! Lady Olivia," she said, rising with a smile. "How kind of you to come. Can you stay for a while? Thomas and I are due for our dinner."

"Of course. Off you go and no need to rush back. Grandmama and I will have a pleasant chat while you are gone."

"Lovely! Or you could read to her. We're working our way through Deuteronomy at the moment. I've marked the place."

The two disappeared. Olivia pulled a chair nearer to the bed and sat beside the Dowager, taking the age-mottled hand in hers. Her face was even paler today, the skin as fragile as tissue paper.

"Well, Granny, and how are you today? About as usual, I would say, and no worse, which is good. Shall we dispense with Deuteronomy? So serious! You would do better with a lighthearted novel, I suspect, or perhaps one of Shakespeare's comedies, something to lift the spirits, not all that exhortation and doing as one is told. One has enough of that in everyday life, I feel."

She paused, as if waiting for the Dowager to respond, but she slept on, undisturbed.

"Perhaps I shall tell you my news instead, Granny. I am to marry a duke — there! What do you think about that? At least, it is not quite certain, for I have not yet met the gentleman, but Lady Esther Franklyn is to help me, and she is a duke's daughter so she must know all about such people, I should think. So there is a good chance... if I can but meet him. And if he should like me… and I have to kiss him, and I am not sure that I can do that. How does one go about it, do you think? I cannot help but feel that the approach should come from the gentleman." Her voice began to waver. "And even if I meet him and he likes me and I kiss him, he might decide not to marry me after all, because how can an illegitimate girl become a duchess? It is not at all the thing, is it? A future duke should marry the daughter of a duke, and even if he stoops to the daughter of an earl, she should be a proper daughter. Not like me."

Her voice tailed away into nothing, and she laid her head on the bed and wept.

The Dowager shifted a little. "Hermione?" she said in a thread of a voice. "Is that you?"

Olivia wept even more.

***

Olivia loitered optimistically in the castle every day, to be sure not to miss the marquess when he came. She had no doubt that he would come, for Lady Esther was not a person to be gainsaid. Both the butlers, Simpson and Wellum, were told that if the Marquess of Embleton should call, she was to be told immediately, for she particularly wished to speak to him. She was not sure what she would speak about, but she would prepare something, some question or other to draw his attention, something suitably complicated. Then she could say airily, "How fascinating! I should love to hear more about it. Would you care to come to dinner?"

In the event, despite all her precautions she almost missed him. Aunt Alice had asked her to pick some scented flowers for her room, and although she had told Simpson where she was going, he had to search the full length of the flower garden to find her.

"My lady! My lady! He is here!" he cried, racing towards her and flapping his hands about in a most unbutler-like way.

"Papa's study?"

"Yes, my lady. And he has—"

Olivia did not wait to hear what he had. Dropping basket, scissors, flowers and gloves as she went, she ran as fast as she could to the terrace, across the bridge to the parlour, where she finally got the apron off, stuffing it under a cushion. Then on past the stairs, across the great hall and through the anteroom to the library. Here she paused to examine her appearance in a mirror. She was a little flushed from her exertions but not unbecomingly so, she thought. Pushing one or two stray locks into better order, she stepped more sedately across the library to the study door, where Wellum smiled knowingly at her as he threw open the door.

There were two men in the room with Papa, and which of the two was the marquess was impossible to tell. One man was slight and rather nondescript, although a gentleman in appearance. The other was rather handsome, somewhat above average height and with a twinkle in his eye. If he were the marquess, it would add a certain piquancy to her pursuit, she thought admiringly.

Her father looked rather harassed, but at the sight of Olivia his face lit up. "Ah, Olivia! Do come in and meet our visitors. May I present to you the Marquess of Embleton..." Oh. The nondescript one. "...and his brother-in-law Lord Harraby from Thirsk. My youngest daughter, gentlemen."

They bowed, Olivia curtsied and to her disappointment it was Lord Harraby who stepped forward to make the greetings and the usual unimaginative compliments — delighted to meet her, had heard so much of her beauty, charms and accomplishments, and so on and so forth.

"How is it we have never met before, Lord Harraby?" she could not resist asking. "Thirsk is not so very far away, after all."

"No, indeed, not much above ten miles the way we came, and a most pleasant ride over the moors, but we are rarely at Harraby Hall. I do not scruple to tell you that it is a dismal sort of house, never warm no matter how many fires one has burning. We have a very snug little place in Shropshire, and there we stay most comfortably from one year's end to the next, when we can. But my wife feels it only proper that the son and heir should be born at my principal seat, and so here we are until her next confinement. We are all hopeful for a boy this time so that we need not suffer the deprivations of Harraby Hall again for at least a generation."

"I hope the deprivations do not include the coverts on your land," she said, smiling to encompass the marquess. "I am sure the waiting time will pass more swiftly if there is good sport to be had."

To her delight, it was the marquess who answered. "Excellent s-sport, L-lady Olivia." And he smiled back at her.

"You are keen on a great many sports, I understand, Lord Embleton? I have heard much of your success racing your horses, and now I discover from the newspapers that you are a noted fencer, as well. You competed in a tournament at Landerby Hall, I understand."

"I did. Out-c-classed b-by others."

"But you were much admired. Let me see..." She produced the now much crumpled cutting from her reticule. "'*Lord Embleton's performance being much admired for his graceful movements.*' You see? My cousin Mr Bertram Atherton attended the gathering at Landerby Hall, so I have kept the report of it."

"Oh, do let me see," said Lord Harraby, "for Embleton has told us nothing of this. Oh, and the poetry, too! *'Agreed by all to be of the highest calibre, and comparable to the works of the great poets of the Roman era themselves.'* My, my, Embleton, how you do hide your light under a bushel."

Lord Embleton shifted uncomfortably. "Mere f-f-flattery."

"Lady Olivia, may I borrow the cutting?" Lord Harraby said. "We have no newspapers at Harraby, and my wife would be so interested to know what her brother does at these scholarly affairs."

She agreed to it, for she had already copied out the important parts.

Lord Embleton looked pointedly at the clock, and Lord Harraby took the hint, rising smoothly to his feet with murmurings about not outstaying their welcome. The earl rose, too, with a smile that looked suspiciously like relief.

Olivia was not about to let them escape so easily, however. "Must you go so soon? I should very much like to hear more of your race horses, Lord Embleton. Will you not join us for dinner one night soon? Both of you, and Lady Harraby too, naturally."

"My wife is not going into company just now, and I do not care to leave her alone at night, but Embleton will come, will you not?"

The marquess looked slightly panicked.

"Delighted to have you," the earl said. "We have a large gathering this Friday—"

"Not then, Papa," Olivia murmured. "Lord Embleton might think we are parading him before all our neighbours as a spectacle to be ogled and fawned over. A quiet family dinner is what I had in mind. We are such a small group now, and we all know each other so well that we are very dull at table. It would liven us up enormously to have just one extra guest." Then, seeing that the marquess was still looking anxious, and wondering if that might be because of his stammer, she added, "I warn you, however, that I am likely to talk your ears off, for I can never stop when I have new company to enjoy. You will not be able to get a word in edgewise."

The earl's eyebrows rose at this outrageous lie, but he said nothing and it did the trick, for the marquess smiled and said all that was proper, albeit painfully slowly, and a date was arranged.

When they had left, before Olivia could make good her escape, her father said, "What are you up to, you little monkey?"

"Oh, just practising," she said airily. "Since I am never to get to town, seemingly, and we live so quietly since Mama left, I have to take every opportunity to test my company manners."

He smiled, shaking his head at her. Laughing, she skipped out of the room, and went to warn the cook to be sure to prepare an unusually good dinner for the marquess.

3: A Family Dinner

The big evening party cheered Olivia enormously. She had been desperately low in spirits for so much of the year, firstly missing her debut season in town because of Grandmama's imminent demise, and then the summer had been blighted by Uncle Arthur. It was bad enough that a man should contrive to get himself murdered, especially a chaplain, but to discover that he had deceived them for years and years, overturning all their lives — it was the outside of enough! Olivia felt as if she had been weeping off and on for months, and now Mama had gone away, and Cousin Tess and even Walter, and there was no one left at Corland, apart from Papa and her brother Kent, who was twice as annoying as all the rest put together for he was perpetually cheerful and saw life as one long joke. But it was not *his* future which had been destroyed for ever.

At least the people investigating Uncle Arthur's death had gone away for the moment. Captain Edgerton was a funny little man who went everywhere with a sword at his side, as if he was about to be summoned to battle, although he told some amusing stories of his time in India. His wife was very elegant, although too tall for a lady — taller than her husband. They had not managed to discover who had killed poor Uncle Arthur, and now they had lost one of their own people and had gone off to look for her.

All of Olivia's worries were pushed aside for now, however. A big, noisy party with everyone from the neighbourhood and the carpets rolled up for dancing — that was more like it! It was almost like the time before the trouble, when Mama had been at home and there had always been some entertainment or other to look forward to. For once, Olivia was happy. She danced almost every dance, and even mousy little Katherine Parish, who never said a word to anyone and certainly never danced, was dragged to her feet for a reel.

The memory of it would keep Olivia warm for weeks, and even in the dull after-the-party low days, there would be letters of thanks and little posies of flowers and more morning callers than usual. Corland was so remote that their pool of acquaintances was small, so they had to make the most of whatever amusements were to be had.

And now there was a dinner with Lord Embleton to be anticipated! Not just dinner, but a whole evening and breakfast too, for the distance from Harraby Hall meant that he must stay overnight. So much excitement — she could barely sleep for thinking about it. Finally, after all these years, she could begin her campaign to win Lord Embleton's heart. Her amusing little game was about to become very real. What should she talk about? A list, she must begin a list of suitable subjects, so that she could talk at length to him and he would not have to feel self-conscious about his stammer.

He arrived in good time. Olivia watched from the window of an empty bedroom as the carriage drew up and decanted the marquess and his valet. Smiling, she skipped away to her own room to dress for dinner. She had long since decided on the gown she would wear, and settled on a simple string of pearls woven through her hair, an arrangement which Mama always said emphasised the shape of her face. As she peered at herself in the mirror, she could not see the benefit.

"What do you think, Hannah?" she said, twisting her head this way and that. "Something more elaborate, do you think? Pearls are so plain."

"Her ladyship allus said to keep it simple, miss, leastways till you go up to town. Save the diamonds for grand balls, she used to say."

Olivia knew perfectly well what her mother used to say, but it was annoying to have her words parroted back at her by the maid, who had never even been to London. She wanted to be in the drawing room before the marquess, however, so she chose not to quibble.

The marquess was not there, but the room already felt full, since Uncle George and Aunt Jane were ensconced there, quietly talking to Aunt Alice and the earl, while Olivia's five cousins clustered around the fire.

"Olivia!" Bertram said, as Simpson announced her. "How are you, cousin?"

"A little surprised. I did not know you were all to be here tonight."

He chuckled. "Aunt Alice sent a note over to Mother telling us that you had casually invited the Marquess of Embleton to dine here *en famille*, and since that might look rather particular, she begged us to increase the numbers, so to speak. Did she not tell you?"

"No, she did not. I sent word to Eustace, but that is all. At least if conversation flags, you will be able to talk to the marquess in Latin. Oh! She did not invite the Franklyns, did she?"

"She suggested I might like to bring Bea along, since we are betrothed, but—"

"Oh no!" Olivia cried, before she could stop herself.

"You know, then?" Bertram said quietly.

"That Lord Embleton offered for Bea? Lady Esther told me in confidence, but it is not generally known, I think."

"No, or Aunt Alice would never have invited Bea to dine with him, at least not so soon after the event. But Bea would not come, naturally. It would have been dreadfully awkward for him, sharing a table with the person who declined to be a duchess."

"I cannot imagine how she could turn him down," Olivia said without thinking.

Bertram smiled. "Can you not? Perhaps she had a better offer."

"What could be better than being a duchess? Oh, cousin, I did not mean—! I am sure you are... well, you will be an earl one day, which is almost as good," she said kindly.

He laughed out loud. "Now you sound just like Bea used to be, judging a man's marriageability by his rank. She has learnt that there is more to a man than his title, and perhaps you will one day, too."

"I know that, of course. But if there are two good, kind, honourable gentlemen, and one is going to be a duke one day and one is not... well, why not aim for the future duke?"

"Is that what you are doing? Aiming for the future duke? Is that why you invited him to dinner?"

Olivia felt herself blushing, but answered him composedly. "Cousin, I have no idea when, if ever, I might get to town or how I shall move in society there now that my circumstances are so much altered. I am merely taking the opportunity to meet as many distinguished gentlemen as I can."

Bertram smiled kindly at her. "You should go and stay with Izzy. She often has a houseful of distinguished guests."

"Izzy!" she muttered under her breath. As if that would help, to be under the same roof as her prettier, livelier, more popular sister — to be the lesser version, always compared and found wanting, always overlooked.

Fortunately, the marquess was announced just then, the earl moved forward to receive him and introduce him to Aunt Alice, and Olivia was too taken up with watching them to worry about Bertram. Kent appeared at her side and spoke to her, but she paid him little attention, so intent was she on her quarry.

Quarry! Now that was a nasty word, as if he were a fox and she a hound in hot pursuit. No, such a quiet man was more like a rabbit, and she was the fox wanting to devour him. Even nastier! There would be no devouring, for all she wanted was for him to fall in love with her, after which she would undertake to make him very happy. What was wrong with that?

The marquess sat with Lady Alice for a little while, but it was obvious that their conversation was strained. His stammer and her inability to see him made it slow going, and eventually Aunt Jane rescued him and took him away to be introduced to her daughters. Now that Olivia could not allow. She was very fond of her cousins, but she would not stand idly by and watch them making progress with her marquess.

She wandered over to the group as casually as she could contrive.

"Ah, Olivia, dear, there you are. Have you met Lord Embleton?"

What a bird-witted woman Aunt Jane was! Had she forgotten it was Olivia who had invited Lord Embleton to dine?

"We are acquainted," she murmured, dipping into a curtsy. "How are you, Lord Embleton? Well, I trust?"

"Th-thank you, yes. And you, L-l-lady Olivia?"

"I am very well, thank you. Was your journey tolerable? The roads are so muddy after all the rain we have had lately, it is a wonder that anyone can get about at all. But we are delighted that you managed to reach us. I hope you like venison, for cook manages to put twenty different forms of it before us at this time of year. And as for duck..."

In this manner, she managed to monopolise the marquess until Eustace arrived, late as usual, and dinner was announced. The marquess looked round, saw that Lady Alice was being escorted to the dining room by the earl, and offered his arm to Olivia, just as she hoped. She lowered her eyes demurely, for it would not do to be thought to be gloating. His actions were mere courtesy to the daughter of his host, no more than that.

Aunt Jane, who was a great organiser, took charge of arranging the seating, placing the marquess beside Aunt Alice, and Olivia next to him. Olivia had Cousin Bertram on her other side, but she did not mind that. He would not be offended if she devoted more of her attention to the marquess.

At first, Lord Embleton was concerned to attend to Aunt Alice, asking her in his painfully slow way what she wished him to do to assist her. Olivia listened in an agony of impatience as he stuttered his way through his little speech.

"How kind you are!" Aunt Alice said calmly, as he finally drew to a close. "However, I am well attended by my personal footman who prepares my food for me. If I need anything further, I have my brother beside me. Do, pray, enjoy the meal. We shall talk in a little while, but for now you may enjoy my niece's company."

He nodded and turned obediently to Olivia as the soup was handed round, and for a while the whole company attended to the needs of the appetite. As soon as the soup had been removed with the fish, and conversation had begun again, Olivia began on her list of topics with which to entertain and, she hoped, beguile Lord Embleton.

"I have been following the triumphs of your race horses, sir," she began. "Such a success at Newmarket last year! Two winners, was it not?"

"Yes, I—"

"And a third later, as well. How proud you must have been! Such a proof of the efficacy of your methods. But this year was not quite so promising. So unfortunate! Crown Star must have been having an off day, such as all horses must have from time to time. My own horse is much the same. Some days he is full of life and keen to take me wherever I wish to go, and other days there is a reluctance in him, as if life is an effort, somehow. But then, people are just the same, is it not so? We all have good days, when we are full of energy and anything seems possible, and bad days, when we do not particularly wish to leave our beds."

She was forced, by the tempting aromas of the fish on her plate, to pause while she ate a few mouthfuls, and the marquess politely jumped into the breach.

"I have f-f-found that m-m-m…" He stopped, took a deep breath, and tried again. "*My* horses are not t-t-t…" Another deep breath. "Temper-am-m-m…"

"Temperamental," she said, without thinking.

"Yes. C-c-crown S-s-s…"

"Crown Star. Oh!" She clapped a hand over her mouth. "So sorry."

His lips flickered into a smile, instantly lost. "Everyone d-d-does it. Think n-n-nothing of it."

"But it is so *rude* to draw attention to your…" She was about to say *'disability'*, but some vestige of good sense prevented her.

There was a flash of anger in his eyes as he said in curt tones, "My affliction. Indeed. Your fish will get c-cold."

Thus rebuked, she could only fall into miserable silence and fork tiny bites of fish into her mouth, but everything tasted like ashes. She wished she could crawl away and hide in a dark place, for tears were not far below the surface.

The marquess turned to Lady Alice for a while, who listened to his hesitant words with her customary placidity. On Olivia's other side, Bertram leaned towards her and whispered, "It takes extraordinary levels of restraint *not* to finish his words for him."

"It must be so irritating for him, poor man," she whispered back. "I do try, but I cannot always stop myself in time."

"At least you try," Bertram said. "So many people do it all the time, and flatter themselves they are being helpful."

The fish was removed with a haunch of venison and a chine of mutton, and the dinner guests devoted themselves to the interesting business of sampling the many tempting dishes laid out before them. Lord and Lady Rennington had for many years prided themselves on the generosity of their table, and even though Lady Rennington was no longer at the castle and the diners numbered only fourteen, the cook made no reduction in the amount provided. There were always to be two full courses every day except Sunday, and the table laden to capacity.

Olivia ate sparingly of the first course, knowing that the second would be well supplied with her favourites — tarts and cakes and various creams and jellies. When she next fell into conversation with the marquess, she had herself fully under control. She talked a great deal herself, as planned, to spare him from the necessity himself, but when he did speak, she listened courteously and patiently as each word limped to completion. He would never be a scintillating conversationalist, but she felt that their discussion had been as enjoyable as possible under the circumstances.

After dinner, it was merely a matter of waiting for the gentlemen to make their way back to the drawing room. Olivia was too astute to approach the marquess directly he reappeared, so she stayed beside Aunt Alice while Aunt Jane and Cousin Penelope attempted to get a coherent sentence from the poor man. Half listening to their conversation, and trying not to smile whenever Penelope jumped in to finish for him, she wondered for the first time what it would be like to be married to such a man. It was incomparably better than a husband who gambled himself into debt or kept a series of mistresses, but that stutter might come into the category of irritating little habits which one could easily survive for an evening or two, but which would drive one to distraction over a lifetime. Or would one simply stop noticing after a while?

And yet... he was a marquess and would one day be a duke, so he and his wife would live the sort of lives typical for their class. He would be out and about, seeing to his estates and tenants and so forth, while she would make sure their current home ran smoothly, raise the children and dispense charity amongst the deserving poor, and possibly the undeserving poor, too, if she felt especially charitable.

She would hardly see her husband except at dinner, when they would be at opposite ends of a very long table. There would be very little occasion to actually talk to him, except perhaps to report on the children's doings. *'Henry's Latin is coming on wonderfully, his tutor says, and he will be quite ready for Harrow next year.'* Or perhaps it would be Eton. Where had the marquess been educated? She knew so little about him. Schools, she must ask him about his schooling.

Oddly, this little vision of her perfect future as a duchess did not sound quite as alluring as she might have supposed. That might be a typical life for the nobility, but it differed markedly from her own family. With two older sisters and three brothers, not to mention a host of cousins, she had always had someone to talk to, to joke with and tease. Her sisters had married and gone away, her brothers were seldom there and even Mama had left. She felt her present loneliness acutely, so why was she so keen to embrace an even lonelier life?

For a moment, her resolve wavered, but then she recollected that, as duchess, she could order her life how she chose. One of her cousins could bear her company — Emily, perhaps, being the same age, and so shy that she would make the perfect retiring companion. Or she could follow Izzy's lead and fill her house with amusing guests. She would never be lonely then, would she?

She had, she felt, made some progress already with the marquess, after a somewhat shaky start. But her next step was clear to her — she had to kiss him, and she already had a plan for that. But first, she needed to get him alone, for kissing was not a thing one attempted in a crowded drawing room. Thus, when the tea things came out, and there was a general mingling, she dared to approach the marquess again.

"What do you think of Corland Castle, Lord Embleton, now that you have seen a little more of it? A most impressive stronghold, is it not? And yet it is entirely false, a modern construction masquerading as a medieval fortress. But no sieges have ever damaged its stout walls, nor have battles been fought on its lawns, the defenders' pennants fluttering bravely from the battlements. Even the moat is a fraud, providing access to the basement and stables."

"It is a m-most com-m-m..." He paused, took a breath. Olivia held her own breath, practically biting her tongue in the effort to stay silent. " *Commodious* house," he managed at last. "Ch-charmingly original."

"The previous house, which was a real castle surviving real battles, was not in the least commodious, by all accounts. Family tradition is that it was always cold, and everything in it was cold, too. Cold soup, cold bath water..." She shivered. "It makes me feel chilly just thinking about it. But it was exceedingly picturesque. We have a painting of it, before it was knocked down. Should you care to see it? I am no expert, but it is generally accounted a work of great skill. The artist was rather famous in his day, I understand."

"I should be m-m-most happy to see it."

"Excellent! It is in the library, but we can go through the dining room. This way."

With so many people milling about, and the marquess not being a great, tall fellow, they were able to slip away unnoticed. A couple of footmen in the dining room paused in their work to bow as they passed through. Olivia took up a candelabrum that stood on a sideboard and threw open the further door. Beyond, the library lay in darkness.

The marquess stopped, frowning.

"Lord Embleton?" Olivia said. "It is just in here."

"No."

"I... I beg your pardon?"

She turned to face him and saw that his face was dark with anger. "How old are you, Lady Olivia?"

"I am eighteen years of age, sir."

"You have much to learn," he said coldly.

She was more astonished by the lack of stuttering than his manner — when he was angry, he did not hesitate at all. How fascinating! She stared at him wonderingly, while he glared back at her, his nostrils flaring. He was rather splendid in such a mood, and she had a brief glimpse of the duke he might one day be, mostly placid but capable of towering displays of temper when roused. His servants would tiptoe round him, terrified of setting him off

A voice from behind them broke the silence. “Olivia, dear! Ah, there you are. Are you going to show Lord Embleton some of our fine paintings? I am sure he will be pleased with them, but do let me come with you, for in your enthusiasm I suspect you have forgotten your mama’s advice on the subject of being alone with a gentleman, have you not?”

Not exactly forgotten, no, for that was the whole point of the exercise, but it had failed anyway. Lord Embleton was far too experienced a man to be caught in that way. Such an eligible gentleman does not reach the advanced age of thirty still unmarried without developing good instincts for ambitious females. Not that Olivia had any thought of compromising him. No, a kiss was all she had wanted, and let what may come of it, but, with an inward sigh, she abandoned her carefully laid plans and allowed Aunt Jane to accompany them into the library.

“Not that Lord Embleton would ever take advantage of your innocence,” Aunt Jane went on in her bright society voice, “but one must always be aware of the possibility of less honourable men. Shall we go in?”

Olivia followed them in, trying not to laugh at the marquess’s thunderous face. He had already been insulted by Olivia trying to be alone with him, and now Aunt Jane was talking about him taking advantage of her! Poor man, he was not having a good evening. But between her own chatter and Aunt Jane’s, they managed to entertain him for quite some time before Papa came looking for them, to see about making up a four for whist. Lord Embleton’s expression brightened at the thought, and within minutes he was settled at a table with Papa, Uncle George and the fashionable lawyer from London, Mr Willerton-Forbes, who had arrived with the murder investigators and now was involved in Papa's affairs and become almost a permanent fixture.

For some time, Olivia played a little and read a little and even took up her needlework briefly, while trying to listen in to the conversation from their table, but whenever she caught snatches, it was Mr Willerton-Forbes talking about Papa's finances, which was not interesting in the slightest. Eventually, the Westwick Heights family went home and Aunt Alice went to bed, but Kent took over Uncle George's seat at the card table, and they played on.

Olivia gave it up and went to bed. By the time she rose, early by her standards, the marquess had already set out for Harraby Hall, and there was nothing for Olivia to do but to reflect on an unsatisfactory evening, and plan the next phase in her campaign. But next time she met the marquess, she would not attempt to kiss him, for such stratagems would only give him a disgust of her. She would merely be herself, and perhaps he would like her or perhaps he would not, but even if nothing came of it, it would still be good practice for her proper come-out next spring.

4: Harraby Hall

Olivia was most unwilling to wait until the spring before seeing the marquess again, but she could not see how an earlier meeting could be contrived. A conference with Lady Esther reassured her that there would be more opportunities later in the autumn.

"He flits about here and there, but when he moves to his own hunting lodge in Leicestershire, there are possibilities. My cousin lives in the area, and there will be no difficulty in obtaining an invitation. Pretty girls with a good dowry are always in demand. How much is your dowry?"

"Five thousand pounds, although Papa says he could manage ten thousand at a pinch, if necessary. He got Josie and Izzy married off at five thousand apiece, and he always said I would do just as well as them," she said, a little defiantly, for she was aware that five thousand pounds was not a great sum for an earl's daughter.

"Hmm. Of course, Lady Josephine and Lady Isabel married men of great wealth, who hardly needed their dowries."

"And I intend to marry a man of great wealth, too," Olivia said, lifting her chin.

"Indeed, but he will have to love you to distraction, as well," Lady Esther mused. "A great many men will marry a pretty girl from a good family with a large dowry without feeling more than a modest affection for her, knowing that it will be enough, but without the dowry... it is more difficult. And there is the unfortunate matter of your change in status."

"You mean my illegitimacy," Olivia said in a small voice.

"Precisely. Many a man would be put off by such a blemish in the family, even though it was entirely unavoidable. With thirty thousand, he might be persuaded to overlook it, or even twenty thousand... something could be done with that. But five thousand? I am surprised that Lord Rennington has not contrived to put something more aside for you."

"There was something amiss with the money. Uncle Arthur had the management of it in Grandpapa's day, and some of it has... gone missing. Mr Willerton-Forbes is looking into it, to see if anything can be recovered."

Lady Esther raised her eyebrows a fraction. "Is that how it was? In my experience, once money has been taken out of an estate, it vanishes, never to be seen again."

"But Uncle Arthur left Tess a fortune in his will, so perhaps he hid it all away somewhere."

"Even if so, it is of no use to you in your predicament. We will just have to make sure Lord Embleton falls desperately in love with you, that is all."

This was all very dispiriting, and Olivia shed a few disconsolate tears into her pillow each night. Her dreams of being a duchess, so recently given succour by Lady Esther's enthusiastic support, were fast dissipating. Not only could she not find a way to meet the marquess again for weeks and weeks, but now she needed a larger dowry as well. She had always known that being illegitimate would be problematic, but for a brief time, Lady Esther had given her hope. Now that hope was all but gone.

But then hope flared again, for Lord Harraby called once more. He returned her newspaper cutting, which he reported had entranced Lady Harraby with this view into her brother's life.

"I am sorry to say that we have been obliged to increase our subscriptions vastly, to be sure not to miss any further description of Embleton's prowess," he said, with a light laugh. "But that is not my only reason for coming today. My dear wife is dreadfully bored with the limited society afforded by her immediate family, and is set on filling the house with guests for the next month, at least. She wondered whether you might care to be of the party, Lady Olivia. If one of your brothers can escort you to Harraby Hall, Lady Harraby will act as chaperon, since your mama is away at present."

Olivia was almost too excited to speak. "Lady Esther Franklyn — she might be able to—"

"Excellent, excellent! Here is a letter from Lady Harraby," he said, handing it to the earl, "making the invitation in formal terms, but I wished to call to tell you how welcome you will be. Another young lady... and we can offer you some good sport, Rennington, if you are of a mind to leave home at this present."

Papa made some non-committal noises, but as soon as Lord Harraby had left, he said, "Now do not get your hopes up, for we must take your Aunt Alice's advice on the matter, you know. She stands in place of your mama just now. She will know what is best to be done."

Aunt Alice was not encouraging. "My dear niece, do you truly wish to go away on a pleasure trip, as if nothing had changed? If you want a change of scene, then you might go to Josie or Izzy, or to Lady Tarvin at Harfield, for they understand your situation."

"What precisely is my situation?" Olivia said with some heat. "Because if this is about my illegitimacy, I do not see why that should concern anyone. If Lord and Lady Harraby do not regard it, why should anyone else?"

"That is the very best attitude to take," Aunt Alice said, nodding her head. "You must never be ashamed of what you are, for it is not your fault. Nevertheless, it cannot be ignored or swept aside, either, and just at the moment, as news of your father's situation is spreading and we are all subjected to unpleasant gossip — even more unpleasant gossip, after the recent tragedy — it might be best to... well, to..."

"Keep my head below the parapet?" Olivia said.

"Exactly," Aunt Alice said, smiling, her sightless eyes fixed on a point close to Olivia's ear. "Live quietly at home or with relations, and do nothing to attract more comment. Then, in the spring—"

Olivia gave an exclamation of disgust and jumped to her feet. "Spring!" She paced restlessly across her father's study and back again. "By the spring I will be nineteen and practically an old maid."

"In the spring," her aunt said firmly, "under the wing of a new step-mother, if that should happen, or your Aunt Tarvin, perhaps, you can be introduced into a suitable level of society for your new position. You need not fear that you will be unable to marry. Your connections will still ensure you make an excellent match, in time, but you must be very careful not to do anything to invite disapprobation. It is... an awkward situation, to be sure."

It was her father who came to her rescue. "I do not think that Olivia could come to any great harm with the Harrabys, Alice. She wants to move in society a little before her come out and this is as good an opportunity as any. If Lady Esther is willing to chaperon her, new company might cheer her up, instead of moping about Corland with nothing very much to do. I have seen how low her spirits have been these last few months, and I do not want to selfishly keep her by my side if she can be off enjoying herself."

"Her place is by her father, until she marries," Aunt Alice said sharply. "You are too soft with the girls, Charles."

"I want them to be happy," he said, spreading his hands helplessly. "I have Kent to bear me company, and Eustace, now and then. And you, of course, and George and Jane are looking after me."

"Then I may go?" Olivia said excitedly.

He nodded, although he looked a little sad. "I shall miss you, daughter."

"Then come with me. New company might cheer you up, too."

He shook his head. "Your Aunt Jane has another friend coming to stay... someone I might like to marry. I must do my best to find another wife, you know. Your mama insists on it."

"Oh, Papa!" Olivia said, flinging her arms around him and squeezing him tight. "I wish Mama had not gone away."

"So do I, daughter. So do I."

Aunt Alice's well-modulated tones interrupted this moment of family accord. "Olivia, if you will scribe for me, I shall dictate a letter to Lady Esther, to see if she is willing to undertake this venture. If not, it will have to be given up, I fear."

This was a dispiriting thought, especially as Aunt Alice felt it necessary to lay out in the letter in stark terms her own disapproval of the idea, and all the pitfalls awaiting an unwary and inexperienced girl in a strange house. But Lady Esther did not let Olivia down. Within an hour, the note had been delivered to Lady Esther Franklyn, and a positive reply received. Two days later, she set off for Harraby Hall, accompanied by Lady Esther and her rather starchy maid, a coachman and groom, two footmen and a pair of outriders.

And before she left Corland, a little miracle happened. Papa called her into his study, beaming from ear to ear. Mr Willerton-Forbes was also there in his fashionable clothes, looking nothing like a lawyer.

"Well, daughter, I have some excellent news. The money that was removed from the estate over many years has been found, and I shall be a great deal better off. Is it not so, Willerton-Forbes?"

"Indeed, my lord. Very much better off."

"It means I shall be able to do something more for you — twenty-five or perhaps thirty thousand pounds, in total. That will make all the difference to you... your aunt was so concerned... well, so pretty as you are, you will have no difficulty in finding a husband, but we want it to be the right sort of husband... someone worthy of you. With such a dowry, you are assured of making a splendid match, even with—"

"Even with the illegitimacy?" she said.

He had the grace to look abashed. "It does make a difference, daughter."

She was very well aware of that, but she was too happy to care. She was going to Harraby Hall and she would have thirty thousand pounds with which to entice a potential husband. Lord Embleton, perhaps? A girl could hope, could she not?

***

Harraby Hall was not like any house Olivia had ever seen before. It was not vast and imposing, like Lochmaben Castle, nor solidly square, like Corland, nor light and airy, like Westwick Heights. It looked as if a child had thrown together bricks of different sizes and shapes and colours. At one side was a tower, with narrow slits for windows, and on the other, rooms projected outwards from the walls. The central part of the house was a single storey, but behind it could be seen other, higher wings. The roof featured an array of battlements, statuary, oddly curved protuberances, chimneys of varying styles and a clock tower. It made Olivia want to laugh.

In some respects, however, it was like any other great house, for out poured an army of footmen, followed by Lord Harraby, who ushered them into the great hall, with its arched roof supported by wooden beams.

"Forgive my wife for not being here to greet you, but she is taking her mandatory afternoon rest," he said. "On behalf of both of us, may I say how pleased I am that you could both come. You are very welcome to Harraby Hall."

Lord Harraby personally conducted them to their rooms and left them to the ministrations of a friendly housekeeper and a pair of maids. Gowns were changed, hair was brushed, faces were washed, a tray of tea and cakes arrived, then Lady Esther settled down to write to her husband, informing him that they had contrived to survive a journey of fifteen miles unscathed.

Olivia wondered if she should write to Papa, but somehow the excitement of a new house and new people to meet overwhelmed any desire for so sedentary an occupation. Instead, she gazed out of the window at the little patch of gardens which was all that was visible — new gardens to explore, too! Everything was new and thrillingly different. But a solitary walk did not appeal, either. People, that was what she needed.

"May I go downstairs and find some company?" she said.

Lady Esther looked up absent-mindedly, tapping her nose with her pen. “Later, my dear. We should rest before dinner. You may go to your room, if you wish, and read or have a little lie down.”

“Thank you.” Curtsying, she left the room, but as she crossed the passage to her own room, she heard a burst of laughter drifting up from below. As softly as she could, she crept to the top of the stairs and peered downwards. She could hear voices, dim and indistinct, then a louder voice — “No!” it cried. Another burst of laughter. How much she longed to be down there, listening, laughing, part of a big merry group where people talked of happy things, and not of murdered chaplains and illegal marriages and poor, poor Granny, so near to death and yet clinging tenaciously to life.

“You must be Lady Olivia,” said a voice behind her, a voice filled with amusement.

Olivia spun round to see a young lady of her own age, blonde curls piled high under a wisp of lacy cap. Then, with a shock, she noticed that she was large with child. This, then, must be Lady Harraby.

“Oh! My lady! Yes, I am... Olivia Atherton, that is.”

“Harraby has told us all to address you as Lady Olivia. But do you wish to go downstairs? No need to lurk on the landing like this.”

“I should love to... but I must not. Lady Esther has told me to stay in my room until the dinner hour.”

“Then let us go there and have a pleasant coze. I am so happy to have you here — another woman my own age. The house is full of guests but the females are all either matrons who want to talk to me about babies, or else embittered spinsters. I am not yet ready to be a matron — I still want to dance, when my shape permits.” Patting her stomach with a little laugh, she linked arms with Olivia and together they entered the bedroom, the door firmly closed behind them.

"Now do tell me all about yourself, for Embleton said very little about you, except that you are very pretty and I can see that for myself. What a dreadful time you have had of it. A murder! But someone confessed to it, we heard. That must be a relief."

"Except that he did not do it," Olivia said. "It is the oddest thing, and it is all Tess Nicholson's fault — she is the daughter of the man who was murdered, you know — but no one can quite understand it. This man, who was just a village woodworker, was supposed to be in love with her, but now he has married someone else, a dairymaid or poultry maid or some such, and Tess has gone away to marry some man no one has ever heard of at Durham. It is most perplexing."

"Well! That sounds most dramatic," Lady Harraby said. "How fascinating! But the man who was murdered... the chaplain... he was not ordained. And so..."

Olivia sighed inwardly. The *'pleasant coze'* presumably meant prodding her for all the family's scandalous events of the last few months. She told Lady Harraby all that was public knowledge, and had to listen to a great deal of sympathetic verbiage followed by yet more questions.

When she could get a word in herself, she said, "Are there many guests at Harraby Hall at present?"

Lady Harraby rattled off a list of names, none of which meant much to Olivia. But there was one name missing.

"And your brother... Lord Embleton? He is here, too, is he not?"

She laughed, a melodic tinkle. "Oh, him! The embittered spinsters drove him away, but to be honest, he is not good in large groups like this, not unless we all speak in Latin or some such. A whole month with his Cambridge friends, that was no trouble to him, but here he vanishes at the first attack from a marriageable female." She sighed. "You would suppose he would be used to it by now, and have evolved strategies to deal with encroaching persons. He will be a duke one day and is quite unable to step outside his front door without sycophants and parasites attempting to latch onto him."

This was a blow — after all this effort, Lord Embleton was not even there! Disappointment washed over Olivia, so acute that she barely noticed the rest of this speech. It was only when Lady Harraby's maid came looking for her to dress for dinner that she realised that she was herself just such an encroaching person as Lady Harraby described. But at least she had reason to believe that the marquess had indeed evolved strategies against encroachment, for had he not refused to enter the empty library with her without a chaperon? And he had left after the embittered spinsters attacked him.

Well, if there were no Lord Embleton, she would just have to amuse herself with the remaining guests, although she had no warm feelings towards the embittered spinsters who had driven away her quarry. Clearly, they were not very subtle.

Olivia and Lady Esther were early in descending to the saloon, sitting decorously together on a sofa as other guests drifted in. Lady Esther was engaged in conversation with Lady Harraby — *'as one duke's daughter to another'*, as she put it — when a somewhat larger group arrived, consisting of a grey-haired woman, a nondescript man, and two women whom Olivia had no trouble identifying as the embittered spinsters, from their age and sour faces. Lady Harraby eased herself to her feet and began to move forward to greet them, but before she was halfway there, the man gave a sudden exclamation, his eyes fixed on Olivia.

Ignoring Lady Harraby, he crossed the room steadily, his eyes locked on Olivia. When he reached her, he fell to his knees at her feet.

"How come you here to haunt me, fair ghost?" he declaimed, throwing his arms wide as if he were on a stage. "What mischief brings a phantom to this place? Or has my fevered imagination conjured this most beautiful of apparitions? Nay, do not shake your head, fair ghost, for I am in earnest. Tell me, tell me at once what you are doing here."

Olivia was bemused and a little afraid of so much intensity in a man she had never seen before in her life, but there was something ridiculous about the situation, too, that made her want to laugh. Lady Esther, however, was not at all amused.

"Desist, sir! I believe you have consumed too much brandy."

"Not a drop, I swear it, or I should not be so confused, ma'am. For here is one I had no expectation to see, indeed I had word only a few days ago that she was settled elsewhere and therefore cannot also be here. Yet here she is! It is extraordinary!"

Olivia began to understand. "Can you not think of an explanation, sir? For I assure you I am no ghost."

She smiled at him, and he cried out. "A dimple! You have a dimple just there, so I must conclude… I was mistaken in you, fair ghost. But you are so alike, it is incredible. Except younger… you are younger."

"Six years."

"Is it so? And yet… you are almost the age she was when I first saw her. Until you smiled and I saw the dimple, I could have sworn you were Izzy as she was. But she has no dimple, and I see now, you have the better figure."

"Sir!" Lady Esther said coldly. "Pray do not continue in this vein, when you have not even been introduced to us."

Lady Harraby was hovering, shaking with laughter. "Ma'am, may I present to you the Earl of Kiltarlity from Strathinver, in Scotland. Lord

Kiltarlity, this is Lady Esther Franklyn of Highwood Place in the North Riding, and your fair ghost is—"

"A daughter of the Earl of Rennington and younger sister of Izzy, now Lady Farramont of Stonywell, although I have forgot your name, my lovely ghost," Lord Kiltarlity said.

"Olivia. I am Olivia Atherton," she said, laughing at him, as he rose from his knees and sat beside her, his eyes brimming with amusement.

"Lady Esther," Lady Harraby said, "shall we leave them to talk, while I introduce you to Lady Kiltarlity and the Miss Osborns?"

Reluctantly, with another glare at Lord Kiltarlity, Lady Esther allowed herself to be drawn away to the grey-haired woman and the embittered spinsters.

"Osborn," Olivia said in satisfaction. "You are Izzy's suitor, Robert Osborn."

"I am, or rather I *was*, but now I have this wretched title to contend with. I never wanted it, you know, and certainly never deserved it, but my loyal, honourable, courageous brothers all fell in the King's service, and I ended up as an earl, for my sins."

"I am the opposite," Olivia said. "I have *lost* my title, for no longer am I Lady Olivia."

"Then let us both revert to our former happy state," he said, with a smile which lit up his face. "You shall be Lady Olivia to me, and you may call me Robert, as Izzy did. You are extraordinarily like her, you know."

"Except for the dimple. I know."

"And the better figure," he whispered. "The *much* better figure. Are you like her in ways, too? Do you explode and throw things and yell at people?"

She giggled. "No, sir, I do not."

"Thank God! One Izzy in the world is enough, I think. Ah, there is dinner ready for us. Will you sit beside me and tell me all about yourself?"

She lowered her eyes demurely. Lord Embleton may not have been present but here was someone new and exciting to talk to. "I should like that, Lord Kiltarlity."

"Robert, if you please."

"I cannot possibly call you by your Christian name."

"Then Osborn. All my friends call me Osborn, even now, and we are going to be friends, are we not?"

"I hope so... Osborn."

As he led her into the dining room, Olivia felt a little bubble of warmth inside. A friend! Yes, she would like to be friends with this curious man. She would like that very much.

5: The Charming Earl

Olivia soon discovered there were two sides to her dining companion. Robert Osborn was a charming, lighthearted man, who flirted with her very gently, teased her a little as if she were a sister, listened with seeming interest to everything she said and even laughed sometimes as if she were truly amusing. But occasionally, the Earl of Kiltarlity broke through and some remembrance of his present situation rendered him morose.

"It is so difficult," he said in one of these phases. "How am I supposed to know what to do? My mother says I need to raise more sheep, because that is what is profitable these days. I have three stewards, and one tells me to develop a four crop rotation system, one tells me to stick to traditional ways and the third tells me it is imperative I invest in coal. My banker is telling me to increase rents and the attorney says the tenants won't hear of it. And all the while, the parson keeps lecturing me on shepherds looking after their flock, so we are back at sheep again. I tell you, my head is spinning. It is not easy, being an earl."

"Is it so very difficult? Papa seems to manage very well, but then he does tend to leave everything to the steward and the gamekeeper. So long as there are enough birds to shoot, he is not much concerned about the rest of it."

Osborn laughed. "Perhaps I should do that! It sounds very restful. The trouble is that my father was such a decisive man, and everyone expects me to be the same."

"You are not your father. Your ways are bound to be different."

"Exactly! I just cannot decide what my ways should be. I cannot decide on anything."

Olivia shook her head. "You are in such a muddle, Osborn! Think of it this way — who do you most want to be happy? Your mother? The stewards? The banker? The attorney? The parson?"

He chuckled. "Ah, an interesting perspective! Well, my mother, in some ways, because she hounds me so. That is why we have instigated the improvements at Strathinver, because she kept on about it. My father never let her do what she wanted there, you see. He said it was fine as it was, unchanged since his childhood, so now she is belatedly bringing the old place into the nineteenth century. But for the estate... I cannot say. Not the banker or attorney, and certainly not the parson, although to do him justice, his sermons enable me to get an extra hour's sleep on the Sabbath. But I cannot see why I should make the stewards happy, either. I pay them to do a job, and so long as they do it, I do not much care whether they are happy with the results or not."

"But are they happy with the conditions of the job? Are they comfortably housed? Are they paid enough to have a family, and given little offerings from the estate — game and fish, that sort of thing? Are you a demanding master, or one they respect and admire?"

"Oh. Are they happy as *people*, you mean? I had never thought of that."

"And your tenants, too — are they happy?"

"The tenants are never happy," he said, with a wry grimace. "There is always some complaint. If it is not a leaky roof, it will be damp walls, or a door that hangs badly, and never, ever mention the weather to them, not if you want to be away from there before the end of the century."

"And can you afford to put these things right? Not the weather, perhaps, but the roofs and doors?"

"Oh, yes, but— You think I should?"

"I think that if you have contented tenants and stewards, they will work better, and that means that the land will be more productive. Mama always said that if the kitchen maids and footmen were contented, a house will run more smoothly, and I should think the same rule would apply to estates. Do you not agree, Osborn?"

"I do!" And almost as quick as blinking, the lighthearted man was back. "Thank you, fair ghost, for your words of otherworldly wisdom. And now I am going to move that dish out of your reach, for there is a serious risk you will turn into a raspberry cream, and who then will advise me how to go on?"

"But I like raspberry creams."

"Do you really? I would never have guessed it. After all, you have just eaten five of them."

"I have not! It is only four."

"Five."

"Four, and they are only a mouthful so I could manage one more."

Laughing, he slid the dish back to her, allowed her to take one, then pushed the dish away again. "That is a big difference between you and Izzy. She only ever played with her food, but you eat properly."

"Is it—" she mumbled, her mouth full of raspberry cream, before she remembered her manners and swallowed first. "Is it proper for a lady to eat five raspberry creams at a sitting?"

"Six."

"Oh! You... you...!"

He laughed at her, and shook his head. As Lady Harraby rose to lead the ladies out of the room, Olivia felt she had indeed made a friend, or an extra brother, perhaps. And for an hour or two, she had not thought at all about murder or illegitimacy or poor Granny.

Lady Esther drew her aside into a quiet corner of the drawing room. "Goodness, there is a dreadful draught from that window. How sensible you were to bring a thick shawl down with you. Perhaps we should move nearer to the fire, but everyone else is there and we cannot talk so easily."

"Shall I fetch a shawl for you, ma'am?"

"Oh... what a thoughtful girl you are! Thank you. In the chest of drawers, third drawer down on the left. The green woollen one. It will not match this gown, but in a draughty house like this, one would rather be warm than stylish, I feel."

When she returned, and Lady Esther had disposed the shawl about her shoulders, she said, "This is an interesting development, Olivia. Do you think we should abandon your original plan and look elsewhere?"

"Lord Kiltarlity? He is a dreadful rattle. Papa called him a fribble."

"But he likes you."

"No, he likes *Izzy*. His only interest in me is that I remind him of her."

Lady Esther nodded thoughtfully. "But something might come of that, and his mother made it clear to me that he is looking for a wife. The last of her sons, and the heir presumptive is a very distant cousin. I greatly approved of your original plan, as you know, for I firmly believe a girl should aim as high as she can, and in your case... Olivia, I do not scruple to tell you that I long to be the instigator of a great match. One of the advantages of my marriage, I felt, was that Mr Franklyn had a daughter of the perfect age for me to mould into a lady and settle successfully. Well, Beatrice has gone her own way, and I am happy for her, but she was not an easy girl to mould. Whereas you... you are a born lady, with your delicate ways and perfect manners. I never have to remind you not to slouch, and of course you have the looks. You are every bit the equal of Lady Farramont, and you have the same ability to sparkle in company, but without the restlessness that characterised her. That is why I was delighted to offer to help you, even though I should probably be at home preparing for Beatrice's wedding just now."

"And I appreciate it, truly I do, Lady Esther. I was so miserable trapped at home all the time, and Papa and Aunt Alice were not very encouraging. It cheers me up so much to be in company again, and meeting new people, even if... *he* is not here."

"You see? Perfect manners. But here we have a charming earl who clearly likes you, and perhaps a charming earl who is looking to marry is a better target for our efforts than a marquess who may be a much tougher nut to crack."

"I do not think you should pin any hopes on Lord Kiltarlity. He was one of Izzy's most ardent suitors, desperately in love with her, and he sees me only as a pale shadow of her. That intrigues him, but I am *not* Izzy, and as soon as he realises that, he will be disappointed and move on. I find him amusing, but I cannot take him seriously. I believe we should keep to the original plan. Since *he* is not here, we need not stay more than a few days."

"Very well. I cannot fault your ambition. I shall find out where the gentleman in question has gone, and in the meantime, you have a few days to enjoy the attentions of your rattle. And if he should care to advance his interest with you, he knows where you live."

***

"What are you about, Kiltarlity? I sincerely hope we are not to be treated to a repeat of the nightmare of five years ago."

Robert took a deep breath before answering. A summons from his mother at bedtime was always bad news, but there was no point antagonising her when she was already tired and fretful from the aching hip which troubled her these days.

"You are talking about the Lady Olivia, I collect? A lady whom I met for the first time four hours ago?"

"Lady Olivia, indeed! She is the illegitimate daughter of Lord Rennington, and I will thank you to bear that in mind in your dealings with her. Even if she were still *Lady* Olivia, I do *not* want you to fall under her spell and treat us to another mortifying spectacle. *Then* I said nothing for you were just a younger son and your marriage of little consequence, so I put up with the embarrassment of watching you grovelling for the least sign of favour from that dreadful girl, but now — the hopes of the whole family rest on your shoulders. Do not betray our trust by humiliating us all over again."

"She is amusing, Mama, that is all," he said mildly. "She is like Izzy, and yet unlike her, too."

"You see? You *are* falling under her spell! It will not do, Kiltarlity."

He noted for the first time how frail she looked. Propped up against the pillows, her grey hair not quite concealed under a voluminous cap, she looked small and vulnerable. His indomitable mother, who had ruled the household with her strong will and managed even his determined father when she needed to, had an unexpected wobble in her voice. She might tell him firmly that *'it will not do',* but he saw fear in her eyes. She had lost three sons, a daughter and her husband in a very short time. No wonder she feared for him, too.

"Mama," he said in his most soothing tone, sitting on the edge of the bed and taking her hand in his. "You must not worry so. That time with Izzy... it was a kind of madness that afflicted all of us, not just me. It was five years ago, and I have no intention of repeating it, not for any woman. I am different now, older and, one must only hope, just a trifle wiser. When I saw Izzy a few weeks ago, I realised just what a disaster it would have been for me to marry her. She would not have suited me at all. Let Farramont put up with her tantrums and wildness, for he seems to relish it."

"Ha! Yes, he is welcome to her, but this child may be just as bad, for all her meek ways."

"She may be, but I like what I have seen of her so far, and I should not object to knowing her better."

"A bastard! Really, Kiltarlity, you can do better than that."

"Until three months ago she was legitimate and eminently suitable, and it is not her fault that her status has changed. When she marries, her husband will give her legitimacy and this interlude will not matter tuppence."

"If you think that, you know nothing about society."

"Oh, there are always a few high sticklers, but who cares about them? A husband gives his wife the respectability of his name. Besides, most people judge by a woman's behaviour and actions, not by legal niceties, and no one could fault Olivia on that score."

His mother only grunted.

"She said something very wise to me this evening," he said, smiling at the memory. "She said I should consider the happiness of everyone when I make my decisions for the estate, and that seems like good advice to me. I already have some ideas of how to proceed. But when I come to marry, whoever it may be, it is my own happiness which will be my primary concern. I cannot marry, or not marry, simply to please you, Mama. You and Papa gave me such a clear example of a happy marriage that you can hardly blame me for wanting the same for myself."

His mother gave a wry little smile. "Pft! Such flattery! Oh, go along with you, and leave an old lady to sleep."

Laughing, he went, closing the door softly behind him.

In his room, Maurice helped to ready him for bed, but when he had gone, Robert sat at the small table drawn up near the fire for warmth, and drew paper and pencil from his writing box. Then across the top of the paper, he wrote Olivia's words, for they were still ringing in his head and he wanted to remember them. *'If you have contented tenants and stewards, they will work better, and that means that the land will be more productive.'* Such sensible words!

He began to write, tentatively at first, and then with growing confidence, a list of actions to be taken that would ensure the contentment of his people... his flock! The parson was in the right of it after all. What Robert needed to do was to tend his flock, not extravagantly or foolishly, but carefully. It could be done! Finally, he began to feel that he was in control of his inheritance.

***

For three days, Robert spent as much time as he could with Olivia. There were shooting parties with the men each morning, and on one occasion, when the London newspapers arrived in a great batch, there was a peers' discussion of Parliamentary business in Harraby's study, but otherwise he felt free to seek her out. She was pleasingly receptive to his company, her rather starchy chaperon was complacent and even his mother only grumbled now and then, having learnt that she would have thirty thousand pounds in her dowry.

His sisters disliked Olivia, but they had disliked Izzy, too, and for the same reason — jealousy, for the Atherton girls were ten times prettier than Lizzie and Lucy, and more accomplished, too, not to mention livelier in company. Izzy had had men swarming round her when she came out, and Olivia would, too, that was beyond question, illegitimate or not. It was hard for his sisters, who had never experienced that kind of success. Now the two of them were drifting steadily towards settled spinsterhood, forced to watch a girl like Olivia emerge with all the qualities they lacked.

For Robert, Olivia was fascinating. She was so like Izzy, and yet also her own self. She was never impatient with him, for one thing. He talked to her about his list of improvements, asking what she thought, and she considered each point carefully and then gave her opinion. Izzy would never have done that! She would have got bored after five minutes and looked for some more interesting diversion. Olivia was quite different in that respect, but sometimes an expression or a gesture would be so like Izzy, that it was almost as if the years had rolled back. Each night when he went to bed he wondered if this interest he felt in Olivia was for her own sake, or whether it was just an echo of his passion for Izzy, so intense that it still haunted him.

Once, he even called her Izzy by mistake, and although he caught himself at once and made her a grovelling apology, she was cool with him for the rest of the evening. When the card tables came out, she contrived to sit at another table from him.

On the third evening, when he entered the saloon and found her sitting quietly near the fire, he came straight to her side, as usual. "This settled spell is likely to last for a few days more. Would you like to ride tomorrow? Harraby has a horse in the stable which is trained to a side-saddle."

"Thank you, that would have been lovely, for I have scarcely left the house these last few days, but we are to leave tomorrow morning."

"Leave?" he said, stupefied. "But you have only just arrived! You cannot leave yet."

"But we must. We never intended to stay long, and we only came because— Well, no matter. We must go, and that is all there is to it."

"You only came because... what? What were you about to say?"

She had gone rather pink, but she answered him composedly. "Because we understood that Lord Embleton was here. I met him at Corland recently, and it seemed a good opportunity to further the acquaintance."

Robert felt as if he had been punched in the stomach. "Oh, so you fancy being a marchioness, do you?"

"A duchess, in fact, but there are very few of them to be had." She chuckled. "A girl must aim high, you know. Of course, it is quite hopeless, I am perfectly aware of it, but I met him, I liked him, so why not? Oh, do not look so horrified. It is a game, that is all. One sees a man of high rank who is amiable and so forth, so one puts oneself in his way to see if anything should come of it."

He was stupefied. Was she truly as calculating as that? "Must it be a duke? Would no lesser rank do? A baron, say, or a viscount?" He wanted to say *'or an earl'* but it might sound too much like a declaration, and he was a long way from that point.

"It must be a duke," she said, with a quick laugh. Normally, he liked her melodic laugh, but tonight it grated on his ears. "Why should I not set my sights so high?"

"Because—" He stopped. There was no reason at all. She was truly lovely, well mannered, brought up in the nobility and with a good dowry. She would make an excellent duchess, and Embleton would be lucky to get her. *Any* man would be lucky to get her.

"I mean him no harm," she said softly, laying one gloved hand on Robert's arm. "I would never try to trick him into it, but he must marry someone, and so must I. All I wanted was to get to know him better, but I have missed him this time."

He gave an embarrassed laugh. "That was my sisters' fault. They saw an unmarried future duke, and it went to their heads rather." He sighed. "Poor Lizzie and Lucy! They are so desperate for husbands that they will try anything."

"How is it they have never married?"

He sighed again. "Lizzie... she brought it on herself, for she fell in love with a most unsuitable man, a naval man and not of good family. They tried to elope."

Olivia gasped, for eloping was the worst crime an unmarried female could commit, according to Mama, except for one other which she would not explain, but merely pursed her lips and said that there was a reason for a girl to be chaperoned. But to think that Lady Elizabeth Osborn had eloped! With a sailor!

"Of course, he is a captain now, and probably has prize money and so forth," Robert said musingly, "but it is a bit late to wonder what might have been. As for Lucy, she had a few offers but she dithered and wavered and could not settle on one, and naturally, there is only so long a man can wait before he goes off and marries someone else."

"Then such a man cannot have loved her," she said stoutly. "True love would wait forever."

That was the confidence of her eighteen years speaking, not yet jaded by the experiences of life. From the perspective of his thirty years, Robert had known many men who had not waited, true love or not. Some had held on for years before deciding that if the ideal woman was not to be had, then one might as well settle for a lesser variety. A man had an obligation to his family, his inheritance and to his own happiness to provide himself with a wife, after all.

But he had no wish to be distracted from the main point. "So what will you do now? Go chasing after Lord Embleton, I suppose?"

"Chasing?" she said, with a little grimace. "That sounds so... forceful, as if I had a right to him, and saw him trying to escape. I should like to know him better, that is all. He usually goes to his hunting box in November, and if so, Lady Esther knows one of his neighbours, so we shall go, too."

"To do some hunting of your own," he said sourly.

"No, no. For good company, that is all, and to meet old friends."

He said no more on the subject, for he could not trust himself to stay calm. She made it sound so reasonable, yet it was so calculating and cold. At all costs Embleton must be protected from her!

When he returned to his room that night, he wrote two letters.

'To the Right Honourable the Viscount Farramont, Stonywell, Nottinghamshire. Monty, my old friend, I am engaged in a silly little game with Izzy's sister Olivia, and I would be obliged if you would let me know of her movements and destination whenever she leaves Corland Castle. Do not let her know of it, for I should like to surprise her. My regards to Izzy and congratulations on the impending addition to the family. Yours, Kiltarlity.'

"To Godfrey Marsden Esq, Chilford Lodge, Melton Mowbray, Leicestershire. Marsden, my old friend, are you settled in for the winter now? If you want company, I should be very happy to shoot a few of your birds, since my mother is determined to render Strathinver uninhabitable for several months at least, and who wants to be in town at this season? Do put me out of my misery, and if you are minded for female company, I can bring my mother and sisters, too. Yours, Kiltarlity.'

Then, smiling, he retired to bed, there to beguile a surprising degree of wakefulness with thoughts of shining eyes, a delicate heart-shaped face and an enchanting dimple beside very kissable lips.

6: A Grand Ball

Olivia returned to Corland Castle in unsettled mood. She had enjoyed her brief stay at Harraby Hall, naturally, for lively company was always exciting and Robert Osborn had been amusing, but it had not advanced her objective at all, and now she had to wait a full month before she could move forward. Lord Embleton was staying with a different sister, in Gloucestershire, far from her reach, and only the certainty that he would be at his hunting box in Leicestershire for the whole of November and possibly December too kept her spirits up.

It was fortunate that there were many entertainments to enjoy. Ever since the ghastly murder, the family seemed to have retreated into its shell, hardly venturing out at all, but now there was a positive spate of large gatherings. First, there were the celebrations surrounding the marriage of her eldest brother, Walter. Then, the Cathcarts, not noted for their hospitality as a rule, held a charming little party for Katherine Parish to which all the young people of the district, but none of their parents, were invited. With the wedding of Bea Franklyn to Cousin Bertram rapidly approaching, Lady

Esther and Aunt Jane seemed to be competing with each other in providing a host of elegant and increasingly ambitious parties, all of which was to culminate in a grand ball at Corland Castle two days before the wedding.

As if this were not enough excitement for Olivia, there was much more of the same to look forward to, since both her remaining two brothers had become betrothed. She did not much care for Eustace's future wife, Miss Rosamunde Wilkes, although she could not say why. She seemed pleasant enough, but Olivia could not warm to her. Kent's betrothed, Katherine Parish, she liked well enough. She had thought her dreadfully shy at first, with hardly a word to say for herself, but when she saw how happy she made Kent, and how he managed to bring her out of her shell, she understood that it would work very well.

And then had come the astonishing news that Tess Nicholson had eloped! *Eloped!* Run off to Scotland to be married over the anvil, as the saying was. And even though it was a respectable, indeed eligible, match, to Lord Tarvin, which everyone approved, and they then went straight to London to be married properly by special licence, it was still an outrageous thing to do. The second worst thing a lady could do, yet everyone seemed pleased about it. "At last, the girl has acquired an ounce of common sense," Papa said, and even Aunt Alice smiled at it, and wrote at once to give her permission, since Tess was not yet of age. Olivia did not understand it at all, although she was pleased for Cousin Tess, naturally.

But there were unhappy moments, too. The murder investigation was still going on, although Captain Edgerton and his team never seemed to make much progress. A few weeks ago, one of them, Miss Peach, an elderly spinster who had once been governess to Mrs Edgerton, had disappeared, and now her murdered body had been found at a farm near Pickering. Olivia had not known the lady well, for she had not dined with the family when she had lived at Corland, and so had been rarely seen, but another murder was a dreadful thing, and poor Mrs Edgerton was very upset.

And then there was Papa. He had been so glad to see her when she returned from Harraby Hall, he had hugged her and made her sit beside him at dinner.

"How much we have all missed your lively chatter," he said over and over. "So dull we have been without you. Do not go away and leave me again, daughter, for I am sadly bereft now. Your mother gone, your sisters far away, and now your brothers... what am I to do without you all? But *you* will stay with your poor, lonely Papa, will you not?"

Then he had been thrown from his horse and dislocated his shoulder, and although he mended quickly, he was very sorry for himself. Olivia went to see him the day after the accident, when he was sitting up in bed, wearing an ornate nightcap.

"I should know better at my age," he said glumly. "Trying to keep up with a younger woman, but Miss Quick outrode me, there is no doubt about it." He sighed heavily. "I wish... well, what I wish makes no difference, for your mother is not coming home. She wants me to find a new wife, so that is what I must do. It will be for the best."

"Will it?" Olivia said. "I do not much want a stepmother, Papa, and I do not see why there should be one at all."

"For legitimate sons," he said sadly. "It is important."

"Is it? There is Uncle George to inherit, and then Bertram, and they will make sure Corland stays as it always has. A new wife would change everything. It would be horrid. Do you not think it is time to give up this quest for a new Lady Rennington? Aunt Jane has produced five candidates so far, and none of them have answered."

He sighed again. "That is true. Perhaps you are right. I shall tell Jane not to invite any more just now, and perhaps in the spring we shall all go to town, and I can look about me for a wife while you look for a husband, eh? That might be amusing, and at least I shall have the winter free from any more of these women. It does not come naturally to me any more to do the pretty to a young woman. My courting days were so long ago, I have got out of the way of it."

"I think that is a splendid idea," Olivia said. "And perhaps you should think about going away from Corland, with all its sad memories. A week or two somewhere else would be just the thing to lift your spirits. My few days away did me so much good."

His face brightened. "Actually, that is not a bad idea. Not too far away, mind you, in case your grandmother... well, I should not like to be out of reach if... although she has clung to life most tenaciously. After her last turn, we all thought she would not last the winter, and here she still is, a year later, although not very coherent. Does she know you, when you visit?"

"No. She calls me Hermione. Who is Hermione?"

"Her sister, who was the Duchess of Lochmaben. Long dead, of course. She calls me Gabriel, and I have not the least idea who he might be. Poor Mother! Such a strong woman, reduced to a mumbling shell of herself. Old age is very cruel, sometimes, and harder to bear for those of us who have to watch a much-loved relation in sad decline. I think you are right, daughter. I should get away for a while. Perhaps after this wedding of Bertram's to Bea Franklyn I might go to Izzy or Josie."

That would not do for Olivia's purposes! "Lady Esther knows some people in Leicestershire... hunting people. That would be more fun, would it not? Ian and Aubrey are not really sporting types."

"Hmm, that is true. Farramont has good shooting on his land, but he is not really interested, and as for Woodridge — and they would both be talking politics at me, which is not my strong suit. But Leicestershire..."

"Near Melton, apparently."

"Ah," he said with a little smile, and she knew the argument was won.

But there was still a month before that could happen, so Olivia settled down to wait with what patience she could muster. Lord Embleton was still in Gloucestershire, Lady Esther informed her, for she had acquaintances who were intimate with the marquess's family and knew his movements, but even so it was hard for Olivia to do nothing. Every day he was out of her sight was a day when he might be meeting some other young lady who would steal his heart away.

But she could not be entirely downhearted, not with a grand ball to contemplate, so even though she often wept a little in pure frustration, she had much to occupy her. A few days before the ball, Eustace arrived with Miss Wilkes. Olivia had only seen her briefly on her previous visit, but this time she was to stay longer, and Olivia was determined to get to know her better.

"You are from Northumberland, I understand?" was her opening question, finding Miss Wilkes alone with her needlework in the parlour one day.

She looked up with a faint blush. "Yes. It is not far from Berwick." Her voice was quiet, and she seemed subdued, but although Olivia smiled at her, there was no answering smile. If anything, she looked nervous to be approached, even with such a gentle question.

"Goodness! Practically in Scotland, then."

"It is nearer to Edinburgh than Newcastle."

"I shall have to look it up in the atlas. Are your parents pleased with the match?"

This time she blushed deeply. "I... You see, my mother is dead, and my father... we fell out. He knows nothing of it."

"Oh dear! But when he knows, he will undoubtedly be pleased that you are to marry so well. Eustace has his own house and an independent income, so he is a very eligible *parti.*"

She nodded, but said nothing more.

"Your father... does he have a large estate?"

"Not as large as *your* father's," she said, with a sudden laugh, which made her look much more approachable. "It is called Warriston Hall. He is a baronet, Sir Reginald Wilkes. I have two brothers and two sisters, all married now."

"So you are the last to be married. I am sure your father will be pleased to have you settled." She wanted to ask about the quarrel, but it would be unpardonably rude to pry, so she said instead, "Have you fixed a date for the wedding yet?"

"No, we cannot marry until my father knows... and there has been a reconciliation. For now, it must all remain secret. Eustace did not want to tell anyone about it, but he had to tell Captain Edgerton about me... to do with the murder investigation. So now your family knows, but you must not mention it to anyone outside the family, and no one must tell my father until I have seen him. I live with... with my aunt in Scarborough, so I am well cared for."

"And you have Eustace, of course."

"Of course," she said, but there was no smile, only a little frown.

Poor girl! What a strange life, to have fallen out so spectacularly with her own family that she could not go home, or even tell her father her good news. It seemed odd that she would not simply hurry along her wedding to Eustace in order to have a settled home again, but perhaps it was important for her father to give her hand in marriage. Olivia could understand that. She would not want anyone but her own dear Papa to take her to the altar to meet her husband.

That led to some pleasant speculation on the nature of that husband, but although she knew quite definitely that he would be the Marquess of Embleton, and placed him firmly beside her at the altar rail, when she turned to face him and take his hand for the plighting of troths, it was Robert Osborn's laughing eyes which gazed down at her. How very odd.

The day of the grand ball was happily free of rain or other depressing weather events, for it was not unheard of for Corland to have snow in November. Olivia had early planned her attire from the bejewelled fillet for her hair to the dainty slippers on her feet, so there was nothing to do but watch the clock, bemoan the slow movement of the hands, and go upstairs half an hour before the usual time, just to be sure not to be late.

Naturally, it took a great deal of time to ensure her appearance was exactly right, so the great hall was already filling up when she arrived, with more guests pouring in every moment. Papa saw her, his face lighting up, and waved her across.

"That is just what I need, a lovely lady on my arm, and who better than my own charming daughter?" he said, smiling down at her affectionately. Happily, she rested her hand on his arm as they moved from group to group, smiling, greeting everyone, enjoying the crowds. They were alike in that respect, in being at their best in company. Olivia was so excited she practically bounced from one group to another.

After a while, Olivia saw Captain Edgerton and his wife descending the stairs, eyeing the armoury display on the half landing with a baleful glare. It was Eustace's little hobby, to collect weapons of various sorts, and the castle too had a fine collection, so he amused himself by arranging various displays around the castle, including the one on the half landing, flanked by two large Chinese urns. The axe which had been used to murder poor Uncle Arthur had come from that display, hidden in one of the urns until it was needed, but even now, five months after the event, no one knew who had wielded it.

A murmur ran round the great hall. The principal guests were arriving. There was a general milling around as some people made their way outside to watch the arrivals, while others moved aside or reformed into new groups. Olivia pulled her shawl tighter around her shoulders and ventured through the passageway to the entrance hall, and out of the front doors.

Corland Castle was a modern construction, but the architect had designed it to resemble an authentic castle as much as possible. Thus, it boasted a dry moat, which surrounded the basement level and allowed access to underground stables and store rooms. There was no drawbridge to be pulled up, there being no enemies to defend against in modern times. Instead, a sturdy stone bridge connected the carriage drive to the entrance of the castle.

Here on the bridge a number of people gathered to watch the arriving carriages. Torches all around and light spilling from inside the castle lit up the early evening gloom, showing two carriages approaching. The rather stylish new one belonging to Lady Esther and Mr Franklyn arrived first, from which also emerged Uncle George and Aunt Jane. The second carriage pulled up behind it, a more old-fashioned affair, belonging to Uncle George and Aunt Jane. The butler opened the door and let down the steps, Cousin Bertram stepped into view, followed by Bea Franklyn's smiling face and black curls. Bea waved exuberantly to the servants gathered at the top of the service steps to the lower level, then they moved towards the bridge.

Olivia caught a glimpse of something, a movement, perhaps, in the bushes further down the drive. Abruptly there was a blinding flash and a thunderous bang that echoed off the castle walls. Someone screamed, there were shouts and people running. Someone pushed past Olivia — Mrs Edgerton, running forwards to the carriages.

Was that a gunshot? What on earth was happening?

"Quick, back inside, everyone!" someone shouted.

Olivia froze, still clinging to Papa's arm, who was craning his neck to look this way and that.

There was a general movement of retreat, some ladies scurrying, picking up their skirts and racing across the bridge towards the safety of the castle, while the men gathered protectively behind them, like a wall. Lady Esther and Aunt Jane were hustled past to safety by Uncle George. Some men ran the other way, forward to the carriages or down the drive. She saw Captain Edgerton in amongst the bushes searching for something, then Lucas ran down to join him. Mr Franklyn had a narrow sword in his hand, as if prepared for a duel, his gaze scanning backwards and forwards, this way and that, before he, too, ran down to join Captain Edgerton. And all the time a thin, keening wail rent the air.

"You had better go inside," her father said to her in urgent tones. "If there is a gunman on the loose—"

"He has gone," she said. "The captain is looking just where he was, but there is no one there. Is someone hurt? I cannot see."

"Bertram," he said, his voice harsh. "Bertram fell. Come, daughter, let me take you back inside. This is no place for a lady."

"That is Bea crying," Olivia said. Shaking with terror, nevertheless she could not bear to see Bea in such distress. Running forward to the little crowd of men clustered around the door of the carriage, she saw Bertram lying unmoving, a dark pool emanating from his shoulder. Crouched over him, Mrs Edgerton was pressing a shawl against the wound, its pale wool already sodden with Bertram's blood.

"Do you need another shawl?" Olivia said, removing hers.

"Thank you, I will need it very soon. Leave it on the ground. Can you see to Miss Franklyn? Convince her if you can that he is not going to die."

"Of course."

Olivia had never much cared for Bea Franklyn, who had set out with ruthless determination to marry Walter and thereby make herself a countess. When the disaster had happened and she learnt that Walter could not inherit the earldom, she had turned her sights on Bertram instead. But now she was a lady in the utmost distress, and Olivia could not withhold the comfort she needed.

So she wrapped her arms round Bea and held her in a fierce hug. "It is all right, Bea. He is not going to die. He will be well, just you wait and see. Mrs Edgerton knows what she is about." Just then, a groom galloped past at full pelt and was away down the drive. "There, he will have gone for help. Mrs Edgerton will keep Bertram safe until the surgeon arrives. You are not hurt?"

Mutely she shook her head, but Olivia could see spatters of blood on her gown and cloak. Bea wept piteously, and Olivia wept too, the two clinging to each other in desperation.

Mr Franklyn returned, the narrow sword now hidden away in a cane. "No sign at all of the miscreant, and Captain Edgerton feels it is safe."

Eustace came out of the house at a run. "Whatever happened? There is such a commotion inside and I thought I heard a shot. Dear God! Bertram! Is he... will he...?"

"He will live," Mrs Edgerton said calmly, without looking up.

"Thank God!"

"A pistol was fired, a single shot, from those bushes down there where Edgerton is looking," Mr Franklyn said, "but there is no sign of the fellow. He seems to have got clean away."

"Down the drive?"

"No, or we should have seen him. Nor has he jumped over the wall into the lower level."

"He would break his neck doing that," Eustace said. "But what can have happened to him?"

"It is a mystery," Mr Franklyn said grimly. "Another mystery to pile onto the great mountain of them already accumulated with the death of Nicholson. And the greatest of them all, in my view, is this — who on earth would want to shoot Bertram Atherton?"

7: The Cheese Store

Captain Michael Edgerton rested his hands on his hips, and uttered a curse. He had examined the whole stretch of shrubbery edging the drive, no more than thirty feet or so, and found nothing — no lurking gunman, nothing but the acrid smell of gunpowder in the air. There was a thirty foot drop over the wall behind the shrubs to the void below, and not so much as a patch of grass or bush to break a man's fall. He could not have escaped that way. But nor could he have run down the drive, for it was wide open and clearly visible, lit by lines of torches.

"Anything?" Lucas Atherton, Bertram's brother, had been the first to help in the search.

"Not a thing. He has vanished into thin air."

"Let me look."

Lucas went over the ground in the same way as Michael, slowly and methodically, shifting aside every bush to look at the ground. The light was dim with deep shadows, but the lines of torches along the drive cast enough light to show that no gunman was lurking in the shrubbery.

Eustace Atherton came up just then. “I wish I had not stayed inside with Miss Wilkes,” he said ruefully. “Another pair of eyes might have seen something.”

“It is not another pair of eyes we need, it is ideas for how the fellow managed to disappear so completely,” Michael said.

“Are you quite sure this was the place? Might the shot have come from the castle… an upper window, perhaps?” Eustace said.

Michael frowned, pondering. It was an interesting point.

Kent Atherton ran up to them bearing a torch, his usually smiling face solemn. “Any sign of him?”

“None,” Michael said, gazing up at the windows, assessing the likelihood of a shot from there. “He has vanished.”

“What about the gun?” Kent said. “Have you looked for it?”

“He would have taken it away with him, surely?” Lucas said.

Kent shook his head. “Not necessarily. He must have been in a great rush to get away, so he may have just tossed it into a bush. Lucas, hold the torch, will you, while I look?”

“No, no, let me,” Eustace said. “Those silk knee breeches will be ruined if you crawl around in the dirt out here. At least I am wearing black.”

For some time, Eustace crawled about under bushes. Eventually, he gave a yell. “There! Kent, hold the torch a little lower. Ha! Got it!”

He rose triumphantly, waving a pistol.

“Well done!” Michael said. “Hmm, a fairly nondescript affair. What do you make of it, sir?”

“Is it one of yours, Eustace?” Kent said, to general laughter.

“Oh yes, I brought one of my own pistols and then tried to shoot my own cousin with it, did I?” Eustace said, laughing too. “This is a naval pistol, I would say, but not one I recognise.”

"Perhaps it is from the castle collection?" Michael suggested. "I do not recognise it either, but you would know the collection better than I do."

"There are none of this type in the Armoury," Eustace said. "I know the family collection intimately, and I have never seen this pistol. Well, there is not much more we can do now. We have the weapon, but the fellow has got clean away. We should see to the ladies inside."

"I should still like to know just how he got away," Michael said. "Unlikely he was firing from inside the castle, since his shot would have to cross the full width of the moat and hit a narrow target in relative darkness. If Bertram Atherton was even the intended target."

"Who else?" Eustace said. "Miss Franklyn, perhaps?"

"I will talk to everyone tomorrow," Michael said pensively. "There must be a reason for this. It was such an audacious act, the gunman must have been desperate, yet I can see no reason for an attack on anyone here tonight."

"Is it connected to Nicholson's murder?" Kent said.

Michael heaved an exasperated sigh. "It must be and yet... how can it possibly be? There is something here that I do not yet understand."

Lucas was prowling round the bushes, looking over the wall at the void below, frowning. "Eustace, Kent, what is below this shrubbery, do you remember? It is not the stables, they are further round. It must be store rooms of some sort."

"The apple store, maybe?" Eustace said. "Cheese? What has that to do with anything?"

"I wondered if it might be one of the coal stores, for they have access hatches above so the coal merchant can tip the stuff straight in."

"You think someone clambered over a pile of coal and out through a trap door?" Eustace said. "Not very likely."

"I only ask because we used to play in them as boys, do you remember? When one of them was empty, obviously, but on the back wall there was a ladder up to the hatch."

"The coal stores are on the other side of the castle, I think," Eustace said. "No, I am sure. Opposite the armoury tower."

"But they used to be on this side," Kent said excitedly. "Do you not remember, Eustace? Mama had them moved, and new hatches made, because she was entertaining someone important — the bishop, I think — in the library, and there were the coal merchants huffing and puffing about outside and not very careful about their language."

He began to stamp about, trying to find a solid surface under the layer of earth and fallen leaves.

Eustace looked startled. "Ha! I had forgotten that! But surely the hatches would not still be usable?"

"Mr Franklyn's cane might be useful here," Lucas said, running off to find him.

The two soon hurried back, and Mr Franklyn prodded the ground methodically with his cane. It was not long before there was a solid thunk. Michael was instantly down on his knees, clearing away dirt and debris several inches deep, to uncover a wooden trap door. A metal ring was set into it to raise it, but it would not shift.

"Bolted shut below, I imagine," Michael said, "but in any case, this has not been used tonight, or for some time. But there will be—"

Mr Franklyn gave a shout. "Here! Another one, not covered with earth."

It was tucked away under a bush and thus almost completely hidden, but it lifted easily. Down below, a light burned, showing a solid metal ladder leading downwards.

"There is our answer," Michael said grimly. "The villain came up here, took his shot, then vanished again."

Instantly he was over the edge, and climbing swiftly down the ladder. An overpowering smell of cheese assailed his nostrils, so it was not a surprise when he reached the bottom to find himself surrounded by racks of cheeses. One empty shelf bore a candelabrum, still burning strongly. Passing the cheese racks, Michael reached the outer door, opened it and stepped outside. Looking up, he saw several faces peering over the wall at hi m.

"Cheese store!" he called up, before looking round for the nearest door into the castle, directly below the bridge. The stable yard door, locked only last thing at night. Very convenient.

But so risky! He had called it an audacious act, but it was almost reckless. With the castle full of guests, the servants moving about here and there, the possibility of being seen at any moment, yet the gunman had calmly left the party, gone down to the basement, across the yard and into the cheese store, then climbed up to take his shot before returning the same way to rejoin the party.

Which led to an inescapable truth — *he was still there now.* One of those in the castle at that very moment had just tried to kill a man.

But who was it?

***

Olivia could not stop weeping. If only Mama were there to hug her — there was no one like Mama for bringing comfort to the darkest hour. Tess would weep with her, and listen, even if with only half an ear, for Tess was always more interested in her own concerns. Even Izzy would at least understand, and would rant and rage about the room, which was comfort of a different sort.

But poor Papa had not the least idea how to deal with a distressed female. No man was properly sympathetic. Walter would roll his eyes and pass her a handkerchief, Eustace would creep away as soon as he could, and Kent would tell her to pull herself together.

Instead, she had Bea Franklyn as her only source of comfort, and who would ever have predicted that? Bertram was even now reclining on a sofa in Papa's study, with Aunt Jane at his side, the two most solid footmen outside the only door and Captain Edgerton's Scottish colleague prowling around restlessly. Most of the other guests had gone home except for the Franklyns, and now they and the family had gone in to dinner as if nothing at all had happened. How could they possibly eat? Even Aunt Alice had said calmly, "We all need to restore our composure and dinner will do as well as anything else."

Not for Olivia, and not for Bea, either, so the two of them sat side by side on a chaise longue in the library, weeping steadily, and awaiting the arrival of the surgeon from Birchall.

Suppose the marquess had been there? Surely he would be suitably compassionate towards a poor girl who had had a very trying time of it. And Osborn would probably tease her out of it. That was a more interesting train of thought which cheered her a little... a very little.

Mrs Edgerton came in just then. *She* had not gone off to eat lobster patties, all unconcerned. She brought dry handkerchiefs, and then poured wine for Olivia and Bea.

"I have ordered a tray of food to be brought in here for you," she said. "I know you do not feel like eating, but if you can manage a few morsels and a little wine, it will do you all the good in the world. Miss Franklyn, I am sure the surgeon will confirm that Mr Bertram's wound is very small. The bullet passed directly through his shoulder and out again, so once the surgeon has cleaned it properly and ensured that no fragments of cloth are embedded in it, he will make a very rapid recovery, you will see. The wedding may even be able to go ahead on the day you planned, or not very long after."

"But if someone... wants to kill him... he may try again," Bea said, through her sobs.

"My husband intends to make very sure that he will not succeed," she said grimly. "That is his main objective now, to get you and Mr Atherton married and away to a place of safety for a period, so that he can investigate this new atrocity without the constant fear of an assassin lurking behind every bush."

A footman came in bearing a tray laden with meat patties, fruit pastries and an array of cakes. Both girls dutifully nibbled a cake each, and Olivia soon found she could manage a second one and then a raspberry tartlet. Mrs Edgerton smiled at them encouragingly and urged them to drink some wine as well. It was an odd thing, but Olivia did feel better for having something to eat. She reached for another cake.

"I wish I could see him," Bea said wistfully, setting down her glass.

Mrs Edgerton patted her hand sympathetically. "Once the surgeon has been... ah, here he is now."

A little flurry of activity heralded the arrival of the surgeon-apothecary, his assistant and a cluster of footmen, followed by Captain Edgerton, now dressed in morning clothes, and with his sword at his side. The little cavalcade disappeared into the study, the footmen and the captain emerged again almost at once, and silence fell.

"Miss Franklyn, how are you bearing up?" the captain said to Bea, his voice gentle.

"I am well. Captain, how is he?"

"In excellent shape," the captain said. "Perfectly lucid and calm, although in some pain, naturally. Miss Franklyn, I shall be talking to you and to Mr Atherton in more detail in the days to come, but I wonder if—"

The air was rent with a bloodcurdling scream from the study, followed by a deep silence.

Bea jumped to her feet with a cry, and would have rushed across to the study door, but the captain stood in her way.

"The surgeon will be cleaning the wound with alcohol, I expect. It... stings a bit."

There were no further sounds from the study except a low rumble of voices, so Bea took several deep breaths and sat down again.

"He is not going to die?"

"Miss Franklyn, one can never predict the outcome of a wound with absolute certainty, but in my experience this is an eminently survivable type. I shall profess myself astonished if he does not survive."

"But then you have been astonished several times since you came here," Bea said, with a hint of a wry smile.

The captain smiled too. "That is true, to my chagrin. Nothing about this case has gone as I expected. But then none of us would have imagined that Mr Bertram Atherton would be the victim of a deliberate shooting. Why, that is what puzzles me? Was he even the intended target, or was the gunman aiming at you, Miss Franklyn? Can you think of any reason why anyone would want either of you dead?"

"No, none at all. There are those who dislike *me*, I know that, but not enough to want me dead, I hope, and no one dislikes Bertram — not a soul. He is universally admired and respected."

"So I have always understood. We will talk more tomorrow when you are rested and, I trust, your fears for Mr Atherton have been somewhat allayed. Perhaps something will come to you that might give me a clue where to look." Then he added grimly, "Because the man who shot your future husband was in this castle this evening, mingling with the guests, and I should very much like to know who he is before he does any more harm."

***

The next morning, Michael talked to Bertram Atherton, who was sitting up in bed in the principal guest bedroom, his arm in a sling, looking pale but fierce. Miss Franklyn sat in a chair by the bed, reading to him, while Luce played chaperon in a corner with her sewing.

"Who would do a thing like this, Captain?" Bertram said, before Michael had even sat down. "Why would anyone want to kill me?"

"I was about to ask you the same question," Michael said.

"It is hard to imagine that anyone hates me enough to commit murder," Bertram said. "But to lurk there in the bushes... he must have been there for hours, watching everyone arrive, waiting for me."

"It is worse than that," Michael said grimly, and explained about the hatch to the cheese store.

"You mean... it was someone we know?" Bertram said horrified. "A friend? A relation?" He murmured something in Latin.

"The obvious person would be your brother Lucas—"

"No!"

"— for he stands to gain most by your death, but he was on the bridge in clear sight at the time. No one who was on the bridge could have been responsible. But that still leaves scores of people who were inside the castle. Any one of them could have slipped away, climbed the ladder in the cheese store, taken the shot and then run back to rejoin the party."

"No one dislikes Bertram enough to kill him," Bea said stoutly, taking his good hand in hers.

"And that is patently untrue," Bertram said, smiling at her. "I just cannot imagine who... or why."

"Has anything like this happened before," Michael said. "Not shooting, necessarily, but... accidents, say? Something in the last year or two that looked like an accident but might not have been?"

"No, nothing. I am not prone to accidents, as a rule, so I would notice," Bertram said. "Walter is the one for accidents, but then he tends to be a neck or nothing rider. He had a fall last year that could have been nasty — something broke as he was about to jump — but he landed in the hedge and came off more or less unscathed."

"There was a stray shot near him last winter, too, do you remember?" Bea said. "He had wandered away from the rest of the shooting party and there was a shot very close to him."

"Well, Walter is an idiot, in some ways," Bertram said easily. "He never thinks, and ends up in the line of fire. But I have never even had the smallest accident of that nature, so this has come from nowhere. And why now... here and now? There must be easier ways, less risky."

"Exactly," Michael said. "There is an urgency about this that is very striking. The assassin could not wait, and needed to stop you immediately from doing... something. Your marriage, possibly, or a legal matter. Were you about to make a will, or anything of that sort?"

"I have had a will in place since I came of age, and it was updated weeks ago to take my forthcoming marriage into account."

"Do you have any information that you are about to reveal?"

"Such as what?"

"Anything. The murder of Mr Nicholson, possibly, but it could be anything. Have you recently found out something detrimental to another person?"

"Nothing at all." He sighed. "I think it must be about our marriage, Bea. Do you have any rejected suitors with murderous tendencies?"

"No. Well, not with murderous tendencies. There was the Marquess of Embleton, but I cannot see him hiding in bushes, can you?"

"And he was not here last night," Michael said. "I will check, but it seems unlikely. Anyone else?"

"There was only Eustace..."

"Mr Eustace!" Michael sat up a little straighter. "He wished to marry you, Miss Franklyn?"

"Oh, yes. He offered twice before I was betrothed to Walter, and when that fell apart, he offered again, but he only wanted my fortune, you know. He was never in love with me or anything of that nature."

"How do you know that?"

"A girl knows when a man feels a real passion for her. It is in his eyes, the way he looks at her, the way he hangs on every word, and when he proposes, it all tumbles out. One cannot be in any doubt about it." She glanced at Bertram, blushing a little. "Eustace had none of that. He told me how well circumstanced he was, his income and so forth, and he talked of attachment but it was all so... so *cold*, somehow."

"And as soon as you are betrothed to me, he is betrothed to someone else," Bertram says.

"Exactly! It is hardly a grand passion if he promptly proposes to another woman. He has known her for some time, apparently, so no, he is not nursing a vengeful broken heart, my love."

"What a pity," Michael said. "That sounded so promising, too. Still, the fellow's motive may not be so important this time, because we should be able to discover who it is. He must have disappeared from view inside the castle, and then reappeared sometime later. Hmm... how much later, I wonder? An interesting question."

8: Briar House

Bertram and Bea's wedding went ahead, only a day later than planned, but Olivia was very put out to find that no one was permitted to attend. Captain Edgerton was determined to provide no opportunity for the gunman to have another attempt on Bertram's life, so only the four parents and Mr Dewar were in church, together with Captain Edgerton, the Scotsman and four burly grooms and footmen who were to act as Bertram's body-guard.

Immediately after the ceremony, the newly married couple were bundled into a carriage and driven off to an unknown location, escorted by the captain, the Scotsman and the body-guard.

It was all very dispiriting, but since the wedding breakfast had been arranged long before, and the cake made, the rest of the family celebrated the marriage by eating and drinking to excess, and allowing a few gleams of merriment to break through.

The following day, however, saw a resumption of misery, for the captain had left behind Mrs Edgerton, the London lawyer Mr Willerton-Forbes and another man, by the name of Neate. Their task was to find out precisely where everyone was at the moment the shot was fired.

"How foolish," Eustace said crossly, having been summoned to take his turn being interviewed. "As if anyone is going to say, *'Let me think... oh, yes, I was under the third bush from the right, firing a pistol.'*"

Kent laughed. "No, but what they will also be doing, I expect, is asking everyone who else they could see around them. That way they will find out if anyone claims to be in the great hall but is actually missing. It is quite clever, if you ask me."

When it was Olivia's turn, she discovered that he was quite right. The table in the old schoolroom was covered by a large drawing of the relevant castle rooms — the great hall and entrance hall, the passageway between them, and the two anterooms — together with the bridge and a section of the drive. Little dots, each labelled with a name, were scattered about. There were not very many dots yet, but she quickly found her father's.

"And where were you standing, Lady Olivia?" the lawyer said.

"There... just there, beside Papa. I was holding his arm."

"On that side... his right?"

"Yes, because I was looking down the drive, and I saw the flash of the gun."

They were very excited about that, and for some time plied her with questions about it, the other man taking copious notes for the captain's benefit. Then they all went outside, and she showed them where she was standing and where she thought the flash had come from.

"And what happened after the flash? Did you see anything else... or anyone down there?" the lawyer asked excitedly.

"No, because everyone started moving about, blocking the view, and anyway, we were all looking towards Bertram."

They looked suitably disappointed, taking her back to the old schoolroom.

"Now, Lady Olivia," the lawyer said, "I should like you to tell me everyone you remember seeing near you on the bridge at the time the shot was fired. Not anyone you passed on the way out, or anyone who came out afterwards, just those around you at the time of the shooting."

She gave a few names, and then ground to a halt. "It is very difficult. There was quite a crowd but I was not taking much notice. I was watching the carriages and... and admiring the way the torch flames danced about in the breeze. They were very pretty. That was why I was looking down the drive. I am very sorry. I am not much use."

"That is quite all right. No one has a perfect memory, after all," the lawyer said.

"But if I forget someone, you might think that was the person who shot Bertram."

"No, no," the lawyer said kindly. "The whole point is that no one will remember everyone, but everyone will remember a few people. So if a person was there but *you* do not remember him, someone else will, preferably several someones, and so we will know he is not our villain. But there will be one person who claims to be there, but *no one* remembers — that will be our man. Do you see?"

She did, and like Kent, she had to agree that it was very clever.

***

Olivia received a brief note from Lady Esther Franklyn. *'Are you ready to go to Leicestershire?"* was all she wrote. Without hesitation, Olivia wrote back, *'Yes.'*

Even Papa, previously so resistant to her going anywhere, made no protest, agreed that a change of scene would do them both good and was quite prepared to suffer the tribulations of excessive amounts of entertainment at someone else's expense. With the addition of Mr Franklyn, who declared there was no point in remaining at Highwood with only the two small boys in the nursery for company, they made their way in great harmony to Leicestershire.

Briar House was a neat modern property with no great pretensions to elegance or architectural merit. Its most important parts were the stables and kennels, and its sole function was to maintain the Duke of Camberley's hounds and string of hunters for the enjoyment of whichever of the duke's multitude of relations cared to take advantage of them. This largesse was well appreciated, and from early November until March, the house was generally bursting at the seams, three additional guest houses being also full, and some years the influx was so great that it spilled over into the adjoining village, and the sleepy little inn became a bustle of activity.

This year, the duke's continuing poor health meant that fewer of his immediate family cared to leave him alone at his principal seat while they gave themselves over to pleasure, so there was less of a crowd than usual. Even so, the main house was full, but there was space for the earl and his daughter, and after Lady Esther made rather a fuss, in her refined and ladylike way, a room was found for her and Mr Franklyn, too.

The house was run by Lady Esther's cousins, Mr Jeremiah Bucknell and his sister Charlotte, pleasant, cheerful people whose sole concern, it seemed, was to ensure that their guests enjoyed every minute of their stay. Olivia found her room, prettily covered in a wallpaper of roses and ivy, was already provided with a blazing fire, with towels warming in front of it, and a bath wanting only the addition of hot water, which was quickly supplied.

Within an hour of her arrival, she had bathed and changed, and was making her way down the stairs to the sounds of conversation and laughter.

There was not a soul there that she knew. Neither her father nor the Franklyns had yet reached the drawing room, but Mr Bucknell and his sister, seeing her enter and hover on the threshold, rose from their seats and came across to greet her.

"My dear lady," Mr Bucknell said, "what a charming addition to our company! I only wish we had a few more young men here to entertain you, but you will just have to make do with elderly bachelors like myself and a few married men, ha ha ha!"

Since Olivia knew from Lady Esther that he was only thirty-six, she merely smiled at this raillery and allowed herself to be led around the room and introduced to a great many people whose names she promptly forgot.

Mr Bucknell had just settled her beside a thin-faced woman in a pale muslin gown best suited to someone twenty years younger, who was eyeing Olivia with barely disguised disapproval, when the door opened and the butler entered.

"The Earl of Kiltarlity, the Countess of Kiltarlity, the Lady Elizabeth Osborn, the Lady Lucilla Osborn," he intoned.

There was a surprised murmuring around the room. This, then, was not expected.

Mr Bucknell and his sister sprang forward to greet the arrivals, but Osborn had already spotted Olivia. His face breaking into an enormous smile, he strode past the Bucknells, quite oblivious, and straight to where Olivia sat, making her an elegant bow.

"Fair ghost, how enchanting to see you again... complete with dimple! I am growing excessively fond of that dimple. Have you been here long?"

Before Olivia could answer, the thin-faced woman coughed delicately. Olivia took the hint. “Oh... oh, yes, may I present to you Lord Kiltarlity, ma’am? And this is... erm...”

“Lady Douglas Bucknell,” she simpered, holding out her hand, and with a nod to the empty sofa space beside her, added, “Do sit down, Lord Kiltarlity.”

“Ma’am,” he said, with a the slightest bow of his head, before pulling forward a chair to sit beside Olivia instead. “So tell me of your journey. Are you here with Lady Esther? What do you think of Leicestershire? Shall you join the hunt? Many ladies do, and I am sure you are an accomplished horsewoman.”

“So many questions!” Olivia said, laughing, but her spirits rose inexorably. So much eagerness in his expression, and those laughing eyes! A girl could be quite swept away by those eyes. “Let me see... the journey went as well as could be expected. Yes, I am here with Lady Esther, and also Mr Franklyn and Papa, but they are still settling in upstairs. I have not seen enough of Leicestershire yet to comment on it. What was the last question?”

“I cannot remember,” he said. “How can I think at all when that dimple is entrancing me so?”

Olivia blushed. “Izzy told me you were a dreadful flirt, sir, and I can see that she was right.”

“A flirt? Me?” he said. “You wound me to the heart, my lovely ghost. What have I said of flattery? Is not every word true?”

“I do not think a gentleman should comment on a lady’s dimple, sir,” she said severely. “Ah, there is Papa!”

Osborn’s sigh was audible as she jumped up and hurried across the room to tuck her arm into Papa’s.

"How glad I am you have come at last!" she cried. "You must tell Lord Kiltarlity he is not to flirt with me."

"Kiltarlity, eh? I had no idea he was staying here."

"He is not, I think, but—"

The Bucknells descended to sweep Papa away to be introduced, and although Osborn watched Olivia relentlessly, he made no move to follow her as she processed around the room on the earl's arm.

Eventually, inevitably, they came round to Osborn, who rose to make his bow. The earl, having excellent manners, exchanged some conversation with the simpering Lady Douglas first before turning to Osborn.

"Kiltarlity. It is a while since I have seen you. You have suffered some tragedies in your family since last we met. My condolences. How are you?"

"Well, sir, I thank you. Sadly grieved by the loss of my brothers and father, but we must soldier on, must we not? You have suffered some reverses yourself of late, I understand, and far more challenging than mine."

Papa looked suddenly stricken. "True, but as you say, we must soldier on and find what comfort we can."

"In your daughter I am sure you find great comfort," Osborn said, with a smiling glance at Olivia. "A man whose spirits cannot be lifted by so lovely a companion is a man without a heart."

"Indeed." Papa's face softened, and he patted Olivia's hand where it rested on his sleeve. "Olivia has barely left my side since the dreadful events first unfolded. She it is who has dragged me away from home for the first time, and now that I am here, I find myself already looking forward to getting out with the hunt. There is a meet tomorrow, I understand?"

"There is, at Chilford, where I am staying with Marsden."

"Marsden, eh? Another of Izzy's court. Is Davenport here as well?"

Osborn laughed easily. "I fear not. He is recently married and cannot tear himself away from his beloved, even for the hunt. But we shall have good sport, I am sure. You have your hunters with you? You will need a good string, for there is a meet almost every day just now. Do you still have that big bay you used to boast of?"

They were soon deep into a discussion of horseflesh, and Olivia's attention wandered. Looking around the room, she saw Osborn's sisters waggling their fingers at her invitingly, so she made her way there.

"Lady Elizabeth. Lady Lucilla," she murmured as she curtsied.

"We did not expect to see *you* here," Lady Elizabeth said, looking at Olivia with a somewhat supercilious glare.

"We should have guessed," her sister said. "Robert was so insistent, there had to be a reason."

"Yes, but how did she get an invitation *here?"* hissed Lady Elizabeth. "The Duke of Camberley's hunting box is for the Bucknells."

"And their guests," Olivia said calmly. "Lady Esther Franklyn is a Bucknell herself. She is chaperoning me."

"Who is that older gentleman talking to Robert? Do you know, Lucy? Oh, I recognise him now. It is Lord Rennington."

Lady Lucilla gasped. "Oh! He is... a very well looking man, is he not? For his age, that is, and they do say..."

The sisters turned in unison towards Olivia, who was trying very hard not to laugh.

"Is it true?" one said.

"That he is looking for another wife?" the other said. "For we heard rumours."

"It is true," Olivia said, smiling at them. "He is looking for someone young and pretty, who is not a bluestocking, not excessively pious, will not fuss over him and can ride well, but not recklessly. Do you know anyone like that?"

They exchanged knowing glances, but Olivia was confident they would not be a danger to her father. Lord Embleton was another matter. They had driven him away from Harraby Hall, and perhaps they might drive him away from Leicestershire, too.

The Franklyns arrived just then, and Olivia was drawn into Lady Esther's orbit for a while as she circulated among her various relations. After a while, she noticed that Mr Franklyn was sitting a little apart, a newspaper open on his knee, although he was not looking at it. Instead he was watching all that was going on in the room, a little smile on his lips.

Olivia crossed the room to sit beside him. "Shall you join the hunt tomorrow, Mr Franklyn?"

"No, I am not a hunting man," he said equably. "I like a horse well enough if it jogs me safely from one place to another, but jumping hedges and walls and streams has never greatly appealed to me. I shall watch the departure, I think, for Lady Esther will want to be there, but after that we shall retreat to the house... or perhaps pay some calls. Whatever my wife wishes to do."

"Do you always do as she wishes?" Olivia said.

He chuckled. "Not always, no. A man likes to be the master in his own house and have matters ordered to his liking, but in gatherings such as this... this is Lady Esther's territory. Here I defer to her experience and understanding of the rules of society. I was not born to this sort of life, unlike my wife... or you, Lady Olivia. I was nothing but an ordinary attorney in Newcastle until my unexpected inheritance gave me wealth and the ability to take a higher position in the world. I have been fortunate to find a wife to show me the way, and it pleases me to watch her moving in her proper milieu now and then."

"Do you ever go back to Newcastle?"

"Sometimes. I am not ashamed of my background — no one should ever be ashamed of what he once was, or of what he is, for that matter. We are all equal in God's eyes, after all, from the King down to the lowliest beggar on the streets."

"Even me?" she said in a whisper. "Even someone who is... illegitimate?"

"Certainly," he said. "You are the same person that you were six months ago, and all rational people will understand that and judge you as people have always been judged — by their actions, and not by an accident of birth. And if a few people look down on you now, as some look down on me, why then they are not worth knowing and you need not regard them."

"You do not think it is wrong of me to be... ambitious?"

"I have the utmost admiration for ambition," he said, with a smile. "In my first marriage, I married the daughter of my employer, and for my second I dared to look at the daughter of a duke, and look how well that has turned out. So why should not you be ambitious, and dare to look at a duke... or a marquess, as he is at present?"

"You know, then?" she said in a low voice.

"I know," he whispered back, "and I wish you the very best of luck, Lady Olivia."

"Thank you. I shall need it."

"Not so much as you might think," he said, eyes twinkling. "I believe he is ripe for marriage, and you have such charming manners. I think you would make an excellent duchess."

"His father would not approve of me."

“Now there you would be wrong. When Embleton offered for Bea, he told us that his father would leave him to make his own choice. The duke sounds like a sensible man, so you need not concern yourself over that. But… a word of warning, my lady. My wife is every bit as ambitious as you. Having failed to marry a title herself, she was determined that Bea would do so, and Bea got into some difficulties in pursuing that idea. There was talk of putting a man in a compromising situation, and that is a very bad way to win a husband. I trust you would never be seduced into such a thin g.”

Olivia blushed at the memory of her failed attempt to kiss Lord Embleton, but she answered composedly, “I know how to behave in a ladylike manner, I hope.”

“Of course,” he said easily, and deftly turned the subject.

Lady Kiltarlity soon rose to leave, her daughters also jumping up with alacrity. Osborn, who had been lurking a little apart from the rest of the company, one shoulder leaning against the wall as he watched Olivia, showed a marked unwillingness to depart.

“Must we go so soon?” Olivia heard him say plaintively to his mother.

But the carriage was summoned and in a very few minutes he was obliged to take his leave, throwing just one long glance across the room at Olivia.

9: The Meet

Olivia could not help but be cheered by Osborn's obvious pleasure in her company. She had met enough young men to distinguish genuine interest from mere politeness or casual flirtation, and although Osborn had a definite tendency towards flirtation, there was a light in his eyes that she could not mistake. Those eyes! She *loved* the way he looked at her! No wonder Izzy had been so beguiled by him.

Izzy... And that was the aspect that lowered her spirits again, for what was she to do with a man who was so clearly reprising a former lost love by paying court to her younger sister? For the moment, he was dazzled by the similarity in appearance, but soon enough he would see that she was nothing but an echo of Izzy, a paste copy of her sparkling diamond, a mere shadow of her brilliance. It was disheartening by any measure to be the younger sister of such a creature, but to look so like her and yet to be so unlike at the same time made her excessively despondent.

There was another niggle of concern, too. Why was Osborn even here? She could tell, from the surprised mutterings of the Bucknells, that this visit was out of the ordinary. He had regularly stayed with his friend Marsden for the hunt, she gathered, but he had never made much effort to show himself around the neighbourhood, and now here he was, with his mother and sisters in tow, paying calls. She wished he would go away... and yet, it was such a boost to her spirits to be the recipient of obvious admiration, however unwarranted.

The next morning, finding her father alone in the breakfast parlour, she ventured to say, "Tell me about Lord Kiltarlity and Izzy."

The earl folded the newspaper he had been reading, and smiled at her. "He was one of her most determined suitors, one of the four. The lovelorn swains, as your mother called them. Farramont, Marsden, Davenport and Osborn. The first to fall for her, but the last of them to talk to me, and expecting me to send him away with a flea in his ear. Five years ago, he had nothing but his own charm and a modest allowance from his father, whereas the others had good incomes, or were heir to it. But your mother liked him... I dare say that charm worked on her, too. Besides, she thought that Izzy favoured him, and she wanted her to be happy. We both did. So I told him we would see that there was enough money, if Izzy chose him." He chuckled. "Well, there is money enough now, and a title too, so if you are asking whether he is worth encouraging, I would say very much so."

That was not at all what she was asking, but she could not quite articulate what it was she needed to know. Part of her wanted Osborn gone so that the wretched comparisons with Izzy would stop filling her mind, yet... he was such fun, and delightfully silly, with his *'fair ghost'* business, and she did not want to lose that lightheartedness. Since Uncle Arthur's death, or even before that, with Granny so ill, everything had been dark and gloomy, like midwinter all year round. It was wonderful to leave Corland behind for once, and make new friends and have a man — an *eligible* man — paying her attention.

Still, she must not lose sight of her main objective. Later that morning, the local hunt would meet at Chilford Lodge, and Lord Embleton would be there. The entire neighbourhood would gather to see the riders off and it was imperative that she be noticed by him. Accordingly, she chose a pale golden velvet pelisse and a matching hat, a pairing that she would not normally wear at this time of year.

"Let us hope it does not rain," Lady Esther said, looking her up and down as the ladies gathered in the entrance hall to await the carriages. "Still, an excellent choice, my dear."

The carriage ride was only a short one, for Chilford Lodge was next door to Briar House. There were the hounds, bouncing around excitedly, and the riders enjoying a warming drink before departure. Olivia's eye scanned the riders. Where was he? He was not here! Ah, there he was, amidst a little group of riders, their horses pawing the ground and tossing their heads, picking up the general excitement.

Olivia took a glass of something from a hovering footman, then set off on a seemingly casual stroll towards Lord Embleton. Several of the riders nodded courteously to her, but there were none she knew so no one delayed her. She had almost reached her quarry when a large black horse moved in front of her, blocking her way.

"My fair ghost emerges into sunlight and survives," came the cheerful call, and before she could do more than huff in annoyance, he had leapt to the ground to execute a flourishing bow to her. "How delightful to see you again so soon, my dimpled apparition."

"Really, sir! Such nonsense you talk! And if you see sunshine today, then you are truly prey to apparitions, for all I see are grey clouds."

"No, no! I will not have it so, for there is sunshine and summer beauty here in our midst. I see it before my very eyes, and it bedazzles me, oh golden orb of light."

He held his hands across his face momentarily, as if to shield himself, but his eyes brimmed with mischief.

"You are the veriest rattle, sir," she said, but his antics were making her laugh and she could not be as severe as she wished. "Just because I wear yellow—"

"Precisely! And it is just what we need to bring sunshine to a dull day. Look at all the practical dark colours with which we are surrounded, yet here are you brightening the gloom."

Another rider loomed up, as handsome a man as Olivia had ever seen.

"Kiltarlity, you really must not keep the prettiest young lady all to yourself, you know. It is most unfair. Will you not introduce me?"

Osborn did not look very pleased about it. "Oh... well... Lady Olivia, may I present to you Lord Grayling, whose estate adjoins this one. Grayling, this is the Lady Olivia Atherton, daughter of the Earl of Rennington."

Grayling dismounted, swept off his hat to reveal a mane of golden hair and executed an elegant bow. "Lady Olivia. I should have realised, for you are so like your sister. Enchanted to make your acquaintance. How is it we have not met in town long before this?"

"I have not yet had a season in town, sir, but I shall be there next spring, all being well."

"Excellent! London will be all the brighter for your presence."

Osborn, having grown increasingly impatient with these courtesies, now interrupted. "The hunt is moving off, Grayling. We do not want to be left behind."

"Of course." With a few more words to Olivia, including the hope from Lord Grayling that he would see her again very soon, and not have to wait until the spring, the two men remounted and began to follow the other riders. Behind them came the little group that had surrounded Lord Embleton and last of all the marquess himself. He saw Olivia standing at the side of the drive, doffed his hat and made a small inclination of the head towards her, his face impassive. Then he was gone, swept up into the great crowd of riders and hounds pouring away down the drive towards the fields.

And that was her sole exchange with the marquess. She sighed sorrowfully.

"Well, that was a little disappointing," Lady Esther said at her shoulder, having presumably been watching the whole time. "However, Lord Kiltarlity is becoming very attentive, and I had forgotten Lord Grayling. He would be a very acceptable *parti* if we could ensnare him."

"I do not want to *ensnare* anyone," Olivia said sadly. "All I should like to do is to meet a certain gentleman in a way which allows me to talk to him, so that we may get to know each other better. However, I do not think that is going to be possible when he resides in a different house altogether. If he never leaves it except to join the hunt, I shall never receive more than an occasional bow in passing from him."

"Do not despair, for Jerry and Charlie are aware of the situation."

"Jerry and Charlie?"

"My cousins, Mr Jeremiah and Miss Charlotte Bucknell. They plan to hold a dinner soon to which Lord Embleton will be invited."

"Ah!" Olivia said, smiling. Such words to cheer her! A proper two course dinner, with two hours of conversation, assuming she could manage to seat herself next to the marquess, was just what she needed. It felt a little contrived, with all this manipulation behind the scenes, but there was no ensnarement going on. All she asked was an opportunity to talk to the marquess, nothing more than that, and then... well, she would just have to wait and hope.

***

Robert was disgruntled. The first part of his plan had worked perfectly, and he had successfully intervened to keep Embleton away from Olivia, but then Grayling had poked his nose in. Grayling! A man who had no serious thought of marriage, yet was perfectly capable of turning the head of a young and inexperienced girl who might fall for his meaningless drollery, and that would never do! He must be kept away from her at all costs.

Wait...

Why was he so concerned to keep Grayling away from Olivia? Or Embleton, for that matter. When he had set out on this mission, the intent had been to guard Embleton from Olivia, yet now, in some mysterious way, that had been turned around, and he seemed to want to guard *her* from *them*. It was true that he was oddly protective of her. The similarity to Izzy aroused all his almost-forgotten affection... no, it was stronger than that... his *passion* for Izzy, but there was something vulnerable about Olivia that made him want to shield her from rogues like Grayling. Izzy had never been so unguarded in her dealings with the world. There was a lady who knew exactly how to get what she wanted, for had she not played them all, like fish on a line? There was none of that in Olivia.

He smiled as he thought of her sweet face gazing up at him trustingly, with that adorable dimple beside enticing red lips. That dimple, and the lips it emphasised, were beginning to haunt him, rather.

His interest in the hunt diminished rapidly once the leaden grey skies began to disgorge a miserable, drenching drizzle, and after a couple of hours, he was glad to return to Chilford, a hot bath, dry clothes and a rain-proof carriage to convey him to Briar House.

There he was disgusted to find Grayling already ensconced in the prime seat beside Olivia. Robert was not so ill-mannered as to display the slightest displeasure, however, so he made his greetings to the Bucknells and then dutifully sat beside the oldest matron to make himself agreeable. As he was thus engaged, his eye was caught by a head of striking blonde curls, similar to Grayling's own hair colour. Was it...? Yes, it must be.

Adroitly extricating himself from the matron, he ambled across to the blonde curls. "Miss Grayling, is it not? We met in town once or twice in the spring, I believe, although I daresay you do not remember me. The Earl of Kiltarlity."

"Oh yes!" she said, her voice wispy and high. "You danced with me at the Carrbridges' ball."

"And a great pleasure it was," he said at once, having no memory of the occasion at all. Had he even been at the Carrbridges' ball? "I have been so little in town these last few years that every dance is a treasured moment. Did you enjoy the season — your first, I think?"

That was a guess, for she looked no more than eighteen, but she smiled and simpered at him. "Yes, it was, and I enjoyed it tremendously although Julian — my brother, you know, Lord Grayling—"

"I know Grayling," Robert murmured.

"Of course. Well, he was a bit cross because we did not get all the invitations he had hoped for, so it was not as successful as he had hoped. But I had a lovely time, and now he is taking me to meet all his friends, which is great fun. You were at the meet this morning, I remember, yet here you are. Was the hunt not to your liking, or did your horse hurt itself, like Julian's?"

"My horse performed well, but the hunt was as hunts always are, exhilarating and tedious in equal measure. The chase is fun, but there is also a great deal of milling about and turning aside and plain waiting around, and in the rain that is not terribly amusing. I thought that a hot bath followed by agreeable company would suit me better and I am discovering that I was quite right."

A more sophisticated or subtle girl would have responded to this very mild compliment with a witticism about hot baths, or by a sly reference to the matron he had talked to first, but Miss Grayling was neither sophisticated or subtle. Fluttering her eyelashes, she said with what was no doubt intended to be demureness, "I trust you find *my* company agreeable, Lord Kiltarlity?"

"How could I not?" he said, with practised smoothness. Then, because he suspected she would like a more open compliment, he added, "The company of a pretty young lady is always agreeable."

"Oh, do you think me pretty? People tell me so but that is just flattery, is it not?"

She looked at him expectantly. Should he play along? She was boringly naive and he had no wish to become entangled with her, but if Grayling was going to monopolise Olivia, why should he not amuse himself with Miss Grayling? And she was exceptionally pretty. If Olivia had not been in the room, Miss Grayling would have been the best looking woman there by a great margin.

He leaned towards her and said in a low voice, "But I never flatter, Miss Grayling. I always speak the absolute truth."

Her eyes widened at his closeness, and she rested a hand on his arm in a fashion he found uncomfortably proprietorial. "Then I believe you," she said in her wispy voice. "I must accept it, if you say it is the truth. Do you make a long stay in Leicestershire, sir?"

"I am not sure," he said, with perfect truth, and then mischievously added, "It depends how long other people choose to stay."

He had Olivia in mind, but he knew that she would interpret it as referring to her, and was not surprised when she simpered, and then began to enquire about Strathinver with an avidity which turned his stomach. No, he could not get up a flirtation with this chit of a girl, who made her intentions so obvious. He was a single man of marriageable age, and the title and its concomitant fortune made him excessively eligible, so he never blamed a woman for putting herself in his way. But such obvious stratagems as Miss Grayling employed left a sour taste in the mouth. Olivia was the same age, but infinitely more interesting to him, and with far less artifice.

A shadow loomed over them. "Much as I hate to break up this charming tête-à-tête, it is time for us to take our leave, sister."

"Oh! Of course. How delightful to meet you again, Lord Kiltarlity. I am sure we shall meet very often."

"I shall look forward to it," he said, politely, and hoped she would not enquire just how keen his anticipation would be, and thereby oblige him to lie to her.

Grayling's seat beside Olivia had already been taken, so Robert took a glass of something from a footman and wandered across the room to join a small cluster of men talking about politics, who fell on him as a great expert, being a peer with a seat in the House of Lords. It was one of the many duties that had befallen him since his father's demise, and although he had indeed attended the House now and then, and had even attempted to understand one or two of the subjects under debate, he had not yet fully grasped the currents of opinion that swirled around Westminster. So he made noncommittal noises, and listened and attempted to learn.

He kept his eye on Olivia, nevertheless, but she was now surrounded by several young men, more refugees from the inclement weather, and after a while he abandoned all hope of talking to her, and made his way to the hall. Here he found Grayling and his sister still lingering. Their carriage was outside the door, but Grayling was engaged in a low-voiced discussion with Mr and Miss Bucknell. Seeing him, they broke apart with suspicious haste, the Graylings left and Robert's carriage was sent for.

"What a pity you must leave so soon," Miss Bucknell said with a little smile on her face. "We are inundated this morning, so I dare say you have hardly had a chance to talk to anyone of interest."

"You have many interesting visitors," Robert said smoothly. "I have been well entertained, I assure you."

"But perhaps none of *particular* interest," she said with a knowing smile. "But perhaps... we have had a couple of dinner guests unexpectedly unable to attend this evening. Would you care to...? I do not think we have room for Lady Kiltarlity and the Miss Osborns, but we can certainly find a place for you, if you would care to join us."

A whole evening with Olivia! And it seemed that the Bucknells knew of his interest, and would help him to forward it. His mother might not be pleased, but it was too good an opportunity to miss.

He accepted with alacrity, and spent the entire drive home trying to dream up a suitable explanation for his mother. And at the back of his mind the thought still lingered, that he was chasing the will-o'-the-wisp of his love for Izzy, and not Olivia herself.

10: Lady Euphemia

Olivia did not see Osborn leave, so once the crowd clustering around her had dispersed somewhat, she had the dispiriting exercise of looking for him and slowly realising that he was no longer there. The room had felt brighter, in some indefinable way, when he was in it, and now it was a little dimmer, as if two or three candles had been snuffed out.

There was not long to suffer this disappointment, however, for Lady Esther came hurrying over, or at least moving with more than her customary stateliness, from her post by the window.

"A carriage has just gone past, and who do you think it is?" she said, her eyes gleaming with excitement.

"Lord Kiltarlity," Olivia said glumly. "He has left already."

"Kiltarlity?" Her eyebrows rose in surprise. "Oh... *leaving*. Yes, he departed a few minutes ago, just after the Graylings. No, this is an arrival, and it is very good news. The blinds were down, but I am tolerably certain of the occupant."

"Did you recognise the carriage?" Olivia said.

"No, no! Heavens, who has time to remember carriages? But the coat of arms — *that* I recognised, and I think... I *hope* you will be pleased. Oh, here he is now."

The door opened, and the butler made his announcement. "The Marquess of Embleton, the Lady Euphemia Howland, the Lord Arnold Howland, madam."

Lady Esther gave a low moan of pure pleasure. Olivia was excited, too — not only the marquess himself, but a younger brother and sister, too! She had pored over the Peerage so much that she knew all about the family. These two were the eldest offspring of the duke's second marriage. Lady Euphemia was Olivia's own age, with the sort of features usually described as handsome rather than beautiful. Lord Arnold at seventeen was bidding fair to be a great inspiration to the young ladies of the *ton* in the future, although being the fourth son of a duke reduced his eligibility somewhat. Still, he was tall enough to be in the Guards, and a uniform would aid his cause wonderfully.

The newcomers stood for some time talking in low voices to Mr and Miss Bucknell. Mr Bucknell smiled and rubbed his hands together, but his sister frowned anxiously, and once or twice shook her head. Olivia was sitting near enough to catch snatches of their conversation.

"....m-m-much obliged..."

"...full... every... taken..."

"I would be no trouble at all." That was Lady Euphemia's higher voice.

"...maybe... at a pinch... could move Auntie..."

"...v-v-very... inconv-v-venient..."

"I can squeeze in anywhere."

Olivia jumped to her feet and moved nearer. "I beg your pardon, but I could not help overhearing. If Lady Euphemia needs a bed for the night, there is more than enough space for two in my room. I have been most generously accommodated, and would be delighted to share, if Lord Embleton has no objection to such an arrangement for his sister."

They all turned on her with surprised expressions, quickly transformed into smiles.

Lady Euphemia bounced excitedly. "There, you see, Embleton?"

"How very kind," murmured Miss Bucknell. "But perhaps Lord Embleton... I mean, he may prefer..." She tailed off in a morass of mumbled nothings, but Olivia understood her. *If Lord Embleton prefers his sister not to consort with an illegitimate girl.* That was what she meant.

But Lord Embleton was a gentleman through and through, for he bowed to Olivia. "How v-v-very k-kind."

Miss Bucknell rushed in with introductions, Lord Embleton and his brother were invited to join them for dinner, and then, tucking Lady Euphemia's arm into hers, Olivia led her triumphantly up the stairs to her room.

"Oh, lovely," Lady Euphemia said, giving the room a cursory glance before sitting on the edge of the bed. "So tell me, who is here of interest?"

Olivia named a few people, but Lady Euphemia stopped with an imperious wave of one hand.

"No, no! Spare me the details of matrons and old married men. I mean *young* men, men to flirt with. I thought I was in heaven at Embleton's hunting box, for all his friends are young and have that look in their eyes — you know what I mean, I am sure. Roguish. Game for anything. But Embleton would not have it. No chaperon, you see, and he was all for taking me straight back to Papa except that I thought of the Bucknells and hoped they might squeeze me in. Which they have! Is this not delightful?

And you can tell me all about the young men here. Is there anyone exciting? Or merely amusing? I do so like to be amused."

Olivia dutifully listed the unmarried men, although she made no mention of her father. It was unsettling enough to see him under siege from women looking to become a countess, but she was not going to let anyone of a flirtatious nature near him. To see her own father flirting would be distressing enough, for the father of a grown family should have left off such childish behaviour years ago, but imagine if he should be caught! To think of him in love, or worse, broken-hearted, would be too dreadful for words.

The housekeeper came in just then, with a little train of maids behind her, and then footmen labouring with trunks, with Lady Euphemia's own maid watching them closely. Finally, Lady Esther appeared. Olivia made the introductions.

Lady Esther looked around the room, as if assessing whether it were suitably grand for the daughter of a duke. "Well now, Lady Euphemia, I hope this meets with your approval?"

"Oh, yes. Lovely!"

"Your brother has very graciously allowed me to be your chaperon while you are here. I have Lady Olivia in my charge, so one extra will be no trouble at all, and your brother will be dining here every night, so you will still see plenty of him."

Every night! Olivia fizzed with excitement. Here was an opportunity she had not expected!

As soon as Lady Esther had left, and the lady's maid was busy unpacking, Lady Euphemia grabbed Olivia's arm. *"Franklyn?"* she hissed. "She is not... is she... related to a Miss Beatrice Franklyn?"

"Stepmother. Bea's father is here, too."

"Is *she* here? Beatrice... Bea? I like Bea better. Busy like a bee, which she must have been to catch Embleton in her web... do bees spin webs? Toils, then. Is she here?"

"No. She has recently married my cousin, Mr Bertram Atherton, and is on a wedding tour."

Lady Euphemia's mouth opened so wide she could have swallowed an entire Bath bun. *"No!* Embleton offered for her, and now she is married... to your cousin? How did that happen?"

Olivia laughed. "In the usual way, I imagine. They decided, when they considered the matter carefully, that they would quite like to be married."

Lady Euphemia looked startled, then laughed, a loud, honking noise. "You are funny, Olivia! May I call you Olivia? And you must call me Effie."

"Oh, may I? For Lady Euphemia is rather a mouthful, and Effie is such a pretty name. Oh, what a lovely gown! That has to be the work of a French modiste."

And after that, as Effie's wardrobe emerged from its boxes, the conversation was entirely taken up by a discussion of the relative merits of sarsenet, lustring and Persian silk, whether tippets were in style or completely exploded, the minimum number of pairs of dancing slippers required for the exigencies of the season and many other topics of a similar fascinating nature.

***

When Olivia entered the drawing room that evening, arrayed in her very best gown for Lord Embleton, arm in arm with her new friend, she had no thought beyond the marquess. It was therefore something of a disappointment that he had not yet arrived. Instead, she saw several familiar faces. Lord Grayling and his sister smirked at her from one side of the room, and from the other, Osborn smiled and waved to her.

The two girls were immediately under siege from the bachelors present, at least those from the Bucknell family. Not that any of them were very promising, either as marriage possibilities or as flirts, for in appearance they were either rail thin or tended to stoutness, none were handsome or witty, and being distant cousins or younger sons meant their prospects were poor. Lady Esther had already warned Olivia not to encourage any of them, and she had likewise informed Effie.

"I do not care two straws for their eligibility," she had said airily, "so long as they can flirt amusingly. Flirting is so much fun, do you not agree?"

Now, while she sparred with one or two of the Bucknell men, perhaps as a warming up exercise, she was also looking about her for more promising material. Olivia watched her anxiously, but although Effie's gaze lingered on Osborn, who was still smiling winningly in their general direction, she settled in the end on Lord Grayling.

"Who is the Adonis?" she whispered to Olivia.

"Lord Grayling."

"Indeed? He has that look in his eye. Very promising. Will you introduce me?"

This took very little effort, for Lord Grayling was already ambling across the room with the same objective in mind, his eyes fixed on Effie. Almost before the introductions had been concluded, he escorted Effie to an empty sofa and said something which made her lower her eyes and tap him reprovingly on the arm with her fan.

"Good evening, fair ghost," murmured a voice at Olivia's shoulder.

"Osborn! I did not expect to see you here, or the Graylings, either."

"The invitation was a pleasant surprise. I believe Miss Bucknell is indulging in a spot of match-making. She was whispering with the Graylings as I was leaving earlier, then she invited me to dinner and here they are, too. She steered me towards Miss Grayling as soon as I arrived."

"She is very pretty," Olivia said. "All those blonde curls! I imagine she does not have to sleep in curling papers, or singe her hair with irons to induce a slight twist, which drops out within the hour. Straight hair is a great trial to a lady."

"Your hair curls very prettily," he said, lifting a strand from one side of her face and winding it round his fingers. "Very prettily indeed."

"You cannot imagine how long it takes to make it do so, whereas a man need only run a comb through his locks to be ready. Or perhaps not even that," she added, looking up in amusement at his wayward coiffure.

He laughed, and shook his head. "Ah, the innocence of youth! I would wager it takes my valet longer to arrange my hair than it takes your maid to arrange yours."

"Really, Osborn, do not dignify that disorderly mess with the epithet *'arrangement'*. You look as if you have been dragged through a hedge backwards."

"Which is entirely the intention. This style is known as the Brutus, a Brummell fashion, I believe."

"Oh, him! Well, if Brummell does it, it must be all the crack, I suppose. My eldest brother, Walter, affects something of the sort, but I always assumed he simply fell out of bed looking like that, and forgot to brush it."

The butler's resonant voice stilled all conversation. "The Marquess of Embleton, madam."

Olivia turned eagerly towards the door.

"I suppose you will not want to talk to me now," Osborn said, with a rueful laugh. "I shall make myself scarce."

She barely noticed his polite bow, or his back as he walked away from her, for her eyes were fixed on the marquess. He scanned the room, saw her, smiled and after the briefest of conversations with Miss Bucknell he moved directly across the room to the sofa where she still sat.

"L-lady Olivia." He made her an elegant bow. "I m-must thank you again f-for making room f-for Effie. I c-c-cannot tell you—"

She stopped him with a wave of her hand. "Pray say nothing of it. Lady Euphemia is my own age, and nothing could please me more than to enjoy her company. Both my own sisters have married and moved away, so I shall borrow yours for a little while. She is already proving to be an entertaining companion."

He grimaced. "Really? I do not f-f-find her entertaining, p-p-persuading Arnold to bring her here. I have s-s-sent him home in d-d-disgrace, foolish boy. Effie is a m-m-minx."

Olivia laughed. "I do not know about that! If it is so, then you must allow that she is an amusing minx." She patted the seat beside her in invitation, and when he sat, she whispered conspiratorially, "I believe she has only come here to flirt. She is exercising her charms on Lord Grayling at this very moment."

He smiled at her. "Effie is s-safe enough with G-Grayling. He likes to f-f-flirt too."

The butler cleared his throat. "Dinner is served, madam."

Olivia and the marquess rose in unison and then — glory of glories! — he offered her his arm with a little bow. "M-may I have the p-p-pleasure of your c-company, Lady Olivia?"

This was more like it! An hour, or maybe two, in his company, and he seemed amenable to liking her despite her *faux pas* at Corland. She also had a little glimpse of the respect that would be accorded her if she should ever marry the marquess. Even in the Bucknell household, where most of the company was related in some way to the Duke of Camberley, the future Duke of Bridgeworth was a person of great importance. On his arm Olivia proceeded at the front of the procession to the dining room, and found herself almost at the head of the table.

Osborn managed to inveigle himself into the seat on her other side, but she could not object to that. When the marquess was occupied with Miss Bucknell to his left, Olivia would have the frivolous Earl of Kiltarlity to talk to. This did not work so well as she had hoped, for every time she tried to talk to the marquess, the earl would tap her elbow. "A pork cutlet, Lady Olivia?" he would say blandly. Or, "Try the woodcocks, do. They are delicious."

"Thank you, but Lord Embleton will supply me, should I need anything," she hissed at him.

"But he only has access to the mutton and sweetbreads. I can reach so much more. Can I tempt you to a little of the ham?"

By the time she turned back to the marquess, he was talking to Miss Bucknell. It was maddening.

When the ladies withdrew to the drawing room, Lady Esther led her to a quiet sofa and whispered, "It is going very well, is it not?"

"Is it?" Olivia said crossly. "Lord Kiltarlity seems determined to interfere."

"Oh, indeed! Such a good sign. He is jealous, you see, so he tries to distract you from the marquess, but you are managing them both beautifully. If one does not come up to scratch, you will be sure to secure the other."

"But I do not want *the other.* I like the marquess, and he seems to like me, whereas the earl is merely irritating, like a bluebottle, constantly buzzing about to no purpose."

Lady Esther gave a tinkling laugh. "You may see it that way, but I assure you his purpose is very plain to see. Do not push him away until you are absolutely sure of the marquess. You seem to get on well with Lord Kiltarlity. Am I wrong about that?"

"Oh... well, he is vastly amusing, I suppose, when he is not trying to distract me away from Lord Embleton."

"There, you see?" she said triumphantly. "Two exceptionally eligible *partis* already forming an attachment to you. I congratulate you, my dear. You will be married before your first season, I wager. And we may congratulate ourselves on another success, too, do you not think?"

"Another success? What can you mean?"

"Why your father, of course, and Charlie Bucknell."

"Miss Bucknell? And Papa? No!"

"Had you not noticed? I assure you, they are becoming closer by the hour. He is so relaxed in her company, it is wonderful to see, after all his tribulations of the last few months. He looks so happy! You mark my words, it will be a match."

***

Robert watched as the ladies withdrew with mixed feelings. It was a relief that Olivia was removed from Embleton's company for a while, but she was also removed from his own company, and he could not be happy about that. There was a rightness to her sitting at his side, even though she had been cross with him tonight. Yet he knew that he could easily cajole her back to her usual sweet temper, if only Embleton were not there to distract her.

Once the ladies had all left and the door was closed, the gentlemen reformed around Mr Bucknell, and Embleton was drawn away to be the star attraction. Robert stayed where he was, not being minded for the usual male conversation. It would be all horses and sport, the last hunt gone over in exhaustive detail and the prospects for the next analysed to a tedious degree. Robert enjoyed the hunt as much as any man, but tonight his thoughts were elsewhere, with a certain heart-shaped face surrounded by curls — laboriously obtained curls, he now knew. The thought made him smile.

"Do I intrude upon your meditations? Happy ones, to judge by your expression."

The oily voice of Grayling.

"No intrusion," Robert said, and meant it, for Grayling had brought the port with him. Taking the chair so recently occupied by Olivia, his well-honed masculine form and golden hair banished the image of feminine beauty and dark curls that had filled Robert's mind. With the slightest of sighs, he accepted a glass of port and waited for Grayling to say what he had come to say. That he had a point to make was certain, for he would not have wandered down to this end of the table at random.

At first, it was nothing but civil niceties — polite enquiries as to the improvements at Strathinver, and whether he planned to reopen the house in town, but then he added, "You seem to get along rather well with my sister."

Robert had taken little notice of the girl on his other side, apart from the usual courtesies. He had not neglected her, but set against the manifold charms of Olivia, she could hardly compete.

Cautiously, wondering where this was leading, he replied, "Miss Grayling is an agreeable dinner companion."

Grayling smiled. "She is! And pretty as a flower — would you not agree?"

"Very pretty, yes." No lie needed there.

The baron swirled his port thoughtfully. "She seems very taken with you. Chatters on about you constantly."

"She does?" he said blandly.

"Mm. But then you could always charm the ladies, Kiltarlity, even in the days when you were merely the youngest of the brood, with no prospect of the title. But now…" He hesitated, eyeing Robert speculatively.

Robert understood now what was being said. Miss Grayling fancied being the Countess of Kiltarlity, that was the long and the short of it. Well, she would be disappointed in that, but still, it was an opportunity to make use of Grayling. Robert could not be everywhere, and another pair of eyes to keep watch on Embleton and protect him from Olivia would be useful.

He decided to help Grayling along.

"The title changes everything, of course. Having never had the expectation of it, I felt myself to be… free of restraint. Free of responsibility. But now, I have to take my position seriously and consider the future."

"Indeed. As we must all do, those of us who have the honour to inherit a noble title."

"My mother is urging me to marry sooner rather than later," Robert said, grasping the nettle firmly. "It would be sensible… secure the succession, and so forth. I cannot put it off indefinitely. I suppose I shall have to put myself about next spring. "

Grayling smiled. "Indeed. But perhaps circumstances might resolve the matter rather sooner than that, if you should happen to meet the right lady."

"That would certainly be convenient," Robert said neutrally.

"Sarah only has five thousand — that is all I can spare, but you have no need for a large dowry, have you? And she has other attractions that amply compensate. I do not think that is merely my fondness as a brother speaking."

"No, she is a delightful girl," Robert said. "I have no objection to getting to know her better, to see if anything develops."

"She is an affectionate little creature," Grayling said with a smile, thinking the game won.

"I have a small difficulty, however," Robert said. "You have met Lady Olivia Atherton? She is an ambitious little minx, and is determined to get her claws into Embleton. I came here with the intention of keeping him out of her clutches, but I cannot do that if I am to direct my attention towards Miss Grayling."

"Embleton can look after himself, I should have thought," Grayling said, looking amused. "He has been heir to the dukedom from birth, so he must be aware that he is the biggest prize on the market, and have ways to protect himself."

"Oh, I am sure he does, but even a marquess is no match for a determined girl of eighteen, and they have been somewhat thrown together lately. I should not want him to succumb to any underhand tactics."

"Hmm." Grayling refilled their glasses. "I could undertake to distract the young lady, if that would help, Kiltarlity?"

It was not quite what Robert wanted, for Grayling was exactly the sort of handsome, smooth-talking man that an unsophisticated girl of eighteen might fall for, and that would be a disaster. Not that Grayling was the marrying sort. He had kept a string of mistresses over the years, and boasted that no one woman was enough for him. Still, it would keep Olivia away from Embleton.

"That would be a kindness, Grayling."

Grayling grinned wolfishly. "No penance, certainly. A lively little creature, quite charming, and so young and fresh. I love them young, do not you?"

"No foolishness, Grayling," Robert said in sudden alarm. "She is the daughter of an earl, after all, with three brothers."

Grayling chuckled. "You are quick to spring to her defence, my friend. If you had not just described her as *'an ambitious little minx'*, I might suspect you of an interest there yourself. But fret not. I know her brothers, and some of her cousins, too, so I know she is well protected, and seduction of innocents has never been my game. But a little flirtation — yes, that would be amusing."

Robert was left wondering if he had made a huge mistake in pushing Olivia into the clutches of a practised rake like Grayling.

11: Captain Edgerton Has A Theory

Captain Michael Edgerton returned to Corland Castle in an optimistic frame of mind. He had seen the newly married Mr and Mrs Bertram Atherton settled at a secret location, with instructions not to leave for at least a month, an order with which they seemed perfectly inclined to comply. The protective body-guard had been drilled in the necessary discipline to ensure that no assassin could get near to Mr Bertram, and the servants were equally on the alert. Michael was satisfied.

As he rode back to the castle with Sandy, his young Scottish associate, he was confident not only that the couple were safe, but that his colleagues would have the name of the murderer awaiting him. He had left them checking with every single person present at the time of Mr Bertram's shooting to find out not only where that person was, but everyone nearby, too. Anyone seen by multiple witnesses could be eliminated, and surely there would be one man who was not seen by anyone, because he had been busy climbing out of the cheese store with a gun in his hand.

Michael knew the instant he entered the old schoolroom and saw their faces that his colleagues had no answer for him.

"Sit down and have a drink," Luce said, as soon as she saw him.

"Do I need it?"

She merely smiled at him sadly and poured him a large brandy. "If we had known you would be here today, we would have kept some cakes for you, but Pettigrew ate them all. Shall I send for something?"

Michael shook his head. "Just tell me the worst. Is there nobody at all who is unaccounted for?"

"Oh yes," Pettigrew Willerton-Forbes said. "Seven men and two ladies. There are also six couples who are the only witnesses for each other, and nine people who were seen in two places at once... one in three places, in fact. It is a nightmare, Michael."

Michael raised his eyebrows, then sighed and took a long draught of brandy. "Well, perhaps we were overly optimistic. Let me have the list of seven men not seen by anyone."

Pettigrew slid a paper across.

"Ha! There ye are!" cried Sandy, reading over Michael's shoulder. "That's yer man."

"Kent Atherton?" Michael said.

"Aye, and wasn't he late coming out of the castle after the shooting? He was here when the sainted chaplain was done in, he saw Peachy's things at the tower, he's neck deep in the smuggling. Has to be him."

"Where does he say he was?"

"Went to relieve himself," Pettigrew said. "Several of the gentlemen took the opportunity, the servants, too."

"Why was he not seen in the gentlemen's retiring room?"

"He says he was at the far side of the great hall, so he was nearer to a place below stairs that the servants use."

Michael tapped the paper thoughtfully. "Yet no one saw him. What of the others on the list? I doubt Sir Hubert Strong is our gunman."

"He had been arguing a point with Lord Rennington, and went into the library to look something up."

"The library windows would overlook the spot where the gunman was," Michael said excitedly. "I suppose he did not see anything?"

Pettigrew shook his head. "He was on the far side of the room, away from the windows, and the gunshot startled him so much, he knocked over his candle. He had to feel his way back to the entrance hall. As for the rest of the list, Lord Farramont was upstairs fetching a shawl for his wife. One of the footmen was in the dining room, and the other was seeing to the fire in the drawing room. No reason to suspect any of them. The butler and under butler were down in the basement, they say. I think we may assume that neither of the ladies on the list climbed that ladder in the cheese store, not in full evening dress."

"Very well," Michael said. "You said there were six couples who only saw each other?"

"Two gentlemen and two ladies in their respective retiring rooms," Pettigrew said. "Two maids in the buttery, preparing something for dinner. The Cathcart twins, up to mischief in the parlour. The Dowager Countess's nurse and lady's maid, watching over their sleeping charge in the tower room at the far end of the gallery. Mr Eustace and Miss Wilkes were in the Armoury at this end of the gallery."

"The Armoury!" Michael said. "Were they, indeed!"

"He wished to show her an Italian wheel-lock pistol from the seventeenth century," Pettigrew said blandly, as Sandy sniggered.

"Yes, yes, just an excuse," Michael said. "Still, an engaged couple may be permitted a moment alone together, no doubt."

"It would have been highly suspicious if the pistol that was fired at Mr Bertram had come from the Armoury," Pettigrew said.

"If only that were the case," Michael said sorrowfully, wandering over to the sideboard where the pistol now lay beside the axe. "Unfortunately, I have spent a great deal of time in the Armoury over the months we have been here, and this pistol was never part of the collection there, nor on the walls."

"Nor in Mr Eustace's collection," Pettigrew said. "He does not recognise it at all."

Michael carried the pistol back to the table, turning it this way and that, before laying it aside with a sigh.

There was a large plan of the castle's principal floor laid out on the table, with the positions of each guest and servant marked on it. Michael spent some time poring over this, and comparing it with the lists of names.

"Which would be the way the gunman went, do you suppose?" he said at length. "He would no doubt have left the castle by the door below the bridge, but which stairs would he have used? The service stairs are all some distance away."

"Not all," James Neate said. "The service stairs are at one end of the great hall, and used by the servants as they come and go. There is also the wider stair beside the garden door, which leads directly up to the great hall, emerging below the main stairs. However, there are two other stairs, narrow spiral affairs set into the walls, intended for the butler or a footman to reach the entrance hall quickly when a visitor arrives. One is just inside the gallery, the other in the library. They are rarely used nowadays, it seems, so there is little risk of encountering anyone."

"Hmm." Michael reached for his brandy glass, found it empty and set it down with another sigh. "I was so optimistic that we would find just one person unaccounted for. Ah, well. Nothing about this case has been easy, and this is no exception. Pettigrew, have you heard any more about Miss Wilkes' home, or the quarrel between her and her father?"

"I have had a reply from the Duchess of Dunmorton," Pettigrew Willerton-Forbes said, brushing a stray crumb from his waistcoat. "She does not know the Wilkes family personally, but she has a friend who has a relation in the neighbourhood of Warriston Hall, so she is to write and make more enquiries."

James Neate had been to Scarborough to check on Miss Wilkes' aunt. "She has lived there for some years, a quiet, respectable widow in a quiet, respectable street. She rarely goes into society, but no one has a word to say against her."

"I wonder how Mr Eustace met Miss Wilkes, if the aunt is not often in society," Luce said, looking up from the shirt of Michael's she was mending.

"One might meet anywhere at a resort by the sea," Michael said. "Walking along the shore, in the circulating library... anywhere. One does not have to be introduced at a ball or an evening party. Well, it does not seem that there is anything untoward about Miss Wilkes, apart from the estrangement from her father, which I would like to know more about, but cannot easily ask. Luce, can you—?"

Luce shook her head firmly. "The girl closes up the instant her father is mentioned. Even her brothers and sisters are unmentionable — it does seem as if the breach is a serious one."

"And there are no obvious cracks in her story," Michael said thoughtfully, "so we must accept the alibi."

"We'd have to accept it whoever she might be," Neate said. "The entire household is adamant that no one left the house that night. No horse was taken, remember, and the grooms would know the following morning if a horse had been ridden that distance."

"Now, why do you want the alibi to be broken, Michael?" Pettigrew said, gently. "Do you have suspicions against Eustace Atherton?"

"I have suspicions against everyone," Michael said crossly, "but Eustace is everywhere in this story. It is his tower where the smuggling goes on, and where Miss Peach was killed, and he found the body, remember. He heard me talking about the books needed to decode Miss Peach's notebook, so he could have stolen them. *And* he was inside the castle when Bertram Atherton was shot. He could easily have slipped out of the great hall, down to the basement, up through the cheese store and bang! Back the same way, in time to appear outside, only a little late, to offer his help."

"But Mr Kent Atherton was even later to turn up, and with no one to vouch for him," Neate said. "He is everywhere in the story, too — the smuggling, finding evidence of Miss Peach at the tower, he was at the castle the night of Nicholson's murder and no alibi in his bed, either."

"That is all very interesting," Michael said thoughtfully. "Yet he has an alibi for the time the books were stolen. Both Eustace and Kent have alibis for some occasions and not others. We are assuming, are we not, that all three events are connected? That is, Nicholson's murder, Miss Peach's murder and the shooting of Bertram Atherton."

"It would be incredible if they were not," Pettigrew said.

"Quite so. Three separate events, then, but deriving from the same cause, and two men with only partial alibis. Suppose they were working together? The smuggling… they must *both* have been involved in the smuggling. We know that Kent Atherton was… no, he *is* a part of the operation. Eustace must have known about it, at the very least, since the tower was his. So either he turned a blind eye or he took a share of the profits. Maybe he was more actively involved… we cannot say. But they must both be part of it. So suppose that Nicholson found out about it and threatened to betray them to the Excise men."

"More likely he wanted a cut," Neate said. "He is all about money, the sainted chaplain. Pay out a large sum or Customs and Excise will be told what is going on here."

"Blackmail! Yes, yes! Very likely! So Eustace leaves an axe hidden in the urn at the castle, and Kent slips out of his room one night and does the deed, knowing that Eustace has a solid alibi. Back to his room, clean nightshirt on in time to appear with everyone else when the screaming starts. Then he tells us he thought he saw someone running down the main stairs."

"Which no one else saw," Neate added.

"Precisely. But then, Miss Peach finds out what is going on, and Kent… or Eustace, or both, strangle her, and get the body to Tonkins Farm. It would be easier with two people, I should think, to manage that undetected. Eustace stole the books while Kent had an alibi. And then…"

"And then they shot Bertram, and for what reason precisely?" Luce asked sweetly.

"Eustace wanted to marry Bea Franklyn," Michael said at once. "He was jealous of Bertram, and decided to get rid of him. He arrived on the scene very swiftly when she noticed someone watching her in the woods, so he could have been following her about. And he proposed three times, after all."

"She also refused him three times," Luce said. "Why would she accept him at the fourth attempt, even if Bertram is out of the way?"

"I agree," Pettigrew said. "Eustace is clever, so I doubt he would take such a phenomenal risk for the slender hope of winning Miss Franklyn's hand in the end."

"Then it can only be that Bertram discovered something about the smuggling," Michael said. "Pettigrew, you are looking smug. Where are the holes in my argument?"

"Two holes," he said, with the satisfied smile of a cat seeing the mouse approaching. "Any Excise man is going to be very, very wary of approaching two sons of a belted earl, even if they are smuggling. He has to have an eye to his own career, and making a mistake of that magnitude would end it very swiftly. I doubt that would be much of a threat, to be frank. As for blackmail... Michael, you have not properly considered Nicholson's character."

"He was a devious rogue, up to no good in a multitude of ways," Michael said savagely.

"So he was, but remember when you were first here? I was still in town then, but your letters were full of *'the sainted chaplain'*. No one had a bad word to say for him. However much deviousness he was up to, it was all *secret*. Stealing the tenants' rent money — secret. Cheating the late earl at piquet, which he assuredly did — secret. Making paste copies of his wife's jewellery — secret. Collecting money for non-existent charitable works — secret. His brothel at Pickering, the profits funnelled through legitimate businesses — secret. Even his illegitimate son — secret, until the lady got drunk one night. But blackmail — that is not secret at all. It is a nasty, underhand business, and blackmailers are thoroughly disliked — hated even. It is an excellent motive for murder, but it is not a secret, not from those subjected to it. Nicholson was no blackmailer."

Michael sighed. "I do not know why I remain friends with you, Pettigrew, when you puncture my theories with such enthusiastic glee."

"Oh, not glee, my friend," Pettigrew said, grinning. "Never that. Enthusiastic, perhaps, for that is my rôle in this little band of investigators, to bring my superior intellect to bear on your wilder flights of fancy... Ow!" he cried, as Michael threw a cork at his head. "But I do it more in sorrow than pleasure."

"Of course you do. Sandy, stop laughing, will you? You all enjoy seeing me humiliated, I am sure. It must be very entertaining to listen to me build what seems like a very convincing case, only to have Pettigrew puncture it with a wave of his well-manicured hand. It is only an intellectual exercise to you, my friend, but to me — this is *personal*. I cannot rest until I have exposed this murderer once and for all."

"I know that," Pettigrew said, his face wiped of all amusement. "I know it very well, and we all feel the same. This heinous crime must be dealt with under the law, and the perpetrator brought to justice. But we have not yet got the complete picture. There is one fundamental piece missing."

"Which is?"

"If Nicholson was not murdered because of blackmail, and I am tolerably certain that is the case, then why was he murdered? Until you can answer that question with absolute assurance, you will never solve the mystery, and all this theorising avails you nothing."

Michael jumped up and paced across the room. "Very true, so we must leave no stone unturned. Every loose thread must be followed to wherever it leads. Pettigrew, I should like you to go to Northumberland to talk to Sir

Reginald Wilkes at Warriston Hall. I am sure you can find a good excuse to approach a baronet."

"What information do you want precisely?"

"Anything you can find out about Miss Rosamunde Wilkes. More specifically, what she looks like so that we might have some idea if Eustace's lady really is Miss Wilkes. Sandy, I want you to go to Scarborough, with James as your valet. You are a wealthy merchant from Edinburgh, having recently concluded some business in Newcastle and now looking for a little entertainment of the female variety. I want you to investigate all the high-class brothels in the town."

"Michael!" Luce said, scandalised, as Sandy laughed delightedly.

"He need not avail himself of their services," Michael said hastily. "I merely want to locate Mrs Mayberry and her so-called nieces."

"The light-skirts from Nicholson's Pickering house?" Pettigrew said, leaning forward interestedly. "I thought we agreed that nothing was stolen when they left Pickering so abruptly, so we would not pursue them. I also thought we did not know where they had gone."

"Yes, but it is astonishing how talkative ostlers and postilions can be when plied with beer," Michael said with a smug grin. "The ladies went to Scarborough in two hired chaises and a luggage wagon, so I think it very likely they established themselves there. A resort by the sea, with visitors coming and going all year — what more likely setting for a discreet brothel? Luce, you look disapproving, but Sandy is a grown man. He can decide for himself how closely he wishes to keep to the path of virtue."

"Oh, it is not that," she said. "Sandy has been given strong principles by his kirk in Edinburgh, so I am not afraid of him straying. It is this pursuit of Miss Wilkes. Did you not say just a few minutes ago that you accepted Mr Eustace's alibi? Yet now you seem to be suspicious of him again."

"Until I can be sure of the murderer's identity, I am suspicious of everyone," Michael said quietly.

"But Mr Eustace has been so helpful to us!" she cried. "He looked everywhere for poor Peachy, even more thoroughly than we did, and he it was who found her sad remains and allowed us to bury her decently and grieve for her. I shall never forget what he did for her, never!"

"I do not forget it, either," Michael said quietly. "But there is something else I cannot forget. In this whole investigation, of all the people we have talked to, only three people are known to have lied to us. One was the foolish Tom Shapman and his false confession, and we have dealt with him. But there was also Mrs Mayberry, who told everyone that Nicholson never went to the house at Pickering, yet we found his office there, with records of his Pickering businesses and the safe with all those gold bars. And then there was Mr Eustace, who put forward Daisy Marler as his alibi, to try to keep us away from Miss Wilkes."

"He had good, honourable reasons for that," Luce said. "He was protecting a lady's reputation."

"True, but he still *lied.* And therefore we must be absolutely sure that he is not lying to us about Miss Wilkes. That is what Pettigrew will determine, and Sandy and James will find out if there is anything untoward about Mrs Mayberry and her young ladies. And then, with luck, we can forget about them."

Luce nodded, not entirely convinced, but unwilling to push the point.

"And what will you be doing, Michael?" James Neate said.

Michael grinned. "I shall be conducting a little experiment. I should like to know just how long it takes to run to the cheese store, fire a gun and then get back into the house again. And I should also like to know how well the gunshot could be heard from all these different rooms."

"Everyone claims to have heard the shot," Pettigrew said.

"So they say, my friend. So they say. But there is no substitute for trying it myself."

12: Suitors And Brothers

Olivia found herself unusually ruffled by the thought that her father might be forming an attachment to Miss Bucknell. Now that Lady Esther had put the idea into her head, she watched the two closely and saw at once how comfortably they got along. She was only astonished that she had not seen it earlier.

Before dinner each evening, Miss Bucknell played her part as hostess, greeting guests and moving from one group to another, to help the conversation along. But she contrived to have the earl beside her for the meal, and he was the first of the gentlemen to return to the drawing room afterwards and he immediately sought her out. Then they would be together for the rest of the evening. If there was music, they listened to it side by side. If the card tables came out, they played as partners. And if there were no other entertainment on offer, they sat in quiet conversation.

One wet morning, finding him mooning about the library, Olivia ventured to say, “Is Miss Bucknell not with you today?”

His face broke into a smile — how much she had missed his smile! Poor Papa, he had had such a torrid time of it lately, far worse than the rest of the family.

“Charlie is busy below stairs just now. She has promised that we will have a game of backgammon later.”

Charlie? They were on such terms already, then?

“You like her, I think, Papa.”

The smile broadened. “I do! She is not the equal of your mother... well, how could she be? No one will ever replace my dearest Caroline, but Charlie... Miss Bucknell, I should say, is a most agreeable companion. She is sensible, thoughtful, a good manager... she plays an excellent game of whist or piquet. She does not fuss over me, or preach at me, she rides well —”

“But not too fast, I hope! We do not want you dislocating your shoulder again.”

He laughed. “No, she is more of a gentle rider, but excellent company to be with. We have taken some longer rides together, so that she can show me the countryside, and— Olivia, I know you do not want a stepmother, and nor do I want that for you, to tell the truth. If I could have my heart’s desire, I would have your mother back by my side, where she belongs. But she is not coming back, and... well, in plain terms, I am lonely. Two of my lovely daughters have gone away and left me already, and you will not be long a spinster.”

Olivia blushed and made an inarticulate noise in her throat.

“No, no, I see how they all look at you, these men. As soon as you show your face in town, you will be besieged, I know it, and then you will be gone. And as for the boys... Walter has left, Eustace seldom shows his face at

Corland and Kent is looking to his own future. And then I shall be all alone, just me and Alice rattling around in that great big place, and I shall go mad, I know it. Not that Alice is poor company… my own sister, after all, but she is very self-contained. I shall be in bad case, daughter. A man needs a wife, there is no doubt about it, and not just for sons. Of course, that would be most agreeable, and Charlie is the right age to give me a son or two. There is no certainty, of course, with a woman who has never been married, but there is no reason why not. But there are more important requirements than sons — I need someone to be a friend to me, a true friend, someone I can trust and respect, who is always at my side."

"And Miss Bucknell is that friend?"

"She might be. It is not impossible."

"Papa! You are falling in love with her!"

"No, no," he said, but he looked sheepish. "I *do* like her, it is true, but there is no need to talk about *love*. I loved… still love your mama with all my heart and soul, and no one will ever replace her in that way, but a companion to see me through the rest of my life… that would make me happy, little one."

"Then it would make me happy, too," she said.

***

Robert was cautiously optimistic that his plan was working. Between them, he and Grayling contrived to spend every evening under the same roof, and when there was no sport offered, they met during the day, too. Grayling had thrown himself with enthusiasm into the task of entertaining Olivia, and if he seemed a little too keen to play his part even when Embleton was not present, Robert could hardly quibble at that. It was all part of the game, for Olivia was too quick of mind to be fooled by a man who was attentive only when another, very specific, man was also there. She hovered around the marquess whenever the opportunity arose, but Grayling was swift to distract her.

If Robert had not known better, he would have been very jealous of Grayling's ability to charm her. He was annoyingly handsome, in the manner of a Greek god, with fine features, a head of golden hair and the well-honed form of the habitual sportsman. Charming, too, for he seemed to have Olivia in a constant ripple of amusement, when she was not blushing at his outrageous compliments or protesting at his foolishness. Fortunately for Robert's peace of mind, he knew very well that Grayling was not in the market for a wife.

For his part, he dutifully hovered around Miss Grayling. She seemed complacent at Robert's attentions, and although she too could not resist throwing a little charm in the marquess's direction, she was easily drawn away from him.

The only fly in the ointment was Effie Howland, the marquess's sister, who was determined to flirt with every gentleman who came within her orbit, which included both Grayling and Robert. This disruption to Robert's careful plans was a nuisance, to put it mildly, for she was neither subtle nor easily deterred, and more than once Robert found himself drawn away to a secluded spot before he saw what she was about and was able to scotch it.

One evening, Grayling drew Robert aside over the port.

"Sarah is nagging me to arrange a visit to Grayling Hall one day," he said. "We are between cooks at the moment, so we cannot invite anyone for dinner, but we could manage a cold collation, and the ladies might find the house interesting. Most of it is closed up just now, but it has a long and distinguished history, and there are some fine walks in the garden. It would be a change of scene for them. What do you say?"

"That sounds very agreeable. My mother and sisters would certainly welcome such an outing."

"And you, I hope," Grayling said meaningfully. "It will give you an opportunity to spend a longer period of time with Sarah... get to know her better, and so on. She is very keen to show you her home."

"That sounds most pleasant," Robert said cautiously, unwilling to allow Grayling to suspect that his interest in Miss Grayling was no more than mere courtesy.

But the very next day, these modest plans went awry. Robert spent some time over breakfast carefully explaining the delights in store to his mother and sisters.

"That is all very well, Kiltarlity, but the builders are playing havoc with Strathinver, and we must be there to supervise."

"Builders? I thought it was nothing but a little light redecoration — to freshen the place up, you said, Mama."

"Oh, one or two small improvements," she said with an airy wave of one hand, the ornate rings looking too heavy for her frail fingers. "One might as well get everything done at once. It would be false economy to call the men back later. You did give me a free hand, Kiltarlity."

"Well, yes, but... never mind. You must do as you wish, of course. But we cannot leave now. It would be unconscionably rude."

"How so? We have been here for two weeks already, and there is nothing here to amuse us."

Robert had found a great deal to amuse him, and he had thought his sisters well entertained, too, and said so.

"Pft. That is because you are as besotted as the rest with the Grayling girl. Your sisters do not show to advantage beside such youthful beauty."

"Any woman of sense would appear to advantage beside a girl with more hair than wit," he said acidly. "She has no conversation or ideas of her own."

"Then why do you hang about her, if she is so devoid of ideas?"

A hard question to answer honestly, so he made no attempt to do so.

"There you are, you see?" his mother said triumphantly. "We shall leave tomorrow."

"You must go if it pleases you, Mama, but I have commitments to keep me here, and Lizzie and Lucy may stay with me, if they wish."

"Certainly not!" his mother said with hauteur. "The daughters of an earl stay on as guests in a house with no suitable chaperon in residence? I think not, and no, Kiltarlity, you are *not* a suitable chaperon. If Mr Marsden's wife were here… but she is not. Stay on here for your own pleasure if you must, for I am sure we will struggle through the journey somehow without your escort, but the girls go where I go. That is the proper way of doing things."

So saying, she rose and swept out of the room.

Robert looked ruefully at his sisters. "I am sorry your enjoyment will be cut short."

"It is no matter," Lizzie said. "Mama is right. With two incomparable beauties in the immediate neighbourhood, not to mention Lady Euphemia and her fifty thousand pounds—"

"Fifty!"

"Yes, an uncle took a fancy to her and promptly died. I wish I had a rich, sickly uncle to leave me such a sum. But you must admit, Robert, no one is going to look at two old maids like us when there are such treasures to be had."

"Not that there is anyone one would want," Lucy said.

"Except the marquess!" Lizzie said, laughing. "But we spoilt our chances there. Rushed our fences and no mistake."

"It is not every day one encounters a future duke who is not hideous in some way or other. We could never get near him in London, but when we suddenly found ourselves under the same roof as him—"

"It went to our heads, rather," Lizzie said. "So that possibility is gone, Lord Grayling is far too astute to be drawn into matrimony, and there is no one else here except younger sons — dilatory clergymen and unambitious army officers and ne'er-do-wells, the lot of them."

Lucy nodded. "Not a one has the wherewithal to marry."

"Well... not in a style we would enjoy," Lizzie added, chuckling. "We must just resign ourselves to eternal spinsterhood, sister."

Robert shook his head at them. "Nonsense! Everything has been a bit topsy-turvy the last two or three years, but I promise you, I mean to open up the London house for the season — even the ballroom! So few houses in town can boast of one, so we might as well make use of it. I shall throw a ball or two for you, and you will be sure to find someone to your liking."

"Yes, but will we find anyone who likes us?" Lucy said with a sigh.

He sipped his coffee thoughtfully, wondering how much he ought to probe. But these were his own dear sisters, and he wanted above all to see them comfortably settled. This talk of eternal spinsterhood and desperate grasping at every eligible man who came into view was not helpful. And they were alone, so perhaps they would speak freely.

"You have both of you managed before to find men who liked you... who liked you very well. Lizzie, you would have been the wife of a fine naval officer — a captain! — if Father had not caught up with you on the road north and dragged you back to town. Why did you not wait until we next went to Strathinver? Being in Scotland already makes for a far more convenient elopement, I should have thought."

Lizzie reddened, but she answered composedly, "That was foolish of us, to try to elope from town, but Mark was due to be ordered to sail in a matter of days, and we simply wanted it settled. I was to stay with his parents until he next had leave. But Papa was too clever for us."

"But why did he never return for you? He has not been at sea for all these years, I am sure."

"Papa knew people at the Admiralty," she said, with a resigned shrug of one shoulder. "He could have destroyed Mark's career, and I never wanted that. Better never to marry than to be the means of ruining a good man, Robert."

He nodded, and then turned to Lucy.

"Do not look at me like that," Lucy said. "I know I had offers... several very eligible offers, but— Oh, it was so difficult! You cannot imagine, brother, what it is like to be a woman and have to wait for a man to size you up, like... like a *racehorse*, and decide whether you are worth the wager. And then the offer is made, and how does anyone decide? Should I take this one, who is rich but sniffs constantly, or hold out for the one who is heir to a title but so, so ugly? Why is it that the handsome, charming ones are all fortune hunters and rakes? And if I turn this one down, will that one come up to scratch or leave me dangling? And all the while, the lovely, shy, *perfect* one is nowhere to be seen. It is all too difficult!"

"Was there one who was perfect?" he said gently.

"There was. His name was Archie... Archibald Whitwell, the heir to a barony. He was there in the background for two whole seasons, Robert

— two years! And he was just the sort of man I should love to marry, not arrogant or bumptious or rakish or a gambler, but sweetly solicitous. But we quarrelled over the most trivial thing — I asked him to fetch me a lobster patty at a ball supper and he brought me a strawberry tart instead, and then he claimed it was because I had asked him for it and I had not, Robert, I swear it! I asked him for a lobster patty, I know I did. But we fell out over it and he left the ball and never came back. I never saw him again, and no one else would ever suit me so well. So you see, it does not matter whether I marry or not, for my life is ruined, quite ruined."

She sobbed piteously, and even the combined handkerchiefs of the three of them were not enough to mop up the tears. The two sisters left, Lizzie with her arm round Lucy, for the solace of their room and the dispiriting prospect of packing for the journey north.

***

Olivia was excited at the prospect of a day at Grayling Hall. Unlike most of the hunting boxes of Leicestershire, which were small and cramped, with stables considerably bigger than the house, Grayling Hall was a venerable old manor house dating back to Tudor times. Having only glimpsed it in the distance, she was keen to have a closer look and explore the many highly decorated chambers of which Lord Grayling boasted.

Effie was excited, too.

"Is it not thrilling?" she gushed, as they readied themselves for bed the evening before the proposed outing. "Grayling Hall is not a piffling little place that takes two minutes to walk around. There are all manner of odd corners and forgotten wings — oh, we shall have so much fun!"

"What sort of fun?" Olivia said cautiously, for she was learning to be wary of Effie.

"Oh... you know what I mean... fun with *men!*"

"You mean flirting?"

Effie laughed uproariously. "That is just how one sorts out the men one wants to play with — the soup, if you will, before the meat appears. I have decided who *I* would most like to play with, but he has been following you around like a little puppy dog, so if you want him for yourself, I shall work on Kiltarlity instead."

"Oh! You mean Lord Grayling? You may have him with my blessing."

Effie gasped. "You do not like him? But he is an angel come to earth... in appearance, anyway. I very much hope he is less than angelic in other ways."

"I do not dislike him," Olivia said cautiously, "but Lady Esther told me he is not looking for a wife."

She laughed again, a noisy laugh, not at all delicate. "I should hope not! But there again... that might be an interesting challenge. So you will play with Kiltarlity, will you? You will have to get him away from the Grayling girl first."

"Pft! He is even more of a flirt than Lord Grayling. The only sensible man by some margin is your brother."

Effie pulled a face. "Oh, you will catch cold with Embleton, my dear. Not a man for fun and games — far too serious."

"I do not want to play games with him," Olivia said with dignity. "I should like to get to know him better, that is all."

"I wish you joy of *that*," Effie said. "We all thought that Embleton would never marry. Well, he said so himself. But then... I do not know quite what spell this Bea Franklyn cast on him, but he offered and was rejected, and it seems to have hardened his resolve. He even told Harold — the next in line, you know — to prepare his son for the dukedom."

"Oh!" That was a blow. Had the marquess been so in love with Bea Franklyn that he could not contemplate marriage to anyone else? "I did not know that his heart was broken. Poor man! How he must have felt it!"

Effie chuckled. "Broken-hearted? Not him! He has a heart of stone. Not that he is not a good brother, if a little too restrictive for my liking," she added, with another chuckle, "but he has never been in love."

"But then—?" Olivia stopped.

Effie cried, "Bea Franklyn? If you had read his letter to Papa relating the whole, you would not be so sentimental as to imagine his heart was involved. I never met a less romantic man. My dear Olivia, you have no idea how much more human Embleton would be with a desperate love affair in his past, for I have to tell you, it is very wearing to have a brother who is perfection itself."

"Is he perfection?" Olivia said, fascinated by this glimpse of family feelings.

"Not in his speech, of course, but he cannot help that, and Papa has always said it is character that matters, not glib words, and Embleton has character by the wagon load. Such a gentleman, always. It is so annoying when one wants to do something, quite an innocuous thing, one would think, and Embleton sits one down and lists half a dozen perfectly sensible reasons why it is not to be thought of. And he is always right, that is the worst of it."

"That would be wearing indeed, to have a brother who is always right," Olivia said. "Are all your brothers like that?"

The two ended the day in a harmonious discussion of the annoying habits of brothers, and nothing more was said about Lord Embleton's broken heart.

13: A Visit To Grayling Hall

Olivia woke full of excitement on the day of the visit to Grayling Hall. The breakfast parlour was busy, the ladies who normally whiled away the morning hours in bed being abroad early for once. Lady Esther was deep in conversation with Miss Bucknell when Olivia arrived, but after a while she moved around the table to an empty chair beside Olivia.

"Excellent news!" she said in an undertone. "Lord Grayling has been making enquiries about you."

"About me?" Olivia said, startled. "What sort of enquiries?"

"Dowry," Lady Esther said meaningfully. "Now we have three strings to your bow."

Olivia could not see this as good news at all. Having Osborn as a potential suitor was bad enough, but at least he was amusing. Lord Grayling was nothing but an oily flirt. He looked well enough, that much she had to admit, but she could not trust a man who flattered her so outrageously.

The Franklyns' commodious carriage conveyed Olivia, Effie, Lady Esther and Mr Franklyn the short distance to Grayling Hall. Lord Rennington and many of the gentlemen preferred to ride, but one carriage after another fell in behind them on the road, making a notable procession for a grey November day.

"We shall have rain later, I dare say," Mr Franklyn said, peering through the window at the skies.

Olivia cared nothing for rain, for there would be enough pleasure to be found inside the house, she sincerely hoped. Surely this would be the ideal opportunity to further her acquaintance with the marquess? A whole day under the same roof, with nothing to distract him — there was bound to be time for quiet conversation, and if he was at all susceptible... but Effie said he was not, and had no intention of marrying, so perhaps she was wasting her time. How very difficult it all was.

Approaching Grayling Hall from the road brought the full glory of the house into view. Having previously only caught glimpses of the rear façade, Olivia had not imagined quite such an imposing entrance. A magnificent archway, towering over their carriage, allowed admittance to the walled courtyard, and there at the far side was the house, three wings of differing sizes arranged around an inner courtyard. The exterior was of patterned red brick, with rows of thin chimneys rising loftily above the roof, and a multitude of projections and overhangs and intriguing irregularity. Here was a house worth exploring!

Lord Grayling and his sister emerged with wide smiles to hand the ladies down from the carriage and usher them into the great hall, light and airy with its arched roof and tall latticed windows. Two massive fireplaces provided some heat, and a side table bore a steaming bowl of punch to fortify the travellers after the rigours of a journey of no more than half an hour. There were dishes of sweetmeats, too, which were far more to Olivia's taste, so she nibbled happily as she wandered about, ostensibly admiring the panelling and stone hearths, but in reality looking around for her quarry... wrong word again. He was not prey, merely an aspiration, she reminded herself.

Annoyingly, Osborn appeared first and headed straight towards her. But he was alone, which was unexpected.

"Lady Kiltarlity is not with you?" Olivia said.

"Mama is exhausted by so much jollity and has retreated with my sisters to somewhere suitably dismal to recruit her spirits."

Olivia giggled. "And where is suitably dismal?"

"Strathinver. I love Scotland dearly, Lady Olivia, but I could wish its weather were somewhat less drear. A little sunshine now and then would make all the difference."

"I have never been to Strathinver, but my memories of Lochmaben are all of sunshine and gentle breezes," Olivia said. "I cannot believe Strathinver is so different, for they are only a few miles apart."

He smiled. "Indeed, you quite mistake the matter, for there is a cloud whose sole function is to sit directly above Strathinver and render it grey and chill. The cloud even has a name — it is called *'Winter'*, and it is so assiduous in its devotion to duty that it stays in place for a full ten months of the year."

She laughed, and said, "But winter is wonderful — proper winter, that is, with snow and ice and the landscape transformed into a magical place. Scotland has proper winters, does it not?"

"Oh yes! Indeed it does, as do many other parts of the Kingdom, but I am a creature of summer, myself. I like a warm sun, and beer cool from the cellar and fresh strawberries full of juice and flavour."

Olivia gave a little moan of pleasure. "Ohhh, strawberries! Do not remind me! Winter is all root vegetables and wrinkly apples."

"And bonbons," he added, tapping Olivia's hand, still full of the sticky sweetmeats.

It was strange how Osborn always made her laugh. There was something lighthearted about him which rendered her lighthearted too. No one could be downcast when he was in the room.

But soon the rest of the guests arrived, amongst them the marquess, and Olivia's attention was no longer on Osborn. Before she could make a move in Lord Embleton's direction, however, Lord Grayling was before her, offering his arm for the tour of the house, and she could hardly refuse such a flattering invitation from her host. Osborn was scooped up by Effie, and it was Miss Grayling, an expression of pure triumph on her face, who accompanied Lord Embleton.

Olivia was not so caught up in her own affairs to miss that her father had a smiling Miss Bucknell on his arm. And he was smiling, too, as he had not done since Mama had left. This was truly going to happen, it seemed. There would be a new Lady Rennington, and Olivia would have a stepmother. She resolved to get to know Miss Bucknell better over the remainder of their stay, since not only would she be an important part of Corland life in future, but she would be responsible for bringing Olivia out next spring. Instead of Mama, as she had always expected, it would be Miss Bucknell taking her to Almack's and presenting her at Court. No — of course, there would be no Almack's or Court, not for an illegitimate daughter, but still, she would be moving in society, and Miss Bucknell would be her guide. The thought was unsettling, as if the world had tilted out of alignment somehow, yet she supposed she would grow accustomed, in time.

From the great hall, Lord Grayling, with Olivia on his arm, led the procession from chamber to chamber, explaining the history of the house, which was a hodgepodge of different styles, erected at different times and in some cases, in different centuries. Nothing, however, was less than two hundred years old.

Many of the rooms were shrouded in holland covers, although the shutters had been opened to allow the proportions and decoration to be admired. After several parlours, no two the same size or shape, there was a beautiful chapel, and then another whole wing of comfortably appointed family rooms. Upstairs were bedrooms large and small, and a splendid long gallery with a wooden arched ceiling. Here a billiard table had been set up, which several of the gentlemen fell upon with excited cries.

"Do you want to see the *garderobes?*" Lord Grayling whispered in Olivia's ear.

"Oh! I have heard of such things, but never seen one."

"This way."

"Should we wait for the rest of the party?" she said.

"It is a very small space, with little room. I can show them to the others later, in small groups," he said smoothly.

"Let me just ask Lady Esther if I may."

"Dear me! Do you need permission for every little thing? What a very dutiful girl you must be."

If there was one thing Olivia disliked above others, it was to be thought overly dutiful. One must be mindful of one's parents and one's chaperon, naturally, but only the most pudding-hearted girl would be constantly asking if this or that were acceptable. She was as good as out, after all, and a guest in Lord Grayling's house, so what could possibly be wrong with stepping aside for a moment? What could happen in a *garderobe*, anyway?

So she lifted her chin, told him forthrightly that she was not so dutiful as all that, and allowed him to lead her down a previously unsuspected stair. The *garderobes* were indeed very small rooms, and exactly as Olivia had supposed they might be. Not as comfortable, perhaps, as a close stool, but preferable to an outside privy. Lord Grayling explained that there had been intended to be a moat to wash away the waste, but the distance from the nearest river had made the scheme impractical. Now the waste went into a pit which was emptied periodically to be mixed with stable straw and spread on the vegetable beds.

"We have the best rhubarb in the county," he said with a little smile.

Olivia's trust was rewarded, for Lord Grayling made no attempt to step beyond the bounds of propriety. The voices of others in the party, still wandering about, reassured her that a chaperon could be summoned in moments if she were concerned.

From the *garderobes*, therefore, she allowed him to lead her to another room set in a corner position, with charming views over a rather neglected garden and a small lake.

"This was my mother's sitting room," he said, his tone more serious than she had heard from him before. "She loved to sit here in the afternoon, with the light streaming in, stitching her tapestry. This was the piece she was working on when she died."

He indicated a frame with a half-completed piece still held fast, an arrangement of flowers and birds of an elegant design, although the colours had faded somewhat. The room was just as elegant, the wood panels painted a delicate shade of yellow, and the furnishings light and dainty. It was a very feminine room, but although it was perfectly clean, the wood polished and the windows sparkling, and there were no holland covers, yet it seemed neglected. The lady who had delighted in it had gone, and no later occupant had enjoyed its charms.

"Your sister does not use this room?" Olivia said.

"It reminds her too much of her mama, and makes her sad. It makes *me* sad, too, but one day, I hope to see another lady occupy that sofa and ply her needle, just as she did."

He said no more, leading her on to another, more masculine room — the library, where Olivia was relieved to see the earl and Miss Bucknell examining a pair of globes in a corner. Lord Grayling at once lost the serious tone, and became his light, flirtatious self, showing her some books of engravings of the leading political figures of an earlier age, and explaining the sly allusions to the foibles of each.

Olivia listened with only half an ear, pondering his behaviour. He had deliberately led her aside, and the *garderobes* were merely an excuse, for it was his mother's sitting room he wished her to see. That, combined with his enquiry as to her dowry, was a very clear signal of intent.

If he were looking to marry, he need not waste his time on Olivia, for she was not in the least tempted. She was not sure he was a man to be trusted. But how to deter him? It was a puzzle, until he took her into another room, where a narrow stair was roped off.

"Why is the stair not used?" she said.

"It is not safe. There are some loose slabs — dangerously loose."

"Why do you not have them mended?"

He laughed. "A direct question, indeed! Because I cannot afford to, that is why. This place takes a monstrous amount of money to keep it from falling down, and I have had one or two reverses of fortune lately in my investments. So it will have to wait."

Olivia smiled inwardly. There was the opening she needed!

"You will just have to marry an heiress, Lord Grayling."

He smiled his oily smile. "I have to find her first, Lady Olivia."

"You need look no further than the Lady Euphemia Howland. I imagine fifty thousand pounds would repair any number of staircases."

"I imagine it would," he said blandly, but he seemed rather thoughtful after that.

***

Michael spent two days experimenting with the gun. With the enthusiastic help of Lucas Atherton, who was more than willing to investigate the means by which his brother had been shot, the gun was fired repeatedly from the spot above the cheese store, while Michael stood in different parts of the castle listening for the sound. Then he ran back and forth by way of different staircases, to work out how long it had taken the gunman to reach his spot and retreat again.

And none of it told him anything he did not already know, or explained those parts of the mystery that were still obscure. It was infuriating.

He was standing on the bridge to Corland's entrance, leaning on the parapet and looking down into the void when Luce emerged from the castle.

"Michael? You will be late for dinner if you stay out here any longer." She stood beside him and gazed into the void. "What are you looking at?"

He turned to her with a grin. "What do you see down there?"

"Nothing, Michael. It is dark, there are no lights and I can see nothing."

"Precisely." He grinned even more.

"Oh, you are minded to be enigmatic? Very well, but might you be enigmatic inside, do you think? It is chilly out here." She pulled her shawl more closely around her.

He laughed and they went inside, and up to their room to dress for dinner.

"What is your theory?" he said, as his head emerged from the neck of a clean shirt. "Who do you think killed Nicholson?"

"An irate husband," she said at once. "Mr Nicholson was not faithful to his wife, and I do not believe that the Whyte girl was the only one he seduced."

"Someone from the village or one of the farms? How did he know the castle well enough to find Nicholson's room?"

"Michael, every family for twenty miles in each direction has a son or daughter working at the castle. The inhabitants are talked about constantly. Everything about the place is known."

"Including the garden door having a broken bolt, and most likely being unlocked? Including the platform inside the urn so the axe did not drop all the way to the bottom? Including the hatch above the cheese store, so handy for shooting at people?"

She looked up from the stockings she was unrolling. "That assumes the same person killed Nicholson and shot at Bertram Atherton."

"You think it was someone different?"

"I cannot see the connection. I think the shooting was a prank—"

"A prank!"

"A friend making a silly point — better dead than married. You know what young men are like. No doubt the shot was intended to miss, but it ended up nearly killing him. No friend would admit to that."

"And Miss Peach?"

"Someone saw her walking and offered her a lift, then tried to rob her. When she resisted, he strangled her."

"And left her purse untouched?"

"I dare say he panicked. Besides, ladies so commonly carry reticules these days that he may have forgotten to check for old-fashioned pockets. I can see you are not convinced."

"I understand why you would like it to be this way," he said slowly. "Strangers... outsiders... so much better than a member of the earl's own family. And yet... this feels personal, somehow."

"Must it be a member of the family?" she said forlornly.

"There are so many points that only the family could know... or someone long associated with the castle, perhaps. A servant of many years' standing... it could be, I suppose. But someone intimately familiar with the place, yes."

"Then it must be Kent Atherton," she said sadly.

"Who was in Branton when Miss Peach's lodging room was broken into and her books stolen, on the chance that one of them would be the key to decoding her notebook."

"So he says."

Michael jumped up. "Yes! We only have his word for it that he was in Branton all that time. We only have his word that he saw someone running down the stairs after the murder. But wait — how did he know to steal the books at all? He was not at the dinner where the notebook was mentioned."

"What precisely was said that night?" Luce said. "It was after the ladies had withdrawn, so only the gentlemen were present, but were any of the servants there?"

"The butler was still setting out the port glasses, I think. The under-butler may have been there, too."

"I am not sure it was wise to mention it at all," Luce said, standing up and sliding her feet into her evening slippers. "You are normally so secretive."

"I wanted to watch their faces," Michael said. "First, I told them only that we had found Miss Peach's notebook, and then paused. Then, I mentioned that it was in code, with another pause. And finally, that I had no doubt that we would be able to decode it easily."

"If the murderer had been present, he should have looked worried, then relieved, then worried again. And did anyone?"

"No. It was very disappointing. But there was no mention of books or the means of decoding. And I have just realised... oh, I am a fool, sometimes!"

Luce pulled him to his feet, and began buttoning up his waistcoat. "You are anything but a fool, but this is an extraordinarily convoluted crime. What have you just realised?"

"That whoever took the books is not necessarily the murderer. He may merely be concerned to keep us from finding the identity of the murderer."

"Protecting someone?"

Michael nodded.

"A friend... or a brother?"

"Which leads us neatly back to Kent Atherton. If Eustace, say, thought Kent was the murderer, but knew he was away in Branton and not able to prevent us from decoding the notebook, he may well have intervened himself. Well!" He sighed, and shrugged himself into his coat. "I must think about this. But there is one thing I must do, that I should have done long since."

"What is that?" she said, smiling affectionately at him.

"I must find the saddle from the mule that Miss Peach borrowed. Mrs Markley has her mule back, but we never found the saddle, so I shall go and look for it tomorrow."

Luce laughed. "Sometimes, Michael, your mind works in the oddest ways. It is the other saddle you should be looking for."

"Which one is that?" he said, smiling at her.

"The one that Peachy wrote about, of course. You cannot have forgotten the very last entry in her notebook - *'I am almost certain of the murderer's identity now. I only need to find the saddle, and then I shall have the proof.'*"

Michael laughed, pulling her into his arms and kissing her on the nose. "I have not forgotten, but one saddle at a time, wife. One saddle at a time."

***

Michael left early, his wife still abed and the household only just winding itself up for the day. Autumn was a fine time to be abroad, he had always felt. There was nothing like cantering beneath the russet and gold canopy of well-grown woodland, or alongside a placid stream, catching a flash of brilliant colour from a kingfisher or sending a stately heron aloft in a whirr of massive wings. In all the years he had been in India, it was the softness of autumn that had most filled his memories of England.

But the moors of the North Riding were not in the least soft. The wind was bitter, with a hint of ice in it, and even the small pools that dotted the moor were ruffled and angry today. He was glad to reach his destination, the tower near to Eustace's estate of Welwood, where the smuggling operation was carried on. He turned his horse into the field beside the tower, alongside the sturdy pack ponies and a few donkeys grazing there. The key to the tower was still tucked under its stone beside the door, so he quickly let himself in. It was chilly inside, but at least there was no wind.

He was tolerably sure that the saddle was not hidden anywhere inside the tower, but he searched it thoroughly all the same. The cellar was less full of smuggled barrels now, just a couple with French markings remaining. Several empty barrels stood awaiting filling, and there was a half-full barrel of ale to refresh the workers. But no saddle.

He passed quickly through the storerooms on the ground floor, noting the thin film of grime that now coated every surface. Last time he had been there, everything was spotless, but no doubt that was Miss Peach's efforts. With housewifely energy, she must have filled the long empty hours of her tenure at the tower by sweeping and cleaning. Poor Peachy! The place looked neglected now that she had gone.

Up the winding stairs, he checked every room and even ventured onto the balcony and up the narrow stair to the viewing platform on the roof, but, as he expected, there was no sign of a saddle or anything untoward. For some time he stood in the uppermost room, gazing down at Welwood-on-the-Hill slumbering gently under wintry skies, smoke rising only from one or two chimneys. Eustace was away from home again, then. He was always away from home.

Kent's pride and joy, the telescope, was still facing the house, but it revealed nothing except a maid optimistically draping sheets over bushes to dry them. No one else seemed to be about, not even the grooms at the stable yard.

Michael could not put off the moment when he was obliged to venture outside again. Pulling his greatcoat more closely around him, he locked the door and replaced the key under its stone. Then he stood irresolute. Where would Miss Peach hide a saddle? There were no buildings nearby, and she would hardly have taken it down to Welwood. It must be somewhere near at hand, but where? There was a large patch of woodland running alongside the ponies' field, but that would take some thorough searching. More likely that it was tucked under the hedge surrounding the field.

He began enthusiastically, swishing aside brambles and overgrown detritus from summer with his sword, but his spirits soon flagged. Would Peachy really have left a valuable saddle under a hedge, where it would be exposed to weather and the attentions of rodents? Yet where else?

After covering a hundred yards or so in each direction and finding nothing, he set out with grim determination to survey the entire perimeter of the field. The far side of it brought him to an ivy-covered wall with a gate set into it, where an elderly gelding gazed mournfully across the Helmsley road to the entrance of Welwood, as if awaiting a friend with an apple or piece of sugar. Michael had nothing of the sort to offer, but he stroked the creature's nose and gave him a few words of encouragement.

Looking around beyond the gate, in the furthermost corner of the field he saw a small copse, overgrown with brambles and fallen branches, but a narrow path led into it from the gate. All Michael's senses tweaked into alertness. A gate and a path meant something hidden within the patch of woodland. Eagerly he followed the path into the wilderness, the enfolding greenery hiding him very effectively from the world beyond.

Twenty paces in, he had his answer — a low shed, rather dilapidated and entirely invisible from beyond the trees. It was not locked, the door creaking open at a push. Inside was hay, piled almost to the roof at one side but scattered in heaps elsewhere. It took him no more than five minutes of prodding and poking and kicking aside clumps of hay to find what he was looking for — a mule's saddle, with the letter 'M' neatly stitched into the leather. The saddle for Mrs Markley's mule.

Michael smiled.

14: The Secret Room

Lord Grayling went off to find out if the cold collation he had ordered was ready, leaving Olivia sitting quietly at one end of the long gallery. At the other end, the punch-fuelled billiard players were becoming rowdy, but she hardly noticed, for there was a far more interesting sight nearby.

Lord Embleton was examining the paintings on the gallery walls, a guide book in his hand, with a gushing Miss Grayling in tow. She chattered away unstoppably while he made the occasional abstracted remark and otherwise ignored her. It was most entertaining to watch and when, after some minutes, Osborn and Effie appeared, Olivia waved them over to the bench where she sat, and indicated the object of her attention with the slightest tilt of her head.

Osborn chuckled. "I am enjoying this visit tremendously," he said affably, folding his arms and stretching out his legs, neatly crossed at the ankles. "What a fascinating house this is, with interesting sights in every room."

Effie laughed, too. "Shall I rescue him, do you think? He does not seem amused."

Without waiting for an answer, she strode across the gallery to where her brother continued to ignore his persistent admirer. "Miss Grayling, did I hear your brother mention a secret room? If there is one thing I adore in a house, it is secret places. Do, pray, show me where it is."

Startled, Miss Grayling turned to her uncertainly. "The secret room? Oh, yes… but perhaps you would care to see it, Lord Embleton?"

"Th-thank you, but I p-p-prefer to examine the p-p-paintings."

"Oh. Very well. This way, Lady Euphemia." She then spotted Osborn and Olivia watching interestedly. "Would you like to come, too?"

"No, thank you," they said in unison.

The two ladies went down the stairs to find the secret room, and Lord Embleton wandered further up the gallery, but Osborn and Olivia stayed where they were. For a while they were silent, watching Lord Embleton's slow progress down the gallery, as Olivia pondered Effie's revelation that he had no intention of marrying. Yet she thought he had not been in love with Bea Franklyn, and his sister ought to know the truth. So why had he offered for her? It was a puzzle.

She rather liked the idea that his heart had been broken by that thoughtless minx. It made him more interesting, and aroused all her sympathy. *She* would not break his heart. To take a poor, lonely, unhappy man and make him happy — that would be something! Nor did she mind the stutter, now that she had grown accustomed to it. He was a good, honourable man who did not deserve to be rendered miserable. She would love to help him forget Bea Franklyn, and his rank had nothing to do with it.

After a while, Osborn unfolded his arms and leaned forward, elbows on knees. "Are you not going to follow him? There he is, your quarry, all unattended. An opportunity for you."

"Do not call him that!" she said, quite unjustly for had she not thought of the marquess in just such terms, as prey? "But it is hopeless. He has no intention of marrying. He has told his younger brother to prepare his son to inherit, in time."

Osborn looked startled. "Has he so? That does seem very final. I am sorry for it, if so, for every man needs a wife eventually."

"Does he?"

"I believe so, yes, especially a man of high estate. A wheelwright, perhaps, can rub along well enough as a single man, but the more responsibilities a man has, the more he needs a true companion by his side, to be his adviser, his helpmeet and comforter through the trials and adversities of life."

"And to share the joys of life, too," she said.

He smiled at her. "That, too. It is no different for a woman, is it? She needs a husband just as much as he needs a wife."

"But for different reasons. A woman has no independent life, so she needs a man to support her financially. Whereas all a man needs is food put before him two or three times a day, and enough coals to keep him warm. He needs a housekeeper more than a wife."

"Ah, Olivia," he said gently, taking her hand in his. "Is that why you harbour hopes of the marquess? You see marriage as a practical arrangement, so you may as well have as much wealth and rank as you can manage, is that it? But marriage is so much more than that... or it can be. My sister Anthea... she and John were so happy, so absorbed in each other. Nothing touched them, for they existed in a protective bubble of joy. Even when the first baby died, they recovered from their grief because they were together. Even now, John is content because he had those three years of perfect happiness."

"What happened to her?"

"The second child... she died. They both died." He fell silent, his expressive face unusually serious.

Olivia squeezed his hand. "And your brothers died, too. But you are here, and that must be the greatest comfort to your mama and your sisters. There is some value in being a foolish rattle, you see, for at least your nonsense makes everyone smile."

He gave a little laugh. "Ah, you see? That is how it works — when I am sad, you manage to cheer me up."

"By insulting you?" she said, although she could not help smiling back at him. He was a hard man to dislike!

"By teasing me," he said, leaning back and folding his arms again. "You have no idea how refreshing that is. Everyone in my family seems to be so serious all the time. When I was merely the little-regarded youngest son, they ignored me, but now that I am an earl— Livvy, you cannot imagine how much I hate being an earl. My family, my stewards, my lawyers, my bankers, even my fellow peers talk to me of duty and responsibility and obligation, and I understand that, truly I do. I accept my fate, however unworthy I am for the great honour that has come to me. But deep inside me, buried but not forgotten, is the free-spirited young man I once was, who set out to make the world laugh. It gets harder and harder to remember him, but *you* bring him to life again, my pretty ghost. You make me young and lighthearted again."

"That is because I remind you of Izzy," she said crisply, rising to her feet and smoothing her skirts. "In your mind, you are back in those days when you courted Izzy and had nothing else to think about but pleasure and amusement. But I am *not* Izzy, my lord, and you are not Robert Osborn any longer."

He jumped to his feet too. "No, no, no! Give me no *'my lords'*, Livvy, I beg you. Ah, I should not have said so much, for now that delightful dimple is hidden away and who knows how much nonsense I shall have to shower on your head to reveal it again. Do not hide your dimple from me, sweet apparition."

What was it about this man that charmed her so much? After such a speech, she could not help smiling again, whereupon he cried out in delight.

"Ah, there it is!" He caught up her hand again and dropped a kiss on it. "You see? You are so good for me, my lovely Livvy. If ever you decide to abandon your main project, you could do worse than marry me, you know. We would deal extremely well together, you and I."

"Oh, tush! What nonsense you talk," she said, but she felt herself blushing all the same. "I wish you would not flirt with me. It is not kind."

"Whatever makes you think I am flirting?" he said, looking surprised.

She had no opportunity to reply, for Lord Grayling reappeared just then to invite everyone to the dining room for a cold collation. It was only later that she remembered that Osborn had used her Christian name. Olivia. Livvy, even, which no one had ever called her. And if he was not flirting, had he just proposed to her? How strange! He was an odd sort of man, but so easy to get along with.

Not like the marquess. However was she ever to get to know him better? And was there any point?

***

Robert watched Livvy walk away down the gallery with Grayling, scooping up the marquess and the noisy billiard players on the way. As they disappeared down the stairs, he stood, hands on hips, rather shocked. What had just happened? Had he proposed to Livvy? And how did she become Livvy, all of a sudden? What had happened to '*Lady Olivia*'?

It was madness, complete madness, and yet...

What a wife she would be! So lovely and funny and quick-witted — he never had to explain his jokes to her, and she had given him some excellent advice on managing his estates. Imagine the delight of a wife with whom one might discuss crop rotation or woodland management, who would listen and then offer sensible suggestions. A wife who would always be on his side, who could put his mother in her place and order life around his wishes and not his father's. All that, and an enchanting dimple, too — it would be paradise.

And yet... there was still the niggle of concern at the back of his mind that she was right, and he was reliving his courtship of Izzy all over again, and that would hardly be fair to Livvy... Lady Olivia.

In the dining room, Robert took a glass of wine, and retreated to a window seat. He had no desire for food. The only interest for him in the room was sitting composedly at the far end of the table, eating something creamy with a spoon. Beside her, the marquess sat, his face solemn, listening as she talked to him between mouthfuls. There was no dimple, he noticed sadly. Indeed, she looked as serious as the marquess.

Where was Grayling, who was supposed to be keeping her away from Embleton? He was at the other end of the table beside Lady Euphemia, their two heads bent together in intimate conversation. What was that all about? Still, better that he should turn his flirtatiousness in that direction.

He did not want Grayling working his way into Olivia's heart, which by rights should belong to Robert.

And yet...

His eye was drawn inexorably back to Olivia and Embleton. She had laid down her spoon, and was talking rapidly, her hands gesturing in the air the whole time, her face lit up with enthusiasm, and Embleton... was he smiling? He was! It made Robert want to smile, too, just watching her, yet there was an unaccustomed ache in his heart. She should be directing all that liveliness on him, not on a man as serious as Embleton, a man who had no intention of marrying. He had even told his younger brother so. Poor Livvy! She was wasting her time... yet the marquess was engrossed in what she was saying.

Perhaps... perhaps she was not wasting her time, after all.

What was it she had said to him? Something like, *'Who do you most want to be happy?'* They had been talking about estate business, and she had made him see everything differently. It had given him the confidence to stop being paralysed with fear and actually make decisions, as he was expected to do.

But surely the same principle applied to his pursuit of Livvy, too. He wanted her himself, he could admit that now, for would she not make him the happiest man alive? But could he make her happy? Was it right to interfere between herself and Embleton, if he was what she truly wanted? That was the foolishness that had caught him in its web with Izzy. Four of them had pursued her, four besotted men swept up in the competition, each determined to be the one to win her. Yet now, looking back on it, he could see that Izzy would not have suited him at all.

Olivia, on the other hand, had all Izzy's good qualities — the beautiful face, the liveliness in company, the wit and love of excitement, yet without

Izzy's instability. Livvy was adorable, and would fit so perfectly into his arms, he was certain. But it was wrong, quite wrong to prevent her from making her own choice. She would make a wonderful duchess, and if Embleton was the man she wanted and he could be brought to value her as any rational man would, why then he should have her, and Robert would rejoice to see her happy. He wanted her to be happy, more than anything in the world.

Now, why did that prospect hurt so much?

***

Olivia was thrilled. Finally, some progress with Lord Embleton. Purely by chance, for she had done nothing to bring it about, they had sat together in the dining room and she had talked and he had listened, and seemed... interested. Was it mere politeness? Hard to say, but they had talked about families, and that had seemed to engender a greater degree of intimacy between them.

The guests began to drift away from the table, including the marquess. There was to be a discussion of rare books in the library, followed by an hour in the music room for the ladies to try out the various instruments. Olivia still had one or two delicacies to sample so she lingered in the dining room. Mr Franklyn, watching her in amusement, helpfully fetched her this or that sweet treat.

"You are not drawn by the pleasures of the library, sir?" she said mischievously.

"Ha! I like a library as well as the next man, especially with a blazing fire, a glass of something and no one expecting me to talk to them... or with Bertram pouring Latin into Bea's ears. That was entertainment, to see my lively daughter sitting still for a full hour, and speaking the ancient language as if she had been doing so all her life. My Bea, an intellectual — who would ever have suspected?" He sighed. "At least she will not be far away when she returns from her wedding tour, so I shall be able to haunt her library instead of my own. But rare books? No, that does not appeal. Nor to you either, by the look of it."

"Not when there is syllabub to be eaten," Olivia said, making him laugh.

Lady Esther returned at that moment, an unaccustomed expression of anxiety on her usually serene countenance. "Olivia, dear, have you seen Lady Euphemia at all? She went away with Lord Grayling, and although I was not far behind, I have lost track of them and... well, she is a lively girl and he has a certain reputation..."

Olivia laid down her spoon. "I have not seen either of them since they left this room. Have they not gone to the library?"

"I tried there, but no, there is no sign of them. What are we to do? I am supposed to be her chaperon."

"With three of us, we can search a wing each," Mr Franklyn said, rising to his feet. "Olivia, will you take the great hall wing? My dear, you search this wing, and I will take the gallery wing."

"They might have gone into the garden," Olivia said.

"Unlikely," Mr Franklyn said, pointing to the window, where raindrops chased each other from pane to pane. "Let us meet back here in... shall we say half an hour? One of us will have tracked them down by then. If not, we must notify Lord Embleton that his sister is missing."

Olivia set off at once, but her search was soon accomplished. At the further end of the great hall sat the kitchen wing, and that seemed an unlikely destination. The great hall itself took up the bulk of the remainder, with only a couple of bedchambers to be examined. But she knew in her heart where they had gone — to the secret room, for what Effie described as *'fun'*, whatever she meant by that, but Lord Grayling had *'a certain reputation'*, according to Lady Esther, and that sounded ominous. A duke's daughter might be better able than most to weather the storms of society's disapprobation, and Olivia had heard of some who had risen unperturbed from the most scandalous rumours, but it was still not a sensible risk to take. Olivia herself had had the principles of maidenly behaviour drummed into her from such a young age that she went hot and cold at the very thought that Effie's reputation might be shredded at any moment.

Her fear lent wings to her feet, and she flew on from the great hall wing into the central wing, no doubt following Lady Esther from room to room, but unwilling to give up the search so soon.

Catching sight of the butler, she cried out, "The secret room — where is it?"

He smiled in a superior way. "I regret, madam, that I am not at liberty to inform the guests of its location. You must apply to his lordship for—"

"If I knew where he was, I would not need to ask you," she muttered, and ran on, her steps taking her into the gallery wing.

Here she encountered Lord Embleton emerging from the library, a book in his hand. The discussion on rare books had come to a close, it seemed.

Lord Embleton! Who better to look for his sister, and he at least had the authority to compel the butler to reveal the location of the secret room.

The opportunity was too good to miss.

"Lord Embleton!" He looked up at her in surprise. "Pray forgive me, but Lady Euphemia is lost and we are concerned for her."

His expression softened into a small smile. "Effie c-c-can l-look after herself, Lady Ol-ol-olivia."

"No, no, you do not understand! She has gone to the secret room with Lord Grayling, and I do not think she wants to admire the view from the window. You must come and help me rescue her before it is too late."

His brows snapped together. "The secret room?"

"Yes! The servants know where it is, but you must be quick. Please, you must come."

She became aware of a group emerging from the library behind the marquess, their conversation dying away as they overheard her discussion with the marquess.

The marquess must have been aware of them too, for although he drew himself to his full height and his face looked thunderous, he said only, "Lady Olivia, I make due allowance for your youthful enthusiasm, but I do not believe my sister to be in any difficulty."

"Lord Embleton," she murmured, taking his arm to draw him a little aside, out of earshot of the other guests, "indeed I believe Effie may be in trouble if we do not find her soon. The secret room is—"

He shook her off. "No. This will not do, Lady Olivia," he said, his tone clipped. "Might I suggest you make your way to the music room for the opening of the instruments?"

This will not do? What did he think she was about? Presumably he saw her concern merely as a stratagem to entice him into a compromising situation. As if she would ever do anything so low!

Taken aback, she cried, "How horrid you are! I wish I had never tried to be your friend. But this is not helping Effie. Go back to your book, for clearly you care nothing for your sister's reputation. I shall go myself."

So saying she ran off, almost blinded by the hot tears that flowed unchecked.

15: Searching

Robert had left the dining room at the same time as Embleton, rather torn, for Olivia was left behind, still eating. But after his previous conversation with her, he felt the necessity to keep away from her for a while. Let her take his casual proposal as flirtation, if she will, and perhaps a little distance would give him time to settle his own feelings and decide how to proceed. It was all very well to want her to be happy, and to allow her to pursue her hopes of Embleton, but he was not sure how that was to be accomplished. Perhaps he should simply abandon the two of them to whatever fate befell them, and retreat to Strathinver.

Following Embleton brought him to the library, where an elderly scholar was introducing the more intellectual of the guests to the rare tomes stored there. Robert sighed, and prepared to be bored. Taking a glass of wine from a footman, he retreated to a corner dark enough to permit an unobserved snooze.

It was not to be, however. Within minutes, he was joined in his corner by Miss Grayling, face alight with mischief and clearly hoping to be entertained.

"Is this not amusing?" she said, sitting down in a swirl of muslin skirts beside him, a little closer than he liked, and speaking in a low voice. "Old Williamson is such a dry old stick, so I have a little wager with Julian that no one will last the full hour with him. Julian says they are too polite to simply walk out, but I beg to differ. What do you think?"

"I think... actually, I was about to say that there is nothing at all amusing about a talk on rare books, but a wager would make it bearable, I believe. I agree with your brother that most of these gentlemen are too polite to walk out, but I would be willing to bet on the possibility of at least one in the audience snoring."

She giggled, hand over mouth. "Oh, yes! That is very likely. What will you wager on it?"

"What did your brother offer?"

"A new gown."

"Ah. I cannot buy you a gown, or any personal item. I am not sure it is proper to accept a wager from a young lady at all."

"How stuffy you are! There is one thing you could give me that no one need know about."

"And what is that?"

"A kiss!"

"Miss Grayling, I do not think—"

"Ssh. Dr Williamson is coming this way."

The scholar led his little troop of guests, among them Embleton, to a lectern nearby where an ancient volume had been opened in readiness.

There he intoned at great length on the contents, most of which appeared to be in Greek.

Robert dutifully fell silent, but his mind was not on Greek writings, but on Miss Grayling and their wager, pondering whether he was now committed to the kiss or not. He had not had a chance to agree to it, but equally he had not repudiated the idea, either. Under other circumstances, he would not have minded at all, for she was pretty and warm and appealing, and a little flirtation, even a kiss or two, would be very pleasant. But not now. Not when his lovely Olivia was also in the house. It was the oddest thing, that she had wormed her way so successfully into his mind... his *heart*... that he could not contemplate even the mildest flirtation with anyone else. Even if she found him nothing but an irritant and her ambitions still ran to a dukedom, he could not look at another woman without seeing it as a betrayal of Olivia.

Dear, sweet Olivia! Had she run out of syllabub yet? Perhaps he should go and find out...

"Listen!" Miss Grayling hissed in his ear. "Do you hear it?"

The scholar and his audience had moved away again, to the far end of the library, but not every guest had followed. Emanating from a large, comfortable chair near the fire, was Robert's doom — the unmistakable sounds of a gentleman, soothed by a substantial intake of wine, snoring gently.

"There, you see?" she cried triumphantly, and without a second's hesitation, leaned forward and planted her lips on his.

To say that Robert was unprepared would not do the moment justice. He had been kissed before, naturally, for no lively man could survive to the age of thirty without a little dabbling in the petticoat line. He had enjoyed a number of very pleasurable kisses over the years, and not regretted any of them. But he had instigated them himself, indeed in many cases he had had to work very hard to bring them about, and thus the reward was all the sweeter. This kiss was bestowed on him without the slightest effort, and at a moment when his thoughts were entirely with his lovely Olivia.

After a moment of surprise, therefore, which held him immobile, he gently disengaged himself.

She was surprised, but not embarrassed. "What is the matter?"

"I did not agree to this, and it is most improper, Miss Grayling."

Her eyebrows lifted. "You *are* stuffy!" Rising to her feet, she said loudly enough to be heard throughout the room, "Really, Lord Kiltarlity, I am surprised at you. Do you kiss all your female acquaintances?"

Leaving him open-mouthed in astonishment, and reducing the surprised Dr Williamson to silence, she flounced from the room. The sleeping gentleman grunted awake and looked around curiously before settling down and closing his eyes again.

Robert was too angry to consider his actions carefully. He raced after Miss Grayling, catching her up not far down the corridor.

"What was that all about?" he said curtly.

"You insulted me," she said calmly. "There is a price to be paid for that, Lord Kiltarlity."

He sighed. "You are a wicked girl, Miss Grayling, but I am not to be caught by stratagems such as this. Where is your brother, do you know? He was not in the library."

"Are you going to tell tales of me?"

"I am going to return you to Lord Grayling's care, for clearly you are not fit to be left alone. Why do you not have a chaperon with you, by the way?"

For the first time, she looked uncertain. "She had to leave. My former governess stayed on as a companion and friend, but..." She looked up at him with troubled eyes, seeming very young suddenly. "We could not afford her. Julian is all to pieces, and needs to marry money, and very soon. That is why—"

"That is why what? Who does he have in his sights?"

She licked her lips, hesitating.

But Robert knew. "Lady Olivia. I am right, am I not? She is his target." No wonder he had been so ready to accept Robert's request for him to watch over her!

"She has thirty thousand pounds," she said apologetically.

He muttered an oath, and tore off in the direction of the dining room, but Olivia was gone. Only the servants were there, busy tidying and clearing.

"May I help you, my lord?" the butler said.

"No... I do not think— Unless you know where Lord Grayling may be found?"

"I couldn't say, my lord. The library, perhaps?"

That was no help, for he was certainly not there. Where would he have taken her? Somewhere private, no doubt, to woo her with sweet words and kisses. The very thought of it brought him to boiling point.

He swept out of the dining room, almost knocking over Miss Grayling, who was lurking outside the door.

"What are you *doing?"* he cried, his rage overcoming all gentlemanly politeness.

"I beg your pardon, but I wanted to tell you... they might be in the secret room," she said. "Julian said something about it last night... an opportunity, he said."

"Opportunity! I will knock his opportunity down his throat when I catch up with him. Where is this secret room?"

"This way."

She led him a circuitous route through the house and up a winding stair, then into a large chamber Robert had not seen before. At the far end, a large, moth-eaten tapestry covered a section of wall.

"The door is behind the tapestry," she said. "Shall I…? Or do you prefer to…?"

Robert had no time to respond, for the tapestry rippled and two figures emerged from behind it — Lord Grayling and Lady Euphemia Howland.

That was unexpected! Robert recalled now that the two had sat whispering together in the dining room, and had left together, leaving Olivia behind. What a fool he was! Chasing all over the house after a will-o'-the-wisp, when Olivia was in no danger at all from Grayling. Clearly he had set his sights on bigger prey. What sort of dowry would the daughter of a duke command? More than Olivia's thirty thousand, he would be prepared to wager.

"Julian!" Miss Grayling called out. "There you are, but I thought—?"

"Change of plan," he said smoothly.

"But—?" Her gaze jumped to Lady Euphemia and then to Robert, before returning, frowning, to her brother.

Grayling had not slackened his pace as he approached them, Lady Euphemia smirking as she gripped one arm. As they swept past, Miss Grayling attached herself to Grayling's other arm and was towed away and out of the room, leaving Robert alone.

Curious, he crossed to the tapestry, lifted it and pushed open the door concealed behind it. The room was filled with light from windows on three sides. Alongside the door, a fire in a vast fireplace burned low, clearly lit some time ago and no longer defeating the chill air of a little-used room. On a side table stood a row of decanters and glasses, together with baskets of pastries, cakes and other sweetmeats. Two glasses and a plate with crumbs on a table near the furthest window suggested that the occupants had passed a pleasant hour in there since leaving the dining room.

Robert replenished the fire, then poured himself a glass of wine, and retreated to the corner beyond the fireplace, where some residual warmth from the fire lingered, and pondered the curious situation. He was light-headed with relief — Olivia was in no danger from Grayling! Whatever the precarious state of his finances, he was not in pursuit of her thirty thousand pounds and Embleton had no need of it.

But that was unworthy. If Livvy had set her heart on Lord Embleton, then she should have him, and they had been getting on so well in the dining room, too. He had never before seen the marquess so rapt with a woman. Normally, he had a certain set look to his face that denoted politeness but nothing more, but with Livvy his expression had softened so much, he almost looked like a different man. And if something should come of that...

Robert knew what he ought to do — he must leave. In fact, he should have left days ago with Mama and his sisters, and put Olivia out of his mind altogether. These Atherton girls — what power did they have that drove him to madness? First Izzy and now Olivia. He really should know better at his age. Yes, he would go back to Strathinver. Maybe in the spring when he returned to town he would see Olivia again and... but that was premature. Let him but get through the winter first. The season was four months away, still. So many long, dreary months without Olivia...

Voices, dim and distant, but growing closer.

"Here it is!" a female voice cried from somewhere beyond the tapestry. Was it...? Surely it could not be...?

It was. The door opened, and Olivia half ran into the room, then stopped. "Oh! There is no one here."

If she had turned her head a little more, she would have seen Robert in his hiding place behind the fire, but she did not. He was just about to spring forward and reveal himself when a second voice spoke.

"Of course not."

Embleton! How did he come to be with Livvy? But he sounded angry.

"But I was so sure," Olivia said in a small voice. "She told me... and this is such an obvious place for an assignation."

"Indeed it is," Embleton said contemptuously. Lord he was in a rage! And not the slightest hint of a stutter. "It is despicable what some women will do to trap a man. I hope you will reflect upon this behaviour and act in a more becoming manner in future, for such stratagems will give any honourable man a disgust of you."

"Well!" Olivia cried. "You have a nasty, suspicious mind, my lord, that is all I have to say about it. My only thought was to rescue your sister, but even if I *had* been trying to see you more privately, you need not be so unpleasant about it. A woman may wish to be alone with a man without any thought of trapping him into marriage. Sometimes it is just about becoming better acquainted, because that is impossible when completely surrounded by people who watch one for every minute of the day. One can talk more freely without others constantly listening in, and how else may one begin to understand a man's character? And sometimes, one wishes only to show a man that one is interested in him and would welcome the opportunity for a closer friendship, for there is no easy way to do that. Not all of us are adept at flirting, my lord, or would wish to be. For myself, I only ever wanted to get to know you better, for you are a very private person and I am unused to that. I found it intriguing. But I am sorry now that I ever followed that thought, for I see that you are a nasty, small-minded and suspicious person, who delights in thinking the worst of everyone, and I wish I might never see you again!"

"I beg your pardon," he said stiffly. "I will withdraw at once."

Robert heard the door close rather forcefully. He was still angry, then. Probably no one had ever addressed him in such terms before in his whole life.

Olivia burst into noisy sobs, and walked forward to the window, resting her forehead against the panes as she wept.

At once Robert set down his wine glass and crossed the room in a few strides. "Hush, little one, hush now," he murmured, enfolding her in his arms. "He is not worth so much grief."

She snuggled into his arms as if she belonged there, clutching at his lapels and sobbing piteously into his cravat. He closed his eyes, savouring the warmth of her trembling body, the soft tickle of her hair on his chin, the slight hint of perfume about her. Lavender? Or roses? He could not tell, but he knew that whenever he caught that scent in future, it would remind him of the glory of this moment, when she was unquestionably his.

For a long time, she wept, but eventually the sobs subsided to an occasional gulp.

"Better now?" he whispered into her hair.

For answer, she lifted her tear-stained face to him with a tremulous smile, and he was almost undone. So close! So needy, so sad, so desperately vulnerable — it took every ounce of his gentlemanly training to resist the urge to kiss her.

"Will you try a little wine?" he said, trying not very successfully to keep his voice steady.

"Oh no, I could not!"

"I am persuaded it would do you some good. There are cakes, too."

"Cakes..."

He laughed, settling her on a chair, and fetching wine and a selection of edibles. By the third cake, she was definitely looking happier.

"I am so sorry about your cravat," she said, waving a hand at it. "Your valet will be very upset."

"It is not of the least consequence," he said, smiling. "A small price to pay, if it brings you some comfort."

"You are very good, Osborn, and just the person I needed to cheer me up, although I am not at all sure how you came to be here. How did you find this place? I had to ask four footmen — four! — before one of them would tell me the way. Were you following me... or Lord Embleton?"

"I was looking for you. I gained the impression that you were in here with Lord Grayling, so I came here to rescue you from his importuning. Miss Grayling showed me where this room was hidden. I was sitting in the corner behind the fire when you came in."

"And I thought he was in here with Effie... Lady Euphemia, that is, but we were both wrong."

"No, you were right. He *was* in here with Lady Euphemia, but they left just as I arrived."

She laughed. "So I was right about them all along! That is one in the eye for Lord Disbelieving Embleton."

"Why was he so cross with you? It almost sounded as if... well, that he distrusted your motives for some reason."

"Oh..." She looked sheepish. "I made a mistake. When he came to dinner at Corland, I... I tried to get him alone, I confess, but not to trap him into marriage! Never that! Such a despicable thing to do, and who would want a reluctant husband anyway? Not I! No, I thought if I could kiss him, then he might fall in love with me and that would make everything easy, but he did not give me the opportunity. He refused to enter the library with me, and got very huffy about it, so I have never repeated the exercise. But today, when I truly thought Effie was in some danger from Lord Grayling, Lord Embleton would not believe me! And I was right! Oh, he is the most provoking man!"

Robert chuckled. "I have never seen him angry before. He did not stutter once, did you notice?"

"Oh, yes! It was the same at Corland. He was cross with me there, too, and the stammering quite went away. How strange that is! But what do I care, for he is nothing to me now. I wish I had never, ever thought of him."

"Yet you seemed to be getting on so well in the dining room. He looked engrossed in what you were saying."

"So he was, and yet I cannot tell you what we were talking about. Oh, I remember — Yorkshire, and how beautiful it is. And I was telling him about Corland, the old castle that was knocked down, or fell down, more likely, for it was very dilapidated, and the new, modern one. And I talked a little bit about Howland Manor, for I have looked it up in all the guide books, and it sounds very much like the old Corland Castle... or like this place, all odd rooms and twisty stairs and draughty windows."

"And smoking chimneys," Robert said, as a gust of wind filled the room with choking smoke. "Shall we find somewhere more salubrious to sit? We can take the cakes with us, if you wish."

She giggled. "No, I think I shall last until dinner, now. By all means let us leave, for here we are, quite alone in a room which is hidden away, and that is exactly the situation from which I was trying to rescue Effie. But of course, I am in no danger from *you*, am I? You may be a flirt, but you are not an untrustworthy rake like Lord Grayling."

"I thank you for the compliment," he said lightly. "You are indeed quite safe with me."

But oh, if she only knew the effort it took to maintain the proprieties, when every bone in his body wanted to sweep her into his arms and kiss her thoroughly. He ached to hold her again, to whisper sweet words of love into her ear, to never let her go.

Instead, he smiled, held open the door, lifted the tapestry to allow her to pass and then offered her his arm, every inch the chivalrous gentleman.

16: Hot Milk At Bedtime

Olivia passed the rest of the day without straying far from Osborn's side. If he drifted away from her, she found that she rapidly sank into a melancholy over her falling out with Lord Embleton, but his cheerful company always raised her spirits again. He seemed to have an inexhaustible reservoir of light banter that never failed to amuse her, and she could not be sad when he made her laugh so much.

They caught the end of the musical performances, although the instruments were in such poor condition that she was glad she had missed most of the hour. Lady Esther and Mr Franklyn found her there.

"So, you have been with Lord Kiltarlity, have you?" Lady Esther said, smiling on them both. "We soon came across Lady Euphemia, so that was all right, but you were gone so long we began to wonder if we had lost you, instead. This is such an odd, rambling sort of house, there is no knowing where an unwary wanderer might end up. But I had no need to worry after all, for you are quite safe with Lord Kiltarlity."

It being still too wet to venture into the gardens, the card tables were brought out, and Olivia settled down to whist with the Franklyns and Osborn for an hour before the carriages began to be brought round and the visit was over. She saw nothing of Lord Embleton, and he did not dine at Briar House that evening, so perhaps she had made him so cross that he could not bear to be in the same room as her.

But Osborn was there, with his jokes and his smile and a warmth in his eyes that stirred her heart just a little. Of course he was a wicked flirt, and he only saw her as another Izzy, but it did her so much good to be admired by him. Without him she would have hidden in her room and wept all night, but in his company she could hold her head high and pretend that she had not quarrelled violently with the marquess.

Effie was unusually subdued that evening.

"Are you tired?" she said, when she and Olivia made their way upstairs at the end of the evening. "I confess, I am exhausted after the excitements of the day, but my mind is too active to sleep. I shall send for some hot milk, I think. Should you care for some? It is most efficacious after a busy day, I find."

Olivia agreed to it, for hot milk always reminded her of her childhood, sitting in bed in the night nursery with Tess, sipping milk and nibbling a biscuit while Mama or Josie or the governess read a story to them. Such a comfort, hot milk! So when it arrived and Effie had stirred some sugar into it, she drank it swiftly, and was soon fast asleep.

***

Robert had hoped to see Embleton again that day so that he might explain that all Olivia's fears had been well-founded, and Lady Euphemia had indeed been hidden away in the secret room with Grayling, and who knew what might have happened while they were alone? Embleton's anger had not been justified, not in the slightest, and Robert could not bear Olivia to be upset by such unwarranted criticism. How maddening the man was! So seemingly sober and gentlemanlike, yet so swift to think the very worst of such a sweet innocent.

Still, if he could explain it all to Embleton, he would apologise to Olivia and she could be comfortable again. But there was no sign of him at Grayling Hall, nor was he at Briar House that evening.

At least Robert was able to spend most of the evening at Olivia's side, trying not to flirt too outrageously, since she disliked it, but teasing her gently and finding a score of little ways to make her smile. She had such a lovely smile! Surely every man must be softened by it, and want her to be happy. How dared Embleton make her cry!

However pleasant the hours with Olivia were, there was the dull hour to be endured after dining when the gentle influence of the ladies was withdrawn, and the men settled down with the port to talk about horses, politics, women of the less savoury variety and more horses. None of these topics was of much interest to Robert just now, so he prepared to be bored, but tonight there was a pleasant piece of news.

Jeremiah Bucknell tinged his glass to get everyone's attention. "Gentlemen, this is not officially known yet, and I believe it will not be for a few days yet, but I can reveal in the strictest confidence that my sister will shortly be contracting a most prestigious alliance. Is it not so, Rennington?"

The earl went slightly pink, but nodded his head. "It is true. I have not yet made the offer in form... there are people to be informed first...

well, my former wife, in particular. I should not like her to read about it in the newspapers. However, Miss Bucknell and I have... reached an understanding. I have already written to the Duke of Camberley to inform him of my intentions."

"Whatever for?" Bucknell said sharply. "Charlie is of age, she don't need anyone's permission."

"It is a courtesy to the head of the family," Lord Rennington said mildly. "I should certainly like to know if a nephew or niece were on the brink of matrimony."

"Yes, but— Well, no matter." He gave a dry laugh. "'Tis done now."

"Never thought we should get rid of her," one of the other Bucknells said.

"Yes, yes, she is thirty-two, but that is a perfect age for his lordship," Jeremiah said testily. "No reason why she should not marry, none at all."

"No, no, of course not," the other said hastily. "Never meant— Apologies, Jerry. A good match, a very good match."

There was a murmur of agreement round the table, and Miss Bucknell's health was drunk with enthusiasm, and then the earl's and then Miss Bucknell's again, after which the conversation reverted to horseflesh, and Robert began to watch the clock, wondering how soon he could go back to Olivia.

She was at the instrument when he reached the drawing room, playing and singing with such sweetness that he was almost overcome. Mesmerised, he lingered by the door, watching and listening and admiring. Had Izzy played so well? He thought she had, but then she did everything well. She had certainly played some complicated pieces, and held her audience rapt, but Olivia had such a delightful innocence in all she did that she quite took his breath away. Izzy had never been so innocent, even in her first appearances in town. There was always a sophistication to her, a knowingness that had enchanted his younger self, but now left him unmoved. Whereas Olivia...

But that was a singularly fruitless line of thought. He must resist the temptation to follow it.

As soon as Olivia relinquished her place at the pianoforte, he crossed the room and drew her to a sofa a little away from the others. He had not meant to mention it, but seeing her father enter the room not far behind him and immediately claim a place beside Miss Bucknell, he said cautiously, "They seem to get on well."

"Oh, yes! I am so pleased for him. He has been looking for a new wife for some months now, ever since Mama told him she would not marry him again and went away. He must marry to have legitimate sons, you see, and Aunt Jane invited several of her friends to visit to see if one of them would suit."

"But they did not?"

"No! A dreadful collection, not at all the sort of person Papa would like. But Miss Bucknell... he truly likes her, and she seems to like him, too."

"And do you like her? She might be your stepmother, after all."

"I like her very well. She is easy to talk to, as a mother... or a stepmother should be. But that does not matter, as long as she makes Papa happy. He has been so sad since Mama went away. I should love him to find someone new to love, and who will love him."

"I wonder why she has never married," he said thoughtfully. "She is thirty-two, after all, and a confirmed spinster, one would have thought, yet if she is so agreeable—"

"Osborn, it is not kind to think that way — she has never married, so there must be something wrong with her, is that it? Perhaps she simply never met anyone she wanted to marry before."

"I am sure you are right," he said soothingly, and deftly changed the subject.

When the card tables came out, a very little manoeuvring put him and Olivia on the same table as the Earl of Rennington and Miss Bucknell, giving him ample opportunity to discover that she was a sensible woman, well informed and articulate, who also played an astute hand of cards. She was, then, exactly what she appeared to be, a pleasant and agreeable woman, and nothing more sinister than that.

He returned to Chilford Lodge, to find Marsden and his friends very much in their cups, and free with ribald comments on the nature of the society which drew him away from their company night after night. After allowing them ten minutes to expend their wit against him, he made good his escape to his room where Maurice, his valet for long enough to read his master's moods instantly, wisely attended him in silence.

There was something about the night that brought his conscience out to sit on his shoulder and plague him with unhelpful thoughts. All the disasters of today rose up in his mind to crowd out any possibility of sleep. His impulsive proposal to Olivia. His chase to rescue her from Grayling. The discovery that Grayling was with Lady Euphemia. Olivia's search for the two of them, culminating in that unpleasant quarrel with Embleton.

And all of it was Robert's fault. If he had not set himself to distract Olivia from Embleton, and involved Grayling in his ploys, none of this would have happened. How stupid he was! This was just like that spring of five years ago, when the four of them had set themselves to win Izzy at any cost. Such tricks they had played! No, not Farramont. He had always played a straightforward, honest game, and he was the one who had won her in the end.

There must be no more of such machinations. Olivia was not Izzy, and she deserved better treatment. Izzy had revelled in the attention, but Olivia did not even like flirting. She was very different from her sister, and she deserved to be admired and loved for herself, and to make her own free choice.

Tomorrow, he would go to Embleton and explain what had happened, and then take himself back to Strathinver and try to be a good landlord to his tenants. Perhaps that would be distraction enough that he would forget about a certain heart-shaped face and a mischievous smile with a dimple beside it. Oh, that dimple! Could he ever forget it? But he must, he must.

***

Olivia woke late, with heavy eyes and throbbing temples, as if she had not slept at all. Harper, Lady Esther's own maid, was bending over her, shaking her.

"Wake up, my lady, do, or you'll be late for breakfast. Lady Esther's already gone down."

"What? Goodness, look at the time!" The bed beside her was empty. "Even Lady Euphemia is up before me today."

She tumbled out of bed, and raced across to the washstand for a hasty wash. That was when she noticed the letter propped up on the dressing table. *'Olivia'*, it said, in Effie's distinctive scrawl.

"What is this?" she said, but the maid only shrugged.

Tearing open the seal, Olivia read the note.

'My dear Olivia, I am so sorry about the milk but I hope you wake none the worse for it. You will understand the necessity when I tell you that by the time you read this, I shall have run away—' Olivia squeaked in alarm. *'—with Julian Grayling. There is no need to tell Embleton if you had rather not, for we shall be travelling fast enough that he will never catch us, and I will write to him when I arrive. You need not fear for me, gentle friend, for I know what I am doing. I have my maid with me, and also the footman that Papa insists upon, so I am very comfortable and hope to have a great deal of fun on the journey. Thank you for making my brief stay in Briar House bearable. No doubt we shall meet again in the spring. Your very good friend, Effie.'*

"Oh no!" Olivia cried. "Harper, go and find Lady Esther and bring her here at once. Mr Franklyn, too."

"But—"

"At once, Harper! There is not a moment to lose!"

Olivia wrapped herself in a robe, and then paced about the room frantically until the door opened again. To her relief, both the Franklyns appeared with Harper.

"My dear, are you ill? Whatever is it?" cried Lady Esther, her usual serenity quite absent for once.

"Read this," was all Olivia said.

Quickly they scanned it, Mr Franklyn looking over his wife's shoulder.

"Oh, my goodness! They have eloped!" Lady Esther said fretfully. "And I am supposed to be chaperoning the girl."

"You cannot be blamed if she takes off in the middle of the night," Mr Franklyn said. "Olivia, what does this mean about the milk?"

"She must have drugged me... a sleeping draught in the milk. I woke terribly late, so they must be long gone."

"Nevertheless, they must be pursued. I will go at once to speak to Lord Embleton so that he may decide how best to manage this. I shall, of course, place myself at his disposal, if he wishes it. We were in some way responsible for the girl while she was under this roof."

Lady Esther collapsed onto the bed with a groan. "An elopement! It is of all things the most damaging to a girl's reputation. We must be several days from the border, and how she is to be salvaged from this imprudence, I cannot imagine. She is ruined, quite ruined!"

"Only if it becomes known," Mr Franklyn said. "Besides, there is no mention in the letter of elopement or Scotland. They may have a much closer destination in mind. Let us hope for the best. But we must be very careful not to start rumours flying. Leave this to me to deal with, while you ladies employ yourselves just as usual. You must give no hint in your demeanour that there is anything untoward afoot. Esther, I know you can rise to the occasion magnificently."

Lady Esther sat up a little straighter. "Of course, of course. And the first thing we must do is to get you dressed, Olivia. Away you go, Mr Franklyn, to see Lord Embleton. Leave everything else to us."

***

Robert arrived at Pelham House to see Lord Embleton so early that no one was up except the servants, who were sent into a flap by so unexpected a visitor. He was shown into a chilly, little-used parlour where a fire was hastily lit, and footmen scurried about fetching decanters, then pots of coffee and chocolate, and finally, a basket of breakfast rolls.

After some little time, a more superior servant appeared.

"I am Hoodley, my lord, Lord Embleton's valet. His lordship has sent me to enquire as to the urgency of your business with him this morning, and to invite you to step upstairs to his dressing room if the matter is particularly pressing."

"No, indeed. Not the least need. I wished only to be sure of catching him before he went out for the day."

"Very good, my lord."

The valet bowed, and went away again, leaving Robert to drink coffee and nibble Bath buns and hope that the marquess was not one of those finicky fellows who spent half the morning tinkering with his cravat. In the event, it was no more than half an hour before he appeared, full of apologies for keeping Robert waiting, and since Robert felt obliged to apologise for being so early, they said little else for some minutes.

Eventually, however, Robert was able to discharge his errand, and explain that Olivia had been right in suspecting that Lady Euphemia and Grayling were secreted away in private.

The marquess listened politely, accepted that Olivia's concern was real, and then said, "Even so, K-K-Kiltarlity, I c-cannot believe my sister was in any d-danger. She l-likes to f-f-flirt, Grayling l-likes to f-flirt — where is the harm? Grayling knows how f-f-far to go."

It was at just that moment that a carriage, driven rather fast, was heard on the drive outside, the occupant calling loudly as he descended. The marquess's eyebrows rose at this unseemly arrival, and it was no surprise when the door opened moments later to admit the newcomer.

It was somewhat more of a surprise that it was a somewhat agitated Mr Franklyn.

"Embleton, I have bad news," he said tersely. "I regret to inform you that the Lady Euphemia has run away with Lord Grayling."

"Nonsense," the marquess said robustly. "My sister is a d-dreadful flirt, Franklyn, but she kn-knows where the line of p-propriety is drawn."

"Read this letter she left for Lady Olivia," Franklyn said, thrusting a paper at him, "and then tell me that she knows what she is about."

The marquess held the letter in his hands, frowning and motionless, as if he could not quite grasp the meaning of the words. Then he groaned. "Just when I think that minx has done her worst she comes up with some even more outrageous scheme. What on earth am I to do with her?"

"My carriage is outside and at your disposal, my lord," Franklyn said. "We can be after them as soon as your man can pack a bag for you."

"We?"

"Lady Euphemia was left in my charge," Franklyn said grimly. "The failure is mine and thus I offer whatever aid is at my disposal, but we cannot delay if we are to have any chance of catching them before..."

His words trailed away, but they all knew what he meant. *Before it is too late. Before she is irredeemably ruined.*

"You are right, Franklyn, we must make all haste to follow them, however futile it may prove," the marquess said, crumpling the paper in agitation. "Never mind the bag. My man can follow in my carriage. I need only my greatcoat. Come, man, let us be off at once. Kiltarlity, you will excuse me for rushing away, I am sure."

"Are they gone to Scotland? If you can catch up with them in time, you may take Lady Euphemia to my mother and sisters at Strathinver. That can be passed off as a planned visit. In fact, I can undertake to tell everyone that is what has happened. It will explain your absence as well as your sister's."

"Ah... an excellent notion," the marquess said. "Thank you, Kiltarlity. You are the best of good fellows."

He pumped Robert's hand vigorously.

"God speed, Embleton, and may you find them soon."

And then he was gone, Franklyn in his wake, leaving Robert alone to ponder the strange ways of the nobility. And the foremost thought in his mind was that Olivia could not now fall into Grayling's clutches. It was oddly cheering.

17: Reputations

Robert abandoned any plan to return to Chilford Lodge before he reached the end of the Pelham House drive. That foolish girl had run away with Grayling, and poor Olivia would be distraught. She was such a sensitive soul that she would feel the disgrace as deeply as if it were her own. He would go directly to Briar House and see how she was bearing up. He could also spread the story that Embleton was taking his sister to Strathinver, for who knew what rumours might spring up once it became known that Effie had vanished?

He had expected the house to be as lively as a stirred anthill with one of its inhabitants having vanished, but all was quiet. The butler received him serenely, assuring him that several of the gentlemen were taking an early breakfast, if he wished to join them.

"What of the ladies?"

The butler smiled knowingly. "I believe the Lady Olivia is there too, my lord, with the Lady Esther Franklyn."

Olivia looked rather pale, he thought, as he was shown in to the breakfast parlour. She was holding a bun of some sort, but she dropped it in surprise when he was announced. Lady Esther watched him warily over the rim of her coffee cup. It was Miss Bucknell who rose to greet him.

"Lord Kiltarlity! What a delightful surprise! Will you join us for breakfast? There is a seat beside Lady Olivia. Thomas, some coffee for his lordship." As Robert slipped gratefully into the designated place, she went on, "What brings you to our door so early, Lord Kiltarlity?"

It was the opening he wanted. "I had business with Lord Embleton, but found him on the point of departure."

Lady Esther lowered her coffee cup slowly.

"Departure? Is he leaving Leicestershire so soon?" Miss Bucknell said.

"He is. Lady Euphemia had a whim to be gone, so I invited Lord Embleton to take her to my mother at Strathinver. My sisters will be delighted to have company there."

"Oh." Miss Bucknell gave a little frown of puzzlement. "So Lord Embleton will wish to collect the Lady Euphemia this morning?"

Robert laughed easily, reaching for a bun. "I think you will find that Lady Euphemia has already left, Miss Bucknell. She is a regrettably impetuous young lady. Lord Embleton has his hands full there."

"Already left!" she said in astonishment. "Without a word of farewell? Surely not!"

Lady Esther coughed discreetly. "I believe Lord Kiltarlity is correct, ma'am. Olivia woke to find a note on her dressing table." She flushed uneasily as she spoke.

"Indeed," Robert said, rather enjoying himself. "Mr Franklyn arrived with the note while I was with the marquess. Was there no note left for you, Miss Bucknell? Well, these young girls can be so thoughtless. Mmm, these buns are delicious. Pray send my compliments to your cook. Those chops Mr Bucknell is enjoying look most tempting. I wonder... would there be any left?"

Miss Bucknell rushed away, muttering under her breath. The footman obligingly heaped a plate for Robert and he tucked in with gusto. Lady Esther sipped her coffee, eyeing him thoughtfully, while Olivia, her face anxious, crumbled a bun on her plate. The others at the table had finished eating, and although they lingered hopefully in case of further revelations, when none were forthcoming they began to drift away.

After a little while, Miss Bucknell returned, saying fretfully, "Well, Lady Euphemia has taken her maid and footman, but most of her clothes are still here. What a strange start, to simply up and leave without a word! And she must have been up very early, for no one saw her go."

"I believe it was very early," Robert said, to avoid Lady Esther having to answer and perhaps admit that Effie had left in the middle of the night. "Such an impulsive girl! I suppose she has been indulged all her life, and thinks she can do as she pleases. Whoever she marries will have a fine time of it, trying to control her waywardness. Is it not pleasant to see the sun after so many overcast days? What a pity there is no hunt today. We shall just have to find some other occupation, shall we not?"

Lady Esther set down the empty coffee cup she had been cradling. "A perfect day for a walk in the garden, would you not say, Lord Kiltarlity? Olivia and I thought to take a little exercise and explore the shrubbery, if you would care to join us?"

"That sounds most agreeable," he said affably.

It took some little while for the ladies to array themselves in garments sufficiently warm, for although the sun was shining, the air bore a distinctly autumnal chill. However, they were eventually ready, and the three of them sallied forth into the gardens of Briar House. These were not extensive, and much of the surrounding grounds were taken up with the stables, kennels and kitchen garden, but there was a small terrace, a few gravel paths between forlorn, windblown shrubs, and a pretty little round temple overlooking a stone-edged pool. Lady Esther led them to the far side of the pool, where a marble bench accommodated all three of them.

"So you know the truth of it?" Lady Esther said without preamble. "Lady Euphemia has run off with Lord Grayling, if you please. Her father will not care for *that!* And Lord Embleton has gone after them?"

"He has, with Mr Franklyn, and in your carriage, Lady Esther. He would not even wait for his own carriage, or his luggage. His man is to follow on as best he can."

"The invitation to Strathinver was your idea, I take it? That was quick-witted of you. If they are indeed gone to Scotland, the situation might still be rescued. Foolish girl! What a ridiculous thing to do! She did not strike me as being swept into indiscretion by passion. That she liked him was clear enough, but no one suspected an elopement, although I suppose he is excessively handsome."

"Effie described him as an Adonis," Olivia said tentatively.

"Even so, they have barely known each other a week... ten days at most," Lady Esther said. "I never saw any cause for alarm, but you were closer to her than any of us, Olivia. You must have seen some sign that suggested the attraction was more serious."

"There was nothing at all. In fact, Effie talked of *playing* with Lord Grayling, and having some fun. I imagined she meant flirting and such like. If I had thought for one minute there was anything more to it, I should have told you, Lady Esther."

"I hope you would," she said, but she sounded dubious.

"Of course she would!" Robert said hotly. "Lady Olivia would never condone such an action, and cannot be blamed for the wilfulness of Lady Euphemia."

"No, no, I did not mean..." Lady Esther began, raising one hand to her forehead. "Forgive me, Olivia, I am not myself this morning. Lady Euphemia was in my charge, and although I do not know how I might have prevented her running off in that way, I still feel that I should have done. Lord Kiltarlity, do you think Lord Embleton will be able to catch the runaways? How will he know where they have gone?"

"He will ask at the turnpikes," Robert said at once. "The gate keepers will remember a carriage passing through in the middle of the night."

"What will happen to Miss Grayling?" Olivia said in a small voice. "Has her brother abandoned her, do you think?"

"And she has no companion or chaperon," Robert said.

"Ohhh!" Lady Esther moaned. "That thought had not even occurred to me. The poor child! And I cannot even go there to enquire, for Mr Franklyn has taken the carriage."

"Now there I can help," Robert said, springing to his feet. "I have my horse here. I can ride over to Grayling Hall to enquire, and be back in under an hour."

It took him a little more than an hour, but he returned with a grin on his face. He found the ladies huddled in a corner of the terrace, sheltered from the wind by a statue of Athena.

"This is the strangest elopement I have ever heard of," he said, chuckling. "Miss Grayling is gone with the lovers, accompanied by her maid, his valet and a footman, in two carriages both emblazoned with Grayling's baronial arms. The grooms told me they took only a pair of horses to each carriage, for that was all that was in the stables, but Grayling planned to hire two pairs for each carriage at the first change."

"Eight horses all the way to Scotland! That will empty his purse," Lady Esther said, her elegant eyebrows lifting a fraction.

"Is it known that they are gone to Scotland?" Olivia said, her face so anxious that Robert's heart was wrung. If only he had the right to comfort her! Even to take her hand would be something. All he could do was to tell her everything he had learnt.

"They are certainly gone north, for I went to the nearest toll gate to ask," he said. "As for the cost, I imagine it will be Lady Euphemia's purse which will be emptied."

"Very likely," Lady Esther said. "Well, I cannot like it, but at least the marquess may be comforted by the thought that his sister is well chaperoned, if Miss Grayling is with her. An elopement is very bad, but taking one's future sister-in-law is not quite so ruinous."

"We do not know that they are eloping at all," Robert said.

"That is true," Olivia said, her face brightening. "The note said nothing about elopement or Scotland."

"What else would this be about?" Lady Esther said. "No one runs away in the middle of the night with an unrelated man merely to visit a milliner or take beef broth to the poor."

"No, but Effie has such a mischievous spirit," Olivia said. "She like to play games — perhaps this is just an amusing game to her?"

"It will not be so amusing when her reputation is destroyed and her only hope for matrimony is the curate," Lady Esther said repressively.

Olivia shivered, sending spikes of alarm through Robert.

"Are you chilly, Lady Olivia? Would you not rather be indoors beside the fire?"

"Oh yes, it is a trifle cool out here, but you see we are avoiding Miss Bucknell's wrath," she said artlessly.

Lady Esther winced. "I would say, rather, that we are diplomatically retreating. Keeping our heads below the parapet. Not drawing attention to ourselves."

Robert chuckled. "Inclined to blame you, is she?"

"Not because Effie ran away," Olivia whispered, "but because we did not tell her. She knew nothing of it until you arrived."

"Well, I am sorry for that, but she would have found out soon enough," he said easily. "There she is now, crossing the lawn with Lord Rennington. He will put her in a better humour, I am sure."

Lady Esther smiled. "Yes, indeed. A pleasing match, and a most gratifying outcome for both of them after all their difficulties."

"Has Miss Bucknell had difficulties, too?" Olivia said, turning innocent eyes on Lady Esther.

"Well... not exactly, but then... everyone has *some* difficulties in life. How you do take one up, sometimes, Olivia," Lady Esther said.

"I beg your pardon, ma'am."

She lowered her head, subdued, and again Robert was on fire to hold her tight and reassure her. After all, it was a sensible question given Lady Esther's words. He rather wondered about Miss Bucknell's difficulties himself, which perhaps accounted for her lack of previous suitors, but now, of course, it was impossible to ask.

Quickly he changed the subject, enquiring about Lady Esther's stepdaughter and her new husband, which kept the conversation in safer channels for some considerable time. A footman came out to see if they wanted anything, and shortly thereafter a pot of tea arrived, and several plates of cake, biscuits and sweetmeats. Robert took a glass of wine, and amused himself by watching Olivia tucking into the cake with enthusiasm, while Lady Esther sipped her tea delicately.

Such a pleasant way to pass the morning. This is what it would be like if he were married to Olivia, except that it would be just the two of them. No need for a chaperon if they were married. There would be endless days like this, sitting companionably on the terrace or beside the fire, and only the occasional intrusion of the outside world to disturb their harmony. And there would be visits to the nursery... goodness, how old that made him feel! To have children of his own would be both a glory and a heavy responsibility.

A murmur of voices broke into this pleasant reverie. The butler emerged onto the terrace accompanied by another man, a well-built man who might have been called handsome were he not scowling so ferociously. The butler gestured towards the corner where Robert and the ladies sheltered, and the man strode towards them. He looked familiar...

"There you are, Esther! What are you doing hiding away out here? The servants have been all over the house looking for you."

"Ramsey?" Lady Esther said uncertainly. "Whatever are you doing here?"

"Are you serious?" the man said, looming over her. "After a letter such as this?" He waved a crumpled sheet of paper under her nose. "Did you expect that we would all just smile and let it go? I suppose you have been promoting this match, have you? And think yourself very clever, I make no doubt."

"You mean Charlie? But Ramsey—"

"Of course I mean Charlie! What on earth were you thinking, to let things get to this stage?"

"But they get on so well! So perfectly matched, and Papa has forgiven her so—"

"Honestly, you are the most bird-witted female I ever knew! Well, it must be stopped... if it is not too late. Where is she, do you know? I suppose the whole house will have to be searched again. It is *not* too late, I take it?"

Mutely, she shook her head.

"Then I must find her, at once. Or him. But there they are now!"

He shot off down the terrace steps and strode across the lawn towards the temple, from where Lord Rennington and Miss Bucknell were emerging. Lady Esther jumped up with a cry and ran after him.

"What is that all about?" Robert whispered to Olivia.

"No idea," she whispered back. "Who is he? Do you know?"

"The Marquess of Ramsey, heir to the Duke of Camberley and Lady Esther's brother. Look he has dropped the letter. What does it say?"

"Osborn! We cannot read other people's private letters."

"Well, we can if they drop them at our feet. Whether we *should* or not is another question, but since his lordship is shouting loud enough to wake the dead, I cannot imagine the secret will remain so for very long. Oh... it is from your father, informing the duke that he intends to pay his addresses to Miss Bucknell." He chuckled. "Oh dear! I rather fear the marquess has come to forbid the banns."

"It is not funny, Osborn," Olivia said in a small voice. "Papa was so happy, and look at him now — the very picture of dejection."

Robert saw that she was right. The marquess, Miss Bucknell and Lady Esther were arguing furiously, but the earl stood a little aside, his head low. As they watched, he raised his hands to silence them, and then said something too low to be heard. Then he bowed, turned and walked back towards the house.

Seeing Olivia on the terrace, he diverted and came to sit beside her.

"There is no fool like an old fool, is there?" he said tiredly. "She seemed so pleasant, too. But it will not do."

"Oh, Papa! Whatever has happened?" Olivia cried, wrapping her arm around his as tears of sympathy trickled down her cheeks.

"Perhaps we should not press for a detailed explanation," Robert said gently.

"No, it is best that she knows," the earl said, straightening his spine. "Let it be a lesson to all of us that we should not judge people by appearances but enquire into their hearts and souls. Miss Bucknell, daughter, has greatly deceived me. She has never married, and so I imagined her as innocent as... well, as innocent as you are, but it is not so, for she lived with a man for a number of years without benefit of matrimony. Bore him three children, even! And this she did not see fit to mention to me. No one here thought to tell me of it."

Olivia's mouth dropped open, and she seemed too stunned to speak. This time, Robert could not stop himself from taking her free hand and squeezing it gently.

"That is dreadful indeed, but better to find it out now than later," he said.

"Yes. That is true," the earl said. Then, with a sigh, "We must leave, I suppose. I cannot stay in this place a moment longer."

"Shall we go home, then?" Olivia said.

The earl shuddered. "And have your Aunt Jane drumming up more potential wives for me? No, no, no! I could not bear it."

"Izzy lives just up the road at Nottingham," Robert said. "She and Farramont would be delighted to see you."

"Mama is there," Olivia said softly. "Papa will not go where she is."

"Oh. What about Josie, then?"

"In town."

Robert stopped, daunted.

The argument on the lawn had finally died away. Miss Bucknell, her cheeks flaming, rushed back into the house, while Lady Esther and Lord Ramsey returned to the corner of the terrace. Silently, Robert handed the marquess the letter. He looked rueful, the anger finally burned out of him, but the usually composed Lady Esther collapsed onto the bench, sobbing piteously.

"Lord, I never meant to upset her so much," Ramsey said, rubbing his neck with a sigh. "Never seen her cry before. Come now, Esther, buck up. It is not so bad as all that, and at least they were not actually married."

"It is not that," Lady Esther said, her voice high with distress. "We cannot stay now! We must leave at once, but how can I? Mr Franklyn has gone off with Lord Embleton and taken the carriage and if I just disappear, he will not know where I have gone and how can I go on my own?"

"These are not insuperable problems," Ramsey said, kneeling before her and taking her hand. "Come now, Esther, this is not like you. I have no handkerchief... Kiltarlity, have you a handkerchief? There now, mop up your tears, sister, and let us put our heads together and see what we can come up with. For a start, you can take my carriage, if you wish. I should be delighted to escort you wherever you wish to go."

"I cannot go anywhere!" she wailed. "Not without Mr Franklyn, but I do not know where he is!"

Robert coughed discreetly. "If I might suggest... we could follow Mr Franklyn and Lord Embleton on their journey north. And if we do not encounter them, we may all go to Strathinver and recover from this upheaval, and Mr Franklyn may meet up with us there. We can leave word of our plans along the way. It is far enough away that you will not be pestered by acquaintances, and only my mother and sisters are there at present. I suggested it to Lord Embleton as a place where he might take the Lady Euphemia, for the same reason. Strathinver is far enough from civilisation to be tranquil. I have always considered that a disadvantage, but in this case it would be ideal. And if you should want more lively company, we have the Duke and Duchess of Lochmaben only a few miles away."

"Our cousins," Olivia said, brightening a little. "Perhaps we could stay with them? They are always hospitable."

"I am not much minded for company," Lord Rennington said. "Strathinver... that sounds perfect. A secluded place to recover from this blow."

"Exactly. What do you say, Lady Esther?" Robert said. "If we encounter Mr Franklyn on the way, you may make alternative plans but for the moment shall we all head to Scotland and escape from the travails of England?"

"Very well," she said, straightening her spine a little. "If I may take up the offer of your carriage, Ramsey. I could not bear a hired post chaise."

"No, indeed!" Robert said at once. "The daughter of a duke should never travel in a paltry hired chaise."

It was the right thing to say, for a watery smile broke through for the first time. "Come, Olivia. We have packing to do. We shall leave in... two hours, shall we say?"

The gentlemen agreed to it and they all dispersed to make their various arrangements.

18: A Journey North

Robert could scarcely believe his luck. He had tossed out the idea of following Lord Embleton north on a whim, not expecting it to be taken up, but for one reason or another they had all agreed to it. Now he had the delight of Olivia's company over several days of travelling, and then however long she could be persuaded to stay at Strathinver. Not long, perhaps, with her cousins the Lochmabens so close, but he would take whatever time he could get.

Jeremiah Bucknell, rather shamefaced, was the only person to see them off. The two ladies, Lord Ramsey and Lord Rennington rode in Ramsey's luxurious carriage, while Robert squeezed into an antiquated luggage wagon, borrowed from the apologetic Bucknell, together with the valets and a maid. He did not envy the two footmen, condemned to stand behind their respective carriages through the worst of the autumn weather.

They were not on the road before the middle of the afternoon, so they got no further than Nottingham before the failing light obliged them to find accommodation for the night.

While rooms were being obtained, Olivia wandered out of the inn yard, passing under the arch to the main street. In some fear for her safety in the busy street, Robert ran after her.

"Going to the shops?" he said cheerfully, not wishing to alarm her.

She smiled, but rather sadly, he thought. "Just three miles from Stonywell. We could have been sleeping in comfort at Izzy's house, if only Mama were not there."

"Do you wish to go there? I will arrange it, if that would please you."

"How kind you are! But I cannot leave Papa, and he will not go there. Now that their marriage is invalid, Mama has cut all ties with him — she does not even write to him, or permit him to write to her. She wants him to marry someone else, and she feels it would only confuse him if they were to meet or maintain a correspondence."

"And yet, I do not think he is happy, do you?"

"No, not at all," she said, turning an anxious face towards him. "Even with Miss Bucknell, although he liked her very much, he said he could never love her as he loved — still loves — Mama."

"Then he should go and make his peace with her, and marry her again."

"Oh no! He promised her he would look elsewhere!" Olivia said, sounding shocked. "A man must keep his promises, Osborn."

"A man must listen to his heart, also," he said slowly. "If he knows that no other woman can ever make him as happy as he once was, then he should tell her so. And perhaps after all this time — five months, is it not? — she will have had time to regret her hasty action. Perhaps she, too, would be happy to return to the way things were."

"Nothing will ever return to the way things were," she said sharply. "Those days are gone, when Mama and Papa were together and Walter was

Viscount Birtwell and engaged to Bea Franklyn." She smiled suddenly. "At least *some* things have worked out for the better. Walter is much better off with Winnie Strong, and who would ever have imagined that Cousin Bertram would tame Bea? No one expected that!" Then her expressive face shifted again. "Poor Bertram! I wonder if Captain Edgerton has found out who shot him yet?"

"Unlikely. He has not found out who killed your uncle, has he? He must have turned Yorkshire upside down, and is no further forward, by the sound of it."

"I expect the murderer is long gone," she said. "He would not linger at the scene of his crime, would he?"

"That would depend on why he killed Mr Nicholson," Robert said. "And if it was a member of the family—"

"That is a horrid thought! Of course it is not one of us! Why would anyone in the family murder Uncle Arthur?"

"Well, someone had a grievance against him," Robert said equably. "No one kills someone without a very good reason. This air is very damp, Olivia. Shall we go inside?"

She agreed to it, he offered his arm and she smiled as she wrapped both hands around it. His spirits leapt at her trusting demeanour as she allowed him to lead her into the inn. If only he dared to offer her more than his arm — his heart, his name, everything he possessed. But he had made a vow to let her choose Embleton, if the marquess would make her happy.

Still, it was unbearably difficult to keep to that vow.

***

Olivia generally enjoyed travelling. The novelty of leaving home, and the prospect of new places to see, of visits to be made or shops to be explored always raised her spirits. But this journey was not exciting at all. There was the worry about Effie, to start with, and whether Lord Embleton could manage to intercept the runaways before they could be married over the anvil. There was no longer any doubt of where they were bound, for their route was steadily northward, as their enquiries at toll gates and posting houses quickly revealed. Whether the damage to Effie's reputation could be avoided, even if caught in time, was a further worry.

Then there was Papa, still mired in gloom after the disastrous matter of Miss Bucknell. Poor Papa! She had longed to turn aside at Nottingham and visit Izzy and Ian, and dear Mama, for much as she loved Papa, there was no one like one's mama for comforting one. But naturally she could not abandon Papa at such a time.

As for Lady Esther, her calm composure was almost completely destroyed by the absence of Mr Franklyn at such a critical moment. All she wanted, it seemed, was her husband by her side, although Olivia suspected that her own carriage was missed almost as much. She had apologised to Papa for saying nothing about Miss Bucknell's scandalous past, but all the Bucknells had agreed to keep silent, in the hope that two people with murky pasts could be made happy again.

"I thought I was acting for the best," she said, on the verge of tears again. "I can see now how wrong it was."

"Your intentions were good," Papa said, "but I could not entrust the care of my children to a woman of such dubious morals."

"No, I quite see that," Lady Esther said. "It was very foolish of me. Mr Franklyn will be so cross with me."

On the third day of travel, they caught up with Lord Embleton's carriage, which contained the two valets and a quantity of luggage. They had left Melton no more than two hours behind Lord Embleton and Mr Franklyn, but had fallen steadily further behind, owing to a shortage of funds. Both had assumed that the other would be well supplied with the readies, and so they had been forced to eke out what money they had, and could only afford a pair of horses at each change. They fell upon the new arrivals with smiles of relief, and readily joined their little procession.

Shortly thereafter, they entered Yorkshire, which ought to feel like home to Olivia, except that it seemed they would drive straight through and on towards Scotland. The weather turned against them, too, becoming cold and drearily wet, and Lord Ramsey allowed the footmen to ride with the valets in Lord Embleton's carriage.

Olivia might have been rather despondent at this point had it not been for Robert. There was something about him, some sympathetic twinkle in his eyes which seemed to say that he knew exactly how she felt. Whenever he was around, her spirits were distinctly lifted, even when he was not particularly paying attention to her. There was something immeasurably reassuring in his presence, just like Papa when he was himself... no, not really like Papa. Papa's presence never made her oddly self-conscious, or caused her heart to speed up in the most unaccountable way, as Robert's did. And when he turned his full attention on her, pressing this dish or that on her at dinner, or ensuring that she was not too hot or too cold, or relating little anecdotes that he thought might amuse her, well... the way she felt then was nothing at all like her regard for Papa.

After dinner, Lady Esther was inclined to retire early, and Lord Ramsey liked to talk to Papa about politics and people that Olivia had never met, so as often as not she ended up playing cribbage or piquet with Robert, and that was the most comfortable thing imaginable. Sometimes he teased her gently and sometimes he talked about Strathinver or his other estates and sometimes they ended up talking about the strangest things — shooting stars and why autumn is both the most glorious and the most depressing season and why it always rains when one is feeling dismal and the strange shapes that clouds make as they race across the sky. And some nights she retired to bed wondering what on earth they had talked about that had absorbed them until close to midnight.

On the fourth day, they had a long wait at Leeds for sufficient horses and postilions for their three carriages to get them to Ripley. Lord Ramsey took a parlour for the ladies to wait in, but Lady Esther, who had an aching head, retired to a bedroom to rest with her maid in attendance. Olivia found herself alone in the parlour with Robert.

"Shall I send for your maid?" he said.

"No, no. Let her attend Lady Esther. I do not need her just now."

"No, but... then perhaps I should withdraw. It is not proper for us to be alone here, Olivia."

"Oh, pooh to that. Papa will be here at any moment, I am sure. I am glad of a moment alone to tell you how grateful I am for offering us the shelter of Strathinver. You are so kind, Osborn. I do hope your mama will not be too inconvenienced by our arrival."

He smiled and said, "Do not worry about that. I have written to tell her of our intentions, and the place is big enough to house us all comfortably, have no fear." He hesitated, an odd look on his face. "Olivia... I expect... I hope that Embleton will be there, too, eventually, whenever he has caught up with his sister. Perhaps... well, it will be an opportunity for you to get to know him better. That is what you want, is it not? And... and you will get to know me better, too."

"I should like that," she said in a low voice, for her words caught in her throat rather. What was he suggesting? That he and Lord Embleton were rivals? He had talked of marriage once, but it was so casual that she had assumed he was merely teasing her.

Something flashed in his eyes, before he became serious again. "You see, it is all my fault, this business with Grayling and Lady Euphemia."

"Oh no! That cannot be!"

"It is, I assure you. I have been playing games, trying to keep you away from Embleton, so I set Grayling to... to distract you, and that made him ripe, I think to fall into Lady Euphemia's hands. That day at Grayling Hall, when we were all chasing round after each other... that was the result of my stupid, stupid interference. That was the mistake I made with Izzy, you know, trying to best the other suitors for her hand instead of trusting her to make the best choice for herself. Well, I shall not make the same mistake with you, trying to bounce you into a decision. You must take the time to know your own mind, and if Embleton is the man to make you happy, then... then..."

Olivia felt as if she had been floating gently along a quiet stream which had now turned into a raging torrent, tossing her this way and that. Whatever did he mean? He seemed to be saying that he wanted to marry her himself, but he would not stand in her way if Lord Embleton was her choice. Was all Osborn's teasing and flirtation actually something more serious? And what did Lord Grayling have to do with it? And why on earth did he talk about Lord Embleton as if she had any choice in the matter? He had never shown her more than gentlemanly courtesy, at best, and the edge of his temper sometimes, too.

It was all too difficult, and she was relieved when Papa came in and broke up the tête-à-tête.

***

Late on the fifth day, their little train of carriages arrived at Thirsk, and as they turned into the market square, Olivia cried out in excitement.

"Look! Look! Lady Esther's carriage!"

Lady Esther, who had been leaning against the squabs with her eyes closed, sat bolt upright. "Where? Where?"

"In the yard of the inn we just passed. We must stop! Lord Ramsey, we must stop at once!"

He was already knocking on the roof of the carriage, and almost before it had drawn to a halt, he was fumbling with the window to reach the handle and open the door. Leaping out, he strode back down the street, leaving the three carriages almost blocking the way for following traffic.

In a very few minutes, he returned with Mr Franklyn. Lady Esther gave a little cry, and scrambled in haste out of the carriage to throw herself into her husband's arms.

"There, there, my love. All is well now," he murmured into her elegant bonnet, as she shed tears of joy onto his immaculate coat. Olivia was delighted with this romantic reunion. Having only ever seen the placid surface of what had seemed to be no more than a pragmatic marriage, she was thrilled to discover the depths of affection lurking beneath.

There was a little argument with the postilions, who had arrangements with a different inn, but Lord Ramsey quickly disposed of this problem by decreeing that the postilions may do as they pleased but he and his party would put up at the same inn as Mr Franklyn and Lord Embleton. Mr Franklyn laughed, and shepherded the ladies back down the road and into the inn yard, which was as lively as a spring fair. Horses, postilions and ostlers scurried about, while a number of chambermaids and scullery maids stood at the kitchen door, eyes agog, and several farmers and tradesmen, tankards in hand, watched from the inn door.

"It is even worse inside," Mr Franklyn said, with a chuckle. "You would imagine Thirsk had never seen a marquess before. Mind you, Embleton is in the most towering rage. This way... we have a very pleasant parlour, very snug."

"He might feel better if he knows that we have Hoodley with us," Olivia said.

"His valet? And is Eastwood with you, too? I confess, I shall be very glad to have properly starched cravats again," he said. "I only packed for an overnight stay, and this has turned out to be very much longer, and now Grayling and Lady Euphemia have disappeared."

Olivia gasped. "No! But where have they gone?"

"If only we knew," Mr Franklyn said with a smile. "They must have turned off the main road at some point, but— Here we are."

He threw open a door and ushered them into a parlour so hot from a blazing fire that Olivia almost felt her cheeks melting.

"Goodness," Lady Esther said, fanning herself with her hand. "A window, I think, Mr Franklyn, if you please, unless you wish us all to collapse with heat stroke."

There was bread, cheese and cold meat laid out on the table, together with various wines. While Mr Franklyn went off to secure accommodation for the new arrivals, and Lady Esther fanned herself beside the open window looking down on the street below, Olivia discovered that she was hungry and set about remedying this deplorable state of affairs. She was polishing off a large piece of cheese and wondering whether she could manage another slice of ham when her father came in, looking glum.

"Well, this is a quandary, is it not? All this way to find the runaways, and they have vanished from the earth. Ah, food," he said, brightening a little.

"May I slice you some ham, Papa?" Olivia said.

"If you would, daughter." He poured himself a glass of wine and sipped appreciatively. "Excellent, excellent. There is nothing like a drop of claret to improve the spirits. Lady Esther, may I offer you a glass of wine? Most refreshing after so many hours on the road."

"Thank you, no," she said faintly. "A lie down is what would do me the most good, I believe. I shall find Mr Franklyn and ensure that the rooms offered are of a suitable standard."

"May I accompany you, Lady Esther?" the earl said politely, but she waved away his help.

For a while, father and daughter ate in companionable silence. Olivia watched him carefully for signs of low spirits, but she thought he was somewhat less despondent. The familiar northern countryside was clearly doing him good.

The other gentlemen came in soon after, Mr Franklyn reporting that his wife was resting under her maid's ministrations.

"Poor Lady Esther!" Olivia said. "She is dreadfully knocked up with all this travelling."

"She will recover very speedily, I am sure," Mr Franklyn said. "She will be well enough to join us for dinner. Embleton, did you have any luck finding which road Grayling might have taken?"

Lord Embleton shook his head, looking as if he wished to wring his sister's neck. "Vanished!" he muttered. "They have turned off somewhere, but I cannot find out where... or why! Surely having come so far they will proceed all the way to Scotland. Foolish girl!"

"We will find them," Mr Franklyn said easily. "We know they did not reach Thirsk, so tomorrow we will work our way south again and explore the byways. Unless they fell into a river and sank without trace, we must come across some news of them sooner or later."

"Perhaps Lady Euphemia wished to visit her sister," Olivia said diffidently.

Five pairs of eyes turned curiously in her direction.

"Her sister?" Lord Embleton said, his expression darkening. "Given that we are currently in the North Riding, Lady Olivia, do you refer to the sister who lives in Shropshire, or the one who lives in Gloucestershire? For I have to tell you that in either case your understanding of geography is abysmal."

Olivia flushed, but said calmly, "I refer to Lady Harraby, Lord Embleton, who was residing at Harraby Hall the last I heard, not three miles from here. Perhaps Lady Euphemia wished to know if Lady Harraby has had her baby yet."

Lord Embleton looked thunderstruck. *"Harraby Hall!* How foolish of me to forget that Jane is at Harraby! I was there myself not two months since. Lady Olivia, I ap-p-pologise m-most abjectly for insulting your intelligence. In all the upheaval, I had quite f-forgot that Jane is at H-Harraby H-Hall. I shall go there at once."

And without another word, he whisked out of the room and his voice was shortly heard in the yard calling for a horse.

"A man of action," Mr Franklyn said, with a smile. "I had forgotten about Lady Harraby myself. Well done, Olivia. But how ironic if we have been chasing after a potential elopement only to find that it is nothing more than a family visit."

"It would be a strange manner of undertaking a family visit to leave in the middle of the night with a gentleman to whom one is not related," Osborn said sardonically. "I await Embleton's report with interest. One of us may yet be called upon to act as second in a duel."

Olivia gasped. "He would not… would he?"

Mr Franklyn laughed. "Embleton has more sense."

But Olivia could not be easy about it. "Surely someone should go after him? To prevent him from killing Lord Grayling?"

Osborn stood up at once. "I shall go, if it will set your mind at rest, Lady Olivia."

"Thank you! At all costs, they must not fight!"

"Believe me, I shall do everything I can to prevent it."

He bowed to her, and was gone, leaving her with nothing to do but wring her hands and pace about the room in abject terror.

19: Strathinver

Robert found Embleton pacing about the inn yard, shouting at the ostlers.

"What is the problem?" Robert said.

"They are reluctant to lend me a riding horse without a postilion to lead the way."

"Perhaps we should take a carriage instead? I should be glad to come with you."

"That would take even longer," Embleton said tersely.

"I do not see the need for such haste," Robert said equably. "Either Lady Euphemia is at Harraby Hall or she is not, and ten minutes sooner is neither here nor there."

Embleton stilled, hands on hips. "You are right," he said slowly. "I am b-being irrational, I s-suppose."

"You are being a brother who is concerned about his sister," Robert said. "Perfectly natural. You there! Forget the riding horse, and put a pair to Lord Embleton's carriage."

That was an order the ostlers were well trained to comply with, and within a very short time they were on the road. Robert could not honestly say he was thrilled by this, for he would far sooner be sitting in the parlour with Olivia, a glass of wine in his hand and her sweet face before him, but if it spared her a little worry, he would do it gladly.

Although her concern for Lord Embleton brought him a worry of his own. Would she have been just as concerned if it had been anyone else potentially tearing off to call a man out? If it had been Robert, for instance? Was her fear merely for an acquaintance? Or was there that deeper fear, driven by affection... by love? That was too dispiriting a thought for words.

Embleton sat stony-faced and silent in the carriage, his anger still close to the surface, but Robert was more optimistic than he had been since they had left Leicestershire. A visit to a sister about to be confined was so very far from the elopement they had all feared that his spirits were quite lifted.

"I wonder if this is what Lady Euphemia intended all along," he ventured. "She never said it was an elopement, after all."

"If she had wanted to visit her sister, she had only to ask," Embleton said tersely, his anger still keeping his stutter at bay.

"Lady Olivia thinks that she likes to play games... to tease. She might have thought it a good joke."

"She still ran away in the middle of the night with Grayling," Embleton said. "She needs whipping! As for him, what was he thinking? He cannot imagine I would ignore this."

"Still, if she is safe at Harraby Hall, then—"

"*If* she is safe, then perhaps I shall only box her ears."

"And she has had Miss Grayling with her as chaperon, and her own maid and footman."

"Two girls of eighteen cannot chaperon each other, nor are servants adequate protection for a duke's daughter," he said haughtily. "You would not think so if it were one of your own sisters."

Robert could see that the marquess was determined to maintain his anger, so he gave it up and the rest of the journey was accomplished in silence.

The carriage had no sooner drawn to a halt before the entrance steps to Harraby Hall than several servants ran out, followed by a very agitated Lord Harraby. His face fell when he saw the marquess.

"Embleton! Well! I thought you were —"

"Is Effie here?"

"Yes! Locked up for the sanity of all of us."

"And Grayling?"

"Gone away, very disgruntled. Will you—?"

But Embleton had already gone inside, taking the steps two at a time and barking orders to the nearest manservant.

"Well!" Harraby said, turning to Robert with a wry smile. "Kiltarlity. Are you here about Effie too?"

"In a way. I am charged with preventing Embleton from calling Grayling out. I take it the lady is unharmed?"

"Unharmed and entirely unrepentant. Thought it all a great lark, if you can believe it. Grayling supposed they were on their way to Scotland, but that chit of a girl only ever intended him to escort her here. It would have served her right if he had forced the issue, but then I suppose Embleton would have been obliged to meet him. I very nearly called him out myself. Happily, he is gone back to wherever he came from, with his sister, poor child. She looked quite bewildered. Ah, this must be the midwife now," he added, as a carriage travelling rather fast bowled up the drive.

"Then we have arrived at an inopportune moment," Robert said.

Harraby's face clouded. "It is, rather. Effie's unexpected arrival with Grayling threw Jane into a dreadful spin, and that started the baby off. Only a little early, but still, one does not like surprises in these matters. Mrs Jopling, I am so pleased to see you. Kiltarlity, you will forgive me if—"

"Of course, of course. Go and see to Lady Harraby. I will find Embleton."

This proved to be unexpectedly difficult, for the household was in rather a flap, and no one seemed to know where the marquess had gone, or even where Lady Euphemia was being housed. Eventually, however, the housekeeper was found who showed Robert by a tortuous route to a bedroom on an upper floor, where two footman stood impassive guard, pretending that they could not hear the argument being conducted at an irate bellow within.

Suppressing the desire to laugh at this family dispute, Robert pushed open the door and went inside, causing the two combatants to stop mid-sentence. Across the room, two boxes were open, clothes strewn about, while a maid cowered in a corner.

"Lord Kiltarlity!" Effie turned to him, her red-faced anger melting at once into welcome. "What are you doing here?"

"I came to prevent your brother from calling out Lord Grayling."

"Calling him out?" She laughed merrily. "What a silly notion! Embleton would not be so stupid... would you?"

"I should have been obliged to, naturally. Matter of honour," Embleton said tersely.

"Oh, pft! Honour, indeed! You men are so foolish. Grayling has not laid a finger on me, and I have had Sarah Grayling with me the whole time, as well as my own servants."

"As if that makes a particle of difference!" Embleton said, his voice rising to anger again.

"Fortunately," Robert said, loudly enough that they both turned to him again, "we were able to provide a plausible explanation for your departure from Leicestershire, Lady Euphemia, so with luck you will escape this episode unscathed. Embleton, if any rumours do surface, a meeting with Lord Grayling would only serve to confirm them. It cannot serve any useful purpose at this stage."

"It would make *me* feel better," Embleton said, but his tone was reduced to its normal level. "Effie, you are the m-most t-troublesome chit. What am I to d-do with you?"

"Let me stay here. Jane will chaperon me."

"Jane is in the midst of her confinement," Embleton said more sharply. "We are very much in the way, but if I take you back to Marshfields, you will just run away again, I suppose."

"Bring her to Strathinver," Robert said at once. "Nothing for miles around. My mother will chaperon her ferociously, I can guarantee it. She will not run away from there, and if she thinks to try it, we can lock her in the dungeon."

Effie squeaked in outrage. "Do you truly have a dungeon?"

"Truly I do, complete with manacles. There are probably rats, too, although I have not been in there to check for some time."

She squeaked again, but Robert smiled benignly at her.

That brought a glimmer of a smile from the marquess. "Strathinver... yes. Why not? Pack, Effie. We leave in one hour."

"Surely we can wait long enough to hear how Jane goes on... whether it is a son this time."

"Harraby can write to us. Pack. Now."

***

While relieved that Lord Embleton was not, after all, to meet Lord Grayling in a duel, Olivia was thrown into despair by the Franklyns' proposal that they should now turn for home. Thirsk, after all, was only a few miles from Birchall and Corland, and would they not be more comfortable in their own houses at this time of year, rather than lumbering up to Scotland? Lord Embleton might go with Lord Kiltarlity if he chose, but surely Lord Rennington and dear Olivia would prefer to curtail their travelling until the better weather?

Dear Olivia would certainly not prefer to curtail anything. If her friends were going to Strathinver, then she would rather like to go there too, for it would be more fun than being cooped up at Corland again. Not that she could say so. Girls of eighteen were seldom asked their opinion on such matters. Instead, the discussion at the inn that evening was carried on between Lady Esther and Olivia's papa, and happily Papa was not minded for home, either.

"You know how it will be, Lady Esther," he said. "Jane will whistle up another improbable candidate for me to marry, and I am not at all in the right frame of mind for doing the pretty to anyone just now. I should like to hide away at Strathinver for a while until I feel up to facing the world again."

"Then I had better come with you, to chaperon Olivia," she said.

"No need for that," he said. "I can protect my daughter perfectly well on the road, I hope, and at Strathinver, she will have Lady Kiltarlity's chaperonage."

And so, to Olivia's satisfaction, it was agreed, and the next morning Lord Ramsey and the Franklyns drove off to the east, while those remaining, in Lord Embleton's carriage and a hired chaise, proceeded northwards.

The journey to Strathinver took four long, tortuous days, through dreary autumn weather, bad roads and horses that plodded along in a dispirited manner. Olivia's companions were no more lively, for Lord Embleton was stonily silent for much of the time, Effie sullen and Lord Rennington gloomy.

Olivia was not downhearted, however, for who could be miserable when Robert Osborn was of the party? His mere presence never failed to lift her spirits. It was a fortunate circumstance that Effie was so irate at being hauled up to Scotland by her implacable brother that she chose to travel for much of the time with the servants in the second carriage, thereby leaving a seat for Osborn in the principal coach. However taciturn Lords Embleton and Rennington might choose to be, Osborn managed to keep Olivia thoroughly entertained. She had no idea what they talked about, but whatever it was, it beguiled away the hours splendidly.

As they finally turned aside off the rutted track laughingly described as a road onto the even more rutted drive of Strathinver, Olivia flattened herself against the window of the carriage to catch the first glimpse of the house.

"Wait until we emerge from the trees," Osborn said, smiling understandingly at her. "You will have a perfect view from this side."

And there it was, a solid building with a high central tower and two lower arms set at a right angle, with smooth lawns sloping down to a sinuously meandering river. From one of the arms, another long wing with a multitude of towers protruded, giving a wide façade overlooking formal gardens. As Olivia watched, a shaft of sunlight broke through the heavy clouds and set the stonework sparkling.

"It is beautiful!" Olivia said, rather awed.

"I am glad you like it," he said, smiling at her. "I like it too — in small doses."

"Oh, you are funning, I am sure! Who could not like living here? Look! Deer! How lovely! And you have your own river."

"Every self-respecting Scottish estate can manage that," he said. "So much rain means many, *many* rivers."

"And fish," she said. "I am very fond of salmon... or whatever is in your river."

"Yes, salmon, also trout and grayling."

"That sounds delicious," she said with a sigh. "Edible grayling instead of wayward Lord Grayling. How strange to be named after a fish! He might have been Lord Eel or Lord Haddock. But how lovely everything looks in the sun! I do not know why you complain about the weather here, Osborn. It seems perfectly benign to me."

"That must be your doing. You have brought the sunshine with you."

The carriage drew to a halt before the front door, which nestled in a narrow turret set between the two principal arms of the building. It was fortunate that it was not raining, for their carriage could not get very close to the door itself for the assortment of carts, ladders, buckets, boxes and other signs of work going on.

"Oh, heavens! I had almost forgotten the builders," Osborn said gloomily. "Now we shall have nothing but hammering all day, half the rooms out of commission and the house filled with the smell of new paint."

"I like the smell of paint," Olivia said. "Mama is always refurbishing one room or another, and when she runs out of rooms at Corland, she visits

Josie or Izzy, and refurbishes there, too." Then, sadly, she added, "I suppose nothing will be done at Corland from now on. Every room will stay just as it is, without Mama to change it."

"You miss her," he said, with such sympathy that she could only nod wordlessly, feeling tears prickling.

"We all miss her," her father said, his voice trembling.

Effie's footman found a route through the builders' detritus to open the carriage door, and they all carefully picked their way to the entrance, where the door remained firmly closed. The footman rang the bell, then lifted the heavy knocker several times, and then, when nothing happened, rang the bell again.

"Oh, let us not stand about in this ridiculous manner," Osborn said, moving forwards. "The door will not be locked, I should hope."

He had barely set his hand to the doorknob when the door was heaved open and several men in smocks and brightly coloured neckerchiefs barrelled out, almost knocking him over. One of them cursed loudly, and Osborn picked him up bodily, lifting him clean off his feet before setting him down none too gently.

"Language! There are ladies in the vicinity. Who are you, anyway, and why are you using my front door instead of the servants' entrance?"

The man visibly paled. "William Page, if it please your lordship, sir, and... and... we're doin' the 'all, sir."

"Doing the hall, are you?" He sighed. "I suppose it could be worse. It could be the dining room... or my book room."

"Dinin' room next week," the man said helpfully. "Book room? We doin' the book room, Bill?"

"Week after."

Osborn groaned.

By this time, a butler had appeared and in a stately manner shooed the painters away and ushered the arrivals into the entrance hall. The painters were indeed *doing* the hall, for the entire floor was covered with sheets liberally spattered with paint of a multitude of colours. Buckets of paint stood about and ladders leaned against walls as several men worked away at the ceiling, one end of which was a dingy brown and the other freshly painted a soft, creamy colour. The wood panels on the walls had already been painted a pale golden colour, to match the balustrade of a balcony running the full length of one side.

"This will be lovely when it is finished," Olivia said, leaning backwards to admired the intricate plasterwork on the ceiling. "Such pretty colours! It will feel like sunshine every day."

"I suppose it was very dismal before," he said. "These walls were almost black, and the floor under these sheets *is* black — black marble, so that will still be dark."

"Some rugs will lighten it," she said, "or you might replace it with a paler marble, or a pattern of some sort."

He laughed. "You must talk to Mama about it. All this is her doing."

"Then she has excellent taste."

More servants now began to stream out of the service stairs to attend to the visitors. Olivia was shown to a bedroom which had not yet been refurbished, for it featured dark wood panels and heavy, old-fashioned furniture. The bed looked comfortable, however, and there was a delightful view over a part of the river and the woods beyond, with the tip of a tower projecting above the trees. A continuous stream of maids arrived with the usual bed linen, hot water and warmed towels, but also plates of cakes and delicate pastries, which Olivia nibbled appreciatively as she washed and changed into a fresh gown.

Another maid arrived, and bobbing a curtsy, said in a charming Scottish brogue, "Lord Kiltarlity's outside, milady, asking if ye've everything ye need."

Trying not to laugh, for her mouth was full of deliciously crumbly pastry, Olivia went to the door and peeped out. He was lounging against the wall, smiling, eyes twinkling. Oh, those eyes! How could she resist a man who looked at her that way?

Swallowing hastily, she said, "Come in, Osborn. There are a dozen maids in here to protect my virtue, so you need not worry about that, but you must tell me what the tower is that I can see from my window."

"It is not exactly a tower, but the ground rises in that direction, so it appears above the trees. It is the local gaol."

"The gaol! Is there a town there, too?"

"No, which is the problem. We are so far from any town that we have to deal with our own lawbreakers here. I have promised Embleton that if Lady Euphemia is troublesome, I shall have her thrown in the dungeon. She is not quite sure whether I am serious. Do you like my cook's creations? She has such a light hand with pastry."

Olivia could only agree, and they sat in companionable comfort on the window seat, working their way steadily through an assortment of edibles, and talking of who knows what, when the door burst open and Lady Kiltarlity swept in, her face stormy.

"Here you are, Kiltarlity! What are you about, to be skulking here instead of attending to your guests?"

"Lady Olivia is my guest, too, Mama. May I not attend to her, also?"

"Not in her bedchamber, no. Miss Atherton, may I—?"

Osborn jumped to his feet. "*Lady* Olivia, if you please!"

Lady Kiltarlity looked him up and down imperiously. "In my house, Kiltarlity, we use correct forms of address."

"And in *my* house, we employ courtesy above correctness."

For a moment, they glared at each other.

Olivia laid a hand on his sleeve. "You are very kind, Lord Kiltarlity, and I appreciate that you still call me *'Lady Olivia',* but I am not entitled to that form of address any longer. Above all things, you must not fall out with your mama on my account."

He smiled at her, patting her hand. "Then I will not, and I shall bite my tongue whenever she calls you *'Miss Atherton'*, for your sake. And she is certainly right in other ways, for I should not be here in your bedroom, no matter how many maids are here, and I should be attending to my other guests. Shall we make our way downstairs? I shall undertake to convey the pastries in safety."

"There are more in the drawing room," Lady Kiltarlity said, with the hint of a smile. "Leave the platter here in case our guest... in case *Lady Olivia* should feel hungry in the night."

"How very kind you are!" Olivia cried, jumping up and wrapping an arm around Lady Kiltarlity's. "Both kind and with a wonderful eye for colour. I was just telling Osborn... Lord Kiltarlity how much I admire the new scheme in the entrance hall."

"Oh! You like it, do you? Then do come and see the winter drawing room. I am rather proud of my choices there."

And the two went off arm in arm, leaving Osborn to trail behind them.

20: Fishing

Robert could scarcely believe how wonderful it was to have Olivia at Strathinver. Every night he went to sleep smiling, knowing that she was under the same roof, and when he woke, joy burst over him as he remembered. He could not suppress the well of happiness that bubbled up in him constantly, even though he knew she was there solely to further her acquaintance with Embleton.

As far as that went, he had to concede that her gentle temperament and pleasing manners were beginning to make inroads with the marquess. It would perhaps be too much to say that he was developing an attachment for her, since Embleton was not a man whose wishes and feelings were easy to read. If he were falling in love, he kept the signs well hidden. But still, Robert noticed every time the marquess offered Olivia his arm as they were walking or chose to sit beside her at table or showed her an interesting tidbit from a newspaper or book. The argument at Grayling Hall and Olivia's tempestuous outburst that she wished she might never see him again had all been forgotten.

For himself, he found it increasingly difficult to keep her at arm's length. He wanted her to be happy, certainly, and if her happiness lay with the marquess, he would do his very best to smile and wish them both well. Yet with every day that passed, he became more certain that his own happiness was inextricably linked with her, and he grew more and more dissatisfied with his resolution. Such madness, to concede the battle without a shot being fired! If only he dared to fight for her himself, to tell her how much he loved her and wished to share his life with her.

She was so perfect for him, he knew that now. She had managed to wrap his mother round her thumb, merely by admiring the improvements being undertaken. On entering the winter drawing room, Olivia had exclaimed at the vibrant yellows and greens, and cried out, "Oh, but it is just like spring! It will always be spring in here, even when there is snow on the ground outside. How lovely!"

And Mama had melted in a moment, and said yes, that was exactly the intention, and how clever of her to surmise it, and would she come and look at the music room and see what she thought of the plans for that? And somehow, the two had spent the rest of the day examining samples of wall coverings and paint, deep in discussion.

Robert had retreated to his book room, a dark, untidy but irredeemably masculine hiding place. It was depressing, because the desk was piled high with letters and bills and terse little notes from one or other of his stewards, full of words like *'urgent'* or *'immediate'* underlined three times. But, mindful of Olivia's advice that he should consider the happiness of the people over whose lives he now had dominion, he began to open the unopened letters and quickly read the others, assigning them to suitable piles, pondering how happiness might be assigned to difficulties with a waterlogged field or low water at a mill somewhere in the West Country. Why did he own a mill in Cornwall anyway?

He was still puzzling over it when his mother and Olivia arrived, in full improvement mode, to discuss strategies for his book room. He sighed, and put his head in his hands.

There was a gurgle of merriment near his left ear. "A brandy, my lord? You look as if you might need it."

He looked up into Olivia's laughing face. "Make it a large one."

Obediently she crossed to the side table where the decanters stood, read the labels and then poured his brandy. Still holding the decanter, she looked at him thoughtfully and then doubled the quantity in the glass.

"There! That should sustain you. But really, ma'am," she said, turning to Lady Kiltarlity, "I do not think this room can be improved upon. I imagine it is much as the late Lord Kiltarlity left it, and as such, perhaps it should remain so, in his memory."

"It is true, it was very much his domain, and I suppose it may be left, for now. Kiltarlity will not wish to change it, I am sure. Very well, the dining room next."

So saying, she swept out, and with a mischievous smile, Olivia followed. Robert sipped his brandy, then laughed. What a woman she was, his Olivia! Such a clever little thing, managing to preserve this one room from his mother's determination to refurbish the house from top to bottom. Even his father's bedroom, now his, had been repainted, although the furniture was the same. But this room, the only one that was truly his, would remain untouched, thanks to Olivia.

***

Strathinver was perfect, Olivia decided. Indoors, she drifted from room to room with a permanent smile on her face. Only a few of the rooms had been refurbished, but when Lady Kiltarlity's plans were fully implemented, the house would be one of the finest in the Kingdom. Outside, there were formal gardens for strolling about, the planting somewhat neglected although that merely added to the charm. However, the greater park was, by the designer's art, seemingly untamed, yet with a multitude of paths wandering over hills and along valleys, winding through woods and along the gently flowing river, broad but shallow, its clear brown water burbling merrily over a stony bed. It was all enchanting.

The men were drawn to the river for a different reason. Lord Embleton was delighted with the fishing to be had there, calling it the best sport he had ever had. Olivia's father was very happy to spend hours there each day, too, and since the rest of the party liked to be nearby, it became a habit for the servants to erect a small pavilion on the bank near the fishermen, supplied with a brazier and a mountain of thick woollen blankets, where the ladies, well wrapped against the autumnal chill, could sit to read or chat, and enjoy a light repast.

Olivia found that the two Osborn sisters, with whom she was quickly on terms of intimacy, were not at all the embittered spinsters that Lady Harraby had asserted. They were watchful of Lord Embleton, and lost no opportunity to talk to him, but they did not put themselves forward, and joked that there was little point with Olivia around.

Osborn was not always there, for he had a multitude of duties to attend to, but sometimes he would arrive and pull a chair near to Olivia, and recount some difficulty he had encountered with the tenant farmers or one of his many holdings and investments scattered all over the Kingdom. Surprisingly often she would find herself saying, "Have you thought that you might…?", and he would listen intently, his anxious face gradually lightening. Then he would smile and say, "What a clever little thing you are, Livvy! That sounds precisely the thing to do." And sometimes, to her delight, he would linger in the pavilion, his shapely legs stretched out and a glass of wine in his hand, keeping her in a ripple of amusement with his lighthearted repartee. If she could not talk to Lord Embleton, his whole focus on the river, then Osborn was a most acceptable substitute.

Effie came on these outings too, but she was not a comfortable companion. Having spent the first few days in a fever of impatience to know how Lady Harraby and the new babe were going on, as soon as word was received of a sturdy son and heir, her impatience switched to the lack of company. Even when she joined the fishing expeditions, she remained restless. While Lady Kiltarlity, her daughters and Olivia sat decorously in the pavilion, she paced restlessly about on the river bank, getting in the way of the fishermen, annoying the gamekeeper charged with assisting them by a succession of pointless questions, and quarrelling with her brother as much as she could. He ignored her most of the time, but every once in a while, he would explode into a tirade of stutter-free invective. Then she would retreat to the pavilion with a little smile on her face.

"You do it deliberately," Olivia said to her one day. "You intentionally provoke him."

"Of course!" she said, with a quick laugh. "If I annoy him sufficiently, he will send me away from this God-forsaken place."

"But Strathinver is wonderful!" Olivia protested. "Why would you ever want to leave it?"

Osborn smiled at this praise for his home, but Effie pulled a face. "Oh, it is well enough, I suppose, but one grows bored with the same few faces every day."

"And you have no one to flirt with," Olivia said.

"True, since Lord Kiltarlity is most disobliging in that way, for he will only flirt with you."

Osborn gave a bark of laughter. "Certainly, for your brother is a fierce defender of his sister, and I have no wish to meet him at dawn. He is both a crack shot and a fine fencer, too. I value my life too highly to take the risk, Lady Euphemia."

"Pft! Men are such cowards. Oh, if only I could escape from here!"

"There are some fine rides around Strathinver," Osborn said. "You could escape at least for an hour or two, if you wish."

"Do you have any decent horseflesh in your stables? I like a mount with some spirit."

"I would expect no less of you," Osborn said gallantly. "Would you like to inspect the possibilities now? It is a little late in the day to set out today, but I would be happy to accompany you tomorrow. Olivia, would you care to join us?"

"I suspect I would not be able to keep up with Effie," she said, smiling. "Besides, I must write some letters tomorrow. I have neglected my pen abominably since I arrived here, and must remedy the situation soon. Poor Mama will want to know how Papa is coping, and then there is Aunt Alice, Aunt Jane, Josie... so many letters."

"Not Izzy?" Osborn said.

"Mama is staying with Izzy, so one letter will inform both of them," she responded, although a little disappointed in him. Still thinking of Izzy! He had never got over the fact that she had married Lord Farramont instead.

"Then tomorrow I shall take Lady Euphemia out for a long ride — if Embleton gives his approval, that is."

Effie glowered at him. "As if I need *his* approval for anything I wish to do!"

"Unfortunately, you do," Osborn said, with a wry smile. "You are but eighteen years of age, he is your older brother and he is responsible for you while you are in his care."

"But he keeps me a prisoner here!" she cried. "Surely there is no need for it. Why can we not make some visits? Or receive visitors here?"

"If anyone calls, you may join Mama and my sisters to receive them," he said, "but Embleton has told me not to make a carriage available to you, and not to permit you to leave the estate. Happily, the estate is large, so we may enjoy some fine riding without breaching your brother's conditions."

"There is an old abbey that you might find of interest," Olivia said. "Not that there is much of it left, but it is a fine place for a picnic in the summer, or an interesting ride at any time."

"You have been there?" Effie said. "I thought you had never been to Strathinver before."

"I have not, because there was usually no one here, but I have stayed at Lochmaben many times. It is only a few miles from here, and the abbey is a favourite spot with the family."

"Lochmaben? The home of the Duke of Lochmaben?"

Olivia agreed to it. "They are our cousins. Grandmama's sister married the previous duke. You would find men enough to flirt with there, for the duke and duchess always have the place filled to the rafters with visitors. What a pity you cannot even call there."

"What a pity indeed," Effie said lightly. "Olivia, have you eaten all those raspberry tartlets? Not even one left?"

"Oh dear," Olivia said, staring guiltily at the empty plate. "I did not notice."

That evening was perhaps the most pleasant Olivia had passed at Strathinver. At dinner, she found herself without the least manipulation on her part seated beside Lord Embleton, and although she carried most of the conversation, out of consideration for his poor stutter, he was more than usually talkative. He was surprisingly forthcoming about his home at Howland Manor, and the new house which was being built.

"B-B-Bridgeworth, it is to b-be c-called," he said. "V-Very unim-maginative."

"But most appropriate, to have your father's principal seat named after his title," she said. "Is it to be very large, like Blenheim? One always feels that a ducal seat should be very grand, much grander than a normal house."

He pulled a face. "The architect would m-make it so, but m-m-my father only wants it to be m-m-modern."

"Ah! I understand. Light and airy, and a proper range in the kitchen."

He smiled. "The k-kitchen! How p-practical you are, Lady Olivia."

"Kitchens are very important, Lord Embleton, together with draught-free windows, chimneys that do not smoke and no mice in the wainscoting."

That made him laugh out loud. "You must c-come to visit us one day, to advise m-my father."

"Surely your mother—?"

But he shook his head. "Not interested in d-domestic affairs. She is a p-painter."

"Oh!" A duchess who preferred to paint rather than take an interest in kitchens was somewhat outside her experience. In Olivia's view, nothing could be more conducive to family harmony than an efficient kitchen, and, after the nursery, it was the principal duty of the lady of the house, but she could hardly say so. Her ambition to be the next Duchess of Bridgeworth had veered back and forth lately, as the marquess's temper had waxed and waned, but it had not quite evaporated, and that precluded her from any hint of criticism of the present one.

The marquess must have read her thoughts, however, for he smiled and said, "A duchess may do as she p-pleases."

That too was a new concept, and as the marquess was drawn away to talk to Lady Kiltarlity on his other side, Olivia was left to eat in thoughtful silence, mulling over the oddity of anyone, even a duchess, who could do as she pleased. If *she* were a duchess, would she do just what she pleased? And what would that be? She could think of nothing except the tenets that her mother had drilled into her head for many years — that she must put her husband first, always, then her sons, followed by her daughters and the servants, and finally the tenant farmers and villagers and tradesmen and all those who depended upon her. There was nothing about painting. An unmarried girl might indulge in sketching or watercolours, just as she learned to play an instrument and sing Scottish airs, as an accomplishment to attract a husband, but once she married, she had more serious responsibilities.

She considered her sisters and their marriages. Josie was besotted by her babies, that seemed to be her primary concern. As for Izzy, she liked to host society dinners, which she claimed helped her husband with his political interests, but she simply loved surrounding herself with lively company. So in a way, both of them were doing as they pleased. Only Mama, still refusing to marry Papa to leave him free to have legitimate sons, was determinedly doing what she felt was best for him and the family.

But what of Olivia herself? What would her life be like if she married Lord Embleton, leaving behind all the familiarity of home, and everyone she knew, and becoming part of an entirely new family? She would grow accustomed, she supposed. It was the fate of all women who married to leave their natal home and transplant themselves into alien soil, and with an amiable man, that would be no hardship, would it? But then how amiable was Lord Embleton? He could be very pleasant when he chose to be, but she still shivered at the memory of his reproofs when he thought she had stepped out of line. Well, she would just have to be very sure not to do so once they were married.

And somehow, this thought did not please her.

After dinner, the marquess approached her directly, and suggested a game of backgammon. Much as she wanted to enjoy a tête-à-tête with him, she had to confess that she was unskilled in the game.

"Chess?" he said with a smile. "Or cribbage, perhaps?"

"Oh, yes! Cribbage! I know that one! I play with my cousins all the time."

And so they played cribbage, not talking much beyond the needs of the game, but to Olivia it felt for the first time as if Lord Embleton was courting her, or at least seeing her as a person worthy of his attention. And she would not be human if she did not glory just a little in the undivided attention of a future duke. So when she woke early the next morning, she sat down at the small writing table in her room, and dashed off a whole series of letters to Mama, Aunt Alice, Aunt Jane and Josie, to reassure them that she and Papa were well, and mentioning, quite as an aside, that Lord Embleton had talked of his family home to her at some length. There was not much else to say of the marquess, but she knew her relations would be amused by Osborn's funny little sayings, for he was vastly entertaining. That filled the rest of the letters most satisfactorily, and she went down to breakfast in a cloud of virtuous awareness of a duty well completed.

Papa was still a little downcast, but the prospect of another day at the river brought a smile to his face when Osborn suggested it.

"Embleton?" Osborn said. "Would you care to fish again, or shall I open up the gunroom for you?"

"You are to ride w-with Effie this m-m-morning, I understand, K-Kiltarlity, in which case I shall ride with you. That g-girl needs to be watched. Is she not usually d-down by this t-time?"

"She is, yes," Olivia said. "Shall I go up and see what is keeping her? Perhaps she is having a tray in her room this morning."

But before this impulse could be acted upon, loud voices were heard outside, and the butler entered in some dismay.

"Whatever is it, Winthrop?" Osborn said, frowning a little at the unseemly disruption.

"My lord... I am afraid that—" He glanced at Lord Embleton. "It is the Lady Euphemia, my lord. She went riding this morning, and naturally a groom went with her, but..."

Lord Embleton set down his coffee cup with a crash. "Tell me the worst, Winthrop. Where has she gone?"

"To Lochmaben, my lord. The groom could not catch her to stay the horse, and once she was there, she declared that she would not return here. She sent him back with a letter for you, my lord."

"A letter? Where is it?"

"He has instructions to deliver it into your own hands, my lord. He is in the hall now."

They all trooped into the hall, where the groom, wild-eyed with anguish, and muttering apologies repeatedly, handed over a note. Lord Embleton read it, then, with a growl, crumpled it into a ball and pressed it into Olivia's hand.

"This is your fault! You truly are the most meddlesome female it has ever been my misfortune to encounter. Now look what you have done! Kiltarlity, you can lend me a horse, I am sure."

He stamped away towards the stables.

The note was brief. *'Embleton, Since Olivia was so obliging as to remind me of the existence of Lochmaben, I have sought refuge there from your tyranny. Effie.'*

Olivia shook her head in disbelief. It was so unfair! How could Effie's wildness be laid at her door? And now that foolish girl had destroyed all Olivia's hopes of Lord Embleton. Surely there could be no return from this final disagreement? She would never now be a duchess.

21: Quarrel And Reconciliation

Robert watched Olivia's retreating back. Every instinct urged him to go after her, but he had Embleton to deal with, not to mention a very upset groom, sure that he was about to be turned off without a character for allowing Lady Euphemia to escape. By the time he had reassured the groom, urged the rest of the guests back into the breakfast parlour and arranged for a fast horse for Embleton, Olivia was long gone.

He searched methodically room by room, but it took him some time to discover that she was not in the house at all. Her maid discovered that a bonnet and cloak had been taken, so Robert fetched his own greatcoat and began a systematic search of the grounds.

She was pacing up and down a small clearing in the shrubbery, quite hidden from the house, head down, holding the cloak tight around her, for the air was chilling. Her face, usually smiling and happy, was pale and drawn.

"Olivia? Are you quite well?"

She stopped, looked up at him, then commenced pacing again. "I am quite well."

Her voice was flat, and his heart went out to her. His poor Olivia! If only he could take her in his arms, purely to comfort her, as he would a sister... perhaps not quite as a sister, but she so badly needed comfort and yet he dared not offer it.

"I am so sorry," he said quietly, feeling utterly helpless. "You were getting on so well with him, too. I truly thought—" But he could not, *would* not put the thought into words.

She looked up at him then, a rueful little smile flickering across her face. "Oh yes! Last night... cribbage... and he talked about his house! That seemed so promising. But I shall never be a duchess now. So much for my foolish hopes."

"Not foolish!" he said, although the words almost stuck in his throat.

The head dropped again as she paced, this way and that across the clearing, slowly and without purpose. "You are very kind to say so, but I do not think Lord Embleton ever saw me in a romantic light. He has not a romantic nature, I suspect, so there was never the least possibility that he would fall in love with me."

"How could he not?" Robert cried, before he could stop himself. She looked up at him then, her lips parted in surprise. And somehow, he could not say how, for he had not intended it, the words tumbled out of him in an unstoppable flood. "Livvy, you must not despair, for you are the most lovable girl in the Kingdom, and even if Embleton does not see it, there are plenty who do. *I* do, for one. I can never make you a duchess, which is what you deserve to be, for no one could grace such a position more than you, but if you think you could put up with only being a countess, then marry me instead. You are so good for me, Livvy, for you always know what to do with the estate business, and you make me feel it is not so onerous... that perhaps one day I shall be able to manage it without becoming blue-devilled. I would love to play cribbage with you, whenever it pleases you, and I know you like Strathinver and you get on with Mama and my sisters, and heaven only knows, I never thought I would find anyone who would. Izzy never did and—"

"Izzy!" she hissed. "It is always about *Izzy*, not about me, because how could I ever compare with the Incomparable? So beautiful, so witty, so clever, so *everything,* while I am nothing but a shadow of her!"

"No," he said faintly. "No, that is not how it is at all. It is *you* I love, Livvy, far more than I ever loved Izzy..."

He stopped, realising his mistake at once, for her face darkened with rage. *"Izzy, Izzy, Izzy!* You are obsessed with her."

His own anger was rising, for he was offering her his heart, his name, the very soul of his being, and she just tossed it all aside as if it were nothing. "I think it is you who are obsessed, Livvy. Why do you compare yourself with her? Why think of yourself as a mere shadow of your sister? You are yourself, and it is you I love, not Izzy. You are *better* than her in a thousand ways."

"Now I know you are lying to me!" she cried, tears falling although she appeared not to notice. "I am not... will never be better than her, because she is the Incomparable and I am just a ghost, remember? A ghost who looks like her but falls short in every way. Oh, leave me alone, Osborn! I do not want your platitudes. Go away!"

The small corner of his mind that was still rational reminded him that she was a guest at Strathinver, so there would be other opportunities when she was less overwrought to press his suit. He would prepare better for the next time, and choose his words more carefully. What a fool he was to allow himself to be swept away by his own emotions! After controlling himself while she put herself in Embleton's way, he should at least have given her time to recover from her disagreement with him.

And now he had made her cry! She had turned her back on him, her shoulders heaving as she sobbed. Never had he wanted to hold her more! He raised his arms to reach for her without any conscious thought. But he must not. That was one thing he could do for her, to obey her last words to him and leave her to her grief. Quietly he crept away, but inside his heart ached with a pain so physical he wondered how on earth he was to get through the rest of the day. Could he appear as his usual insouciant self? He must, for Olivia's sake.

Hardly aware of his whereabouts, he was shocked to be hailed by a male voice. Surely it could not be—? But it was indeed Embleton.

"Kiltarlity! W-w-where is she? L-Lady Olivia?"

"I thought you had gone to Lochmaben," Robert said, realising as he spoke how stupid that sounded.

"Later. Must ap-p-pologise."

"Oh." An apology! Then Olivia's hopes had not foundered irretrievably. Robert's spirits, already low, sank even further. But perhaps he could put Embleton off? Say he had not seen Olivia... but no. She deserved her chance of happiness, however bitter that might be for him. "She... she is down that path. Or she was. That is where I saw her."

Eagerly, Embleton raced off, and Robert was left to wonder whether it was too early in the day for brandy. A lot of brandy.

***

Olivia paced and wept, and wept and paced, back and forth across the small clearing, her feet crunching on the fallen leaves strewn everywhere. Why did Robert Osborn torment her so? Why did he pretend to love her, when Izzy was still uppermost in his thoughts? He had loved her passionately five years ago, and he still loved her now — loved her so well that he would take even Olivia, the pale imitation, to have some trace of Izzy in his life.

Maddening man! And yet, so kind, so charming, so amusing. He never failed to lift her spirits, whereas Lord Embleton— But no, that was not a thought she wanted to pursue. The marquess was a serious man, not a fribble like Robert. And the stutter, too, was a hindrance to the lighthearted banter of which Robert was such a master. It was wrong of her to compare them, for the quiet marquess could not fail to be the loser.

And now there was no point in thinking about either of them, for she had quarrelled with Robert and Lord Embleton had shouted at her *again*. This time it truly was not her fault... was it? She could not be blamed if Effie had taken her casual words and used them to run away. But he was angry with her all the same.

It was all so difficult, and there was no one to talk to about it. Papa was still sunk in gloom about his own romantic affairs, and there was no one else. No Mama, in particular — how she longed for Mama to hold her tight and tell her briskly that everything would come right in the end, and not to worry about it. It would even be good to unburden herself to Aunt Jane or Aunt Alice, for although they never quite made her feel better in the way that Mama would, at least they would not shout at her and tell her she was a meddlesome creature.

Oh, if only Robert had not tried to propose to her! If only he had simply held her, as he had that day in the secret room, when she had wept all over him and he had hugged her until she felt better and then fed her wine and cakes. Robert always made her feel better, she thought wistfully. Even in this year of all horrible years, with Granny so ill and that terrible business with Uncle Arthur — murdered in his bed with an axe! Such an unspeakable thing to happen! Then the whole business with being illegitimate, too. And the poor lady who disappeared, Mrs Edgerton's friend, had been murdered and then Bertram had been shot! Such a dreadful succession of events that would have rendered her quite prostrate with horror, except that Robert had managed to lift her spirits. And now she had fallen out with him, and she was not sure that the breach could ever be mended. That thought filled her with longing for the happier times when he had simply flirted with her and—

A sound. Footsteps nearby, scuffing through the leaves.

Before Olivia had time to prepare herself for an intrusion, the Marquess of Embleton burst into the clearing. His face lightened when he saw her, then immediately darkened again.

"No, no, no!" he murmured, closing the distance between them in a few steps. "No t-tears! M-My fault. So s-s-sorry!"

Quite unable to speak, Olivia waved a hand about, trying to convey… she hardly knew what. Her mind was too overwhelmed to formulate a coherent response.

"M-must not cry!" he said, sounding rather frantic. "No tears. Never meant… please… marry me."

And then, somewhat clumsily, he put his arms around her and patted her back, but that just made her cry even more.

"No, no!" he said again, more loudly. "Sorry! S-Stupid of me. Forgive me. Marry me. Please."

What else could she do? It was what she had wanted for years, and here it was, her life's ambition achieved at last. So she lifted her head and, quite unable to speak, nodded her acceptance.

He smiled, taking her by the shoulders to hold her at arm's length. "B-better?" he said.

And she nodded again, although oddly she could not stop crying. Tears of happiness, she supposed, for what else could they be? She could not be sad... could she?

***

Robert returned to the house, and sat quietly in his study, his arms resting on the empty desk. And then he waited. He was not quite sure what it was that he was waiting for, but he knew there would be something. Another quarrel, perhaps, between Olivia and Embleton, which would restore him to equanimity and that tiny sliver of hope that had never quite left him.

Or would it be something worse, something to bring him to total despair?

He had not long to wait, for before the clock on the mantel struck the next hour, he heard voices outside and then, after a brisk knock, Embleton came in. He looked... Robert could not quite interpret his expression. Bemused, perhaps. Well, Olivia could have that effect on a man.

Embleton gave a little cough, but said nothing. Now he looked awkward, almost guilty. Robert's insides clenched. It was bad news, he knew i t!

Another cough, then Embleton said, "L-lady Ol— Ol— Ol—"

"Olivia," Robert said, his nerves too shredded to wait.

With a quick nod, Embleton went on, "Betrothed. Going to Lochm-m-maben now."

And without another word, he turned and left the room.

Robert poured himself a large brandy, but then he set the glass carefully down on his desk and sat in his chair, head in hands. His desolation was too great even for brandy. Betrothed! That was the end of it, then. She would marry Embleton and be a marchioness and in time a duchess, and Robert would have to try to live without her for the rest of his life. Somehow.

He was vaguely aware of disturbances going on, of carriages on the drive, voices in the entrance hall below, and feet tapping up and down the stairs and going past his door. He did not care. If the house was on fire, presumably someone would inform him, but nothing else was worth moving for.

After a while, a tentative knock on the door was followed by the apologetic figure of the butler.

"Beg pardon, my lord, but the Duchess of Lochmaben and the Marchioness of Galloway are here."

"Are they?" Robert said dully, not much interested. "Why?"

Winthrop gave a deprecating cough. "Lord Embleton, Lord Rennington and the Lady Olivia Atherton are removing to Lochmaben Castle, my lord. They are about to depart." Then, after a long pause. "Shall I tell them you are engaged at present, my lord? Or indisposed?"

Robert stared at him blankly.

Giving up, the butler bowed. "I am sure Lady Kiltarlity will say all that is proper on your behalf, my lord."

And then he was gone, and before long all the voices moved outside, and after a little while, the Lochmaben carriages crunched away down the drive, the doors closed and all was quiet again.

For a long time, no one intruded upon Robert's misery. Occasionally he heard footsteps on the passageway outside his door, or in the entrance hall below, but no one disturbed him for some time. But then the door opened and a face peeped round. His sister Lucy.

"I came to see if you wanted anything."

Mutely, he shook his head.

Undeterred, she came in and closed the door, then placed a sheet of drawing paper on the desk in front of him.

"I am not sure whether it will help or not, but I took a likeness of Olivia just a day or two ago. I thought you might like to have it. To remember her by."

Picking it up, he smiled a little. "Thank you! It is very good — very like her."

"I think it is one of my better efforts, yes. Rob..." She hesitated. "We are all sorry about it. Even Mama liked her, and you know how hard to please *she* is! Well, she was so against Izzy, but Olivia is quite different. In ways, I mean, not in looks. They are like twins in appearance."

"Do you think so?" Robert said, frowning as he gazed at the portrait. "Well, yes, superficially they are alike, but once one comes to know Olivia, one sees a multitude of small differences. The chin, for instance, or the eyes. Izzy's eyes are closer together, I am sure." *And there was that dimple*, he thought with a wrench of pain.

"Perhaps. Rob... you will get over this. I know how much it hurts to lose someone you love, but trust me, it will fade."

"How long does it take? To forget, I mean."

"Forget! Oh, one never *forgets.* One simply grows accustomed. The pain becomes duller, something one simply lives with every day, but one never quite gets over it. Do you remember when I fell off my pony when I was nine? I broke my arm — the left one, fortunately, and it healed perfectly well, but I am still aware of it, when someone grabs hold of me too forcefully in the dance, or when I roll over in bed awkwardly, or just lean on it too hard. Then it hurts and reminds me. A failed love is like that. But you must know that, after Izzy."

"No," he said slowly. "It was never like this, not with Izzy. I was angry, more than anything else. Jealous of Farramont, of course. But I realised very quickly that she would never have suited me. But Olivia..." He took a ragged breath. "She was perfect, Lucy. Perfect for me, I mean. She would hate me making the comparison, but she had all the good parts of Izzy without the constant high drama. Izzy would have been the most wearing wife, I imagine. Look at the dance she led Farramont this summer. The poor fellow had to follow her all over the north."

"And had to kidnap her in the end to stop her running away," Lucy said giggling. "I am not quite sure what Lord Farramont sees in her, to be honest, although she is very beautiful, and lively in company, but then so is Olivia."

"Exactly!" Robert cried. "Oh, Lucy, what am I going to do?"

"You are going to hide away here and keep away from the brandy," she said firmly, moving the glass out of reach. "You never know, she might yet realise what a mistake she has made, giving you up for a blockhead like Embleton."

"He is not a blockhead," Robert said, feeling an obligation to be fair, despite it all. "In fact, he is reputed to be very clever — writes Latin poetry and such like."

"Wrong. He is a blockhead. Olivia has been delicately putting herself into his path for weeks now, far more subtly than Lizzie or I could ever manage, and he has taken virtually no notice of her, until now. I am not sure what brought about the change, but it seems very sudden to me, so either of them might have second thoughts. So do not despair, brother dear, for Mama, Lizzie and I will go to Lochmaben to see how the betrothal is progressing, and perhaps drop a little hint in Olivia's ear that you are very sad just now. She is a gentle-hearted creature, and maybe that will bring her back to you, who knows?"

But Robert could not find any cause for optimism, for Olivia now had everything she had ever wanted. What could possibly tempt her back to Robert's side?

Nothing.

22: Lochmaben Castle

Olivia hardly knew what was happening. She was betrothed! Lord Embleton had finally proposed, although it was not the world's most romantic proposal. *'Forgive me. Marry me.'* That was all. No words of love, no kiss, no smiles of happiness, simply that rather awkward hug and then a nod of acknowledgement when she had accepted him. Almost as if he were resigned to his fate. Which was not at all how a lover should be, was it? Robert would have been more affectionate, she was sure.

Now why was she thinking of Robert at such a time? She must make allowances for Lord Embleton's difficulty with words. He would never murmur passionately to her, after all. But at least he could hold her and kiss her, she thought with just a little resentment. At least he could show some enthusiasm.

But then he had gone haring off to Lochmaben after Effie, and not an hour later had returned with the duchess and her daughter-in-law.

"You will not want to stay here, Olivia, not now that you are betrothed to Embleton," the duchess said briskly.

"Why not?" Olivia had said, bewildered.

The duchess had exchanged a glance with Lady Kiltarlity. "It is better so. Come and stay with us for a while, dear. Embleton will be there, too, so you can… well, make plans and so forth. Goodness, betrothed before your first season! What an astonishing girl you are."

Since Papa was agreeable to the move, to Lochmaben they went. Olivia had felt remarkably settled at Strathinver, with just Papa, Lord Embleton and Effie, as well as Robert and his family. Despite the number of builders and painters and carpenters underfoot, it had felt very restful, almost like home.

Lochmaben was not restful at all. It was a very different place from Strathinver, being both larger and also filled to the rafters with the most amazing assortment of guests. The duke and duchess loved nothing better than to fill the house with guests, and on her previous visits, Olivia, being of a sociable nature, had enjoyed the constant bustle. There had been long outings into the Scottish hills, or picnics beside gently flowing rivers, with visits to small towns of pretty stone-built houses. There were balls and musical evenings and afternoon parties on the castle's sweeping lawns.

The middle of December was less conducive to entertaining. Sleety showers kept all but the most intrepid indoors, where the only recourse was to arrange one's own entertainment. One group was working on a performance of Julius Caesar, while another was engaged in reciting poetry, preferably learnt by heart. Several ladies had commandeered the gallery to practice archery, and some of the matrons were busy renovating a large and very dilapidated tapestry.

Olivia would normally have been eager to join in one or other of these projects, but more often than not she found herself listlessly sitting in a window, watching the wind tossing the trees about, and listening to icy rain spattering against the window panes. Sometimes Lord Embleton sat with her, and then she made an effort to be her usual lively self, for what man would want a silent wife? But he himself seemed glum, and she could not honestly say that their betrothal brought happiness to either of them.

When she was alone, and especially in her bed at night, her thoughts were drawn to Robert, and that strange conversation they had had. '*You are yourself, and it is you I love, not Izzy. You are better than her in a thousand ways.*' So he had said, but she had not believed a word of it. She had refused even to listen to him. But what if she had? What if she had asked him what he meant by that... would he have convinced her? He had said he *loved* her, and she had hurled his words back in his face as if they were nothing.

And the worst thought, the one that had crept into her mind and buried itself there, so that she could not quite dislodge it was — did it matter if he only loved her because she was like Izzy? Love is love, however it arises, and he was too kind to turn away from her later because he discovered that in fact she was nothing like Izzy. And even if he loved the ghost of Izzy now, over time he might grow to love Olivia for herself in very truth.

If only she had paused for a moment, and *talked* to him, like a rational being, instead of shouting at him. But she had been so shaken by Lord Embleton's accusations that she had hardly known what either of them said. And then she had been so upset by quarrelling with Robert that she had accepted Lord Embleton's proposal without a thought. And now...

She hardly knew what she felt now. She ought to be happy, but she was too confused to know whether she was or not. All she was sure of was that a little corner of her hoped that Robert would come to Lochmaben. Not to fight for her, perhaps, but to show her that he was not still angry with her.

It would be some comfort, in all the strangeness of her betrothal, to know that they could be friends again.

But he did not come. Lady Kiltarlity and her daughters came, and stayed for the prescribed time and then left again, but when she asked how Robert was, they said only that he was a little out of spirits, which told her nothing. No doubt he had a difficult problem with a tenant or a coal mine or some such thing. That always put him out of frame.

It was the oddest thing, but she had never felt so alone as now, when she was surrounded by company and all of it lively and willing to amuse and be amused. At any other time she would have thrived in such a situation, delighting in the multitude of friendly faces. Yet she felt disconnected from everyone there. Her cousins cheerfully assumed she was happy and talked excitedly about her wedding and future life as a marchioness, and even Papa, who sighed and shook his head at the prospect of losing her, had no doubts about her betrothal. "What a wonderful thing for you," he said more than once. "You will be a great lady and rule over society. I congratulate you, daughter."

As for Effie, the friendship with Olivia had fallen into abeyance as quickly as it had arisen. Effie found fertile ground for her talents at Lochmaben, naturally, for there were innumerable young men, and a few beyond the years of youth, who were willing to indulge her desire for flirtation, and she skipped from one to another with a roguish twinkle in her eye and a definite spring in her step. Her brother made no effort to restrain her, and barely even seemed to notice her, so Olivia, who disapproved violently of such behaviour, felt that she could safely ignore her former friend. If Effie were to go her length while under the duke's roof, as seemed to be somewhat likely, the responsibility would be her brother's.

But the loss of her friend left her with no confidante, no one to whom she could turn and say, "Why do I feel so unsettled? Am I doing the right thing?"

Even with Lord Embleton, who should be her greatest friend and comfort, she could not be at ease. Olivia found she spent surprisingly little time with him. He was one of the crowd at breakfast, of course, and in the evenings he punctiliously sought her out and escorted her into dinner. Yet there was no eagerness on either side, and an awkwardness that she had not anticipated. Having devoted all her efforts to attracting his attention, now that she had it, she was not quite sure what to do with it.

There was a complication, too, in that he had made a new friend amongst the other guests at Lochmaben, and one not from his own level of society. Olivia had noticed her on their first evening at the castle, overhearing one voice at dinner that was most definitely from the merchant class, yet the girl seemed to be quite a favourite with the ladies of the castle, and Lady Galloway in particular.

"Who is she?" she asked one of the cousins at dinner that evening.

He smiled knowingly. "Ah yes. A gift from Izzy. That, my dear cousin, is Miss Ruth Plowman, the daughter of... well, I am not quite sure. A mill owner or wool merchant or some such. One of these northern men of enterprise. She was supposed to marry Sydney Davenport — you remember the Davenports, I am sure. Anyway, Izzy blew in like a summer storm, scotched the betrothal, scooped up the Miss Plowmans and brought them here, where they rapidly made themselves indispensable."

"The Miss Plowmans? How many of them are there?"

"Only the two, Miss Plowman and Miss Marian Plowman. That is the younger girl over there — the one in the pale blue dress. Very quiet, though — barely says a word."

"Her older sister makes up for it, however. Well, how like Izzy to stir things up!"

He laughed. "Indeed. Never a dull moment with her. Nor with you — betrothed to Embleton, indeed! Not the marrying kind, one might have supposed, but there we are. You Atherton girls draw us poor men like moths to the flame."

"I hope we do not burn anyone," Olivia said, rather offended. "Like bees to the blossom, perhaps, would be a more flattering description."

But he only laughed before turning to his companion on the other side.

Later that evening, however, Olivia's attention was drawn to Miss Plowman in the most unexpected way. The gentlemen had just begun to rejoin the ladies after dinner, amongst them Lord Embleton, who was deep in conversation with the duke, in his usual stuttering way. Miss Plowman broke off her own conversation with an *'Oh!'* of surprise, then, to Olivia's astonishment, she rose and with quick steps crossed the room to place herself before the marquess.

"No, no, more slowly," she said, loudly enough that half the room heard her. "Take a deep breath, look into my eyes and above all, speak slowly."

The marquess frowned, and the duke murmured, "Miss Plowman, I do not think—"

"No, it's possible to overcome it," she said briskly. "All he has to do is to speak more slowly and stop thinking about it so much. I've done it with Marian, and though she'll never be a chatterbox, she doesn't stutter any more. Why don't you try again? Deep breath, look into my eyes and speak slowly."

"I... d-do not th-think—"

"Slowly!" she cried. "Very slowly."

By this time, the room was almost silent, conversations drifting into nothingness as all eyes were fixed on the little grouping near the door.

"I... do... not... think... we... have... been... intro... duced, ma'am."

"Oh, very good!" she cried, clapping her hands together excitedly. "Ruth Plowman. And you are—?"

"The M-M-Mar—" He gave a huff of annoyance, then breathed in and exhaled slowly. "The... Mar... quess... of... Emb... le... ton."

"Ooh, another marquess! Pa will be so proud of me, mingling with all these great people. Are you going to be a duke, like the Marquess of Galloway? He'll be the next Duke of Lochmaben."

"I kn-know. I... know. My... father... is... Duke... of... Bridge... worth."

And he spent the rest of the evening locked in slow but unstuttering conversation with Miss Plowman and her sister. From then onwards, he seemed to spend an inordinate amount of time in their company, Miss Plowman chattering away, the marquess responding in a ponderous way and even Miss Marian Plowman taking a share in the conversation. It was not precisely that Olivia was jealous, for she was engaged to the marquess and Miss Plowman was not, but she could not help noticing that, although he was taciturn with Olivia, as with most people, he was much more talkative with the Plowman sisters, and even smiled occasionally.

***

About a week after Olivia had arrived at Lochmaben, the great bell in the tower above the entrance clanged to announce the arrival of visitors. This was a regular occurrence, for the duke and duchess were hospitable, and even in December there were guests arriving to stay or simply to pay a morning call. The bell was the signal for the duke and duchess and those of a curious nature to make their way to the entrance hall to greet the arrivals, and Olivia was amongst the many who thronged there, waiting to see who walked through the great double doors, and how wet or bedraggled they would be, for the weather was foul.

A man walked in dripping from head to foot, despite the valiant efforts of a footman with an umbrella. As soon as he removed his sodden hat, Olivia knew him, for no one else had quite such a distinctive head of golden hair.

"Lord Grayling!" she said, but before she could move forward, a figure shot past her.

"Julian!" cried Effie. "Have you come to rescue me?"

He smiled at the sight of her. "I have, but I am afraid you will have to marry me first. Your father insists upon it."

"You have talked to Papa?"

"I have, and he has given his permission. I have been chasing about to find you ever since. I thought you were at Strathinver."

"It was too boring there for words. Can we leave at once, before Embleton can interfere?"

"Grayling is welcome to you," came a voice from behind them, as Embleton emerged from the throng. "You are the most pestilential female any man was ever saddled with, and I shall be heartily glad to be rid of you."

Effie laughed. "And you are the stuffiest brother any girl could have. Give me half an hour to pack, Julian, and we can be away."

"Of course. We will go to Carlisle to obtain a bishop's licence and be married forthwith."

"Oh Julian, we shall have so much fun! And who cares if we get married or not?"

"Your father, for one, and Lord Harold, for another."

"Harold? What does my brother have to do with this?"

"He is waiting in the carriage as we speak. He will travel with us to ensure there is no fun until we are respectably married, so if your objective is to put off the wedding, then you had best say so now, and we will part with no hard feelings."

She pulled a face. "Harold is almost as stuffy as Embleton. How long will it take us to reach Carlisle?"

"Three or four hours, if we are lucky. We might make it before dark."

"I can last half a day without fun," she said. "Very well. It shall be as you wish."

She scampered away to organise her packing.

Lord Embleton shrugged and offered Lord Grayling his hand. "Good l-luck, Gray... ling. You... will... need... it."

"Thank you, my lord. I shall try my utmost to keep her out of mischief, or if that proves impossible, at least out of your way."

They shook hands with smiles all round and within the hour Effie was gone to be married to Lord Grayling, leaving Olivia a little breathless and bemused, but quietly pleased.

***

The very next day, the arrivals bell clanged again, even though the rain had now turned to light snow, and again a crowd flocked to the entrance hall to greet the newcomers. Three figures arrived in a veritable cloud of snow, their breath steaming in the cold air despite the massive logs burning in two great hearths. Three figures shrouded in thick winter garments and swathed in blankets, but Olivia knew them at once, although they were the last people she had expected to see at Lochmaben.

Beside her, Papa said dubiously, "Surely that cannot be—?"

"I think it is," Olivia said. "Look, the tall man has removed his hat, and no one else has such distinctive red hair."

"Farramont? Then the ladies must be..."

"Izzy, yes." And in a whisper she added, "And Mama."

Her father made a strange noise in his throat, like a growl. "Caroline... Caroline!" And then he was off across the entrance hall, cutting unseeingly through little knots of people, practically knocking over one hapless footman. *"Caroline! Caroline!"*

Mama turned, saw him, her face melting into a smile. "Charles."

He came straight up to her, wrapped his arms around her, heedless of the snow clinging to her cloak, and burst into tears.

"Oh, *Charles!* My dear!" Her arms were around him, and she was crying too, oblivious of the crowd gathering excitedly around them.

Eventually he surfaced, his face still streaked with tears. "Dearest Caro, I have missed you abominably. I have not been right since the day you left. Everything has gone wrong. I cannot manage without you, my love. Will you not come back to me?"

"Charles, are you proposing to me?"

"Yes!" he yelled, then laughed suddenly. "Marry me, Caro. No, no, I have to do this properly." Dropping to his knees, he took her gloved hands in his. "Caroline Horncastle, will you make me the happiest of men once more and do me the very great honour of becoming my wife again? Because my life is insupportable without you."

"And mine without you, I have discovered," she said. "Oh Charles, but you will have no legitimate heirs. I am far too old for that."

"I have no legitimate *sons*," he said, rising gracefully to his feet, her hands still firmly in his, "but I have a brother and several nephews who will take very good care of the earldom after I am gone. How soon can we be married, dear heart? You will not make me wait, I hope?"

"But how can it be done?" she said, frowning. "A special licence can only be had from London, and even a bishop's licence will take several days to obtain with this weather."

The Duke of Lochmaben chuckled. "We can do rather better than that. You are in Scotland now, so you need only say you are married in front of witnesses, and it is so."

"Truly?" Papa said. "So I need only say… *we are married?*"

"Congratulations," the duke said smoothly. "I now declare you man and wife. Rennington, you will want to show your wife where she will be sleeping."

There was a burst of cheering from the assembled crowd, but Olivia's throat was too tight from weeping to cheer. At last, Papa would be happy again and Mama would come home to Corland, where she belonged, and at least there would be some semblance of normality after the last terrible six months.

She felt an arm round her shoulders. "Come, sister, let us escape from this mêlée. Where is your room?"

"Izzy? What are you doing here?" Olivia said between sobs.

"I was just about to ask you the same question," Izzy whispered. "We thought you were at Strathinver. Farramont, where are you? Ah, there you are. Will you see about rooms and luggage and such like, while Olivia and I have a cosy chat? No doubt you will have letters to write, as well."

"No doubt I will," he said, smiling affectionately at her, before disappearing towards the footmen dealing with mounds of luggage.

The two sisters retreated to Olivia's room, where a fire burned low in the hearth.

"Let us get a bit of a blaze going," Izzy said, taking up the coal tongs and rapidly tossing lumps of coal onto the fire. "Goodness, but I am chilled! One forgets how dismal the roads are in December. I cannot remember the last time I was warm. Will you ring the bell for some wine for me? The fire will warm my hands and feet, but I must have something to warm me inside, as well."

"Why on earth are you travelling at all?" Olivia said. "In your condition, you should be safely tucked up at Stonywell, warm and snug."

Izzy only chuckled. "I am past the sickly stage and not yet at the elephant stage," she said with a little shrug. "Besides, when one travels with Ian, nothing can possibly go wrong. He will not allow it. As to why, we came because of you, sister dear. We were concerned for you."

"For me? But I have Papa with me. There is nothing to be concerned about."

"Is there not? Your last letter — six pages, Olivia, and on the one hand telling all your hopes for Lord Embleton, and on the other rattling on for pages about the oh-so-amusing Lord Kiltarlity — or Osborn, as you are pleased to call him. You sounded in a sad muddle, and Mama insisted we come haring up here to sort you out. But what has brought you to Lochmaben, sister? We quite thought you were settled at Strathinver with the two men you are dithering over. What happened? Did you fall out with Lady Kiltarlity? She can be a bit of a she-dragon sometimes."

"No falling out."

"Then...?"

"I am betrothed to Lord Embleton."

Izzy gave a squeak of surprise. "That was sudden! My goodness, so you have achieved your ambition, young lady, and Josie and I are quite put in the shade. A marchioness... and a duchess, eventually. My dear Olivia, my sincere felicitations. If you knew how many caps have been tossed Embleton's way over the years, and he has ignored them all, yet you, not even properly out of the schoolroom, have succeeded where everyone else has failed. How did you do it?"

Olivia gave a rueful smile. "I have no idea. I was crying... about something... and he just proposed."

"You were *crying?* Well, you often find something or other to cry about. A broken lace, the stable cat bringing home a dead bird..."

"It was nothing like that!" Olivia said sharply. "I may cry easily, Izzy, but I am not a *child* any more, or perhaps you have not noticed?"

"I beg your pardon," Izzy said. "It is abominable of me to tease you at such a time. But will you not tell me the whole story? Of both your young men, that is, for there is more to this than meets the eye, I fancy."

So Olivia told the tale, what little there was to tell, as Izzy walked about the room, a glass of wine in her hand, asking the occasional question but mostly simply listening. Tea and cakes had arrived with the wine, so Olivia fortified herself suitably as she talked, and gradually she began to feel better. As she laid out the whole of her dealings with the marquess, she began to feel it was all perfectly reasonable. There was nothing there to unsettle her, was there? She had set her heart on the marquess, but she had not flirted or tried to compromise him or even thrown herself in his way. And when he proposed, she had accepted, so what was wrong with that? She was happy, was she not?

At the end of the recitation, as she reached for another cake, for there was nothing like cake for reassuring one, Izzy laughed.

"Oh sister, what a mess you have made of it!"

"Have I?" Olivia said, dropping the cake in surprise.

"Of course. Can you not see it? You quarrelled with Lord Embleton, and you were angry. Robert proposed but you were too angry to listen. Then you cried, Lord Embleton found you crying, thought it was all about him, so he proposed."

"And I accepted," Olivia said. "It is what I want."

"Has he told you he loves you?"

"No, but—"

"Has he kissed you?"

"No, but—"

"Do you want him to?"

Silence.

"Do you want Robert to kiss you?"

Olivia burst into tears.

23: Of Love And Happiness

Olivia wept for a long time, while her sister held her tightly. What she was weeping for, she could not quite say, except that she wished it were Robert holding her, for only he had the power to make her feel better, whatever the crisis. Nothing was so terrible when Robert was with her.

"Do you think," she said, when the sobs had abated somewhat, "that I have chosen the wrong man?"

"I cannot answer you," Izzy said. "What do you think?"

"How can I tell?" she wailed. "How did you decide? You had four men chasing you. What made you settle on Ian?"

Izzy laughed throatily. "His title, principally. And his income."

"But… there must have been something more than that? Who was the bald, fat, wheezy one who offered for you at Almack's, in front of half the patronesses? He had a title and a huge income, did he not?"

"Oh, yes, and he was sixty if he was a day! If I had been minded to be a merry widow in very short order, he would have done perfectly, for he is dead now, you know. But one must have *some* standards. The four who persisted were all men I could willingly marry. Godfrey Marsden, who was rich as Croesus. Sydney Davenport, who wrote poetry for me — so romantic. Robert Osborn, the charming flirt. And Ian, the steady one."

She smiled, her face radiant with affection.

"Dear Ian!" she went on. "The moment I knew it would be him was at some impossible squeeze at Carlton House. We were so late, the place was full to overflowing, and I was terrified that we would be so late that we would arrive after the Prince of Wales and be ostracised for ever more. I had never been to Carlton House before, so it was all new and thrilling, but frightening, too. I was beginning to realise how easy it would be to make a misstep in society, and my confidence was dreadfully wobbly. But as we entered the room, there on the far side was that distinctive head of red hair rising above the sea of turbans and tiaras, watching me, and I knew it would be all right. I would always be safe with Ian."

"You felt safe with him," Olivia repeated wonderingly. "Is that what love is, feeling safe with a man?"

"That is part of it, certainly. Do you feel safe with Lord Embleton?"

"Oh yes! He is very steady, like Ian. Very dependable. Although... he gets angry with me, too. When he thought I was trying to trick him into compromising me, and I was not, not in the least! That would be despicable, and I would never stoop so low. I was insulted that he would even think it of me. And his sister... he thinks it is my fault that she ran away from Strathinver, but honestly, if he could not control her himself, he should have taken her home for her father to deal with, for she was not fit to be in society, I swear. She did nothing but flirt with every unattached mal e."

"Did? She does not do so any longer?"

"No, for she will be married to Lord Grayling by now, and I imagine he will not be amused if she tries her games with anyone now."

"Grayling? Goodness! I had no idea he was looking for a wife, but then there were rumours that he was all to pieces and I dare say Lady Effie has a fine dowry."

"Fifty thousand pounds."

"Well! I am sure I wish them joy of each other, the flirt and the fortune hunter. But did she flirt with Robert?" Izzy said, picking up her wine glass again.

"No, for she said he was very disobliging and would only flirt with me," Olivia said, giggling.

"Did he flirt with you?"

"Well… he talked a lot of nonsense. I assumed he was flirting."

Izzy's eyebrows rose. "Even when he proposed to you?"

Olivia jumped up, too agitated to sit still. "Oh no, *that* was not flirtation! That was an insult. Do you know why he wants to marry me, Izzy? Because I look like you! He fell in love with you five years ago, he has never found anyone to compare with you and now that he is the last son and has to marry, he thinks to have me because I remind him of you, in a small way. Insufferable man!"

The tears were prickling again, but she dashed them angrily away.

Izzy sipped her wine, frowning. "I think you are wrong about that, sister dear. I saw Robert in the summer, remember, when I was briefly unmarried, and he made no effort to attach me. In fact, he told me very clearly that he no longer had any wishes in that direction, so if he proposed to *you*, it is you he wants. Did he tell you that he loves you?"

Mutely, Olivia nodded. It was true! He had said that he loved her but she had not believed him, had in fact thrown his words back in his face contemptuously. Oh, what a horrid, ungrateful girl she was!

Sitting back down beside Izzy in a swirl of skirts, she said in a small voice, "What am I to do?"

With a chuckle, Izzy said, "It seems Mama and I arrived not a moment too soon! You are already betrothed, so Robert is out of the question, for now. The first thing you must do, little sister, is to talk to Lord Embleton, and discover, if you can, his feelings on the matter. It may be that he has a deep passion for you, and your tears merely brought things to a head. But if not..."

Olivia nodded. "But what am I to *do*, Izzy? Must I marry him? *Should* I marry him? I have wanted this for so many years, yet now that the moment has come, I cannot decide. Whatever decision I reach will affect my whole life... decades and decades to regret my choice, perhaps. How do I know that I will be happy with him... or not?"

"Sister," Izzy said gently, "all I can tell you is that I chose Ian for largely pragmatic reasons, and I never regretted it. Marriage to a good, honourable man brought me great contentment, and whatever unhappiness I felt was within myself, and nothing to do with Ian. But I did not know true happiness until he showed me the passion within him, the love that he had kept swathed in secrecy for five years. If Lord Embleton can show you that sort of passion, then you may be sure that he can bring you happiness."

"But he cannot express it!" Olivia cried. "Words are so difficult for him."

"Love does not need words," Izzy said firmly. "Love is in the way he smiles at you, the fire in his eyes, the ardour with which he kisses you." She paused with a little sigh, and a faraway look in her eyes. "And if he does not even kiss you... then you have your answer."

***

Olivia eventually tracked down Lord Embleton in the sewing room, a tiny apartment high in one of the castle's many towers. The two Miss Plowmans were there, both with stitchery in their hands, and one of the elderly Lochmaben cousins acting as chaperon, reading a book beside the fire. She and the younger Miss Plowman were silent and industrious, but Lord Embleton and Miss Plowman had their heads close together, laughing — laughing! Olivia could not recall seeing the marquess so light-hearted before.

The scene was so intimate that she cried out, "Oh, forgive me for intruding!" before remembering with a spear of resentment that she was engaged to Lord Embleton and need never apologise for claiming a little of his time.

He looked up at her, the laughter dying away, leaving his usual imperturbable expression. He rose and bowed politely. "Lady Ol... Olivia."

There was no pleasure in her arrival, no expression of delight to see his future wife, not even so much as a smile. Almost she had her answer on the spot, but she owed it to him to give him the chance to explain himself fully.

"I wonder if I might have a word with you, my lord. In private. If Miss Plowman can spare you."

"Of c-c-..." A huff of annoyance, then he took a deep breath. "Of... course."

"Well done, Ralph!" Miss Plowman trilled. "Remember, deep breaths, speak slowly. We'll leave you two to have a coze. Come on, Marian. Lady Sophia."

Ralph! They were on first name terms, then.

The ladies left, and only Lord Embleton remained, his expression wary. Olivia took the seat vacated by Miss Plowman, right beside the marquess, so that if he should wish to hold her hand or press impassioned kisses on her lips, he would not have to do more than lean forwards a short distance. She was not sure she wanted him to do either of those things, but she felt she ought to give him the opportunity.

"Lord Embleton, I believe we should talk seriously about... well, about ourselves. We never have, and I know you are not a great one for talking but it is a conversation we need to have, I believe."

He nodded. "Indeed. I have... written... to... my... father... telling... him... about you, but... he... will... not... dis... approve."

"No, no! That is not what I mean. I suppose what I am saying is that I should like to know why you so obligingly offered for me."

He looked at her blankly, a little puzzled. "I..." He stopped, frowning.

How could she explain it to him? It was awkward, for she could hardly say, *'Are you in love with me?'* She had no wish to push him into a corner where he might feel obliged, by some obscure gentlemanly rule of honour, to declare an affection for her that he did not feel. And he could hardly say, *'I do not love you, but I am quite prepared to marry you anyway.'* It was not exactly chivalrous, even if true.

But she needed to *know* beyond all doubt what was in his heart, and perhaps the most honest way to approach the problem was to tell him what she herself felt.

"Well, let me explain my position first," she said. "When my older sisters married, both of them to viscounts, I determined that I would outdo them. For my husband, I decided, nothing would do for me but a duke. Or the heir to one." His eyebrows lowered alarmingly, but he said nothing. "So I set myself the task of identifying the most likely prospects. There are not very many of them, as I am sure you are aware. Once I had eliminated all those who were married, too young or too old, or lived in Scotland, I—"

The eyebrows rose again. "Scotland! Wh-what is... wrong... with... Scotland?"

"Nothing at all, in fact, I like Scotland very well, but you must acknowledge that it is a very great way from London. Or from almost everything except mountains and bogs. In any event, I decided that I would prefer to live further south, within easy reach of the Metropolis. And yours was the name I settled upon." Down came the eyebrows again. "For several years now I have followed your exploits in the newspapers and journals, so you may imagine that when I had an opportunity to meet you... to know you as a real person and not merely a name in a newspaper, I grabbed it with both hands."

He said nothing, merely looking dazed, so she hastily continued.

"Now, you must not be imagining that I planned to trick you into marrying me, for I despise stratagems of that nature. I heard that you offered for Bea Franklyn after she kissed you, so I thought I might try to kiss you, too. Nothing more than that, I assure you. And I confess, I went into Leicestershire because I knew you would be there, and I wanted to get to know you better. It worked very well, in fact, for I did indeed get to know you better and I liked you very well. I liked you well enough to be content to follow you to Scotland. Indeed, I liked you well enough to accept your proposal."

She licked her lips, wondering if he wished to say anything, but he seemed stunned by her confession.

"However, I must be honest with you, Lord Embleton. I am not in love with you. I am not quite sure what I feel for you, to be perfectly truthful. More than liking, perhaps, but definitely not love. It is important that you understand exactly what sort of a bargain you will be making, if we marry. We must be totally candid with each other, do you not agree? There should be nothing withheld regarding our feelings and expectations."

"N-n-nothing w-w—" He gave an exclamation, then jumped to his feet, stamping agitatedly around the room, saying nothing but throwing her sideways glances.

She waited, having said all she wished to say. Now it was for him to decide how to answer her, although the glowering countenance did not betoken a sympathetic hearing.

After some minutes of silence, while he continued to prowl about restlessly, she rose to her feet. "Very well. I shall see you at dinner, Lord Embleton."

He growled low in his throat. "Is that all you have to say? Hounding me for months — *years* — inveigling me into a proposal and not a word of apology?"

"What would you have me apologise for?" she said, her chin lifting. "For wanting to marry well? That is all any woman does who has a care for her own future. And do not insult me by suggesting that I tricked you into offering for me, for I did no such thing! You are unspeakably rude to suggest it. You are a grown man, Lord Embleton, so take responsibility for your own behaviour. You freely chose to offer for me, although you still have not explained why, and I was free to accept. And now, just because I want to talk more openly, as a betrothed couple might expect to do, you berate me as if I were a child and expect me to apologise."

"You only want to marry me because I shall be a duke one day!"

"Every woman of marriageable age wants to marry you because you will be a duke one day. There is no shame in that! It is sensible. Do you think we are all romantic fools who will marry just for love, even if the beloved is only a common labourer? Women are more practical than that, I assure you. We take into account a great many things before we decide on a man, and a duke at least has the advantage of great wealth, so if he turns out to be a bear after the wedding, at least one may be miserable in comfort. And if he turns out to be a bear *before* the wedding —"

She stopped, seeing the obvious conclusion to this train of thought.

But he seemed to deflate before her eyes. "A b-b-bear?" he whispered. "Am I?"

The stricken look on his face had her instantly awash with guilt. And yet, she could not face a future where her husband might at any moment turn on her in anger, and without the least provocation. It was unthinkable. She wanted a husband like Izzy's, who meekly followed her about in adoration. Or like Josie's, whose face lit up whenever she came into the room. Or like Papa, who simply disintegrated when Mama was away.

She wanted a husband who teased her and never failed to lift her spirits. A husband who asked her advice and listened to her. A husband who loved her.

She wanted Robert.

Licking her lips, she said gently, "I think perhaps you are only a bear very occasionally, and only with me. Something about me seems to rub you the wrong way. I do not think we are suited to marriage, do you?"

He gazed at her, raw misery on his face. "You were c-crying," he said softly. "I c-could not b-bear to think I m-made you c-c-cry."

"I had quarrelled with Lord Kiltarlity, that was why I was crying," she said crisply. "It was nothing to do with you. Lord Embleton — Ralph — you made the same mistake with Bea Franklyn, I think. She kissed you, naturally you supposed her affections were engaged so you proposed. And with me, we quarrelled, you found me crying, you proposed. Your problem is not that you are a bear, but that you are entirely too soft-hearted. You must learn not to propose marriage to every woman for whom you feel sorry. You need to find a woman who makes you feel glad to be alive. My lord, may we at least part as friends? Will you shake my hand?"

She held it out to him, and at once he took it and lifted it to his lips, with a warm smile that lit up his whole face. "You d-d—" He took a deep breath. "You de... serve... to... be... a duchess."

Olivia smiled too. "You are very kind, my lord, but that was merely the foolish conceit of a child — to outdo my sisters. I have discovered that it is not the rank of a man which matters, but his character. And whether I love him, of course. I shall never be a duchess. I might perhaps, if I am very fortunate, one day be a countess."

"Kil.. tar.. li.. ty?"

Her smile broadened. "Yes. Wish me luck."

"I do. And happiness. And I... shall... look... for a woman... who... makes... me... glad to... be alive."

"Then I wish you good fortune in your search, my lord."

With a curtsy, she turned and left the room, free of her engagement and freer of heart than she had been for many weeks.

***

Robert could not tell how many days passed as he slid slowly into a despair so profound he wondered how he could even breathe. He sat in his book room all day, a glass of something in his hand, staring into space, wondering where his darling was and what she was doing and whether she was happy... surely she was happy? She was going to be a duchess, just as she had always wanted, so she must be happy. And Embleton had won a priceless jewel, so he must be happy, too. It was only Robert who was overwhelmed with grief.

At first he managed tolerably well, arriving on time for meals, although he ate nothing, and dragging himself through the usual activities — meetings with his stewards and gamekeepers, a visit from his attorney and another from a neighbouring landowner, and even, once, attempting to play whist with his mother and sisters, until his ineptitude became too great even for his fond relations to tolerate.

They treated him as if he were a valuable piece of porcelain, liable to break at any moment, and he could not say they were wrong. He felt as if he might simply crumble to nothing at a single loud word, so he was grateful for their soft voices and the gentle reminders of appointments. His valet came to fetch him when it was time to dress for dinner. Somehow, he got through each day.

But every day was a little worse than the day before. He woke late each morning after a few restless hours' sleep hoping that this was the day when he began to feel better, but it never was, and eventually the day came when the pain became too much to bear. He went into his book room, locked the door and reached for the brandy bottle.

24: A Kiss

Robert woke to grainy eyes, a thundering head and the sound of birds twittering. Moving, or even opening his eyes, was far too difficult, so for a while he simply lay, wondering why his bed was so wretchedly uncomfortable. His pillow had gone missing for one thing, and his cheek, which should have rested against smooth linen, was lying on something else entirely. Wool, his befuddled brain decided. How very odd.

The twittering came and went and there was some sort of perfume in the air, that made him think of spring flowers and warm sunshine. There was a rustle of... was it silk? The perfume grew stronger and faded away, leaving him with a wisp of memory of walking by the Serpentine in London. None of it felt threatening, however, so he lay still, allowing it to wash around him.

Whispers. The twitterings were whispered female voices, low and melodious. Not his sisters, whose voices were rarely low and never melodious. But there was one who sounded so... surely it could not be...?

With difficulty, he opened one eye, cried out in shock, closed it tightly again.

The whispers became giggles. "He is awake. Open your eyes, Robert."

"No, no, no!"

"Why not?"

The voice was familiar, but he could not quite bring its owner to mind. "Seeing double."

More giggles.

"Open your eyes."

That voice... was it...? Tentatively, he opened his eyes, but it was no good. "Still two of you. Two ghosts." He snapped them shut at once.

They giggled again.

"Will you not sit up?"

It *was* her, it was! He opened both eyes. Still two ghosts. His eyes flicked from one to the other. How was that possible?

Why was he lying on the floor, clutching a bottle?

One of the ghosts knelt on the floor beside him, her head tilted to one side. A different perfume, less strong, reminding him of— Was it really her, or had his brandy-befuddled brain conjured an apparition?

"Robert, try to sit up. I am persuaded you will feel much better."

Whether she was flesh and blood or not, he could not disobey her. With a struggle, he pushed himself up and leaned against the wall. The bottle rolled away under a chair. He was in his book room, he realised. No wonder his bed had felt uncomfortable, for he had been lying on the carpet.

The room shifted and swayed, and he closed his eyes again.

There was a sigh, another rustle of silk and the stronger perfume came nearer.

"Have a drink of water." Her voice again.

A glass was pressed against his lips, and a little cool water trickled into his mouth. Gratefully, he opened his eyes again. She was smiling, and oh, there it was!

"Dimple!" he cried triumphantly. "'Tis you. Knew it." His eyes were drawn to the other ghost, standing nearby with the water jug. She was smiling, too, but there was no dimple. "Izzy? What you doin' here?"

"My little sister was making a hash of things, so Mama and I came to fix everything." She bent down and reached under the chair to retrieve the bottle. "Heavens, Robert, how much of this stuff have you drunk?"

"Lots. Too much. Not enough."

They both laughed again. "What are we going to do with him?" Izzy said.

"Throw him in the river?" Olivia said. "That would sober him up."

"We should throw him off the roof, more like. Foolish man!"

"I should not like him to be hurt, Izzy."

"Then you will just have to kiss him."

Robert made a strangled sound deep in his throat, and squeezed his eyes shut again.

"No, no! Open your eyes!" Olivia cried.

He shook his head, then winced as brandy-induced pain lanced through him. "Want to keep dreaming."

"This is not a dream, silly boy. You truly are as drunk as a wheelbarrow, and I truly am here."

"No, no, no, no! If I look at you, you'll disappear like a soap bubble popping or... or just fade away. Couldn't bear it, Livvy. Too horrible for words. Have to throw *myself* off the roof."

"Hush now! No talk of that nature, if you please. I am as real as you are."

He shook his head again, pleased to find that the explosion of pain was lessened this time. "Can't be real. Can't be here. Goin' to marry Emblaton... Embling... the marquess."

She giggled, but said softly, "I am *not* going to marry Lord Embleton."

"Oh!" His eyes shot open, to find her face just inches from his. He could hardly breathe! She was free! The nightmare was over. "Will you marry me, then?"

She knelt back on her heels, her face solemn. "Well, I might, but I should like a proper proposal, if it is all the same to you, and I should like you to be sober, so that I know you mean it. But I should very much like to kiss you."

He smiled at her, wanting nothing more than to reach out to her, touch her, sweep her into his arms, but painfully aware of his dishevelled state.

"No. First kiss... has to be romantic... beautiful. The lady... lovely 'n' eager 'n' enticin', which you are, always. The gentleman... 'maculately groomed... new coat... carryin' a posy, which I'm not. If you will wait... what time is it?"

"A little before noon. We arrived first thing, but you had locked the door, silly boy, and there was some trouble finding the spare key."

"Ah. Sorry. Might be... couple of hours to make myself p'sentable enough for a kiss. Will you wait or—?"

"I will wait."

"Then meet me in... winter drawn... draw... drawin' room... two hours."

***

It was more than three hours, in the end, but Olivia did not mind. He would come, he would kiss her, he would propose, and then this strange, unsettled, not-quite-belonging feeling would disappear for ever. She would be with Robert, and everything in her world would be in alignment again.

Izzy stayed with her as she waited. Lady Kiltarlity and her daughters sat with them for a while, but eventually they had other matters to attend to and then it was only Izzy.

"Will it be strange for you, if I marry him?" Olivia said. "You nearly married him yourself, after all."

"That just shows what excellent taste in men we both have," Izzy said with a smile.

At last, Robert came, freshly bathed and shaved, wearing a coat of blue superfine that seemed moulded to his form, and bearing a small posy. He saw Olivia, smiled and marched straight across the room to the window seat where she was perched. He did not so much as glance at Izzy, as she crept quietly out of the room.

"Where did you find flowers at this time of year?" she said, burying her face in them. "Oh! They are silk!"

"Yes, but pretty, are they not? Lizzie found them for me when the footmen came back from the hothouses empty-handed. I had promised you a posy, so a posy there had to be."

"As if I would have minded!" she said laughing. "But it is quite delightful that you went to the trouble."

"Do you like them?"

"I love them!"

"Ah. Good. So perhaps you will forgive me for keeping you waiting all alone for such an abominable length of time."

"I did not mind waiting, and I have not been alone. Izzy was here."

"Was she?" He looked about vaguely as if he expected her to pop up from behind a sofa.

"She has just this minute left. Did you not see her?"

"I confess I saw only you," he said, his voice husky. "There is only you."

Olivia found it hard to breathe suddenly.

"My sweet Livvy," he murmured, "whatever Izzy once was to me is long gone. When she chose Farramont... I was cross, but not heart-broken. What I felt then is nothing at all compared to what I felt these past days when I thought I had lost you forever. I wanted to die, Livvy. I could not see how I could struggle through the rest of my life without you. The brandy was just a feeble attempt to shut out the misery for a few hours. And then... there you were! My lovely ghost had come back to me."

"Then... it is not just that I remind you of Izzy?" she said.

"I love *you*, my darling ghost, and I love you all the more because you are *not* Izzy. I will always be grateful to Izzy for being the first to unlock such tender feelings in me, and your likeness to her drew me to you when we first met, but she and I would have driven each other mad within weeks. Whereas you, my love, bring peace to my poor mind, and calmness to my life."

He was standing bare inches away from her, but he still had not touched her... he had not *kissed* her, and Olivia was almost driven wild by his hesitation.

He sighed, and took her face in his hands, his warm, strong hands. "You are *not* Izzy, my dearest one. You are yourself and unique and very precious to me."

Closing his eyes, he leaned his forehead against hers with the softest of sighs. She could feel strands of his hair tickling her skin, and smell the soap he used — a strong scent, very masculine.

And still he hesitated, with some anxiety lingering in his eyes.

"Are you going to kiss me now?" she said hopefully.

With another sigh, he released her, his face troubled. "I *want* to, of course. There is nothing I should like more, but sooner or later it will stop and then it will be over and that will make me sad."

She giggled. "The first kiss will be over, but there will be a second and a third and so on."

"Will there?" His face was alight with affection.

"I promise you, there will always be one more kiss. If you want it."

"I shall always want it. I shall always want *you*," he whispered.

Then his arms were round her and his lips were on hers, burning her with a fire that set Olivia aflame. It was a long, long time before they broke apart, rather breathlessly.

"Oh dear," Olivia said. "I am afraid the posy has become horribly crushed."

"Never mind," he murmured, bending to kiss her again. "I will buy you more. I shall fill the house with flowers for you, my love."

This time when they parted, Olivia said, "You may propose to me now, Robert. A proper proposal, mind."

He shifted a little further away from her, although with his arms still around her waist. "Do you know, I think I will not."

"What!" Olivia screeched. "Have you been taking advantage of me under false pretences, Robert Osborn? Shame on you!"

"Olivia, how old are you?"

"Nineteen. Well, almost."

"And you have been nowhere, met no one, not even had a season. But you should. You ought to go up to town for the first time unattached, so that you can be fêted and mobbed and swamped with suitors, just as Izzy was. You will be the season's Incomparable, just as she was. That is what you deserve, before you settle into marriage. And I shall be just one of your horde of admirers. I shall court you in proper form, and take you driving in Hyde Park, stand up with you at Almack's and fight for a glimpse of you at the theatre. I shall come to every event you attend, just to see you, hoping for a dance with you at balls."

"I shall keep every supper dance for you."

"Shall you? That will be wonderful. And at the last ball of the season, my love, I shall take you out onto the balcony in the moonlight. The air will be filled with the scent of roses, there will be a fountain splashing gently and peacocks will be strolling on the lawn. There under the stars I shall kiss you and propose... or I might propose first and then kiss you. No, because if you turn me down, I should not get a kiss at all, so definitely kiss first."

"How absurd you are!" she said, laughing. "And what happens if it is raining?"

"Then we will huddle under umbrellas and it might be a fairly rapid proposal. But I am serious, Livvy. I want to court you properly, as you deserve, but I also want you to have the chance to meet other potential husbands, and if you choose one of them..." He stopped, taking a ragged breath. "I will try to accept it with equanimity. I shall, of course, be doing my best to prove that I am the best of them, but I want you to have the choice and not be tied to me before you even show that adorable dimple in town."

"Very well, but..."

"What is it? What have I forgotten?"

"What about you? What if you change your mind... or meet someone else?"

"My mind is entirely unchangeable at this point, Livvy, my love. I would have proposed to you here and now, and I am as bound as if I truly had. In fact, I should do this formally so that you know precisely where you stand." He cleared his throat ostentatiously. "Lady Olivia, would you do me the very great honour of receiving my proposal of marriage at the final ball of next season?"

That made her laugh again. "I am very much obliged to you, Lord Kiltarlity, and I should be honoured to receive your proposal of marriage at the final ball of next season. And I mean to accept."

"Those words will sustain me when I have to watch you stand up with every eligible suitor in the Kingdom," he murmured.

After that, they found that words were no longer necessary.

***

Captain Michael Edgerton waited impatiently for his fellow investigators to return with news. Mr Willerton-Forbes had gone to Northumberland to find out more about the baronet's daughter Rosamunde Wilkes, while Sandy and Neate were visiting brothels in Scarborough in search of the ladies from Pickering. Michael was not optimistic that anything valuable would be unearthed, but every avenue had to be pursued.

While he waited for news, he relieved his frustration in long rides over the moors. As often as not, he would find himself near the tower at Welwood, and if there was no one about, he would turn his horse into the field with the retired donkeys and pack ponies, and retrieve the key from its hiding place under a stone. The tower was still used for Eustace's smuggling operation, although the work must have been carried on at night, for although Michael never saw anyone else there, the number of barrels in the cellar rose and fell regularly.

The smuggling operation was of no interest to him, however, so after a cursory inspection he would climb to the uppermost room of the tower. There he sat, gazing down at Eustace's house and brooding on the progress of the investigation. Sometimes he looked through the telescope, still pointing towards Welwood, but as often as not he simply read through Miss Peach's notebook for some clue that he had missed.

It was a pity that her notes had been so cryptic. If she had been more open about her investigations and shared her findings with Michael, he had no doubt that he would have had the murderer under lock and key by now, and Miss Peach would still be alive. Instead, she had left only a jumbled collection of fragments — of laudanum and mule droppings, of a person of the greatest interest, of a saddle that would be found in the obvious place. If only she had been less secretive!

One day, he saw a man walking across the field from Welwood towards the tower. Even without the telescope, he recognised the form of Mr Eustace Atherton. He waited patiently, hearing the door open and close several floors below, and then measured steps on the stairs.

"Good day to you, Captain Edgerton," Eustace said, setting down a bottle and two glasses on a small table. "I saw your horse in the field. A glass of port? That was the only bottle I could find."

"You do not drink the brandy, then?" Michael said, bowing respectfully, for Eustace might be a smuggler but he was also an earl's son.

"Not straight from the barrel, no. What brings you out here, Captain? Should I be concerned?"

Michael smiled. "About my visit? No. I had time on my hands and a need for some exercise, that is all. This is just the right distance for an invigorating ride, and a good place for pondering, I find."

"Is your pondering productive?"

"Not very, no. I am just about at a standstill with my investigations, yet I find myself reluctant to admit defeat."

Eustace sprawled, one leg over the arm, in a battered leather chair that had obviously been expensive library furniture once, sipping his port. "That is a part of your character, I suppose, that reluctance to let go. Such determination is presumably why you have made a successful career from investigating murders."

"Perhaps. That and insatiable curiosity. I always like to know who and where and when, and most of all, *why*. And you are a case in point, sir. You are the son of an earl, a man of honour — a gentleman. Unlike most younger sons, you have an estate of your own and a modest independence. Yet you choose to involve yourself in the risky business of smuggling. I very much wonder why."

Eustace smirked. "It is the risk that makes it enticing, Captain. The secrecy, the night adventures, the hidden barrels, the coded messages. Such fun! I think that is something you understand very well, unless I have mistaken you entirely. Some of those tales of India that you tell border on the reckless. Then there was the business of climbing the drainpipe to see if a man could have entered the castle that way. There must be safer ways of finding that out than climbing it yourself, and dangling in mid-air."

Michael grinned. "We are cut from the same cloth, then, except that my risky ventures would only end with broken bones, whereas yours could bring you to the hangman's noose."

"Highly unlikely," Eustace said, the smirk widening. "Everyone in authority for twenty miles around is receiving from us, and as for the Excise men — ha! So far they have been persuaded to ignore us."

"How do you persuade them?"

"Oh, one generally knows something about them. A less than honest past. A wife whose adventures would be better not noised abroad. A bribe, if all else fails. I never met an Excise man yet who could refuse a bribe. There is always the chance that a new man might arrive who is... less persuadable and then we should be in trouble. But so far my persuasions have been successful."

"Ah, you have thought of everything, I can see," Michael said.

"I believe so, yes. One tries to take care of every detail." And he grinned at Michael in such a smug and self-satisfied way that it was all Michael could do not to punch him on the nose.

He hastily changed the subject, asking if Eustace had added any new weapons to his already impressive collection, and for some time they talked animatedly, as one connoisseur to another, of broadswords and pistols and rapiers. To Michael's intense disappointment, no invitation was forthcoming to view any of these interesting items. Just once he had seen the Welwood collection, but since that day, months ago now, he had not been invited back.

Eventually he had no choice but to make his departure and ride slowly back to Corland Castle, wreathed in thought.

25: A Murder Is Planned

Sandy and Neate were the first to return from their quest in the brothels of Scarborough.

"That was the most amazing fun!" Sandy said, with a boyish grin.

"Really, Sandy!" Luce said, in her severest tone.

"No need to worry, Luce. We didnae take advantage of the facilities, so to speak, but there's nae harm in looking, is there?"

Michael only laughed. "Let the lad be, Luce. He could hardly be blamed if he had a bit of passing fun. I liked a bit of passing fun well enough myself, until I met you."

"Not brothel women, though, Michael."

"No, but there were plenty of married women looking for amusement, and one must always oblige a lady."

Luce raised her eyebrows speakingly, and shook her head.

"Well, I didnae have any fun that ye need worry about, Luce. Mind you, I cannae speak for Neate."

"My lips are sealed," Neate said, pasting an angelic smile on his face. "You would not believe how many brothels there are in one small seaside resort. However, we found Mrs Mayberry and her merry band of nieces eventually, hidden away in a discreet side street. Seven nieces, now, so the family is expanding, and very exclusive they are. We had to grease a lot of palms to gain access."

"Did you talk to Mrs Mayberry, and ask her why she lied to us?"

"No mystery about that, is there?" Neate said. "Nicholson wanted to keep his involvement secret. Once she realised we knew everything about the Pickering house, she confessed the whole. Very talkative she became, with enough coins in her hand. She was afraid to cross Nicholson, but now that he's dead, she's more cooperative."

"And ye'll never guess, Michael!" Sandy burst out excitedly. "Eustace's light-skirt isnae there anymore."

"Ah," Michael said, smiling. "Did you find out why?"

"She has a protector," Sandy said. "She's some man's mistress, and we can guess whose — Mr Eustace Atherton."

"Did Mrs Mayberry tell you that explicitly?" Michael said sharply.

"No," Sandy said sadly. "Even Neate wasnae able to winkle a name from anyone. But it must be, wouldn't ye say?"

"Possibly," Michael said, frowning. "But... that would be an odd coincidence. His lightskirt from the brothel becomes his mistress, and at the same time he betroths himself to a baronet's daughter, who is not above warming his bed for him."

"So are you suggesting that they are one and the same?" Luce said. "That Miss Rosamunde Wilkes became Miss Rochester?"

"It is certainly possible," Neate said. "While Sandy was enjoying himself in the brothels, I ingratiated myself with the manservant from Miss Wilkes' aunt. Apparently all the Wilkes daughters spent time with the aunt as they grew up, a month or so every summer, but the other two married so it was only Rosamunde for a while. Then came the falling out with the girl's father, and she arrived in a big rush one November, stayed for a few months and then vanished."

"To a brothel in Pickering?" Michael said, frowning. "That seems quite a stretch."

"Not at all," Neate said. "Suppose that the lady had an eye for the gentlemen. Her father sent her away when he found out, but she turned out to have a little reminder of her dalliance, so the aunt threw her out when it became too obvious to hide, and the breach became permanent. What happens to a woman in that situation, Michael? Desperate, and with no other option, I suggest she joined Mrs Mayberry's little enterprise, where she met our friend Mr Eustace. He's using her respectable family to bamboozle us into believing he's going to marry her."

"Very possible," Michael said. "If Pettigrew comes back from Northumberland with a description that matches, then I shall accept your theory, Sandy."

Pettigrew Willerton-Forbes returned with a smug smile on his lips.

"Description? I can do better than that. I spoke to Sir Reginald Wilkes, and he has no portrait of Miss Rosamunde, having had her painted out of the family gathering hanging over the drawing room fire. However, the other daughters drew and painted numerous portraits of her and he very kindly allowed me to take one of them. There," he said, producing it with a flourish. "Is that not the image of the lady?"

"Did you mention Eustace to Sir Reginald?" Michael said.

"I did not feel it was my place to do so," Pettigrew said. "It is for Mr Eustace or the lady herself to approach her father... or not, as they feel best. Sir Reginald thinks she has gone abroad with her lover, and it is not for us to disabuse him of that notion."

"Very true," Michael said.

"Besides, it hardly matters who she is," Pettigrew said. "She is Mr Eustace's alibi, but not his sole alibi, after all. His entire household swears he never left his house that night, and even if Miss Wilkes is lying, I believe that the household servants and grooms are telling the truth. It is an unbreakable alibi."

Michael laughed. "No alibi is unbreakable, Pettigrew. It is always possible for a man to sneak out of a house unobserved, if he is careful. The question in this case is why he would want to do so. That has always been the difficulty with this case."

"So what's next, Michael?" Sandy said. "Ye've a plan, I'm sure."

But Michael sighed. "I seem to have run out of plans, my friend. I think we may have reached the end of this particular road."

Silence fell. Even the irrepressible Sandy could not think of a single stone left unturned. The investigation was over.

But before the end of the day, an event occurred which wiped the murder of Arthur Nicholson from their minds. The Dowager Countess of Rennington, slowly declining over many months, finally breathed her last.

Corland Castle was immediately thrown into frenzied activity. Quantities of black crêpe, bought months ago against this eventuality, were brought forth to drape about the deceased's room and muffle the door knocker, and to fashion caps and armbands for the servants. Clocks were stopped, the pianoforte was locked and the maids crept about in soft slippers.

It was unfortunate that Lady Alice Nicholson was the only member of the family still in residence. Her brother, George, and her nephew, Mr Eustace, who both lived nearby, were sent for, but the rest of the family was scattered about the country. Luce immediately offered her services to write the necessary letters to Lady Alice's dictation, to be sent off by express to the far corners of the kingdom. Lord Rennington and Lady Olivia were in Scotland. Mr Walter was in London, and Mr Kent in Lancashire. The two married daughters were in County Durham and Nottinghamshire. Lady Alice's daughter was in London. And in time, one by one, carriages drew up on the drive and black-clad figures crossed the bridge over the moat and were received into the castle.

The Dowager Countess was buried with all the ceremony due to the relict of an earl. Afterwards, with Christmas so close, and the weather uncertain, and other entertainments forbidden so early in their bereavement, the family settled down with almost audible relief for a protracted stay, to catch up with all the news, as families always do when meeting after long absences.

There was much to celebrate, too, with so many marriages in the family, not the least of which was that of the earl and countess, reunited after a long separation, both by Scottish custom and, more solidly, by a bishop's licence in Carlisle, and delighting in their status. The gathering seemed likely to turn into quite a party.

Michael and his friends made themselves useful when they could, and otherwise kept out of the way. They took to eating dinner in the old schoolroom, not wishing to intrude on the family's mourning. Yet even when the funeral was over, Michael made no move to leave. It was Luce who raised the issue.

"Is it not time for us to go?" she said. "The investigation is over, Michael. There is nothing else for us to do here... is there?"

Michael grinned. "Just one thing. Do you remember in the early days, how I tried every point of ingress to the castle, to see how the murderer might have gained access?"

"The drainpipe!" the others said in unison.

"And recall how we recreated the shooting of Bertram Atherton. We did exactly what the perpetrator must have done, and showed how long it took. Well, why should we not try recreating the murder of Nicholson? We have everyone here who was present on the night of the murder, after all. We might glean some new insight, or someone may remember something, some seemingly trivial point, long forgotten. It is worth a try, is it not?"

"Yes!" Sandy cried, jumping to his feet. "And we'll be able to *see* how it happened!"

"Precisely! We can find out whether a figure fleeing down the main stairs would be visible to Kent Atherton passing the aperture above."

"And the timing," Neate said. "How long everything takes — that would be so useful to know."

"Excellent plan," Pettigrew said. "I commend you, Michael. But if this does not work —"

"Then I shall give it up. It will haunt me to my dying day, but six months is long enough. If we cannot resolve the matter with this one last attempt, then it will be over and I shall accept my failure."

***

Michael timed his request carefully. He suspected that if he simply approached the earl, he would be inclined to refuse on principle, but some of the younger men might be more amenable. He waited one evening, therefore, until the ladies had withdrawn from the dining room and then made his request to speak to the remaining eight gentlemen.

He was not given to nerves, as a rule, and had dealt with lords from the rank of duke downwards, but there was something intimidating about so many peers of the realm gathered in one room. Apart from Lord Rennington, there was another earl, Lord Kiltarlity, who was courting Lady Olivia. The two viscounts were Lord Woodridge, husband of the eldest daughter, Josie, and Lord Farramont, married to middle daughter, Izzy. The lowest ranking, a mere baron, was Lord Tarvin, husband to Tess, the mercurial daughter of the murdered chaplain and Lady Alice. Only Lord Rennington's three sons, Walter, Eustace and Kent, were commoners, but despite their illegitimacy, they were still the sons of an earl and not to be treated lightly.

"My lords, gentlemen," Michael said, with his most respectful bow. "Thank you for allowing me to speak to you."

"Still here, Edgerton?" Eustace said languidly, twirling his port glass as he lounged in his chair. "Thought you would have left by now."

"I shall be gone soon, sir, I assure you, but there is one more test I should like to attempt before I give up entirely on this case. It occurs to me that we have everyone at Corland just now who was also here in June, when the murder of Mr Arthur Nicholson took place. With your permission, my lord, I should like to stage a recreation of the event."

"Recreate it? How?" Lord Rennington said.

"Someone would play the rôle of the murderer, creeping into the castle and up the stairs, collecting the axe from the urn on the way, then pretending to murder Mr Nicholson before creeping away again. Everyone else would behave precisely as they did at the time."

"What would that accomplish?" Lord Rennington said.

"It would enable me to *see* how events unfolded," Michael said. "I might be able to spot discrepancies in the various accounts I have received, and there is always the possibility that one of the participants might recall something previously forgotten."

"We are a house in mourning, Edgerton," the earl said sharply. "It would be disrespectful to my mother, so recently deceased, to be putting on a performance of this nature."

Before Michael could respond, Kent said eagerly, "We are also celebrating, Father, are we not? You and Mother are reunited, and despite all the upheavals of this year, every one of your children is now settled in life, and either married or about to be so. Even my wild Cousin Tess has found a man willing to be tormented by her for life." They all laughed, even Lord Tarvin. "Grandmother had a long and happy life, and she would not want us to mope about on her account. She was so full of life, she would be happy to see us all so contented."

"She was fond of amateur theatricals herself," Walter said. "Remember her in *Coriolanus?* She was magnificent. She would doubtless have joined in Captain Edgerton's scheme with enthusiasm."

"I cannot see that such a performance would achieve anything," Eustace said, "except to dredge up unhappy memories. It was a night we would all wish to forget, I am sure."

"It was rather terrifying at the time," Walter said, "but after so many months, and as long as Aunt Alice is not upset by it, why not?"

"Far be it from me to influence what is purely a family matter," Lord Farramont said, "but it seems to me that it would be an excellent scheme. There is nothing like seeing a thing for understanding it fully. Captain Edgerton has done everything in his power to find the murderer, and although he has not yet achieved that objective, he managed to recover a great deal of your fortune along the way, Rennington. I believe the captain is owed one last throw of the dice to solve the mystery, and there will never be a better opportunity than now, when we are all gathered together. I should be delighted to offer myself as an impartial observer, if the captain will tell me what to look for."

After that, all resistance crumbled and the earl reluctantly gave his permission.

***

Michael gathered everyone in the library after dinner to plan the recreation of the murder.

"The time of year is quite wrong," he said with a frown, "but if we hold the enactment at dusk, that would be close enough to the situation of near-dawn in June."

"I hope you do not expect me to reprise my rôle in the events of that night, Captain," Lady Alice said.

"No, indeed, my lady! Under no circumstances! If you wish, you may choose to be elsewhere — not in the castle at all. Or, you may stay with those who were not present that night. I suggest that those not participating may wait in the great hall, since we know that the murderer must have passed that way twice. I shall invite Sir Hubert Strong to be a witness, also, as magistrate, and if the lady's husband approves, I propose to invite Mrs Walter Atherton to play your part, Lady Alice — to find the body and raise the alarm."

"Winnie!" Walter said. "Why Winnie in particular?"

"Because she is exceptionally calm and sensible, sir. She was a great help to me in the early days of the investigation, and she has already acted as Lady Alice once before, when I was testing whether a lady would be strong enough to wield the axe."

"I should be happy to help in any way I can," Winnie said, "but I draw the line at screaming."

There was a ripple of amusement around the room.

"No screaming needed," Michael said. "There is a loud hand-bell in the old school room. That will serve the purpose very well. Everyone apart from Lady Alice who was here that night should be in the room he or she occupied then, and should react precisely as they reacted at the time. The servants, too. I shall explain what is expected of them. What I hope is that someone will remember something... some trivial thing that may have been forgotten or overlooked at the time. Or notice something, perhaps. Mr Kent recalled seeing someone going *down* the main stairs, so we will find out if our fleeing murderer is indeed visible on the stairs. The timing will be an important consideration, so Mr Willerton-Forbes and I will be noting how long everything takes. Is everyone clear on what is to be done?"

"I believe you have forgotten one point," Kent said.

"Have I?" He smiled widely.

"The murderer. Who is to play the leading rôle in this little play? You?"

"Not I, no. I need to watch what happens. Who would like to be the murderer?"

There was general laughter.

"It sounds amusing," Izzy said, "but I imagine you will want a male murderer."

"Hardly amusing, Izzy," the earl said. "We are talking about the recreation of a real *murder*, not some foolish Drury Lane farce."

"I do think the murderer was male, yes," Michael said hastily. "Long skirts are a great hindrance to speedy movement, I imagine, and the murderer must have moved fast."

"Must he?" Lord Farramont said. "Might he not have crept about through the castle for some time before blundering into Mr Nicholson's room?"

"That is certainly a possibility," Michael said evenly.

"Might he already have been inside the castle?" Lord Farramont said. "One of the inhabitants, perhaps."

There was an intake of breath around the room at this suggestion.

"One of us?" Olivia cried. "What a horrid idea!"

"And a most unlikely one, my lady," Michael said quickly. "Someone living in the castle would hardly have needed to resort to an axe to murder anyone. A drop of rat poison in the brandy decanter or the morning chocolate would do the job most effectively. No, this was someone — a man, certainly — who entered the castle from outside."

She nodded, still looking rather anxious. Lord Kiltarlity, who sat beside her, squeezed her hand reassuringly, and was rewarded by a tremulous smile.

"We cannot know how long the villain was here before the murder was committed," Michael went on, "but for the purposes of recreating the crime, I wish to know what is the shortest time it would have taken him. Therefore, I propose that he enters by the garden door where the bolt was broken, proceeds up the service stairs to the great hall, collects the axe, and then goes directly to Mr Nicholson's room. Given that Mr Kent Atherton saw a fleeing figure, I further propose that Mrs Walter Atherton, in her rôle as Lady Alice, should hear something and enter Mr Nicholson's room immediately."

"So this is all guesswork?" Eustace said. "You have no idea how it happened, have you?"

"No one can know precisely what happened leading up to the murder," Michael said carefully.

"Except the murderer," Kent said, to more laughter.

"True. If anyone would like to reveal his identity, we can ask him," Michael said. "Until then, I propose to work with the most likely situation, which to my mind is that the murderer wished to get in and out as quickly as possible, before he was spotted by a servant up early. So... does anyone apart from Lady Farramont wish to be the murderer?"

Lord Woodridge shook his head decisively. "I do not think I have the temperament even to pretend to be a murderer."

"Nor the eyesight," Josie said. "You would undoubtedly have to stop to polish your spectacles on the way up the stairs."

"I suppose it has to be someone who was not here that night," Lord Farramont said slowly.

"That would be you or me or Tarvin," said Lord Kiltarlity.

"Or me," Eustace said. "I was not here that night either."

"Indeed," Michael said, "and you have the inestimable advantage over the other gentlemen that you know the castle intimately. Besides, it does not seem right to ask a peer of the realm to portray a murderer. Would you be willing to undertake the rôle, sir?"

"If it will help, of course," Eustace said, languidly. "I agree with Izzy, in fact — I think it will be a lark, and the tale of it will keep me in ale at the White Horse for years. But you need not worry, Captain. I shall take it very seriously. I know how important it is that this fellow is caught, once and for all, and I am happy to offer whatever assistance is in my power."

Michael made him a sweeping bow. "You are very good, sir. Shall we say tomorrow afternoon, then? If we gather at two, say, there will be time to settle everyone in their initial positions, and arrange a bolster in the bed to represent Mr Nicholson."

"You want me to murder a bolster?" Eustace said.

"I am depending on it," Michael said, with a grin.

26: The Captain Understands

It took a little more than an hour to arrange everyone in their starting positions, family and servants alike. Michael had emphasised again that they should react exactly as they had done on the night of the murder, so if they were slow to wake up, they should be slow this time, too. It would not be precise, for it was impossible to recreate the events exactly as they had happened, but there might be something, some clue that would point him in the right direction.

All those who were not present on the night in question gathered in the great hall, together with Sir Hubert Strong, as magistrate, and Lady Alice. Mr Alfred Strong had insisted on being with her, so that he could describe what was happening to her.

"Very well, but keep the sound very low when the murderer passes through. The great hall should be silent and empty, so please, everyone be as quiet as you can, and do not delay Mr Eustace. Now, Sandy, have you the axe?"

The Scotsman brandished it with a grin.

"Mr Eustace, sir, will you please deposit the axe in the left-hand urn?"

"Why me?" Eustace said.

"You are the murderer, Eustace," Kent called out. "You have to know where the axe is."

"Ah, so I can retrieve it. Of course."

Confidently, he took the axe and ran lightly up the stairs to the half-landing where the two giant Chinese urns stood, and moved directly to the right-hand one.

"The left is the other side, Eustace," Walter called out, as a murmur of laughter ran round the assembled crowd.

"Ah. Of course."

"Heavens, Eustace, you make a terrible murderer," Izzy said. "You should have let me do it after all, Captain."

That brought more laughter.

"Now, sir," Michael said. "Outside, as soon as you can. The light is fading fast."

He led the way down to the basement and out through the garden door. Outside, the air was chilly and damp. "You know what you have to do, sir?"

"Through the door, up the service stairs to the great hall, retrieve the axe from the urn—"

"The *left-hand* urn."

"Yes! Then on up the stairs to Nicholson's room, murder the bolster, drop the axe and straight back down the stairs. Is that right?"

"It is, and as fast as you possibly can." Michael pulled out his pocket watch. "At all costs, you want to get in and out without being seen. I shall be timing you. Right, off you go, sir."

Eustace went. Through the garden door, and up the service stairs two at a time, straight along the narrow passageway, then erupting into the great hall. Michael followed three paces behind. On the half-landing, Eustace hesitated, moved to the right, stopped, moved back to the left, and then to the urn. He pulled out the axe, waving it triumphantly at the assembled watchers.

Then he set off up the left-hand stairs.

"Other stairs, sir," Michael murmured behind him.

Down, across the landing, up the right-hand stairs to the very top, out onto the landing that ran round all four sides of the castle, and through the door directly opposite. There was the bolster in the bed, a mop head representing Nicholson's hair. For a moment, he hesitated, axe held loosely in his hand.

"This is definitely a bolster, yes?"

"Definitely."

Then, as Michael watched, Eustace set to with a will, releasing clouds of feathers into the air. For a moment he paused, then dropped the axe beside the bed where it fell with a thud, before brushing away the feathers that clung all about him.

He turned and left the room, closing the door softly behind him, and took two brisk steps towards the top of the stairs. Almost at once the bell clanged loudly behind him. That was quick!

Eustace swore with realistic fervour, and ran for the stairs. He had not taken more than two steps down when there was the distant sound of a door opening. Someone tripped over something, cursing, and passed by on the landing, as Eustace pressed himself against the wall and froze. Walter Atherton, first on the scene because he had not stopped to light a candle. Then more doors opened further round the upper level. The wavering light of a candle appeared. Eustace stood, paralysed.

Michael said nothing, leaving him to work out what to do. Down below them, the great hall was in darkness, the fire extinguished and no candles lit. Only a dim gloom from the glass roof far above cast enough light to see the stairs.

The candlelight disappeared, hidden behind a pillar. Abruptly, Eustace made a decision, and ran on down the stairs to the great hall. There he would have stopped, but Michael urged him onwards, along the narrow passage, down the service stairs and out of the garden door. Then and only then did Michael check his pocket watch.

"Seven minutes," he said with satisfaction. "Thank you, sir. A very proficient performance."

"Did it give you any new ideas?"

"New ideas? No, but it was interesting all the same." And he grinned wolfishly. "Shall we go back inside?"

By the time they reached the great hall, arriving more slowly this time, there was a great deal of excited chatter amongst the watchers. Michael left them to it, and went upstairs to Mr Nicholson's bedroom. The earl, Kent, Walter and Mrs Walter, together with several footmen, were milling about, while Neate and Sandy were making notes of who arrived when.

"Ladies all sent away," Sandy said. "Everyone's here who was here on the night."

"Excellent," Michael said. "Mr Kent, sir? Did you see the murderer running down the stairs?"

"I did, Captain, although... not so far down the stairs as the real murderer. I was looking for him, this time, so it was not just a glimpse in the corner of my eye. Alexander saw him, too."

"Aye, I did. He was lucky to get away with it — the real murderer, that is. Mrs Walter came through as soon as she heard a noise, and because she raised the alarm so swiftly, we saw Mr Eustace running away. But Mr Kent saw the real murderer running away, so Lady Alice must have raised the alarm almost as swiftly."

"That is true," Michael said. "She must have been awake already. No doubt the murderer did not expect that. Mr Eustace responded well when he found the alarm raised so quickly. Hmm... not so far down the stairs. Well, we cannot expect everything to be precisely the same. Did anyone remember anything new?"

Neate and Sandy both shook their heads.

"What about you, Captain?" the earl said. "Did you gain any new insights from this exercise?"

"No, my lord. It has confirmed one or two matters which were uncertain before, but no more than that, I regret to say."

"You have done your best," the earl said. "No one could have done more."

"But it was not enough," Michael said sadly. "Now he will get away with it, and justice will never be done." He sighed heavily. "You have been wonderfully patient, my lord, but we will importune you no longer. Tomorrow we will be gone."

"What do you want to do with this?" Sandy said, proffering the axe.

"I suppose it can go back to Mr Eustace now," Michael said disconsolately.

Downstairs, the candles and fires were lit, and the servants were busily handing round drinks and platters of pastries and cakes.

While the rest of those assembled in the great hall seemed to be in celebratory mood, Michael's spirits could not be lifted. He stood glumly at the bottom of the stairs, gazing up at the two Chinese urns and the armoury display between them.

Luce tucked her arm into his. "Stop thinking about it."

He chuckled ruefully. "That is difficult, when I have thought of nothing else for six months."

"You have to let it go, Michael. It does no good to keep fretting over it like this."

"But I am so close! There is but one piece of the puzzle missing, if I could only see it."

"I see it more like a maze," she said. "However long we spend wandering about, we can never find the centre, and if we could, it would be just as difficult to find our way out again. Probably we should have turned left instead of right at the first branch and then— Michael, are you listening?"

"Oh... *of course!*"

"Michael?"

"The belt was broken," he murmured. "Laudanum... the saddle... and the painters... Of course! The *painters*! It must be so!"

He stood as if in a trance, eyes far away, mouth slightly open.

"Michael?" Mrs Edgerton said, puzzled. "Michael, what is it? Oh! You know! You know who killed the chaplain."

The captain turned astonished eyes on his wife. "Yes, I know. Actually, I have known *who* it was for a while now, but the rest... It is like one of those images one sees... it is a vase, you think, but there are supposed to be faces there. You cannot see it no matter how hard you try and then suddenly...

there it is. The answer. It all makes sense now. Oh, but I have been so unbelievably stupid. Why did I not think—? But at last I know, and not o nly *who* killed Mr Nicholson, but *why*. That is what has puzzled me all this time, which has kept me gnawing away at it like a dog with a bone, but now I *know*, and it is so clear… so blindingly obvious."

His voice was loud enough to drown out the other conversations rumbling round the room, and everyone drifted nearer.

"Well, you had better tell us at once," the earl said gruffly. "Is it someone here this very minute? We have Sir Hubert with us to effect an arrest. Come, man, do not keep us in suspense."

"No, I will not," the captain said distractedly, "but I must check my notes first… and the plan! The plan of the castle that Mrs Walter was so good as to label for me." He dashed away, was halfway up the stairs before turning and racing down again. "My lord, would you be so good as to gather everyone into… the library would be best. I shall be back in five minutes."

And then he dashed off again.

***

They were all there, the ladies and some of the gentlemen on chairs set in a loose semi-circle by Pettigrew, who was still helping to arrange them, while Luce and Sandy passed around glasses of what looked like brandy. Some of the younger gentlemen stood at the back, and Lady Farramont prowled back and forth, a glass in her hand.

Michael ran a quick tally in his head, and decided that everyone was there. No one had sneaked away. They all turned expectantly towards him, as Neate and Sandy moved unobtrusively into place in front of the two doors.

"My lords, ladies and gentlemen," Michael began. "Thank you all for helping to recreate the murder for me, and for being so patient with my bumblings. It has taken me an unconscionable time to understand this murder, but perhaps there are good reasons for that. The murderer was clever, for one thing, and threw me quite off his trail. And then I was looking at it all wrong. I could see very clearly *how* the murder was done, but the point that evaded me all along was *why* anyone should want to murder Mr Arthur Nicholson, a chaplain, a well-liked man, in general, and a man who, whatever his faults, appeared to have no enemies."

He turned to Lady Alice with a bow, even though she could not see it.

"Lady Alice, you will forgive me, I am sure, if I say that your husband was no saint. He set out, almost from the earliest moments of his arrival here, to amass a great fortune. We may never know why he felt impelled to do so. Perhaps it was envy of those around him, so wealthy and so careless of that wealth. Or perhaps he thought that his lack of ordination would one day be discovered and he would have to leave in a hurry. Perhaps a man cut adrift from his own family and not fully rooted in his new one simply needed the security of money. We cannot say. But whatever his motives, he embezzled great sums from the late earl's estate, he won suspiciously often at cards, he sold his wife's jewellery and substituted paste copies, he solicited charitable contributions from acquaintances and he ran a brothel in Pickering, channelling the profits through legitimate businesses to hide th em."

He paused, gazing round the room, seeing the surprise on some faces. The full extent of Nicholson's perfidy had been known to few people.

"But none of this," he continued, "provided sufficient motive to kill him. The late earl made no complaint about his losses, and probably knew nothing of them. Lady Alice had no idea about her jewellery. No one questioned where all those charitable donations went. His connection to the brothel was not generally known. Even his unacknowledged illegitimate son was not at all resentful. No one, it seemed, hated Mr Nicholson enough to kill him. And only one person benefited from his death, his daughter, who inherited that vast accumulated fortune."

"I did not kill him!" she cried.

Michael bowed. "No, indeed you did not, my lady. You shared a room with your cousin, so you could only have left your room at night if you had drugged her into a deep sleep — laudanum, perhaps, which is so easy to obtain. So very easy... Yet when the murder was discovered, you both went to the scene, very much awake. So no, you did not kill your father. But again, it left me with no one who had a reason to murder Mr Nicholson, and was in a position to do so."

Again he paused. Part of him relished the drama of the situation, but he knew he was about to distress the earl and his family greatly. How much easier this would have been if the murderer had been nothing but a random stranger!

But the truth, however unpalatable, must be faced.

"And I was exactly right about that. No one hated him enough to kill him. No one wanted him dead. He was not supposed to die that night."

"Whatever do you mean, Edgerton?" the earl said tersely. "Just get to the point, will you?"

"Of course, my lord. The point is this — Mr Nicholson was not supposed to die because he was not the murderer's target. He died by accident. The murderer took the axe from the urn on the stairs, and then he made a fatal mistake. He went up the *wrong stairs*, entered the wrong room and killed Nicholson."

"How could anyone—?" someone began, but then stopped. Already eyes were beginning to turn in one direction.

It was Lady Rennington who voiced the fear in everyone's mind.

"You mean Eustace. You are saying that Eustace murdered Nicholson. Impossible!"

"But why?" someone cried.

Michael said nothing. Surely they would work it out?

"That is nonsense!" Olivia cried robustly. "The room at the top of the other stair is the guest suite, which was empty that night."

"No," Walter said slowly. "It was not empty. I was sleeping there, because my own room was being repainted. You are saying that *I* was the target, and therefore it must have been Eustace because he was next in line to inherit."

"Mr Atherton," Michael said slowly, "if you had died that night, as I believe was the intention, Mr Eustace would have become the heir, he would have been Viscount Birtwell, and he would also have been able to claim the woman he loved obsessively, Miss Beatrice Franklyn. She was betrothed to you as the heir, and had you died, she might very likely have transferred her affections to the new heir. And then Mr Eustace would have had everything that was yours. Now *there* is a motive for murder if ever I heard one."

27: An Ending

One of the ladies gave a low moan, but Eustace laughed.

"Bravo, Edgerton! A fine tale. But you have forgotten, I think, that I was in my own bed twelve miles away at the time, as my entire household will tell you... have already told you, I believe."

"I have not forgotten that, sir. If his lordship will permit the indulgence, I should like to describe how I see the murder arising in the mind, and then taking place."

The earl nodded his agreement. One or two of the gentlemen at the back exchanged wry glances, and Eustace was still smiling, quite sure of himself. But Michael was very sure of himself, too, and had dealt with enough murderers over the years to understand how good a face they could put on impending disaster.

So he settled down to tell them just how the murder must have happened.

"It began, I believe, a week or ten days before Mr Nicholson's murder," he said. "Perhaps there were earlier attempts on the life of Mr Walter Atherton, or Viscount Birtwell, as he was then. There were certainly a number of odd incidents — accidental or otherwise. Whatever the truth, there is no longer any hope of pursuing them, so let them be left in the past, if they existed. But certainly Mr Eustace must have been considering how his brother might be disposed of. A second son must always be a little envious of his elder brother, who has so much, when he has so little. Mr Eustace is better off than many a second son, for he has a modest independence, enough to enable him to live as a gentleman and not need a career, but that does not compare with his brother's future prospects, of eight thousand a year and a great title, as well as Corland Castle and much other property."

Pettigrew pushed a glass of something into Michael's hand. Gratefully, he took a sip. An excellent brandy, and French, no doubt. He knew, now, where that had come from. But that was not his concern.

"And now he has something else that Mr Eustace wanted, as well," Michael went on. "His future wife is Miss Beatrice Franklyn, whose personal attractions are enhanced by a dowry of forty thousand pounds. Mr Eustace had already offered for Miss Franklyn twice at this point, and been rejected both times. If only Walter were not there! Then both the inheritance and Miss Franklyn would be in Mr Eustace's hands. Yet time was running out, for surely Miss Franklyn would soon set a date for the wedding, and then all would be lost. If only there were a way to get rid of Walter. So he must have thought, as he arranged the armoury display on the stairs on that day. If only! But he could see no way it could be done, because he would be the first to be suspected."

The men were listening quietly now, thinking about it, and he could see the frowns on some faces, and the curious glances thrown Eustace's way, as if they were beginning to wonder — could he truly have done this? Could he have wanted to kill his own brother? Someone was sobbing quietly — Lady Rennington, he thought. Lady Alice looked ashen, but dry-eyed. The younger ladies were clearly shocked, but they listened in silence.

"But then, a strange mischance occurred. Mr Eustace was arranging the armoury display on the stairs one day, and the belt which was meant to hold the axe in place, broke. Or perhaps it was already broken, who can say? However it was, it could not serve its purpose and the axe could not be displayed. The broken belt is one of those niggling little points that always worried me. I assumed at first — we all assumed, I think — that the belt was broken by the murderer wrenching the axe from the display on the night of the murder. A weapon seized by chance, as he passed by. But my own experiments proved that the slightest touch would bring the entire display crashing down, as many of you will remember."

There was a murmuring around the room, recalling the devastation at the time, when the armour and weapons had cascaded noisily down the stairs and scattered across the great hall.

"So it would have been impossible to remove the axe from the display on the night of the murder without waking the whole household. Where, then, was the axe, if not secured by the belt? The maid who cleaned the display never saw the axe at all, so it must have been hidden, and thanks to Lady Tarvin, we know precisely where — it was inside the urn overlooked by the balcony. Light shining through the roof windows on a sunny day illuminated it, and she realised what it was. So I suggest that Mr Eustace, when arranging his display and discovering that the belt was broken, tossed the axe into an urn. Perhaps he intended to come back and repair or replace the belt, but when he thought about it, he realised he now had the perfect opportunity to remove his brother. Mr Walter was not in his usual room, near to the rest of the family, but in the guest suite, surrounded by empty rooms with no one to overhear. There was a hidden weapon, ready to be retrieved at any time, and the murder would look as though a random stranger had simply walked in, picked up the axe from the display on the stairs and wandered into Mr Walter's room by chance. All Mr Eustace had to do was to arrange a rock solid alibi for himself."

"Yes, how do you explain that, Edgerton?" Lord Rennington said testily. "He was at home all night, his servants vouch for him."

"Laudanum," Michael said crisply. "He chose a day, and invited a lady to join him to dine and stay the night, as witness. To ensure his servants slept soundly, he gave them a bowl of punch, and sleep soundly they certainly did. I interviewed every one of them, and they all reported it. Let me read you some of their remarks. *'Never overslept before.'* That was the head groom. *'Don't know what was in that punch but I went out like a light and woke ever so late.'* Or this one. *'The master made the punch with his own hands, and it must have been strong because I fell asleep at the kitchen table.'* It has not been mentioned, but I would wager that Miss Wilkes was offered a bedtime glass of something, too."

She nodded. "It's true, but it was just wine, and he poured it from the bottle, two glasses."

"But did he drink any of it?"

"I... don't remember," she said, frowning. "I don't remember much, to be honest, until I woke up next morning, and the sun was well up. I was ever so late getting back to—"

Eustace made a noise deep in his throat. "Rosamunde!"

"Oh!" She flushed, and subsided at once.

"It is quite all right, Miss Wilkes," Michael said smoothly. "I believe I can finish the sentence for you. You were late getting back to Pickering, to Apstead House, a rather exclusive brothel. Miss Rochester, that was your name then, was it not?"

She turned terrified eyes on Eustace, who made a small shrug with one shoulder. "What of it? So she was once a light-skirt, and now she is my future wife."

"I thought she looked familiar!" Tess cried. "I saw her when I worked there as a housemaid briefly."

"A housemaid!" said Lady Alice and Lady Rennington in unison.

Izzy laughed. "Tess, you are the most outrageous girl!"

"Although she had black hair when I saw her," Tess said.

"That is true," Michael said. "I think with a black wig, as she used to wear when she visited Welwood, she looked somewhat like Miss Beatrice Franklyn. Your little fantasy, Mr Eustace. And perhaps, if you had succeeded in killing your brother, it would not have mattered that your alibi was a light-skirt, but when you realised you had killed Nicholson instead, the owner of the very house she lived in, you had to avoid any connection with Pickering. Hence the use of Daisy Marler, instead."

"This is all very fanciful, Edgerton," Eustace sneered. "So I drugged my entire household and rode here in the middle of the night, did I?"

"You did," Michael said, with a swift grin.

"And how did I do that, without rousing the grooms who slept above the stables?"

"You rode one of the horses kept in the field across the road from your entrance gates. You keep a saddle in the shed there, for your various night-time activities, most of which do not interest me, but it was very convenient on that night in June."

Eustace shook his head, but said nothing.

Michael went on, "You rode to Corland — I wonder how you chose the right direction? Did you check with the markings on your own gateposts, or does the horse know its way better than you? But that is of no consequence. You reached Corland, left your horse in the woods to the north of the lodge gates, climbed the wall — there is a very convenient point where the coping stone has fallen off — and entered the castle, probably by the garden door, where the bolt was broken. I wonder if you broke it yourself? Possibly you did. The rest we know. The dogs knew you, so even if you encountered them, they would not have barked. You came up the service stairs and out into the great hall, a clear route with no confusing turns, you retrieved the hidden axe and then... then, sir, you had to choose a stair. Left or right? And in the darkness, in a panic in case you encountered a servant up early, you went up the wrong stair, entered the wrong room and murdered the wrong man. I can only imagine your dismay when you discovered your error."

"He was astonished," Walter said. "He came over that afternoon, and was amazed to hear that Nicholson had been murdered."

"He did not usually call in that casual way," Kent said, frowning. "He must have expected to be summoned as soon as Walter's body was discovered, and came to find out why he had not."

"For heaven's sake, Kent!" Eustace cried. "Anyone would think you *believe* this farrago of nonsense!"

Kent lifted his head and looked his brother straight in the eye. "I do. I do believe it, Eustace. Because when you heard that Nicholson had been murdered, you did not say *'Murdered?'*, as anyone might, on hearing such a thing. You said *'Nicholson?'*. I thought it odd at the time, but now it makes sense. You were not surprised to hear there had been a murder. You were only surprised to hear that it was Nicholson who had died. Yes, you killed Nicholson, but you intended to kill Walter. I am sorry Nicholson died, but I am extremely grateful that you did not succeed in the crime you planned."

It was Winnie who made the other obvious point. "And yet he did succeed, in a way. He managed to deprive Walter of both his inheritance and his intended wife, although at least Walter has been spared any further attempts on his life."

"But he tried to kill Bertram," Kent said. "The inheritance was out of his reach for all time, but Bea was not. He had one last shot at winning her. Happily, he failed there, too."

"And yet, what audacity!" Michael said. "To slip away from the gathering, run down to the basement, across the open space to the cheese store, climb the ladder to the hatch, take the shot and run back inside, emerging in time to aid the search for the gun, and at any moment risking discovery. Incredibly brazen, and carefully planned, too. He wore black that evening from head to toe, to make himself less visible as he crossed the void beneath the bridge. In the darkness, perhaps with his collar turned up to hide his white neckcloth, he would have been impossible to see. We can only be glad that his shot failed to achieve its objective."

"But he succeeded in killing Miss Peach," Luce said quietly.

"Yes," Michael said. "I am afraid he did. She knew just too much for his comfort. She hid herself away in the tower, spying on Mr Eustace and all the comings and goings at Welwood. She no doubt saw Miss Wilkes leave the brothel in Pickering and step into Mr Eustace's carriage, recognising it just as Lady Tarvin did. So she went to Welwood, to the tower, discovered the field between the tower and the house contained a few horses capable of making the journey to Corland, experimented with laudanum to see if it would be possible to induce an entire household to sleep soundly, and we can guess the answer to that. She wrote in her notebook that it only remained for her to find a saddle secreted in *'the obvious place'*, as she described it. The obvious place being the shed in the field where she had herself hidden the saddle for her mule. That would complete the picture of the murder."

"But she was killed before she found it," Luce said.

"Unfortunately, she made a fatal mistake," Michael said. "The laudanum caused her to oversleep one day, and she was almost discovered by Mr Kent Atherton. Her bag *was* discovered, and Mr Kent reported that to his brother. Mr Eustace went to the tower to confront Miss Peach, and... we can only guess what was said at that meeting, but we know the result."

"What nonsense!" Eustace said. "You should be writing novels, Captain Edgerton, with such a fanciful imagination."

"It is not my imagination, however, that there was indeed a saddle hidden in the shed at the far side of the field. I had already found the saddle for Miss Peach's mule buried in the straw, but when I looked further, I found another saddle, one designed for a full-sized horse. It was very well hidden, by the way. I had to shift a vast amount of hay before I found it. I should have liked to discover a green leather bag there, too, or even blood-stained clothing, but you were sensible enough to dispose of those. A saddle, however, is much harder to get rid of. So you buried it in the hay. It is all very ingenious, sir," he said, gazing steadily at Eustace, "and you almost got away with it. You were greatly aided by Miss Peach's love of conspiracy. If she had been less secretive, we could have arrested you months ago, and she would be alive today. But there are no more secrets and you will answer for your wickedness, both in this world and the next. Sir

Hubert, will you arrest this man for the murders of Mr Arthur Nicholson and Miss Philomena Peach, and the shooting of Mr Bertram Atherton?"

"I will indeed," Sir Hubert said grimly.

Lady Rennington gave a great wail of despair, her daughters clustering around her protectively. Even Lady Alice, the most phlegmatic of the Corland ladies, had her hand covering her mouth, eyes closed in distress. The men looked grim, but no one questioned Michael's summary. He had expected objections, but apart from a few murmurs about finding the best lawyer from London, there was no resistance. Lord Rennington had his head in his hands. He believed it, and that was more telling than anything el se.

Eustace himself, his face set, had nothing else to say. Sir Hubert led him out of the library and into the entrance hall, with Michael and Sandy following.

"Do you have somewhere secure to house him until he can be conveyed to York Gaol?" Michael said.

"There is a room in my cellar fitted up for the purpose," Sir Hubert said.

"You will allow me to pack a few things first?" Eustace said. "I trust you would not have me incarcerated with only the clothes I stand up in?"

"Of course," Sir Hubert said. "Lead the way to your room."

Eustace had been housed in one of the guest rooms on the first floor, so they made their way up the stairs and after only one false start in the wrong direction, found the room.

Eustace hesitated, his hand on the doorknob.

"Might I be permitted to do this alone? I cannot escape, after all. Edgerton has proved that the drainpipes will not bear a man's weight."

"What do you say, Edgerton?" Sir Hubert said.

"I have no objection," Michael said. "Mr Atherton is entitled to a few moments of tranquillity to contemplate his future."

Eustace went inside, closing the door softly behind him.

"Yer very trusting, Michael," Sandy said. "He could be out of the window in moments."

"There are no trees or climbing plants anywhere on the castle walls, and the nearest drainpipe is well out of reach. If he jumps, he falls clear to the basement level and breaks his neck."

"He could knot sheets together, and climb down that way," Sandy said.

"Then he will find Neate waiting for him, pistols at the ready."

"Ye've thought of everything," Sandy said.

"I certainly hope so," Michael said sombrely. "One never knows how these occasions will end, and one is prepared for all eventualities — he might not hang, and if he is transported there is always the prospect of him turning up on the doorstep one day with that oily smile of his, looking for revenge."

"Ye used to like the man," Sandy said.

"I did," Michael said shortly. "He was always so affable and so helpful — looking everywhere for Miss Peach. Luce thought he was wonderful for finding the body, but it was not exactly difficult when he put it there himself. He was stalking poor Miss Franklyn, too... Mrs Bertram Atherton, I should say. It will be safe for them to return now. I must write to—"

The explosion inside the bedroom was shockingly loud. Sandy jumped away from the door, and even Michael, who had half expected it, was startled. Only Sir Hubert was unmoved.

"Ah," he said. "He retains some shred of honour, then, and his mother and father will not have to suffer the shame of a son tried for murder."

"Has he—? Is he—?" Sandy whispered. "Should we—?"

He set his hand on the doorknob, but both Michael and Sir Hubert called out, "No!".

"I will deal with it, Sandy," Michael said gently. "I have seen a great many dreadful sights in my time, and this one will be no worse than many, but you need not share it."

"Captain Edgerton and I will deal with this," Sir Hubert said grimly. "You may stand outside the door and ensure no one enters, understood?"

Already the sound of the gunshot was bringing anxious faces up the stairs.

"What shall I tell them?" Sandy whispered.

"The official story will be an accident with a gun," Michael said.

"Accident with a gun," Sandy said, nodding.

He turned to face the first worried arrivals, as Michael and Sir Hubert slipped into the bedroom to take care of the devastated remains of Eustace Atherton.

28: Afterwards

Olivia was numb. It was too terrible even for tears. The recreation of the murder had seemed almost like a silly game, but the outcome had been more horrible than she could ever have imagined. Eustace, a murderer! He had tried to kill Walter, his own brother, just like Cain and Abel in the Bible, and she could hardly imagine a worse sin. Brothers and sisters should love and cherish each other, surely, and even if it happened that they did not get along, it would be utterly disloyal to act upon it. One should not so much as speak disparagingly about a kinsman. But murder!

And then the even more horrible news that Eustace had shot himself. *'An accident with a gun,'* everyone said, but what was he doing cleaning his guns at such a time?

It was Robert, dear, gentle Robert, who explained it to her, and persuaded her that it was for the best. Now there would be no trial, and no possibility that an Atherton might be hanged. He sat with her for hours, holding her hand with gentle sympathy, but nothing and no one, not even her beloved Robert, could ease her grief.

***

The next morning, the investigators met for the last time in the old schoolroom. On the sideboard, the axe sat once more, beside the gun used to shoot Mr Bertram. No one knew quite what to do with them now. Pinned to an old blackboard was the plan of the castle, showing where everyone was at the time of the murder, and on the table, weighted down at the corners with two decanters and a writing standish, the larger plan which showed the position of everyone at the time of the shooting of Bertram Atherton.

"This is not the ending everyone hoped for, Michael," Pettigrew said sombrely.

"Would you have preferred a trial at the Assizes and a public hanging?" Michael said.

"I had begun to hope we would never find the answer," Pettigrew said. "It might have been better so. This family has suffered enough."

"But then he might have tried again to kill Mr Bertram," Luce said. "At least this way his death can be passed off as an accident and no one outside the family need know the dreadful truth."

"Let us hope so," Pettigrew said. "Now it can all be put behind them. Thank God you realised yesterday who the murderer was, Michael."

"Oh, I already knew it was Eustace. I could not work out why, that was all, until I saw the importance of his inability to distinguish left from right, and remembered that Walter was not in his usual room."

"How did you know it was Eustace?" Luce said. "Because he lied to you?"

"That made me suspicious, certainly. I was investigating the brutal murder of his uncle by marriage, after all. Any innocent person would have told the truth at once. Yet I could not find a flaw in his alibi. Even if it was not Daisy Marler in his bed, he had *someone* with him, and an entire household who swore he could not have left the house that night. He was involved in so many ways, and yet that seemed an unbreachable difficulty. Kent Atherton was equally involved, and had no alibi. And yet... Kent has such an open, honest face. Eustace always had a darker side to him."

"Even a murderer can look honest," Pettigrew said. "I never suspected Eustace for a moment."

"It was the gun that first made me wonder, the gun used to shoot Mr Bertram Atherton." Michael crossed the room to pick it up, laying on the table in the centre of the room. "Such a nondescript weapon, is it not? So many guns are works of art, beautiful and memorable, but naval issue guns are merely practical. Unusual to see outside the navy, too. There are none in the Corland collection. But Eustace had several at Welwood, I have seen them, yet he swore he did not recognise this one. Now that may have been true — he might know his own collection so well that he could confidently say , '*This is a gun I have never seen before.*' But he should have mentioned his own naval pistols. He *should* have said, '*I have several of this type, but this is not one of mine.*' That is what an honest man would have said. Instead, he allowed everyone to think he had never seen such a thing before. That was what made me start to think about him seriously."

"He wanted to marry Miss Franklyn, too," Pettigrew said thoughtfully. "If Mr Bertram had died..."

"Precisely," Michael said. "He wore black that night of the grand ball, did you notice? Everyone else wore pale silk breeches, but he wore black. All the better to pass unnoticed as he ran to the cheese store, and to hide any scuffs of dirt when he hid in the bushes awaiting Bertram. So then I fell to thinking about it. I wondered, if he was the murderer, how he might have done it. Laudanum, of course, to drug everyone into a deep sleep. One of the old horses from the field opposite. And a saddle… he must have had a saddle hidden somewhere. And then I remembered Miss Peach's words."

"'I am almost certain of the murderer's identity now. I only need to find the saddle, and then I shall have the proof'," Luce said softly.

"Precisely. She said she would look in the obvious place for it, and where would be more obvious than the place where she had hidden her own saddle for the mule? So I set out to find that, and when I did, I had only to search a little further to find the saddle Eustace must have used. Once I knew that his alibi was worthless, everything else fell into place and I knew he must have killed Nicholson. But I did not know *why* until yesterday. You set me thinking, Luce, when we stood on the stairs and you talked about mazes, and going to the left and right. All of a sudden, the words of Lady Farramont popped into my head."

"She said he made a terrible murderer," Luce said, puzzled.

"Exactly," Michael said. "He was confused over left and right, even in his own home from childhood. On the night of the murder, when it was dark and he would have been on edge in case he was discovered, he could easily have taken a wrong turn and murdered the wrong person. The wrong person! Once that thought had occurred to me, I wondered who his real target might have been and then it was obvious."

"If he had not made that mistake," Pettigrew mused, "if he had succeeded in murdering his brother, would the case have been easier to solve, do you think?"

"There would have been a clear motive, certainly," Michael said thoughtfully. "Eustace would have been the obvious beneficiary. But he had a solid alibi, and it would have looked like a random intruder who snatched up the axe opportunistically, just as he intended. And since we had not the secret life of the sainted chaplain to investigate which kept us here for months, our enquiries would have run into the ground almost at once. We would have abandoned the case in a month or less."

"Then you think he would have won?" Luce said sharply. "He would have been Viscount Birtwell, the heir, and we could not have done anything about it? Michael, I am disappointed in you. Surely it would have been easier to solve the case if he had murdered the right man?"

"Only if I had realised the importance of his inability to distinguish left from right," Michael said. "I knew of it very early on, but it was not until I had seen him take a wrong turn on the stairs that I understood he could get lost even in his childhood home. Think about it, Luce. Every other important clue — the gun, the saddle, the laudanum, stalking Miss Franklyn, recreating the murder — all happened recently. If Walter had been the one murdered, we would have been long gone before discovering anything useful. It is only chance that the case has now been solved, and not by any skill of mine."

"Except that of dogged perseverance, Michael," Pettigrew said. "If Walter had been killed, you would have suspected Eustace right from the start, instead of being... how shall I put this? Let us say you were swayed by his apparent affability in showing you his collection of weapons. You liked him, in short, so although you suspected him as much as you suspected anyone, you put no extra effort into investigating him. Not until you discovered that he had lied to you, anyway."

Michael smiled ruefully. "It is true. I *did* like him, and not just because of our shared interest in weapons. He seemed to be so helpful, looking everywhere for Miss Peach. He truly *was* looking for her, of course, to ensure she knew nothing vital, but I confess, when he found her body, and showed me the many places he claimed to have looked for her, I was convinced he was on our side. He is very plausible, and if it had been Walter he killed, I would not have uncovered his perfidy at all, I am convinced."

"I do not like to contradict you, but you know I am always right," Pettigrew said smugly. "If Walter had been killed, Eustace would have been the obvious suspect, and therefore you would have been haunting Welwood every day to work out how he did it. You would have noticed that the field opposite held not just donkeys and pack ponies, but a few riding horses, too. Then you would have looked for the saddle, and you would have found it before long. The case would have been far easier to solve. In fact, I would go so far as to suggest that you would have solved it within a we ek."

Michael shook his head. "You are very kind to say so, Pettigrew, but no, I have displayed nothing but ineptitude from start to finish this year. Maybe it is time I retired altogether."

They all protested loudly, and eventually he laughed. "Very well, very well. Have it your own way." He picked up the gun again. "I think I may keep this, if the earl does not object. The axe, too, perhaps. I doubt any of the Athertons wish to keep it. They will be reminders of my own fallibility, if I ever again become overconfident."

***

Michael was helping Luce finish packing when a knock on the door heralded the appearance of Mr Kent Atherton.

"May I come in?"

"Of course, sir. If you want the room, we shall be gone in a few minutes. The carriage is already ordered."

"Oh, no rush, but it is about the carriage that I wanted to ask a favour, since you will be returning to Hartlepool—"

"Hartlepool!" Michael said, startled. "What makes you think we are bound for Hartlepool?"

"Is that not where you live?"

"No. Mrs Edgerton's house is in Bedfordshire, although we spend much of our time in London, too."

"How strange!" Kent said. "All this time we thought you came from Hartlepool and now find out it is no such thing. I wonder how such a story got about?"

Luce chuckled. "It was Michael's most famous case. The Hartlepool hat-pin murder."

"Ah! That would account for it. But if you are bound for the south, that would work even better, since you will pass through Helmsley. It is Miss Wilkes, you see. She wishes to return to Scarborough, and we thought, since you are to be on the road yourselves, that you could convey her to the stage coach stop. Mr Willerton-Forbes' carriage is also bound that way, but we do not like to call upon a single gentleman."

"Where is she?" Luce said, a martial look in her eye. "Let me talk to her."

They found Miss Wilkes sitting forlornly in the great hall, a single small box at her feet, dressed in travelling clothes. Her face was white and tear-streaked.

"My dear Miss Wilkes," Luce said, sitting down and taking both her hands in hers, "you cannot go back to that dreadful place. You cannot wish it, I am persuaded."

"Where else can I go?" she whispered.

"Home to your father?" Luce suggested. "We doubted you for a while, but you truly are Rosamunde Wilkes, are you not? So go home and beg his forgiveness."

She shook her head violently. "No, no, no! He made it very clear that he never wanted to see me again. He said it would be as if I were dead. He crossed out my name in the family Bible and had me painted out of the family portrait. No, there is no place for me there."

"Your sisters? Brothers? Your aunt?"

She shook her head again. "A woman once fallen is lost, Mrs Edgerton. She can never be respectable again."

"Nonsense," Luce said briskly. "What about Eustace? Perhaps he has left you something in his will."

"I doubt it," she said. "He promised to pay me well after this was over. You are very kind to concern yourself with me, but my best hope is to find a wealthy man to offer me protection."

"No, your best hope is to come home with us. I can find you work at Rudgewood House, my home in Bedfordshire, until you find a husband, which with your looks should not take long."

"What sort of work?"

"As my companion. Michael is away so much that I shall need company. I move in the very best circles — my cousin is an earl — so you will be able to meet some very eligible gentlemen. There, that is settled. We have only to finish our packing and then we will be on our way."

Michael followed her back up the stairs to their room, and quietly closed the door. "Companion, Luce?"

She would not quite meet his eyes. "Yes. Why not? She is a baronet's daughter and has obviously had an unexceptionable upbringing until her fall from grace."

"I have no objection to Miss Wilkes. I merely wonder why you need a companion. I am not sure she will be an asset to our investigations."

"Oh... well... I shall not be travelling about with you so much in the future." She bent over her box, fussing with the contents, her head down.

"Tired of me, Luce?" he said quietly, fear clutching at his insides.

"Never! You know that. I would always rather be with you than not, but... I will not be able to for much longer."

"Are you ill? Please do not be ill! You must not leave me, Luce!"

"No, no!" She looked up then with a mischievous smile. "Nothing like that. It is just that... something unexpected has happened."

"And?"

"I am with child."

For a moment, Michael was stunned into silence. Then, pulling her to her feet, he wrapped his arms round her and swung her in a full circle with a shout of pure joy.

"Truly? Oh, Luce... my darling! We are going to be a family!"

"You are not cross? I was afraid you might be, since I will have to stay close to home from now on. I cannot abandon a child, not when it took six years to conceive this one and there might not be another, and even you cannot expect me to take a baby about the country looking for murderers."

"No, but this solves a problem that I have been pondering for a little while now," he said, still holding her close. "I have been wondering whether it is time for me to settle down myself. Not retiring exactly, but leaving the more active side of things to younger men. Sandy is turning out to be very adept, do you not think? So I shall settle down at Rudgewood House with you and put my experience to use in training men to investigate, rather than doing the investigating myself. I can teach fencing, gun use, boxing, tracking, how to interview people, how to examine the site of a crime and so on. Pettigrew can teach them the law, what they can and cannot do, and Neate can teach them to pick locks and how to move about unnoticed. How does that sound?"

"Very good, except that I would advise you to teach a few women, too. A woman can talk to other women, and move about shops easily. Men are better in tap rooms and coffee houses."

"An excellent point. I can initiate cases, but I will not undertake anything dangerous myself. No more drainpipes."

"Will you be able to resist?" she said, smiling at him.

"I will have all the motivation I need to do so. A child needs a father and a stable home life, and that is what I intend to provide for our son... or daughter. And *I* need *you*, so you may believe me when I say that I shall not stray far from your side."

"Oh Michael!" For a moment, she leaned her forehead against his as he held her tight. "It all sounds a bit tame. You will be bored."

"Not at all. I shall spend my days playing with swords and guns, and who could be bored with that? I shall still travel a little to set up new investigations, but none of these jobs with no foreseeable end. Truly, Luce, I came close to giving up this investigation several times recently. It grows wearisome after a while. I am happy to leave the heroics to others."

"You will always be my hero," she said softly.

"And that is exactly as it should be," he said. "A man should be a hero to his wife, and a wife should be a shining beacon of joy to her husband. As you are, my love."

"Oh, Michael," she breathed, "you are *talking* to me. As a husband talks to his wife."

"As a man talks to the woman he loves," he whispered. "Impending fatherhood can do that to a man, it seems. It can break the dam of silence, and loose the words of... well, of love. Because I do love you, Luce. You know that, I am sure."

"I do, but you have never said it before. Perhaps you will never say it again, but I shall treasure this moment forever, my love."

He reached up to kiss her, and for a long time they stood immobile, wreathed in pure bliss.

Eventually, she sighed, but said, "This is very pleasant, husband, but we should get on the road soon, or we will not reach our overnight stop before dusk."

"Very well. If we must. Let us go and collect poor Miss Wilkes and be on our way."

Epilogue

LONDON: THE FOLLOWING JUNE

There were few houses in London large enough to boast a ballroom, but the residence of the Earl of Kiltarlity was one of them. By some quirk of land division, the house had an unusually large garden, and an ambitious ancestor had contrived to squeeze in a proper ballroom, not the usual two or three rooms with doors thrown wide that most were able to manage. It was not the largest ballroom in town but it was more than adequate for the purpose.

Robert had promised his sisters two balls during the season, and the first, a modest affair, had passed off tolerably well in the early days of the season when there were few competing events. Now it was time for a greater challenge — a grand ball in the height of the season, when every night was filled with other enticing occasions. His mother had planned the occasion with military precision, and Lizzie and Lucy had joined in with enthusiasm.

There was nothing for Robert to do but play the part of genial host on the night.

He felt the usual frisson of excitement before a ball. Not for the occasion itself, for he had been a part of London society for more than ten years now and the novelty of an endless procession of shiny-eyed debutantes fresh from the country had long since worn off. Since his older brothers had died and left him the heir to the earldom, he had lost much of his interest in the usual entertainments of the season. As often as not, he had arrived late to an event, lounged at the side of the room for a while and then, bored, retreated to the card room.

But now... oh, now there was Olivia! Whatever event she attended, there he would be, too, catching her eye across a packed room at a rout, waving to her at the theatre, fetching her an endless supply of cake at a Venetian breakfast or riding beside her carriage on outings. And at a ball, he had the joy of dancing with her, sharing secret smiles and delighting in the touch of her hand when the movement brought them together. And she kept her word to save the supper dance for him, so he was then able to take her in to supper. Half an hour or sometimes a whole hour sitting beside her, drinking in her lovely face and making her laugh with his teasing, watching her blush when he hinted, very subtly, at his affection for her.

Affection! Such an inadequate word. Fondness... no, that was worse. Love. Devotion. Adoration. Idolisation. That was closer. Every moment spent with her was precious to him.

Yet he had found it almost impossible to spend an entire ball with her. It was difficult enough waiting impatiently for his own share of her attention, but watching her dance with other partners was a peculiar form of torture that twisted his insides with painful intensity. He agonised over every expression on her lovely face. Was she smiling more than usual at that one, or laughing at a jest by another one? Was she more enthusiastic with another partner than she was with him? It almost drove him mad. He had taken to arriving later and later, arriving just in time for his own dance with her, staying only for supper and then leaving as soon as he decently could. It was less heart-rending that way.

But tonight he was the host, so he would be there from the first arrival until the last merry reveller staggered away home, and he was not sure he could bear it.

The Athertons were early arrivals, having dined together and then proceeded to the ball in several carriages. The butler, relishing his rôle, made the announcement in stentorian tones.

"Lord and Lady Rennington, Lord and Lady Farramont, Lord and Lady Woodridge, Mr and Mrs Bertram Atherton, Mr Lucas Atherton, Mr and Mrs Walter Atherton, Miss Olivia Atherton."

Robert supposed he said the proper words to each of them, but he only had eyes for Olivia. She looked enchanting tonight in a cream coloured gown that sparkled in the candlelight, and tiny white flowers threaded through her hair.

"I am last, of course," she said, her eyes laughing up at him.

He lifted her gloved hand to his lips. "You are first *and* last, Lady Olivia."

"Oh!" she breathed. "You do pay me the prettiest compliments, Lord Kiltarlity."

And she smiled at him so charmingly that any witty or clever response flew straight out of his head, and he could only mumble, "Supper dance?"

"As always."

She was forced to move on by the press of arrivals awaiting their turn to greet the host, but his eyes followed her until she was absorbed into the crowd and lost to view.

It was some time before the musicians began to tune their instruments and Lady Kiltarlity allowed Robert and his sisters to escape from the receiving line and open the dancing. Robert had already been told he was to partner one of the Medhurst girls, who was widely acclaimed as the season's Incomparable. There were many who held that Olivia should hold that title, but the Lady Angelica Medhurst was the legitimate daughter of a duke, and Olivia was only the illegitimate daughter of an earl, and to many in society, that made all the difference. Olivia's loveliness, her sweet nature, her graceful deportment and her charm meant nothing. Even her thirty thousand pounds melted no hearts amongst the highest sticklers.

Amongst the gentlemen, however, she was the absolute favourite. They swarmed around her so closely tonight that her diminutive form was scarcely visible in the crush. In the end it was Lord Thomas Medhurst who triumphantly led her onto the dance floor for the first dance.

Robert was not sure he was the best company for Lady Angelica that night. He did his best but he kept being distracted by glimpses of Olivia, eyes shining, the curls framing her face flying out and her gown shimmering in the candlelight.

Eventually the interminable dance was over, and as Robert was escorting Lady Angelica back to her mother, he saw Bertram and Bea sitting together at the side of the room, with Lucas lounging against a pillar.

Bea waved cheerfully to him, and called out, "You are a clumsy oaf, Lord Kiltarlity. You nearly trod on your partner's gown."

Lady Angelica laughed. "A friend of yours, I take it? She looks lively. Do introduce me."

"Of course. Lady Angelica, may I present Mrs Bertram Atherton and her husband, whose father is brother to the Earl of Rennington. That fellow by the pillar is their brother, Mr Lucas Atherton. And this is the Lady Angelica Medhurst, sister of the Duke of Wedhampton."

"Delighted to meet you, Lady Angelica," Lucas said, stepping forward eagerly to execute a deep bow. "Would it be presumptuous of me to hope to engage your hand for the next dance? I promise not to step on your gown."

With a smile, she said, "Unfortunately, I am engaged for the next two... here he comes now to claim me."

She had turned away almost before she had finished speaking, disappearing into the throng on the arm of her next partner.

"Ah, well," Lucas sighed. "It was a little ambitious. The daughter of a duke will not look at an untitled man. A parson's daughter is more my level, I imagine."

"Nonsense, Lucas," Bea said robustly. "You are a gentleman of means now, you know. Why should you not look as high as you please?"

"Because a modest house and an income of fourteen hundred a year is not enough to keep a duke's daughter contented, that is why."

"Combined with the duke's daughter's dowry of fifty thousand, she could be kept very contented, I imagine," Robert said.

"Fifty thousand? Is that her portion?" Lucas's eyes were wide.

"So it is said in the clubs. That was what her father promised her, and the new Wedhampton has agreed to honour that. She is a lovely lady."

"She is!" Lucas cried. "But then... I am discovering that London is full of lovely ladies."

"You are seriously looking for a wife, then?"

"Oh, yes! Now that I have my house, I want to put a wife in it as soon as possible."

"How are you liking it at Welwood? That was a most unexpected bequest, I understand."

Lucas laughed. "Indeed, and I was the last option. Eustace left his estate to his eldest son, if he had one, or failing that, his eldest daughter, or failing *that* his wife. And failing that... me. Because I am a second son, seemingly, and Eustace had a sympathy for those in that position. However it came about, I am deeply grateful, although I have not been there very much, only to clear out Eustace's things. So many weapons! I got Captain Edgerton to come and take them all away. He is very happy to take care of them, and gave me a good price for them."

"And the smuggling? Is that still going on?"

"Heavens, Kiltarlity, for an outsider you know a great deal about our family business!"

"Olivia is a chatterbox," Robert said, with a smile.

"So she is. No secrets from you, then. I have told all the Welwood people that I want nothing to do with anything illegal, and if it goes on, I have no wish to know about it. Mind you, the brandy in the cellar at Welwood is of exceptional quality."

Robert chuckled. "I am sure it is."

He encountered Lord Embleton and his new bride, the former Miss Ruth Plowman, a most improbable match but one that, judging from the smiles of contentment on their faces, seemed likely to be a happy one. If only he could be so sure of his own future happiness!

Robert felt obliged to stand up for the next pair of dances, but this time he found Olivia and her partner were the next in the line, so he was dancing with her almost as often as with his own partner. It made him the stupidest dancer in the set, with no conversation and little attention to his steps, so that he had to apologise abjectly to his partner afterwards.

"It is not of the least consequence, Lord Kiltarlity," she said, smiling at him. "Everyone must bow to the demands of true love without demur. My brother had some ambitions there, but he stepped aside smartly when he saw that you were high in the lady's esteem. She is the sweetest girl and will make an admirable countess, I am sure."

Robert hardly knew how he answered, for he was watching Olivia being claimed by her next partner, and when he turned around, his own partner had gone. He was in such a muddle that he could not even remember her name.

He decided it would be safer for everyone if he sat out the next two and awaited the supper dance. Accordingly, he propped himself against a pillar and watched the commencement of the next dance. But it was not safer for his own sanity, he discovered, for he now had nothing to do but watch Olivia with her new partner, smiling and even laughing with him, and the pain tore at his insides. How could she be so carefree? Did she feel nothing for Robert, if she could enjoy herself so wholeheartedly with another? Useless to tell himself that this was exactly what he had wanted for her — a season free of any prior understanding so that she might choose the man who suited her best. He could not bear it, and how was he to wait until the last ball of the season before speaking? He would be fit only for Bedlam by then. No, it was impossible.

"Kiltarlity?"

"Mmm?" For a moment he could not place the man at his elbow. "Um..."

"Strong," he said helpfully. "Alfred Strong. Sir Hubert's brother."

"Ah, of course. Forgive me... Um... did we...?"

"Invite me? No, but your servants very kindly permitted me over the threshold." He smiled genially.

"I am sure the lack of an invitation was an oversight," Robert said.

He chuckled. "I do not usually attend such events, but tonight I was supposed to dine with Winnie and Walter, and I was delayed, so I am come to apologise. Ah, here they are now."

"Uncle Alfred!" cried Winnie, excitedly. "Well? Is it done?"

"It is."

She squealed with delight. "Then, may I be the first to congratulate you — *Sir* Alfred."

Walter shook his hand, Winnie hugged him and Robert was moved to offer his own felicitations. "Bart? Or knight?"

"His Majesty has seen fit to bestow a knighthood on my unworthy self, to mark my retirement from the Treasury," Sir Alfred said. "A baronetage is of no consequence to me, since I shall never now have a son to inherit."

"Oh, never say never," Robert said. "There is still time for you to marry a pretty young thing. Shall I introduce you to one or two who might like to be Lady Alfred Strong?"

Sir Alfred went slightly pink, but it was Winnie who answered. "I think he may already have a lady in his eye, Lord Kiltarlity. Is it not so, Uncle Alfred?"

"Well, the secret is out, I see," he said, in some embarrassment. "It is true that the Lady Alice Nicholson has given me to understand that my addresses would not be unwelcome."

"Aunt Alice!" Walter said in tones of astonishment. "I never thought she would marry again, but now that I think of it, I have noticed that you have been spending a lot of time in her company."

"I have always admired her," he said, "but I could not aspire so high when I was merely a lowly Treasury official. But now I am comfortably situated and... well, since Mr Nicholson's demise, I have been able to offer her some assistance. Not that she needs a great deal of help, for she copes with her blindness admirably, but having someone to read the newspapers to her and discuss the reports with is useful. And perhaps I was some comfort to her in the darkest days after her husband's death. We have become… close, and I have hopes that we will be married before the summer is out."

"You will have to live at Corland Castle," Winnie said. "You will not mind that, I dare say."

"No, not at all. Alice cannot leave her home, so necessarily I must make my home with her. I have already spoken to Rennington, and he has no objection. Who would have thought I would marry at my time of life, eh? One never knows what is in store for one."

"How lovely for both of you!"

They drifted away to find the other members of the family, but Robert stayed beside his pillar, watching the dance and pondering the strength of character that enabled a man to admire a woman for years… for decades, without giving a sign, and then step into the breach only when she was widowed. Could he have done as much if Olivia had married Embleton? He was not sure he could. And yet… if she had been happy, that would have made him happy too.

She was happy now, he could see. Her smiles, the jaunty way she danced, her animation when she talked to her partner all told him of her pleasure in the occasion. And there was that familiar twist of pain inside him… perhaps she would turn him down in the end? The uncertainty gnawed him constantly. He had to know!

As the dance drew to a close, he saw her eyes scanning the room, looking for him. She saw him, and her face lit up in its widest smile yet. Oh, that smile! It was sunshine and wine and the promise of a warm summer day, all rolled into one. A man could die happy with such a delight near h im.

The music ended, she curtsied to her partner and steered him towards Robert's pillar, where he bowed as he left her.

"My supper dance at last," she said with such obvious pleasure that he was heartened again. Perhaps she would accept him after all? "Shall we take our places?"

"Not yet. I have promised something special for Lizzie and Lucy."

"How exciting!" she said, taking hold of his arm and snuggling close to him. "Here they are now."

His sisters arrived, still puffing slightly from the dance. "Who are these mysterious partners you have promised us, brother?" Lizzie said. "Has he told you, Olivia?"

"No, not a thing."

"He is being very secretive," Lucy said. "They are extremely eligible, he says, and very keen to meet us, but he will say nothing about— oh! Oh, Lizzie, *look!*"

Winthrop was leading two men into the ballroom. "Mr Whitwell and Captain Lingard," he intoned, and then gestured towards the pillar where Robert stood.

"Archie!" Lucy whispered, while Lizzie stared at the captain open mouthed.

The two men approached, they bowed in unison, their eyes fixed on the two sisters.

"Lady Elizabeth, may I have the honour of this dance?" the captain said. Too stunned to speak, she placed her hand on his proffered arm and he led her away.

Whitwell could not even manage so many words, merely holding out his hand to Lucy, who accepted it with a smile of pure delight.

"Who are they?" Olivia whispered into Robert's ear, as they watched the four join the set now forming.

"Mark Lingard is the man Lizzie tried to elope with several years ago, and Archie Whitwell is Lucy's lost love."

"But you found him... you found both of them," she said. "How wonderful you are."

"Oh... well... I cannot take all the credit, Livvy. It was you, if you remember, who told me to ensure that everyone was happy, and I thought that ought to apply to my sisters as much as anyone else. I found the two men, discovered they were both still single, and both suffering just as Lizzie and Lucy were. So I arranged for them to arrive in time for the supper dance. I think... I hope I did the right thing."

"Oh yes, for look how happy they are... all four of them. Are we going to dance, too? We can still join the bottom of the set, if you wish."

"Would you care to take a stroll on the terrace?"

"Oh!" She leaned away from him to look up into his face. "It is not yet the last ball of the season, Lord Kiltarlity."

"I know, I know, but I cannot wait a moment longer. Do you mind?"

She chuckled. "Not at all. It is so hot and stuffy in here, anyway, too hot for dancing. I had rather be on the terrace with you. *Much* rather."

And she smiled up at him in a way which warmed him through and through. It was going to be all right! Surely it would be all right?

Robert had forgotten how small the terrace was, for half the guests seemed to have spilt out from the ballroom to stroll about there, the ladies fanning themselves vigorously. He and Olivia could not take three steps without being greeted by someone, and there was no hope of talking privately.

"Well," he said ruefully, "this is not how I imagined it."

She looked up at him with laughter brimming in her eyes. "No, indeed, for I see no peacocks on the lawn, nor is there a fountain playing."

"And there is no moon and no stars tonight, with so many clouds about." He paused, as a passing couple made some complimentary remark on the success of the ball. "Thank you, thank you! Most kind."

"And it is just a trifle crowded out here," she murmured, as they inched past a loud group of young men to reach the low balustrade that separated the terrace from the narrow garden beyond. "But I distinctly smell roses nearby, so that is all right."

He laughed. "I am sorry, Livvy. I cannot speak to you as I would wish with so many people here."

"They are all watching us, too," she said, then lowered her voice to a whisper, "so we cannot even steal a kiss."

"What are we to do?" he whispered back.

"We could kiss anyway, and cause a scandal," she said.

"Certainly not!"

"Oh. Then we could presume that you have already made your speech and I have made mine."

"I should not like to presume anything," he said softly, "and I certainly want there to be kissing involved."

"Then you will just have to come and see me tomorrow, and we will imagine the peacocks and so forth."

He sighed. "I suppose so. At least then we can be sure to be private."

"True."

As they stood, gazing out into the darkness, ignoring the conversations going on all round them, she slipped one hand out of its glove and, hidden in the folds of her gown, her hand touched his and held it fast.

And he smiled, reassured. It was definitely going to be all right.

For a long time, they stood hand in hand. The music inside died away into a burst of clapping, and then a miracle happened. With the time for supper arrived, the crowds on the terrace drifted indoors until, when Robert dared to look, he and Olivia were the only ones remaining.

"Still no peacocks, sadly," he said.

"I do not need peacocks or fountains or moonlight," she said. "All I need is you, Robert Osborn."

He was too overcome to speak.

With a little chuckle, she went on, "I am very grateful to you, you know, for giving me this season free of entanglements, and I have enjoyed myself. It was not perfect, for with such recent bereavements there was much I could not do. I should still be in black gloves for Granny and poor Eustace, by rights, and I am still illegitimate, so Almack's was out of the question, nor could I be presented at court. Despite all that, I have had a great deal of amusement, and do you know what made it especially enjoyable?" He shook his head mutely. "Knowing you were there, that there would always be the supper dance and that eventually there would be a proposal and we could be... entangled. As we ought to be." She paused, reaching up to touch his face gently. "You may propose to me now."

"I had a charming speech prepared," he said hoarsely, wrapping his arms around her waist, "but I am so befuddled I cannot remember a word of it, not when you are here, so close, so enchanting, so *real*. I cannot believe I ever thought of you as a ghost."

"I do not need a speech, Robert. Four words will do it." When he still could not speak, she chuckled and said, "Repeat after me... will."

"Will."

"You."

He gave a little laugh. "You. Marry me."

"There, you see? Not difficult, was it?"

He smiled down at her. "What about you? A speech... or just one word?"

"And what word would that be?" she said, a mischievous glint in her eye.

"Do not tease me! I cannot bear it, Livvy. You have no idea how much it hurts to be so much in love."

"Oh, but I do," she whispered. "I love you to distraction, my poor befuddled earl. *Yes*... that is the word you are waiting for, is it not? Yes, I will marry you, and live at Strathinver, if that is what you want."

"I have a house in Kent, too."

"Do you?"

"And one in Hertfordshire, and an estate in Cornwall, and—"

"Great heavens, what do you need with so many?"

"There is bound to be one that you like above all others, so we shall go on an extended honeymoon and visit them all and you may choose. And if you dislike them all, I shall build you another. You must have whatever makes you happy, my love."

"You make me happy," she said. "Just you. I care nothing for where we live, except that I would like to spend the winter at Strathinver, and enjoy proper snow."

"Then you shall, and next spring, when you are the Countess of Kiltarlity, my mother will present you at court and your illegitimacy will not matter tuppence."

"Oh!" Her eyes widened. "That would be lovely. There is something that would make me very happy right now," she said, her eyes twinkling.

"My darling must have whatever she wishes."

"Supper," she said, then, seeing the horrified look on his face, added quickly, "But first, a kiss, perhaps?"

"You are a minx," he murmured, before complying with her request with great enthusiasm.

THE END

This concludes the story of the Earl of Rennington and his family. The next series, *Black Sheep*, follows the fortunes of the Duke of Brinshire, his new heir and extended family, as the mysterious Mr Goodenough sends seemingly random strangers to the duke's door. You can read a sneak preview of book 1, *The Duke's Architect*, after the acknowledgements. For more information, go to my website at https://marykingswood.co.uk.

Thanks for reading!

If you have enjoyed reading this book, please consider writing a short review on Amazon. You can find out the latest news and sign up for the mailing list at my website at https://marykingswood.co.uk.

A note on historical accuracy: I have endeavoured to stay true to the spirit of Regency times, and have avoided taking too many liberties or imposing modern sensibilities on my characters. The book is not one of historical record, but I've tried to make it reasonably accurate. However, I'm not perfect! If you spot a historical error, I'd very much appreciate knowing about it so that I can correct it and learn from it. Thank you!

About the series:

Book 0: The Chaplain: a man adrift, dreaming of a home (a novella, free to mailing list subscribers).

Book 1: Disinheritance: a man freed, looking for a new purpose in life

Book 2: Determination: a man pursued, forced to outwit his adversary

Book 3: Anger: a woman alone, trying to choose a different path in life

Book 4: Secrecy: a woman neglected, scheming to secure her own happiness

Book 5: Loyalty: a man of dreams, torn between the past and the future

Book 6: Ambition: a woman thwarted, unswervingly set on making a brilliant debut in society

Any questions about the series? Email me at mary@marykingswood.co.uk - I'd love to hear from you!

About the author

I write traditional Regency romances under the pen name Mary Kingswood, and epic fantasy as Pauline M Ross. I live in the beautiful Highlands of Scotland with my husband. I like chocolate, whisky, my Kindle, massed pipe bands, long leisurely lunches, chocolate, going places in my campervan, eating pizza in Italy, summer nights that never get dark, wood fires in winter, chocolate, the view from the study window looking out over the Moray Firth and the Black Isle to the mountains beyond. And chocolate. I dislike driving on motorways, cooking, shopping, hospitals.

Acknowledgements

Thanks go to:

Allison Lane, whose course on English Architecture inspired me.

Shayne Rutherford of Darkmoon Graphics for the cover design.

My beta readers: Charles Crouter, Kelly Darpinian, Julie Desbrus, Sharon Flaherty, Melissa Forsythe, Donna Sue Holly, Corinne Lehmann, Leanne McKinley, Tina Miles, Pat Oen, Kristen Pinto-Coelho, Rosemary Paton, Melanie Savage, Wendy Stubbs, Carol Sturtz, Jeanne Thomas, Andrea Usami

Last, but definitely not least, my first reader: Amy Ross.

Sneak preview: Book 1 of Black Sheep: The Duke's Architect

FINSBURY SQUARE, LONDON; JANUARY

The Honourable Simon Payne pulled his shawl more tightly round his shoulders and glared balefully at the fire burning fitfully in the grate. It was not the fire's fault that it had so little power to heat the attic room. It was doing its best, he supposed, but there were limits to what could be expected of any fire against the freezing cold air trying to creep through even the smallest crack in the windows.

He sighed, remembering sorrowfully the brilliant blazes of his youth. There was no chill in any room at Edlesborough, no matter how frigid the outside air. But all that had changed fifteen years ago, when he had asked to be articled to an architect, and his father had stared at him as if he had two heads.

"Articled? To an architect? Nonsense! It is the army for you, my lad. That is the tradition for younger sons in the Payne family, since you are hardly suited to the church. John and Matthew are promising in that way, and will take up the two livings I have in my disposal, so you must go into the army. It will do you good — make a man of you, and none of this drawing nonsense. I can get you into the Guards, so you will not have to fight."

"No, sir."

"Good. That is settled. Next year, when you are sixteen, you will—"

"No, sir. I will not join the army."

His father's eyes had bulged like a frog's. "You will do as you are told!"

"No. Chloe said she will take care of me."

That brought on such an outpouring of rage that the physician had to be called, and Mama had brusquely packed Simon off to London to join Chloe at once.

And here he still was, still trying to become an architect, still failing miserably. Yet Chloe's small annuity managed to keep him in paper and pencils, and so he still designed his great houses in the Greek style, although he toyed with Gothick designs sometimes, too. But no one wanted them. They were much admired, but the men of wealth who could afford them preferred the established names like Stewart, Holland or Wyatt. How was a man ever to become an established name if no one would engage him? Just one house would make his reputation, he knew it.

Mary Ann brought him his afternoon pot of tea. It was weak, of course, since the leaves had to be reused and by supper were barely colouring the water, but at least it was hot and would warm him inside. He sipped gratefully, moving closer to the fire. Another quarter of an hour and he could add some more coals to it. Then there would be his glass of wine at dinner to look forward to.

He had barely begun his first cup of tea when Chloe dashed in, unwinding a voluminous scarf, her nose red from the cold.

Simon frowned. "Thought you intended to be out all day."

"Indeed I was, but I called at the post office and there were three letters, which have been there for an age, the fellow said. Since Christmas, almost! Just imagine, and two are for you from your mama, so I brought them at once. Quick, quick, quick! How much is it?"

She tossed two small letters at him which he tried to catch but missed. Swiftly, she bent down to pick them up. "Hurry up, Simon! The suspense is killing me."

He ripped open the first letter. "A hundred!" he said, awed, holding up half of a bank note. Tearing open the other, he held the two halves side by side. "A hundred pounds, sister! We can have beef steak for Sunday dinner."

"Or a turkey, perhaps," she murmured. "Or what do you say to a bit of partridge? I am so fond of partridge."

"Let us not be too ambitious," he said, laughing. "We cannot say how long this will have to last us. It is six months, two weeks and three days since the last note, and that was only twenty."

"She must have had all the aunts and uncles at Edlesborough for Christmas," Chloe said. "You know how she does it — feed them up, pour Papa's best claret down their throats and then gently fleece them at the card table."

"It was only fifty after last Christmas," Simon said.

"So it was. She has had a successful time of it. I wish my mama were still alive, to send me little presents like this. Yours is very kind, and Papa knows nothing of it. The letters were not even franked, but I do not mind paying the postage when the contents are so rewarding."

"Three letters, you said. What was the other? A bill? We can settle for the coal now... and the butcher."

"Oh, yes. In all the excitement, I had forgotten." She fished the third letter from her reticule. "I do not recognise the hand. It is not a bill, I think." Breaking the seal, she unfolded it and read it silently, before looking up with a frown.

"What is it? Not bad news?"

"No... good news, I think, but... strange. Listen. 'To the Lady Chloe Payne, Finsbury Square, London. With humble greetings, my lady. You do not know me, but I am bidden to request you to bring Mr Simon Payne to Staineybank in Brinshire at your earliest convenience, in order to discuss the design for an orangery. Please reply directly to me to confirm your preferred date of travel, and I shall arrange private transportation and accommodation en route suitable to your station. Respectfully yours, A Goodenough (attorney at law), Castle Street, Brinchester'. What do you think of that?"

"An orangery? Nothing else?"

"It is progress, Simon. Nothing but stables and kennels so far, so an orangery is a step up. A gentleman client, at least."

"But Mr Thwaite may yet settle on a design."

"Two years you have been working on designs for Mr Thwaite, and for all his great fortune, we have seen not a penny piece from it, nor has he actually commissioned any of your designs. But this... transport provided... a private carriage, Simon, just think! And suitable accommodation on the way. Oh, to be eating at someone else's expense! And when we arrive, we might even be invited to stay at the house itself. Staineybank… I have never heard of it."

"Campbell," Simon said. "English Palladian style. Built 1722."

She chuckled. "Yes, but who lives there?"

"Duke of Brinshire."

Her eyes widened. "A duke! Oh, Simon, we must go! Even if nothing comes of it, we must go."

"Yes," he said. "Campbell's houses are always worth seeing, and I have never seen that one. Of course we must go."

She shook her head, smiling. "You are incorrigible, brother. Very well, I shall write to this… what is his name? Mr Goodenough, attorney at law, and make arrangements, and you will be able to see Staineybank. And I… I shall endeavour to take as long as humanly possible to discuss this orangery in the hope that the duke will feed and house us both in the meantime. A fortnight, at least, surely, or even a whole month. And if he likes your designs, and who could not…" She shivered in anticipation. "Just think, Simon — we might see out the whole winter in comfort."

"And warmth," he said with feeling. "I hope Staineybank is warm."

***

STAINEYBANK, BRINSHIRE; JANUARY

Miss Sophia Merrington gazed at the image on the page before her and sighed. Such elegance! Such exquisite details! And, sadly, such extravagance. *'A light blue, or grey chemise robe, of gossamer net, imperial crape, or Spanish gauze, worn over white pealing satin, ornamented up the front with French bows and knots of silver'*, quoth the journal. White satin?

Six shillings a yard at the very least, and possibly twice as much. The gauze would be a little less, and the bows and knots... she could make them quite small.

Then she read the next lines and despaired. *'A full melon sleeve, formed of the same material as the dress, and alternate stripes of white satin; finished with bows and knots of silver. A double roll of white satin round the neck of the robe, by way of tucker'.* Full sleeves in stripes of two materials? A white satin tucker? And then the journal went on to describe the diamond comb in the hair, and diamonds for necklace, armlets and ear-rings.

She sighed even more heavily.

The slumbering figure on the sofa stirred. "Georgie? Oh, it is you, Sophia. Have I slept for a long time?"

"An hour or so, no more. Georgie went to see about the jellies. The duke came in to look at you, but I chased him away."

"He fusses so, but I am perfectly well. Just... tired. And enormous."

"Not much longer to wait now, Rowena," Sophia said briskly. She was very fond of her sister-in-law, and was delighted that Richard had married such a pleasant, unassuming woman, but the whole household revolved around her. If she should happen to fancy a certain dish at dinner, an army of gamekeepers and poultry maids and gardeners and still room maids would be mobilised to provide the ingredients. If she sneezed, the servants were thrown into a frenzy of possets and tisanes and tinctures, followed by a stream of midwives and apothecaries and physicians, who all recommended different remedies and stood in the hall roundly disparaging each other.

And the duke was the greatest worrier of them all. Since Richard was his official heir, the child Rowena carried would be the next in line, and oh, the hopes and expectations that rested on her to produce a son. Sophia could only hope for that, too, for then perhaps the trembling excitation that infected Staineybank would dissipate and they could all settle back into their usual activities. Not that there was much to look forward to in January, with the Christmas festivities past and not so much as an evening party on the horizon for months. It was dispiriting.

She sighed again.

Rowena heaved herself into a more upright position. "Now, what is making you sound so out of sorts? No ball to plan for, I imagine. What are you reading? Oh, this is pretty," she said, taking the journal from Sophia's hands. "White satin... French bows and knots of silver. That sounds quite delightful. Shall you have one like it made up?"

"I cannot afford it," Sophia said dejectedly.

"Not even with the additional allowance from the duke? He is very generous."

"Oh yes, the *duke* is generous, but Richard is not. I do not like to speak ill of my brother, for he is an admirable man in every other respect, but he is a nip-farthing, Rowena. Even you must admit it. He insists I must not overspend my allowance, not even by the cost of a single ribbon, and how can anyone be sure to keep to a specific sum? One must have clothes, after all."

"He is careful with money, it is true," Rowena said with a little smile. "Being a man, he does not quite appreciate the benefits of a new gown or slippers."

"Or diamond armlets," Sophia said with another sigh. "Just imagine how glorious that would be. With every movement, I should glimmer and sparkle."

She jumped up, held her arms in the correct position and executed a complete figure with all the steps, and then sighed again. "When, oh when will there be a ball? I cannot tell you, Rowena, how I long for a proper ball, but not when I have nothing to wear."

"There will be no balls before Lady Day when your next allowance will arrive, but perhaps the seamstress might begin work a little early? She will know she will be paid, after all."

"Richard will not permit it," Sophia said dejectedly. "We are never to buy anything for which we could not settle the bill immediately, if required. Nor are we allowed to borrow money, and we are never, ever to gamble to defray debts. Oh, it is hard! There is nothing like a new ball gown to lift the spirits."

"Then you know the answer, Sophia," Rowena said with a quick laugh. "You will just have to marry a vastly rich man who dotes on you so much that he gives you all his wealth to spend on ball gowns and diamond armlets."

"*All* his wealth? But then we should be destitute and how should I survive without any new gowns at all?"

Rowena laughed out loud at her dejected tone. "There is no pleasing you! What you must do, Sophia, is what I was obliged to do for many years, and rework your old gowns. You have some very pretty ones that could be refreshed with very little effort."

It was a strange thing, but Richard had said precisely the same thing to her many, many times, and it had merely made her cross and long even harder for the new gown or gloves or fan. When Rowena said it, however, it sounded eminently reasonable and she could not think of a single argument against it.

Richard himself came in just then, with his sketchbook under his arm, and Sophia had no wish to hear any more about his precious orangery. For months now, he had been drawing up plans for it, so that Rowena might grow oranges and lemons and who knows what exotic fruits, and Sophia was tired of it.

Leaving them to their discussion, she slipped away to her room, and flung open the doors of the two presses that housed all her ball gowns. She had quite a collection now after eleven years of balls and she had bought at least two for each season. Laying them carefully on the bed, she counted thirty-one. Since each gown had danced its way through four or five balls apiece, that was... too difficult a sum to work in her head. She kept a notebook with every ball listed, and all her partners, and what they had danced, together with a few comments about the number of couples and the quality of the supper and any particularly memorable moments, so she could work it out from that.

After some concentrated effort with the notebook, she reached a final number — one hundred and forty-one. That was the sum of her life so far, one hundred and forty-one balls, any number of dances and partners and not a single offer of marriage. Even in the days of her highest bloom she had attracted no suitors, and now, at the advanced age of twenty-eight, it was unlikely that she ever would. She was a confirmed spinster, and even three older sisters in the same pitiable state was no comfort. What was *wrong* with them all, that no man wanted any of them?

She lifted up her favourite gown, her very first. Horribly outdated now, of course — such full skirts! So much material in it, and even Richard had agreed that she must wear silk to a ball. She pressed the fabric to her face, wondering if she would still catch the faint scent of the perfume she had worn on that unforgettable evening... No, it was gone.

With another sigh, she carried it to the window to examine more closely. Such a beautiful silk, that flowed over her hands like cool water. And so much of it... if it could be carefully unpicked, perhaps a new dress could be contrived? And there would even be enough left over for full sleeves, if she should want them.

Gathering up the gown, she rushed off to find Lily. The duchess was almost the same age as Sophia, and also came from a family at the lower edge of gentility, where finding the money for new gowns was a constant struggle. Even since her marriage to the duke, she still dressed frugally, and was adept at fashioning new from old.

"Have you never had to do this before?" Lily said, taking the gown to the window to examine it closely. "Richard must have been very generous with you."

"Not he!" Sophia said. "The trustees were generous, certainly, but as soon as Richard came of age, he leased Leahollow and marched us off to a poky little house in Norwich, and reduced our allowances."

"Oh!" Lily said, wide-eyed. "But perhaps there were debts to be settled?"

"No, he is just horridly cheeseparing. It is not so bad for my sisters, for Charlotte is as tight-fisted as Richard, Augusta is happy so long as she has a riding habit to wear, and Maria cares nothing for clothes when there are books to be read. Mama was the only one who understood, but even she could not sway Richard. His mind was entirely closed to the idea that one cannot exist on only two or three gowns a year. It is just not possible, not if one is to be respectably turned out."

Lily laughed. "Indeed, I cannot fault your logic, cousin, for my sisters and I suffered just as you do. Poor Papa! There were so many of us, and the boys had to be educated and mounted, so there was very little left over for unnecessary items like clothing. We were only allowed new gowns twice a year, spring and autumn, and then it was only one morning gown, one walking and one evening. We spent half our days unpicking and sewing anew."

"How dreadful!"

"Oh, it was a challenge we all relished. Happily for me, my godmother descended on us when I was about to come out, and insisted I needed a veritable mountain of gowns. Papa grumbled about it, and we only persuaded him in the end by telling him that good quality clothes could be handed down for year after year, and serve for several of my sisters."

"I imagine he did not grumble so much when you drew the duke's eye," Sophia said slyly.

"Oh, but he did! He was horrified, and I think he would have forbidden the match if Mama and my godmother had not pointed out all the advantages. And now Cordelia and Amabel have made very good matches, and John has his colours, in a far better regiment than he might have expected, and Henry is a midshipman. There is a living for Charles or Thomas, too, if they want to go into the church. The duke has been so kind to us... to all of us," she added wistfully.

Sophia said nothing, for she found Lily's story heartbreaking. To be forced to marry a man old enough to be one's grandfather! Lily had been eighteen to the duke's sixty-eight, and no matter how kind he had been and still was, for he was clearly fond of his young wife, it was indubitably a dreadfully unequal match. As for the advantages, those all accrued to others — Lily's brothers and sisters, and not to Lily herself, beyond the security of wealth and high standing in society.

But Lily never railed at her situation, except to say now and then that the grandeur and size of Staineybank felt oppressive to her. After her only child had died at the age of six, she had planned to leave it altogether and return to Cheshire, where her family lived, but here she still was.

Now she smiled, running slender fingers over the skirts of the ballgown. "This is a beautiful silk. It will make up afresh very well, you will see. We can look through the journals today, and talk to the seamstress tomorrow."

The two spent a delightful afternoon in the duchess's private sitting room, with journals lying open on every available surface, sipping tea and discussing fashions, for it was a subject of inexhaustible interest to both of them.

Dinner that evening was dominated as so often these days by discussion of the proposed orangery. It was intended as a wedding gift to Rowena, who had admired the Duke of Camberley's orangery at Marshfields, but at the present rate of progress the bride would be a matron with three or four children before it was finished. Not a stone had yet been laid, and the exact location had not even been determined.

As always with Richard, it came down to money. The duke was all for a grandiose scheme on a hill to impress visitors, lined with marble pillars. Richard was more inclined for a simple brick structure, on account of the cost of glass, and as for marble, it was not to be thought of. No matter how many times the duke pointed out that he would be paying for it and the estate could easily bear the cost and it would be a gratifying celebration of the birth of the next heir, it made no difference.

Sophia was glad to creep away to bed and dream of balls and the swirl of silken gowns, of rooms filled with waving feathers and sparkling jewels, and everywhere music and charming young men eager to dance. And surely there would be one, just one, who would look at her and truly *see* her.

***

The next morning, she awoke to steady snow, coating the gardens in white icing. By breakfast, the fall was reduced to a few stray flakes, but there was a flurry of activity amongst the men, anxiously discussing the roads, while most of the ladies had wisely decided to take breakfast in bed.

"Let us escape," Lily whispered to Sophia. "The seamstress will not be able to get up from the village today, but there is much we can do. I thought we might look at the rest of your gowns and see what else might be reworked."

Sophia could see no flaw in this enticing plan, so they left the men muttering about oxen and sweepers, and crept away to Sophia's room.

She was still unused to an entire room all to herself, having shared with Mary all her life. At first, she had confined her things to the accustomed half of the room, leaving ample space for Mary's piles of books, but she had soon realised the luxury of taking up every inch of space herself, if she wanted it. Not that she did. Oddly, the more space she had to fill, the less she wanted to clutter up every surface with abandoned bits and pieces. Only a few small ornaments, symmetrically positioned, graced the mantelpiece, her hairbrushes sat in a neat arrangement on her dressing table, a single journal lay on the bedside table in case she should be wakeful at night and everything else was hidden away in drawers and cupboards.

In under an hour, Lily had selected seven gowns that could readily be converted to a more fashionable style. Only two were ball gowns and one an evening gown, but Sophia could not deny that four new morning gowns would be very welcome, too. Their two lady's maids were summoned to give their advice, a pot of tea brought and all was going on in the most satisfactory manner when Spearman, the butler, came in.

"Beg pardon, Your Grace, Miss Merrington, but there's a Lady Chloe Payne and Mr Simon Payne just arrived."

Lily's face registered bewilderment. "I do not know them. Sophia, do you? No? Are they perhaps acquaintances of the duke, Spearman?"

"Not that I'm aware, Your Grace."

"Perhaps they are stranded by the snow… a carriage breakdown," Sophia suggested.

"I don't think so, madam," the butler said. "They seem to think they're expected… something to do with the plans for the orangery."

"Then Mr Richard Merrington must have invited them," Lily said.

"Oh, yes, of course," Spearman said, brightening. "That will be it, and I dare say he forgot to mention it, what with the snow and all. It's a pity he's out with the oxen team just now. I'll let Miss Hester know. She can arrange rooms and deal with them."

"Oh, no, indeed, I must receive them myself," Lily said at once. "As a noblewoman, Lady Chloe will expect it."

The two visitors stood rather forlornly in the Marble Hall, their luggage in a puddly heap near the door, while an assortment of servants awaited instructions. Mr Payne was gazing around the Marble Hall with its array of pillars reaching imperiously to the high ceiling, his expression of awe one that Sophia entirely understood. She had never quite accustomed herself to the grandeur of Staineybank herself. Lady Chloe, oddly, was engaged in watching Mr Payne.

They were a strange couple. Lady Chloe was tiny, a doll-like figure of around forty, while Mr Payne, perhaps ten years younger, was a large man in every sense, both tall and broad of chest, and as handsome a man as Sophia had ever seen. No… that was not quite true, for there had been a man of ethereal beauty at her very first ball, but he had not even noticed her and she had never seen him again. Nevertheless, he remained an ideal of manhood, but she suspected that Mr Simon Payne, once unwrapped from the many layers of his winter travelling garments, might come very close.

"Lady Chloe, welcome to Staineybank," Lily said. "I am the Duchess of Brinshire."

It was, perhaps, an unnecessary introduction, for the flurry of bows and curtsies from the assembled servants must have suggested her rank, but Lady Chloe turned to her in some surprise.

"Oh! Duchess! I had not expected..." Only then, rather belatedly, did she drop into her own curtsy.

"You are here to see Mr Richard Merrington, I understand?" Lily said brightly.

"Well... I am not sure..."

"It is about the orangery, is it not? Then that is his project."

"Is it? I did not know that," she said vaguely. Then, in a sharper tone, "Simon, do not wander away when her grace is speaking."

"But it is a perfect cube," he said, his face alight with inner fire. "And the pillars... Corinthian, and the frieze is so elegant. Do you not think?"

"Well, I am sure, but do please pay attention when her grace is addressing you."

He turned puzzled eyes on her. "I am complimenting her house, Chloe. She cannot object to that, can she?"

Lady Chloe sighed, but Lily only laughed. "Actually, Mr Payne, I am very pleased that you admire Staineybank, but I find it oppressively grandiose myself."

"Oh no," he said solemnly. "It is beautiful. Campbell, you see. Wonderful architect."

"I am sure he was," Lily said diplomatically. "But if you are not here at Mr Richard Merrington's behest, who was it who invited you?"

"Goodenough," Mr Payne said. "Attorney. Brinchester."

"Mr Goodenough!" Sophia cried. "But there is no such person!"

"I assure you there is," Lady Chloe said robustly. "He wrote to us and then brought us here himself from London in the most commodious style. The carriage is still outside, awaiting our instructions."

"I am afraid it is quite true," Lily said. "Mrs Richard Merrington arrived here last year in precisely the same manner — a letter from a person calling himself Goodenough, who brought her here, whereupon he disappeared. There is no attorney in Brinchester by that name."

Lady Chloe turned and almost ran across the Marble Hall, wrenched open the door before the footman could reach it and raced outside. The others followed more slowly, knowing what she would find.

The drive was empty, only the twin tracks in the snow betraying that a carriage had arrived and had now left, making its way down the drive and not to the Staineybank stables.

"Then it is true," Lady Chloe said. "We have been duped. But *why?* Why would anyone play such a cruel trick on us?"

But no one had an answer to offer.

END OF SAMPLE CHAPTER of *The Duke's Architect;* for more information or to buy, go to at my website at https://marykingswood.co.uk.

Made in the USA
Middletown, DE
14 September 2025